THREAD AND STONE

THE ZHYRRAK
BOOK 1

MAEVE BROOKS

CONTENTS

Cover Art by Eric Andren

Published in the United States by Binary Star Press.

eBook ISBN: 979-8-9936042-0-6

Print ISBN: 979-8-9936042-1-3

CONTENT CONSIDERATIONS

This story contains themes and depictions that some readers may choose to avoid, including on-page portrayals of PTSD, slavery/forced labor, violence, and open-door sexual interactions, as well as off-page mentions of combat trauma, familial death, and alien abduction.

For a full list of content considerations, please see https://maevebrooks.com/thread-stone-content-considerations/

For those who fight back, even when victory seems impossible.

1

UNRECOGNIZABLE

AMARA

THE OTHER TWO nurses go statue-still, faces turned towards their shoes like the lack of eye contact might save them from a little work and discomfort. Selfish pricks. It's times like these I wish I were a shittier person.

Hand raised, I step forward and say, "I've got it."

Solta waves in confirmation and returns to her datapad with complete disinterest. If no one had volunteered, she would've randomly assigned someone and never checked whether they'd done the job. She doesn't care if the gladiator lives or dies, as long as she doesn't have to deal with him. Fucking infuriating.

Gripping my med-bag, I follow my escort away from the Nurse's Room and down the darkened passageway. Light from the outside world bursts beneath the cell doors in glowing strips that cast strange shadows over the jagged surface of the stone floor. The shadows are fitting, but the warm glow is not. It just adds another layer of incongruity to an already unsettling environment. Like a haunted house with children's songs playing in the background. There's nothing warm here. Nothing comforting. Just stone, death, and the promise of a lifetime spent in perpetual hell.

The walk is short, maybe 30 feet or so, but with each step, my will to continue shrinks. The fetid stench leaking out of Cell 3 is already so thick in the air my eyes are watering, and damn if it doesn't make me want to regret my decision. But I ignore it and keep moving.

Embrace the suck, Amara.

Yuxta, my pain-in-the-ass escort, pushes one of his three-fingered hands into my back, ushering me right up to the door. His face is placid and unmoving, and I can't help but wonder if he even has a sense of smell. Probably not. There's no way his poker face is that good.

I wait for him to sort through the keys while I try to think about anything other than the smell. It's not easy. The species on the other side of that door is a level of rank I didn't know was possible, and that's why I'm here. Fighting for every breath. Because if I don't keep this fucker alive, no one else will, and I don't feel like giving the Magistrate another dead slave.

A clunk reverberates off the orange-hued walls as Yuxta turns the lock.

"When was his last dose given?" I ask.

He shakes his shoulders in what I've determined is a shrug before saying, "Wait inside when you are done."

I bite back a sarcastic remark as I realize the guy who can't remember when he sedated the giant space-spider thinks that I'm the one with memory issues.

Clenching my jaw, I drop my gaze to the ground. Sure, Yuxta seems nice, but I'm not dumb enough to assume he's on my side. A single snarky comment could be the end of my road, and I'm saving my final 'fuck-you' for someone a little higher up the food chain.

The door swings open and I step over the threshold, holding my breath.

"I will return rapidly," Yuxta says.

I nod at the awkward translation and wait for him to partially close the door behind me. When he's gone, I dart past the sedated alien, drop my med-bag on the table, and stick my face out of the hole in the wall that serves as a window.

The rush of fresh air and sunlight is like a drug, and I take my time soaking it in. From here, the view of the sprawling Calidus desert is stunning. Endless, undulating dunes stretch out as far as the eye can see. Distant rocky outcroppings cast long shadows through the morning haze. Sand dances in the breeze, bursting upwards into the pale sky with enviable freedom.

What a beautiful prison.

With a final breath of untainted air, I leave the window and face my task.

My patient, the spider-like Thoratlium, is on the bed with his many legs sticking upwards in the exact way you'd expect. If I were to go off smell and appearance alone, I'd say the guy is dead. But he's not. The creepy bastard is chittering in his sleep.

Taking shallow breaths through my mouth, I slip on a pair of gloves, turn on the adjustable lamp, and inspect his injuries. Deep gouges run along his carapace, and one of his legs is cocked at an unnatural angle. Definitely broken. Or dislocated? I don't know. Alien physiology isn't my forte, and in the year I've been here, no one has offered me any real training.

"Looks like you got quite the ass-kicking," I mumble as I fill a syringe with a fresh dose of sedative. Since Yuxta couldn't tell me when the spider got his last dose, I'm giving him a 'safety-dose'. Dying at the hands—claws?—of a giant space-spider is not at the top of my to-do list, and neither is being deemed a 'criminal' and mysteriously vanishing.

No one will outright say what happens to the nurses who break the law and vanish, but we all know. The Magistrate loves his overcomplicated rules and thinly veiled threats. *God, I hate that fucker.* I can't wait to give him a thinly veiled threat of my own.

The spider's leg twitches as I stick the needle in the joint near his carapace, and I nearly jump out of my skin.

"Holy shit," I gasp as my heart tries to pound out of my chest.

Ok. Calm down. He isn't waking up, he's just twitching.

I'd love to say I'm not scared of the gladiators, but that would be a lie. They're all scary. Even the ones that don't look threatening are here for one reason and one reason only: they're really good at killing. This little guy might be smaller than me, but he's heavier than shit and he's still alive. Since only one gladiator can leave the arena with a pulse, it's clear this eight-legged freak is capable of some serious damage.

With the sedative in his system, the spider's chittering finally quiets down. While I'm grateful for the sedatives, I'm not so grateful for the reason we use them. A while back, I asked Solta about it, and she gave me some cock-and-bull story about the nurse's femininity distracting the gladiators, resulting in poor fight outcomes. But if that were the case, why have only female nurses? It makes no sense until you realize the Magistrate is scared of us. I've read enough history books to know that when a subjugated people are allowed to communicate freely, those in power don't last very long.

I work quickly, cleaning and bandaging the wounds while taking frequent breaks at the window for fresh air. Surprisingly, I haven't puked yet. *Yay for me!*

Now to address the leg.

There's definitely something wrong with it, and I'm leaning towards dislocation.

I prod along the joint and frown. The exoskeleton's still intact, and if I remember anything about bugs, they don't have an endoskeleton. But this is an alien, not a bug. And I'm pretty sure bugs can't be this big without having an endoskeleton. Right?

Wishing I had a textbook on alien orthopedics, I grab the leg, say a prayer to whoever's listening, and yank. There's a satisfying pop, and the leg settles into a more natural position.

"Would you look at that," I mutter. Somehow, I nailed it.

Feeling content, I splint the joint, rip my gloves off, and wait for Yuxta by the door.

The gap he left is just wide enough for me to get a consistent flow of fresh air, but I have to lean awkwardly against the doorframe to enjoy it. After a few minutes, my muscles start to burn, and my impatience grows. Yuxta should be back by now.

Resisting the urge to poke my head into the hallway, I grip my med-bag to my chest and try to let my mind wander. Eventually, I hear the familiar thud of boots.

Finally.

The door swings open, and I'm face-to-face with ... not Yuxta.

"Come," Kyvern says. His nearly translucent skin bunches at his nose as he takes a deep sniff of the rank air.

I grimace. *Fucking hell, I think he's enjoying the stench.*

With an obedient nod that feels very forced, I step into the darkened hall and try to appear non-threatening. Kyvern's ability to flip from calm to violent in a heartbeat is shocking, and the last thing I want is to piss him off.

Out of the corner of my eye, I watch Kyvern and wait for him to close the door. But he's just standing there.

I'm about to ask what's wrong when his lips curl and my stomach sinks.

Fuck me, that's a smile. Kyvern doesn't smile.

Forcing myself to stay calm, I keep my eyes low and my breathing steady, but that goes out the window a second later when he lowers his head and fixes his dark, predatory eyes on me.

Instinct takes over, and I run.

A laugh that sounds like breaking glass follows me. *Not good.*

I turn to look, feet still propelling me forward, and watch as Kyvern coils his muscles and slams the cell door shut.

The crashing sound of metal on metal hits me like a thousand knives. Panic swells. I try to breathe through it. *It's just a sound, Amara. You're fine.* But I'm not fine. Terror takes root. Nerve endings scream. Adrenaline burns as my heart works to escape containment. I try to stop the downward spiral, but I'm already too far gone. Past the point of no return. My ears roar as a familiar fog creeps over my vision until all I can see is that bright square of light in a sea of shadow.

I grip my face, trying to push myself back to the present. Back to reality. But it doesn't work. My legs are still moving, but the square of light isn't getting any closer. *Because it's not real.* But it feels real. Something catches my foot. My stomach rises as I drop. I reach out, bracing myself to meet the stone floor. But it's not stone. *No, no, no, no.* Cold metal presses into my skin. The smell of sweat and shit and death surrounds me. And then the screams start.

MY ENTIRE BODY jolts as something touches me. I try to fight back, desperate to strike my attacker, but my arms feel like lead. They're too heavy. And I can't see. *Oh my god, I can't see.* Hysteria rises in my throat until I realize I'm not blind. My eyes are just closed. I try peeling them open. They're sticky, and my vision is blurred.

"You are safe," someone says. Hands touch my shoulders. Non-threatening. Not an attack. I blink a few times, and Roveen's slim face and drooping antennae come into focus. *Not an attacker.*

My head falls back, and I groan at the unforgiving surface beneath me. Something sharp is digging into my spine and my bare thighs. Because I'm on the floor. In the Nurse's Room.

"How did I—" I stop when Roveen's antennae go rigid and she flicks her eyes to the side.

Solta's watching us with an annoyed expression. "She is fine, Roveen," Solta says. "Get back to your duties."

Roveen gives me an apologetic glance and stands. The motion is enough to throw off my equilibrium, and I have to close my eyes to fight the nausea rising in my throat. Eventually, the feeling goes away, and I'm able to open my eyes again.

Neat shelves of medical equipment tower over me from my prone position. Everything looks odd from down here, and the floating, disconnected feeling in my body isn't helping.

It happened again.

I want to scream in frustration, but it won't help. I should get up. Try to act normal. But I can't. Not yet.

The underside of the table catches my attention, and my first thought is, '*Huh, no gum,*' followed by a surge of unwanted memories. The smell of leaves in the fall. The feeling of grass under my feet. The nostalgia of an old book. I push it all down, and I try to ignore the ache in my chest. There's a reason I pretend I had no life before this.

I'm ok. Everything's ok.

Cool stone sucks the unwanted heat from my body as I try to piece together what happened before the flashback. I remember the Thoratlium, and—

Fuck. I press my palms over my eyes as the image of Kyvern's sadistic grin comes rushing back.

Breathe, Amara. Breathe and forget.

Nope. Not working.

I sit up, grab the trash can Roveen must have left, and empty the contents of my stomach.

I despise the weakness of the human mind. I should be able to push past this, to find a way out of the constant flashbacks, panic attacks, and blackouts, but I can't. I'm stuck. And somehow, the flashbacks are worse than the events that caused them. Being in that box was awful, but being a prisoner in my own mind is worse.

When I'm confident my stomach has revolted as much as it can, I drop my head between my knees and drag my fingers over the uneven surface of the floor. Somehow, nothing but rain, wind, and time ate away at this solid slab of stone, changing its unwavering surface into a nightmare of sharp peaks and deep crevices. Changing it until it became something dangerous and unrecognizable.

2

THE OBLIGATION

VEXAR

"I UNDERSTAND THE risks, Marius. We have been over this." I run a hand over my face and scratch the stubble already forming on my chin as Marius continues to drone on about the many risks I am unnecessarily assuming. This is our last opportunity to speak before I sign my contract, and his repetitive nagging has my finger hovering over the mute button of the holoCom.

"If you would just accept the mate that was chosen for—"

"Marius," I interrupt, "I am not interested in accepting that proposal, and I do not need to absolve myself of my vow."

Marius makes a huff of frustration and brings the camera closer to his face. His dark brown eyes look almost black in the sunlight of my home-world as he whispers, "Drusa is a fine mate, and if you just agree to the proposal, we can ensure your safety."

I nearly laugh. He thinks pairing me with Drusa will keep me safe? And that whispering will keep my refusal quiet? This news will spread no matter what we do, so let it. I will not allow my honor to be tarnished by whispers alone. My choice is one I stand by.

"I am not here to ensure my safety," I say calmly. "I am here to prove my worthiness. To fulfill the Obligation. If the Obligation were without risk, there would be no point in doing it."

Marius shakes his head. "If you are truly intent on fighting without medical care..." He trails off when he notices my stern expression. "Apologies. I will not bring it up again."

His tone of defeat stings. I care about Marius, but his desire to protect me has eclipsed his reason and is bordering on disrespect. We are a people of honor and strength. How can I lead such a people if I give in to a pairing with a female whose familial line has violently fought to overthrow my own? It would be a stain on my reputation and a poor way to begin my rule.

No. I will rule the same way my ancestors did. With honor and strength. Besides, I have trained my entire life for this. My vow will not be a hindrance, of that much, I am certain.

"I am grateful for your concern, but I will be fine. You have trained me well, and my opponents will certainly pale in comparison to your skill."

The hint of a smile on Marius's face tells me the flattery is working. "You have seen your matches?" he asks.

I sigh and lean back in my cushioned chair, grateful for these last few moments of comfort. By the end of the day, I will be sleeping on a cot in a dank cell.

"I was given a brief overview," I say. "No specifics, of course, but I know I will be paired with a low-level gladiator today, and the following two fights will be against mid-level fan-favorites. As discussed, Gaius has agreed not to pair me with any of his 'criminals', so all fights will be consensual. There is no need for concern."

"Good. Remember your training and come home safe."

"Thank you, Marius. I will speak to you in three days." Almost as an afterthought, I add, "And please make sure my siblings do not cause too much chaos in my absence."

Marius laughs. "Of course. I will speak to you again, *mek Tyrna.*"

I smile at the premature use of the moniker and end the call.

GAIUS'S OFFICE appears to be more of a museum than a place of work, and I find myself staring curiously at his overflowing collection of artifacts. Every wall is lined with floor-to-ceiling shelves, covered in an array of both strange and familiar pieces of technology from the empire's past and present. While I am certain he did not build this collection himself, it is interesting nonetheless.

"And you have reviewed the contract?" Gaius asks, folding his hands over his ample belly.

I settle into one of the unyielding stone chairs, crossing an ankle over my knee. "I have."

Gaius, the Magistrate of this planet, watches me with a predatory gaze. He is Vhortahi, like myself, but it is painfully clear that our only similarities lie in our DNA. He has never lived on our home planet, nor does he have any interest in our people's values.

In a crowd of Vhorathis, he would stick out like a blood stain on a white tunic. Not because he is different, but because he is insecure about those differences. He is a bit under two meters tall—which is not unusual—yet he wears shoes to give him added height. His horns are underdeveloped and show signs of premature cracking, but he has gilded them to hide their imperfections. He pretends to be fearless, and yet he wears a personal electron shield generator around his neck.

His rule over the Coliseum has been marked by dubious methods and erratic laws, and while his methods are technically legal, they lack any sense of honor. Despite this, he has maintained his position for a surprisingly long time. At least 15 cycles on this planet. Needless to say, his replacement is high on my list of priorities.

"Excellent," he shouts, clapping his hands together. "I am glad you have read and understood the agreement. Just to confirm, you still agree to the addendum on your medical care? You have not had any … life changes since we last spoke?" He raises his brows and scratches the base of one of his gilded horns.

Word does travel fast.

"I understand your propensity for hiring female nurses and the position that it puts me in, yes. And there have been no life changes."

Gaius stares at me, clearly waiting for a further reaction. I hold his gaze and wait for him to continue.

"Right, yes. And you are aware we have not stocked any sedatives for you? Even for an emergency?"

"As I have already stated, I have *read* the contract." This is becoming tedious.

Gaius unfurls a ridiculous scroll and gives me a curt smile. "Of course. If you accept the terms, please place your print here." He points to a blank space at the bottom of the page.

Without hesitation, I sink a fang into the pad of my thumb, squeeze out a bead of blood, and stamp the contract. I was hoping this moment would be more … celebratory, but I suppose that is the way of things. You build them up in your mind until reality has no way of competing.

Gaius smiles. "Excellent. I will have the guards escort you to the preparation chamber."

"When will the fight begin?"

His eyes narrow, and in a voice dripping with disdain and pomp, he says, "You are not a Prince of Vhorath right now. You are a gladiator. *My* gladiator. And you fight when *I* say it is time to fight."

I do my best to hide my amusement.

Now that the power dynamic has flipped, the hungry cretin I have heard so much about appears. Many people try to paint Gaius as mad, but he has held this position for a long time, and I doubt someone lost in the storm of insanity could accomplish that. No. He is not mad. He is just driven by an insatiable thirst for dominance, and now that he has the future King of the Vhorathi Empire in his grasp, he is salivating.

It is as ridiculous as it his hilarious. Yes, we have a contract, but the contract is between him and me. It is only binding while we both draw breath, and he only draws breath because I let him.

I wonder if he realizes that?

Naturally, I could not kill him without consequences, and I would not want to anyway. He is lucky, really. It is not in my nature to disrespect his position of power. But, neither will I allow his arrogance to go unacknowledged.

When I stand, I do so slowly, rolling up to my full height until I am towering over his bent form. Taking my time, I examine a collection of old hand-held holoComs on a dusty shelf, poking one out of its neat alignment while watching Gaius scowl out of the corner of my eye. He does not scold me, and that alone tells me all I need to know.

With a curt nod, I duck through the doorway, gripping the stone arch with enough force to crack it before saying, "I will see you in the stands, Magistrate."

3

VALIANT SPIRES

VEXAR

THE COLISEUM'S CROWD is thunderous. A chorus of thousands—cheers, chants, and violent stomps—that blend into a rabid cacophony. It is both infectious and distracting. But I must focus. I must use my training.

Discipline and control.

I squat and grab a handful of dusty sand, admiring the soft, dry texture. This planet is so different from my home. There is nothing green. Nothing wet. Only dust and death. It is fitting, I suppose.

I spit into my handful of sand, adding some much-needed moisture, before rubbing my palms together and standing.

This moment is one I have thought about many times, but the scale is far more dramatic than I envisioned. On the vidFeeds, the Coliseum appears grand, but in person, it is vast, ancient, and foreboding, carved by the brutality of the desert itself. A massive stone structure weathered and worn to a nearly organic state. It is beautiful.

Where the sandy flat of the killing-floor ends, the rise of jagged stone begins. Vertical walls of heavily eroded rock give way to consecutive, expanding layers of seating that end where the stone peaks kiss the open sky above, as if inviting the gods to bear witness to what occurs within. It is a striking oasis, all valiant spires and dramatic fractures that speak of an ancient, raw power. The power of my people. And I can feel that power radiating from this place and all those who fill it.

Smooth wood greets my hand as I pull my axe from its sheath. It is shocking how effective the high-gravity training was. My body and axe feel featherlight.

Testing my legs, I jump, and a vicious smile crosses my face. I am grateful I heeded my brother's advice. He is wise in the ways of war.

"Today is a momentous day!" Gaius booms from his viewing box in the upper levels. "We have in our midst the Prince of the Vhorathi Empire, the Fury of Solira, the Vanquisher of Verdoon, Vexar Valdís!" The crowd roars its approval and Gaius proceeds to explain my purpose here. When he is finished, the metal portcullis opposite me begins to rise.

I pace, fixated on the shadows behind the rising gate while thousands of curious eyes track me. They are eager for blood. Perhaps too eager.

The sun heats my skin. Sand kicks up around my feet. Sweat drips from my nose. And then, my opponent emerges. I frown. He is not a species I am familiar with, and I have studied every sentient race within 250 light-years of this sector.

The male stalks towards the outer wall of the killing-floor, and an unsettling tightness creeps down my spine. His body is a strange amalgamation of creature types. His bottom half is that of a quadruped—four legs supporting an elongated body. But his top half is similar to a bipedal creature—a torso with two arms and a head. The more I look, the more certain I am that this male was not born. He was *made*.

My eyes flick to the Magistrate's box, halfway up the Coliseum's seats, where Gaius sits in his oversized throne. As certain as

I was that Gaius is not mad, the circumstances of this fight are forcing me to reconsider my assumptions. Bringing an engineered creature to Calidus is highly illegal, and yet, unless I am mistaken, Gaius has done just that and is flaunting the crime in front of me. In front of the future King of the Vhorathi Empire.

Shaking off my confusion, I return my focus to the arena. My opponent lazily walks the perimeter, swinging his longsword dramatically and riling the crowd into a frenzy. He is enjoying the attention.

Good. It is a poor use of his time.

Gaius's voice booms again, but the only word I hear is my opponent's name. "Botar."

My focus is narrow. Singular. Unwavering.

As my opponent parades, I learn. Every twitch of muscle and flash of eyes offers valuable insight.

Botar's head moves slowly under the weight of his oversized horns. *Reduced ability to track fast or unpredictable movements.* Four smooth hooves. *Vulnerable to unstable or slick ground.* Large hind muscles on hinged joints. *Strong forward attacks, but weak lateral movement.* Wide-set eyes. *Poor field of view in front and behind.*

This fight is clearly uneven, and yet, Botar seems unaware of that fact. If anything, he appears confident. Carefree.

Shaking my head, I kick off my boots and leave them in the sand. The soft ground gives beneath my feet, affording me additional leverage that my opponent does not have. As much as I would prefer to call off this fight, that choice is entirely out of my hands. I can only hope Gaius sees reason before the end.

A sharp, sudden blast of sound marks the start of the fight, and Botar charges towards me. Anxiety tightens my chest. I shake out my arms and focus.

He approaches at an angle, his hoofed feet sinking into the sand with each loping step. He expects me to dodge, so I do the opposite. I step in front of him, where I am certain his vision is limited. His head turns under the weight of those massive horns as he tries to track me. But he is slow. Gods, he is slow.

I glance up at Gaius who sits unmoving in his throne. *Does he want a slaughter?* No time to think. I jump, clearing Botar's horns while angling my body to land behind him. His head turns frantically as he searches for me in the wrong place. Frustration blooms, and I swing my axe into Botar's hind legs, sending him tumbling forward.

He regains his footing quickly. Blood coats his rear legs and pools in the sand beneath him, but he does not limp.

I lunge forward, dodge his sword, and land another punishing blow to a front leg. This time, he roars. With some space between us, I risk one last glance towards Gaius. He sits calmly, hands folded, face too distant to read. Everything about this feels wrong. I was promised an equal fight.

When Botar swings his sword again, I hook it with the beard of my axe and pull the blade towards me, letting my fist drive into his abdomen. There's a crack of bone. A wheeze of breath. I pull back to drive into him again. A glimmer of light catches my eye. His sword is free.

I duck, lose my footing, and feel the ripple of air as the blade passes over the back of my neck.

Too close.

I roll away. Sand sticks to my skin, my nose, my mouth. My hesitancy is going to get me killed. I cannot hold back anymore.

Botar's chest rises and falls rapidly. He is winded and bleeding.

I let the handle of my axe slip through my fingers until I am gripping the very end. Like this, it is a weapon of inertia. A brutal object to be wielded with aggression.

Botar lunges and swings his sword again with a hopeful roar. This time, I move towards it, ducking at the last moment and using my momentum to carry my axe into his chest. It lands with a wet crunch followed by a strange cracking sound as Botar crumples on top of me, burying me beneath his titanic weight.

My breath is short and shallow as I push him back and free myself. My vision is spotty. A chill rolls over my skin. I feel ... strange.

The crowd bellows. Gaius's voice thunders around me. And yet my focus does not waver from what I have done. Everything about this feels wrong. This was supposed to be a victorious moment, heroic even, but it feels hollow.

I grip the handle of my axe and wrench it free of Botar's corpse as guilt tightens my chest. He should never have been here at all.

Everything around me clashes in discordant commotion. The turbulent jeering of the crowd; the slumped body of my opponent; the blood covering my hands, my face, everything. I was sent here to prove my worthiness to lead. To show my strength. But this ... this was not strength.

Confused and uneasy, I do my best to appear stalwart, straightening up to my full height and keeping an unreadable mask on my face. My people are watching—not just my fellow Vhorathis watching the feed at home, but every face in these stands—I must not show weakness. Only strength. Only power.

Discipline and control.

I offer the crowd a subtle raise of my chin, grab my boots, and exit the arena.

The cool dark of the hypogeum is a welcome reprieve, but in the stillness, my confusion flourishes. That wasn't a battle; it was a murder. An unnecessary slaying. Botar had no hope of surviving that. Of surviving *me.*

Exhaustion surfaces as the energy of the fight wanes. I move at a sluggish pace, peeling away armor until a painful sting stops me. Something wet coats my hand. Blood. *Red* blood. I remove my leather breast-plate and find a large gash, deep and ugly, that traces a line from the middle of my ribcage to the top of my groin. Streams of crimson run down my body to pool at the waistband of my pants.

How?

I was not struck during that fight. And the wound feels strange. The pain is different from the familiar burn of a blade. Too delayed. Too dull.

Something is wrong. Very wrong.

My mind spins as I grab a towel and press it to my side, trying to slow the bleeding. I need a doctor ... and I do not have access to one. The realization hits me, and I want to tear this room apart.

Marius was right.

Focus. I need to stop the bleeding. I need something better than a towel. I spin and take in the room around me. It is simple and sparse. There is a rack for weapons, two wooden benches, a shelf with towels, and torches for light.

Torches. Fire. I can cauterize the wound.

I reach for a torch on the wall, and nearly roar when I discover the flickering light is coming from a bulb. Imitation flame. Another one of Gaius's many deceptions.

The Coliseum was built to appear ancient and operate in the ways of old—solid-state melee weapons, limited medical technology, and gambling with real chits—but of course, the illusion does not include real fire.

I push down my bubbling rage.

Emotion serves no purpose. Do not let it control you.

A shuffling sound has me spinning on the spot. The guards have come. I abandon the fake torch and turn to face my subjects, who are now my keepers. It is a strange dynamic.

One of them I recognize. He escorted me here but never gave me his name. Honestly, I am surprised he is working as a guard at all. His people, the Undurians, are not known for their courage. The other guard is new to me, but I know his kind well. He is from Palitus—the one planet in the empire I avoid visiting at all costs.

"Come with us," the Palitian says, waving his fat, scaly hand. His home world is a swampy, desolate planet, devoid of all life beyond the species the Palitians keep as livestock. Their appetite for destruction is unparalleled, and their planet has suffered because of that. It is a shock that their species survived long enough to develop language, much less technology.

I move to follow the Palatian, but the pale-faced Undurian slaps a hand over his mouth and points at the bloodied towel in my hand.

"You are bleeding," he says through his slim fingers, as if he has never seen a battle wound before. He is speaking Undurian, but the Palatian clearly understands him. *Translators. I almost forgot.*

"I am," I reply in Undurian.

"We ... uh. We don't have anyone who can..." His fumbling words only add to my rising frustration, and I give him a stern look, waiting for him to finish. "We only have female healers."

I wonder if this interaction is as uncomfortable for them as it is for me. They know who I am, and I doubt it feels natural to interact with me in this way. Perhaps that is why the Undurian is struggling with his words.

"Have bandages and a hot iron brought to my cell," I say as kindly as I can.

"A hot iron?" the Palitian asks, confused.

"To seal the wound," I say.

He shakes his head. "We have nothing like that. We can get you a needle and thread."

I let out a disapproving grunt. "Check anyway." Dying here is out of the question. I must finish my fights.

4

THRUM

AMARA

"AMARA!" A VOICE shouts from the hallway.

With a sigh, I abandon my fresh cup of tea and stick my head out of the Nurse's Room door.

"Pack supplies for a gladiator," Yuxta says.

"What kind of supplies?" I ask, tucking my still-wet hair over my ear. Solta took pity on me earlier and let me clean up. I even got a fresh dress and a pair of shoes. I think it was more for her benefit than mine, but at least I'm clean.

Yuxta gives me a confused stare, so I clarify, *slowly*. "Who are the supplies for, and what's wrong with them?"

"A big cut. He is Vhorathi. Losing a lot of blood."

Vhorathi ... never heard of them.

I duck back into the Nurse's Room, grab a med-bag, and start looking for the correct sedative in the cabinet. There's no vial labeled "Vhorathi". Of course.

Frowning, I pop my head back into the hallway. "Can you repeat the species name?"

"Vhorathi."

Ok. That's exactly what I heard before.

"What's the name of the home planet?" Maybe the vial is mislabeled?

"Vhorath."

Very original.

I duck back into the Nurse's Room and almost collide with Solta. "Gah!" I shout, surprised by her sudden appearance.

"What species did he say?" she asks calmly, her dark eyes and square pupils soft and unfazed. I repeat the name, and she sighs knowingly. "We do not have sedatives for him."

"We don't?"

"We do not. Grab what supplies are needed and give them to the guards. They will handle the rest." With a single graceful stride, she returns to the table and her datapad.

"Wait, so he has to sew himself up?" I ask, walking around the table and back into her line of sight. "Why don't we have sedatives for him?"

"A Vhorathi cultural rule," she says, waving her hand dismissively, eyes still on the datapad. When I don't leave, she looks up, clearly annoyed. "He is not permitted to come in contact with persons of the opposite sex, so there is no point in sedating him. You could not touch him, no matter his condition. Just deliver the supplies."

"You know he won't be able to sew himself up." Even I would struggle with that.

"He agreed to the risks when he signed his contract and refused medical care," she says, lowering her eyes back to the datapad, clearly unbothered by the impending death of another slave. Gladiator or not, she doesn't care. We're all the same to her. Expendable slaves. "Give him what he needs and leave. What happens from there is none of your concern."

Feeling a mix of discomfort and frustration, I bite my tongue and pack the kit as instructed, tossing in a few extra packets of hemostatic gauze. *It probably won't help him, but it's better than nothing.*

Before leaving, I risk one more question. "Do we really not have access to anything he *could* use? Like regen-tape?" I've never seen the stuff before, but Roveen waxes poetically about it like it's some long-lost lover. Supposedly, it's very easy to use and helps wounds heal quickly. Sounds a lot better than sutures.

"No, Amara," Solta says loudly, her voice tinged with annoyance. "Please, just do your job."

I leave the room with a frown etched on my face and a useless bag of medical supplies under my arm. I shouldn't be surprised by Solta's lack of concern—she's part of the problem—but it's hard to reconcile all the different faces she wears. She can be kind and gentle, but at the same time, she's complicit in the kidnapping and forced labor of hundreds of people. I swear, either her cognitive dissonance is robust enough to compete in the unhinged Olympics, or her soul is blacker than tar.

Yuxta escorts me through the maze of hallways in complete silence while I fume.

When we reach Cell 29, the shorter of the two guards posted there stalks towards me. It takes all of my willpower not to reel back. I've seen a lot of freaky aliens at this point, but this guy takes the cake. His face is a horror—scaly ridges covered with what looks like a thin layer of mucus—and he walks with a wide gate, approaching me like a massive salamander, dragging this tail on the ground behind him.

For some sick reason, my brain forces me to check for a slime-trail. There isn't one.

I hold out the med-bag. "The medical equipment you requested, sir."

The lizard grunts a confirmation and takes the bag.

I wait to be dismissed, but he just stands there, staring at me.

"Does the gladiator need help closing his wound?" I ask, hoping to end this interaction.

He answers with a short, angry, "No."

Ok. Noted. I lower my head in a quick bow and return to Yuxta's side. We get a few steps down the hall before I'm forced to a stop by a jarring thud in my chest. Air bursts from my lungs, and I bend over, bracing my hands on my knees as my heart takes off in a series of rapid, uneven beats. My ears roar. Sweat slicks my skin. And a surge of panic follows. *Is this a heart attack?*

"Amara!" Yuxta shouts, waving his hand emphatically.

I force myself to move. *Maybe it's just another panic attack. A really weird panic attack.* The only issue with that theory is that the anxiety showed up after the heart palpitations.

An unhelpful voice in the back of my mind says, '*It's probably an alien heart condition.*'

Great. Thanks, brain. Nothing like the warm reassurance of an untreatable new disease to calm my nerves.

As we near the first turn in the hallway, the uneven beats turn into a steady thrum. My heart's beating too fast, but I'm not feeling any of the negative effects I'd expect from that. *Fuck. If this is some weird heart condition, I'm completely screwed.* I don't have access to medication or human doctors, so any issue with my body is going to tank my life span... and the amount of time I have to act.

I collide with something solid, and an "Oumf" leaves me. It's Yuxta's outstretched arm. "What's go—"

He holds up a finger, his middle finger—which I guess might be considered his index finger since he only has three—and I wait. He tilts his head like a dog, oversized ears sticking straight out and twitching. Then I hear whatever he did: wet thumping sounds. *Maybe punches? I'm not sure.*

Then I hear a scream. A loud scream. Followed by the distant sounds of chaos.

Normally, a scream like that would turn my nervous system into a shaking idiot, but I'm fine. My heart's still beating faster than it should, but beyond that, everything seems normal. No adrenaline dump. No pounding headache. Nothing.

Ok. This is interesting.

Another scream reaches us. This one sounds closer.

Yuxta turns to me. "You must go to the Nurse's Room alone. Can you do that?"

I nod and watch as he takes off around the corner.

It takes a moment before I realize I'm *alone* in the hallway. Fuck. I really don't want to get caught out here, but at least if I am, I won't be the only person whose ass is on the line. Yuxta will be screwed too. Taking that small detail as a sign of his confidence that I'll make it back undetected, I start walking, slowly.

A year ago, I would have killed for an opportunity like this— some time alone to do some recon, maybe find a way to escape —but there's no point in that. The only thing waiting outside these walls is death.

A few days after I woke up in the Coliseum, I was assigned my first patient. A Sikut in Cell 7. The window in that cell is big and close enough to the ground outside for me to be willing to jump. So, instead of patching up the sedated Sikut, I jumped out the window and ran. I didn't have a plan or supplies, but I was free, and I thought I'd figure things out as I went. Maybe I'd find a nice local willing to help, or I'd find a shipyard and sneak onto a merchant vessel, but all I found was endless desert.

By the time the sun was setting, I collapsed at the base of a dune and was found by a couple of guards, sunburnt, dehydrated, and exhausted. They dragged me back here, and the Magistrate had me locked in a cell without food or water for two more days. I thought I was going to die.

At the end of the second day, I was handcuffed and taken to

the Magistrate's office. My head was swimming and throbbing. Lips cracked. Every movement hurt. And the stone chair in his office felt too much like metal.

"Escaping is pointless," the Magistrate said. "If you try to escape again, you will be deemed a criminal." He slowly crept around his desk and lifted the chain between my cuffed hands with a single finger. "The people of this planet hate criminals almost as much as I do." He dropped the chain, and my swollen hands crashed to my lap as he leaned over me. He was so close I could smell the sour odor of his breath and see the pink, raised skin around the base of his horns. "They will hunt you down and skin you alive for sport. No one *cares* if a slave lives or dies. You are nothing more than a set of hands, a sack of meat, a creature of labor. Remember that the next time you see an open window."

He wanted me to be terrified of him, of my situation, of everyone. And sure, I am scared, but not in the way he wanted. He took away his only bargaining chip. The only thing keeping me compliant. The only thing I had left. *Hope.* It's clear he hasn't realized how dangerous a person is when they have nothing left to lose, and I can't wait to watch him figure it out.

The sound of a lock thunking forces me to a stop. I'm barely ten steps away from where Yuxta left me and already someone's opening a cell? *Why?* There shouldn't be any gladiators moving for the next hour.

My heart continues its strange thrumming as I glance around, resisting the urge to run. I want to run, but if I run the wrong way, I risk encountering whoever made that sound, and I'm not ready to get caught breaking a law. Not yet.

I press my body against the stone wall and listen.

Silence.

The most logical explanation is that the guards are opening Cell 29 to deliver the medical equipment, and if that's the case, I can just keep walking the way I was going. But if the sound is coming from somewhere else…

First things first. Check Cell 29.

I move towards the end of the hallway, silently rolling through each step. When I reach the corner, I stop and carefully peek down the hall. Relief floods me. This lizard is opening the—

"Were you able to get a hot iron?" someone says in a voice like rolling thunder.

My skin tightens, hairs stand on end, and the thrumming in my chest reaches a dangerous speed. *That voice.* I slip back behind the wall and squat down, clenching my hands over my heart. I've never heard a voice like that, and the desire to hear it again is overwhelming my sense of reason.

"We do not, but we have other medical supplies," the lizard replies.

I can't stay here, but my muscles refuse to act.

"What do you have?" the thunderous voice asks, each word vibrating through my body with a quiet hum that grows more insistent by the second until I can barely breathe.

"A needle and thread."

"*Zar'vok,*" the voice booms. It's like listening to the sounds of boulders crashing beneath a river's surface during a flood. Both terrifying and hypnotic.

My fingers dig into my chest as the thrumming gets worse.

"This is all we can provide," the lizard says. "I am sorry, Vexar."

The door thuds shut and I'm plunged back into silence, feeling a sharp tension in my ribs and a pooling heat in my belly.

5

BLOOD SWEEP

AMARA

ROVEEN STARES AT me with her wide, gray eyes, antennae flicking back and forth in interest. "He left you?" she whispers in her native language through her too-small mouth. My translator repeats her words in English.

"There was some sort of skirmish happening down the hall. I couldn't see it, but it sounded bad. People were screaming."

She wiggles her antenna more widely this time, showing her confusion. "Strange."

Roveen is the only other nurse willing to risk a conversation with me. The Magistrate made sure I would be seen as a dangerous pariah after my escape attempt, and it worked. I've been properly ostracized. But not by Roveen. She's brave and smart and doesn't take shit from anyone. In summary, she's my favorite kind of person.

Pushing away my empty lunch bowl, I glance around to ensure we're still alone, and ask, "Do you know if Naxiur was sent to meet with the Magistrate before she went to the arena?" While I don't expect Roveen to know for certain, I'm hoping she saw the direction Naxiur was taken after she was found out.

Information is hard to come by here, but if I want a shot at the Magistrate, I need to know how to get back into his office. Obviously, my last run-in with the law got me in there, but as far as I know, I'm the only nurse who's broken a law and lived to tell about it.

"No," Roveen says solemnly. "After Naxiur was caught, I never saw her again."

I do my best to hide my disappointment. Whatever's going on with my heart has lit a fire under my ass, and I know the longer I wait, the less likely I am to succeed. Every day I spend here, I get weaker and slower. Sure, I could wait for more information to trickle into my lap, but that feels less like a plan and more like procrastination.

In the year I've been here, I've only seen the Magistrate twice. Once, after my failed escape attempt, and again when he was giving a tour to someone he kept calling, "my Queen".

I still don't know who that "Queen" was, but the day she was brought into the gladiator's quarters was the only time I've seen the Magistrate down here. My deduction: If I want an audience with the Magistrate, I either have to break a law and hope he wants to admonish me before my death, or wait for the Queen to come back and hope there aren't many guards around. Obviously, the second option is dumb. The first one is too, but it's less dumb than the alternative.

All I know for certain is that I can't keep living like this, and I refuse to die before doing everything in my power to take the Magistrate out. It's clear he doesn't see women as a physical threat, and it's also clear that out of all the nurses here, I'm probably the only one with the training to actually take the fucker down. After spending almost eight years with the Marines, I have a bias for action and the resolve to see that action through.

"I'm sorry about Naxiur," I say to Roveen.

She shows her teeth in a sign of gratitude. "Thank you."

I open my mouth to respond right as the door of the Nurse's Room bursts open. Still seated, I spin around and find the slimy reptilian guard panting for breath in the doorway. Somehow, he's managed to make himself look even more repulsive in the past hour. It's like he's sweating slime.

"You!" he shouts, pointing a hideous finger at me. "We require you!"

I glance at Roveen, and she lowers her antenna, clearly just as displeased by the situation as I am. Nurses aren't supposed to go on emergency calls without Solta's permission, but once again, I can't really say "no" to a guard.

With a reassuring nod to Roveen, I follow the lizard out the door.

He takes off down the hall, his short legs propelling him with anxious purpose while I struggle to keep up. A minute later, we skid to a stop in front of Cell 29, and instantly my heart starts thrumming again. As much as I'd love to stop and consider what that means, the lizard is already shouting.

"He is still bleeding! You must help him. He *cannot* die here." His voice is breathless and frantic with concern. Which is weird. Guards don't usually care about the gladiators. "Help him!" he shouts.

I thrust my hand towards the wall of steel between me and Vexar. "What am I supposed to do through a closed door?"

"Tell him what to do!"

He wants me to talk the guy through it? I'm not a 911 operator, I'm a fucking Corpsman. *Or ... I was. Whatever. Not important right now.* I glance at the other guard, who seems to be more focused on his hands than on what's going on around him. *Unhelpful bastard.* With a sigh, I turn back to the lizard.

"His name is ...?" I ask, not wanting to reveal my earlier eavesdropping as I move towards the door.

"Vexar," the lizard supplies.

"Vexar?" I ask, projecting my voice through the door. A rumbling grunt answers, and my heart stutters uncomfortably. "Can you tell me what's going on?"

"Blood," Vexar says.

It's been at least an hour since I delivered the med-bag. The fact that he's still bleeding and alive is both impressive and concerning.

"How much blood?" I ask.

"A lot."

If his physiology is anything like a human's, he'd already be in shock. But with aliens, there's no telling what sort of adaptations they've developed to deal with blood loss. A month ago, I treated a guy whose circulatory system had cut-off valves that would trade a limb to save his life. It was gross, but effective.

"Where's the injury?" I ask.

"My flank."

I pepper him with a few more questions, trying to gauge the situation, and it's not comforting. If he doesn't pack the wound and control the bleeding, he's not going to last much longer.

"Do you still have fresh gauze?" I ask.

"Yes."

"How much?"

"One roll."

Shit. That's not enough.

"Ok. Vexar, I need you to listen to me carefully. Don't take the gauze off. Layer the remaining roll on top and *keep pressure*. Then add whatever else you have on top of that. Towels, sheets, whatever. And keep the pressure. Can you do that for me?"

"Anything for you," he says in a breathy grunt, followed by what sounds like a chuckle. *Was that ... is he flirting with me?* No. He's clearly delirious.

I turn to the lizard. "He needs more gauze. Hemostatic gauze and bandages."

The lizard orders the pale guard to go, and a few seconds later, the lanky humanoid is sprinting around the corner and out of sight.

"How big is the wound?" I ask the lizard.

He holds up his hands to show me. The wound is big. About the length of my forearm. But wound size is relative. A big cut to me might be a paper cut to an elephant. "How big is Vexar?" I ask.

"Big," Vexar says through the door, his rumbling voice strained but still somehow playful.

I press my lips together and focus on the lizard as he extends his arm above his head and says, "Bigger than this."

"Much bigger," Vexar adds with a rumbling laugh.

This fucking guy. We're in the middle of a medical emergency, and he's joking around like he's still in middle school. Am I blushing? Maybe, but I'm also trying to focus on keeping him alive.

I turn back to the door. "Vexar? How much of the wound can you cover? Is it bigger than your hand?"

"Yes. But not bigger than my—"

I interrupt before he can finish that sentence. "Are you able to put pressure on the entire thing?"

"No. But you..." His voice trails off into a faint groan.

Fuck. If he loses consciousness—

No. Focus on the task.

"Vexar? I need you to take a sheet or something. Something big. And I need you to wrap it around your body to add pressure to the whole area. Can you do that for me?"

There's a long pause. Then he whispers, "Do not leave, Xelora."

I frown. "Vexar? Did you get the sheet around your body yet?"

A weakened grunt, followed by an unintelligible word, is the only response.

"Vexar?"

Silence. My stomach drops, and a surge of adrenaline rushes through me. I don't know why, but the urge to keep him alive is overwhelming. *I can't let him die.*

"Let me in," I say to the lizard, my voice firm and unwavering.

"No."

"Would you prefer he dies?"

"We have no sedatives," he says, crossing his arms over his chest in the universal sign for 'end of conversation'.

I thrust my hand at the door, outraged. "He's already unconscious, and if you don't let me in there, he's gonna die."

The scaly dickweed is impossible to read, but it's clear he isn't moving, and I don't know what to say to convince him.

"Acquired," my translator says as the pale guard sprints towards us with boxes of supplies under his arms.

To the lizard, I say, "If I can't go in there, then *you* have to. Take the gauze. I'll tell you what to do."

I take the boxes from the pale guard and hold them out to the lizard.

"Get away from the door," he orders.

Clutching the boxes to my chest, I take a few steps back. *Maybe this walking biohazard is going to help after all?*

The lizard opens the cell door and lets out a ridiculous shriek.

I dash forward and see a very large, very human-looking man draped over the bed, covered in blood, and clearly unconscious.

My heart slams against my ribs, and it feels like something is tugging at my spine. I shove the boxes towards the lizard and shout, "Go!" He takes a step back, holding his hands up. "Take these, and help him," I urge. His face remains unchanged, and I growl in frustration as I turn to the pale guard. "Then you do it. Take the supplies and I'll tell you what to do."

The pale guard shakes his head and backs away, but I swear there's a shadow of a smile on his wide mouth that sends a shiver down my spine.

I glance at Vexar, helpless, covered in blood, and way too close to death. Something in me knows my decision's already made, but I have to wait for my logical brain to catch up.

This is what I've been waiting for, right? A situation worth taking the risk? I just have to break this one law, and I can save a life and possibly end another. Sure, there's no guarantee, but if there was ever something worth the risk, it's this. Right?

I tighten my grip on the boxes and dart into the cell, expecting some sort of resistance from the guards. None comes.

'This is a bad idea', the voice in the back of my mind says, and I tell it to, 'Get fucked'. That voice is living in the past, where survival was the goal. But that's not the goal anymore. Revenge is. Revenge and resistance.

Fuck the Magistrate.

My feet splash in the dark puddle of blood that's formed on the ground. I drop the boxes, climb onto the bed, and check Vexar's airways. They're clear. He's breathing. I sink to my knees in the middle of the tacky pool, lining myself up with the bleed. Rough stone digs into my exposed flesh. The heavy scent of copper stings my nose. Gauze packets crinkle as I tear them open and start packing the wound.

I shout over my shoulder, asking the guards to get Roveen. She's a skilled surgeon and far more equipped to deal with a wound like this than I am.

No response. *Doesn't matter.* I keep moving. My hands cramp. Sweat drips. And the bleeding slows.

Please be alive.

I press my fingers to the side of his neck. Nothing. Nothing. A thud.

Holy shit, he's alive.

I let out a raspy breath and move my fingers to the inside of his wrist. Nothing. I slide my fingers up until I find the thud of an artery on the inside of his bicep. His pulse is strong. Slow, but strong.

Using the analog stop-watch on my wrist, I track his pulse against the seconds—or whatever this watch actually tracks—do the math, and get twelve. Twelve beats in whatever this planet considers a 'minute'. That's it. Hopefully, that's in range for him.

I jot the number on the bedsheet in blood and keep moving, pressing a bandage over the packed wound and using a twisted section of the bedsheet to add pressure.

Wishing my arms were longer, I climb on the bed and start my blood-sweep. As much as I'd prefer to do this on my feet, the placement of this bed was chosen by a moron who thinks medical care can be completed by a mountain goat.

Seriously, who puts a medical bed in a corner? Up against two walls?

My fingers slip over Vexar's scalp, between his massive, curling horns, and through the thick locks of his braided hair. I move down the back of his muscled neck and to his shoulders. His skin is warm and surprisingly soft—not that I'm paying attention to how his skin feels or anything.

Everywhere I touch, I come back with black blood on my hands. It's not his blood. His blood is red.

As I work my way down, it's clear I won't be able to wriggle my hands beneath him. He's too heavy. So, I check what I can and keep moving. I don't find any new injuries, but I do find scars. Lots of scars.

When I reach his legs, I groan in frustration. His pants are made of a thick type of leather. They won't absorb blood, and there's no way I can remove them. I run my hands over the material, searching for cuts in the fabric or temperature irregularities. Nothing. I pull his shoes off, and his feet seem fine too.

The last thing I do is check the underside of the mattress. The only blood I see is on the edge, where I already knew he was bleeding.

Finished with my check, I lean my forearm over the layers of gauze and bandages on his side and use my bodyweight to apply even pressure. Thank god he's not conscious right now. He's massive, and I have no doubt this level of pain would have him bucking, thrashing, and screaming at me. That's my least favorite part of being a medic. When someone's screaming at you to stop, but if you stop, they die. It makes you feel like a monster, and there's no way around it.

"Any luck on getting Roveen down here?" I ask over my shoulder, hoping the guards are still close enough to hear.

When I don't get a response, I awkwardly turn towards the door, keeping my body weight pressed against Vexar's side.

My stomach drops.

The cell door is shut. Not just mostly closed. Shut.

6

CLAWS

AMARA

T FIRST, I thought it was a mistake, like maybe they bumped the door shut by accident, but I'm seriously doubting that now. It's been at least thirty minutes, and no one's come for me. I don't get it. I just committed a serious 'criminal' offense in front of two guards, and instead of handcuffing me and sending me to my doom, they locked me in here ... with an un-sedated gladiator.

I'm trapped. Locked in a box. *Again.*

I try everything to get the door open—pulling, pushing, kicking, screaming—nothing works. I even toss a handful of bloody gauze through the meal slot in the door, hoping someone will notice it and let me out. But when I check the hall through the slot a short while later, the gauze is gone, and I'm still here.

This is bad. Really, really bad.

My heart pounds in my throat as I lean against the locked door and try to keep my mind from revisiting that living morgue. My head throbs. Chest burns. And every time I close my eyes, all I can see is that bright square of light.

But I can't keep spiraling. I need to calm down and get control of my situation.

I drop into a squat and push my hands against the floor in an attempt to ground myself. I let my emotions flow without interference, and eventually, I find my way to acceptance. I can't do anything about the locked door. I made a choice. I chose vengeance over a life of imprisonment. Humanity over safety. I knew there'd be consequences.

Feeling a little steadier, I push myself back to my feet and let out a dark laugh. If there is a God, they certainly have a sense of humor. After years of dodging bullets in war zones, I finally retire, only to find my death on an alien planet, not in a war zone, while trying to save the life of a wounded warrior. Go figure.

A shaky groan pulls my attention back to Vexar. He's stirring, but still not conscious. Which is good. His body needs time to recover before his brain gets involved. Also, Solta said he opted out of medical care, and I don't know if he's going to be pissed I kept him alive.

I glance at the long claws that tip each of his fingers and can't help but imagine the kind of damage they could do. If he wakes up and wants me dead, there won't be anything I can do to stop him. But I can't just let him die. So, my choices are: Sew him up and risk him mauling me to death, or let him die and gift the Magistrate another dead slave.

Yeah. Option two isn't happening.

I move to check his pulse, and the moment I touch his skin, a warm tingle shoots down my spine. It's strange enough that I jump, but subtle enough that I'm able to ignore it. His heart rate's holding steady, but without a baseline for his species, I don't know if that's a good thing.

"Any chance you know what your heart rate should be?" I ask jokingly.

When I glance up, my stomach flutters like a pre-teen girl seeing her first crush. In my defense, he's shockingly beautiful. Beautiful in the same way a deadly ice storm is.

My eyes trace the sharp line of his jaw up to the high rise of his cheekbones and over the strong angle of his nose. Until now, I hadn't taken a second to really look at him, and I'm ... transfixed.

In the low light of the cell, his horns cast dangerous-looking shadows, like two black snakes curling up from his hairline. I've always associated horns with herbivores, but this guy is definitely not a herbivore. Everything about him screams, "predator".

Even lying down, I can tell he's at least seven feet tall, probably more, and so broad he looks almost stocky. I should be frightened, but the only emotion I feel is a quiet sense of awe, like the first time I saw a great white shark.s

My lack of fear is probably unhealthy, but considering my looming death, it sort of makes sense. Besides, I've already talked to the guy and he seemed ... nice? Funny? Flirty? I don't know. He just didn't seem like a monster.

AFTER GETTING Vexar and the surrounding area as clean as possible, I stare at the med-bag lodged beneath his thigh. Everything I need is in that bag, and I'm dreading having to find a way to dislodge it. The bag might as well be lodged underneath a fallen tree.

I bend at the waist, stretching my tired legs, and groan when I realize my knees are covered in Vexar's blood. "Fuck, I miss pants." Wearing a dress has its upsides, especially in the heat, but right now, pants would be nice.

I could clean my legs, but I have limited resources and I'd

rather not waste them. Besides, I'll most likely be dead before nightfall. No need to worry about alien pathogens if I'm dead.

With a final sigh, I move to the edge of the bed.

"Alright, Amara, time to suck the day's dick." I reach for the med-bag's handles, and ... can't reach. Too far.

I swear, if I ever find the person who designed these rooms...

Setting my jaw, I climb onto the bed, reach over Vexar's right leg, and pull.

No movement. Need more leverage.

I swing my leg over his right thigh, grip the bag, and stop when my eyes catch on the growing bulge between his legs.

Seriously? How does he have enough blood for a boner?

For a moment, it's almost funny. Seconds later, my body reacts with a wave of lustful heat, and I panic. I yank the bag and shout as it pops free, sending me tumbling backwards onto his thighs. Naturally, Vexar lets out a groan at that exact moment, which sends me flying off the bed with a terrified yelp.

Somehow, he doesn't wake.

Feeling my heart pounding in my throat, I shake my head. The reaction I just had was wildly inappropriate. Vexar's an unconscious patient, having a normal bodily reaction, and I'm what? Getting horny?

Fucking hell, Amara.

I slam the bag onto the table and start digging through it while trying to talk myself down.

"Sometimes, uncomfortable things happen when you're a nurse," I whisper. "I mean, usually it's the patient who has an uncomfortable reaction, but that's ok. Usually, the patient isn't a wildly hot alien with a boner."

Fuck... I drop into a squat in front of the table, breathing heavily.

"Ok," I say gently, trying to soothe myself, "just shake it off and focus on the task."

I get a makeshift workstation set up on the side of the bed, wave the sani-light over everything, tuck the extra pair of medical shears between my boobs—I'll need a weapon later— and get to work.

Beneath the gauze, the bleeding has slowed, but the wound is bad. It looks almost cauterized in places. Which is weird. The only injuries I've seen out of the arena are from blades, opponents' body parts, and blunt force. Unless he was fighting a balrog or something, I'm not sure how this happened. The good news is, I know how to deal with it.

If you're wondering why I have experience stitching up partially cauterized wounds, the answer is simple: Marines do dumb shit when no one's looking.

My only real concern with the procedure is the depth of the wound. His fascia is nicked in a few places, and I've never had to suture fascia before. But they say confidence is key, and after a few minutes of swearing under my breath, I stare at my handi-work with a smile. His fascia is pulled back together with five neat little Xs. It's not perfect, but if I just keep doing what I'm doing, I think—

Something darts across my vision and latches onto my wrist.

It's a hand.

Vexar's hand.

A yelp bursts from my lungs as my eyes fix on those deadly claws. I try to pull away, twisting my arm in an attempt to free myself from his vice-like grip. It doesn't work. *I'm trapped.* My lungs expand and contract at an impossible rate. Adrenaline burns.

My eyes snap up and...

Holy shit. Impossibly green eyes lock on mine. Alien eyes. My heart races. Skin burns. I open my mouth, but before I can make a sound, the familiar fog descends, the cold press of metal hits my skin, and my nervous system shuts me down.

7

XELORA

VEXAR

A SERIES OF sharp, burning sensations pulls me from the darkness and into interminable agony. My head pounds. Pain arcs over my torso in searing bursts. Something brushes against my ribs, and in a desire to stop the pain, I reach out and catch it.

A startled yelp breaks the silence and pulls me from the haze.

A female...

Her large brown eyes snap to mine.

Confusion, surprise, and a foreign feeling I cannot identify rush through me. Everything stills. Her warm skin vibrates against my palm. Then the moment shatters. The female's eyes unfocus, and she starts to fold in on herself, collapsing towards the floor. I act without thought, releasing her wrist and catching her waist before she topples.

Bolts of agony rip through the muscles of my side, and with a deep groan, I hoist her onto the bed. Her head lolls back, draping a river of dark hair across my neck.

Is she ...?

I press a finger to her neck and feel the rapid flutter of her pulse.

She is alive.

And she smells ... amazing, earthy and sweet, like warm mornings in the *veladoo* orchards when the soil comes alive in the sun. I suck down the scent and smile as I realize where I am.

I am dead. This is *Zarlysa.*

The memory of what came before is fuzzy, but the image of blood is clear. I was wounded. And I died. There is a short moment of sadness before I allow myself to sink into the pleasure of having a female's skin pressed against mine. I am free. I smile and nearly laugh. This is what freedom feels like. True freedom. The weight of responsibility, gone.

I adjust myself to get a better look at the female's face, and as I shift, so does she. One of her elbows drops against my ribs, and a wave of fresh agony ends the fantasy.

This is not the afterlife.

Tears of rage prick my eyes as the memory of where I am comes rushing back. I am still in the Coliseum. Still injured. Still locked in a cell. And a female is lying across my chest.

"*Vok!*" I shout.

I am not dead, but my vow is broken.

My vow is broken. And I am wounded. A series of panicked breaths shakes my body before I can get control of myself again.

I need information.

My surroundings have not changed from earlier. The door is closed, there are no guards present, and nothing seems out of place—except for this female.

How did she get in here? What was she doing?

I close my eyes, thinking back to the moment I woke up. The female was kneeling next to the bed, her hands were on my flank, and she was doing something to my wound.

Is she a nurse?

If she is a nurse, why is she in my cell? And why is she unconscious?

I take her arm in my hand and examine her wrist, wondering if I harmed her. Her arm feels like a brittle leaf in my grasp, and yet, it appears undamaged. But there is so much blood. Her hands are covered in it.

With a quick sniff, I groan, knowing exactly where the blood came from. It is my blood, and the scent burns my nose and forces me to fight back unwanted memories. *I must focus.*

The female is human, which is odd, considering the empire's treaty with Earth. The fabric of her dress is stained with blood. She wears no identifying marks or badges. And her face...

A jolt of recognition runs through me. The resemblance is too clear. Too undeniable. The slightly upturned end of her nose. The way her mouth curves down at the corners. The striking contrast of her blushed lips, dark hair, and starlight skin.

"Xelora," I whisper.

The only reaction I get is a strange flutter in my chest. I do not know why I expected more. I shake my head, feeling foolish. She is not a goddess; she is a *human*, and I am supposed to be looking for answers, not admiring her. And yet, I am struggling to look away. My willful eyes continue down her body, tracing over the rise of her breasts, along the sloping curve of her waist, and to her hips. A tremor runs through me as the uncomfortable feeling of desire begins to creep in.

"*Vok*," I groan, as I press my head back into the pillow.

Where is my control? I feel powerless against the tempestuous inferno roaring in my chest. I am burning alive from the inside out. My eyes and mind are not my own, my skin is tight and hot, and my heart is fluttering uncontrollably. It is too much to ignore. *She* is too much to ignore. The way her weight presses into me, the warmth of her body, the goddess-like features of her face, the tickle of her hair on my neck, the scent of her skin, the soft curve of her waist beneath my hand.

My hand.

I have been holding her waist this entire time.

I pull back in a panic and knock her arm off the bed. A flicker of light catches my attention, and carefully, avoiding touching more of her than necessary, I pull a shiny object from between her fingers.

A needle.

She *is* a nurse. A human nurse. *On Calidus?*

A quiet moan escapes from between her pillowy lips, and I tense.

"What?" she whispers, her voice carrying with it a thin thread of memory. It is the voice from the other side of the door. She was trying to help me. She mumbles something else I do not understand, and her eyelids burst open. A look of horror takes over her face, and she jumps from the bed, jostling me and sending a wave of pain through my ribs.

"What the hell?" she shouts, breathing heavily and pressing a hand to her chest.

English. She is speaking English.

Gritting my teeth through the pain, I respond in her own language. "You were unconscious. Are you hurt?" The language feels stilted and strange on my tongue, but I am pleased I have not forgotten it.

"Wait ... what?" She looks at me with what I believe is confusion, then shakes her head. "I'm fine."

"Then why did you fall unconscious?"

"I ..." she stammers, looking both puzzled and annoyed. "It's called vasovagal synco— uh, fainting ... because—" She lets out a sound of what I assume is frustration before saying, "What the hell is happening right now?"

"Why did you faint?"

"It doesn't matter! Why did you pull me onto the bed? And ... and ... *you* aren't even supposed to be awake!"

"Me?"

"Yes, *you!*"

Despite her small stature, she admonishes me with such fervent ferality that I find myself captivated. No one yells at me, ever, and it is surprisingly disarming—at least coming from her. She is fearless. But also making very little sense.

"Would you prefer I pretend to sleep?" I ask.

Her eyes go wide, and she presses a fist to her forehead. "What the fuck is happening right now?" she whispers.

"I am not certain. I just awakened." *Is 'awakened' the correct word?*

Her hand drops to her side, and her cheeks turn a lovely shade of pink. "Well, this isn't going the way I'd expected. I thought you'd be ... messed up? But clearly you're some sort of alien miracle, because you seem..." She shakes her head. "Are you ok? You lost a lot of blood."

I move to prop myself up on an elbow, but an intense surge of pain stops me. My injury is worse than I thought.

"Stop moving!" she shouts, rushing towards me. "You're going to ruin my hard work." Her hand contacts my shoulder, and a bolt of euphoric electricity shoots through me.

"*Zar'vok,*" I groan, surprised by the intensity of her touch. "I —" I need to ask her to stop, but the words die on my lips as her hand slides onto my chest and absolute ecstasy spreads across my skin. Gods, is this what a female's touch is supposed to feel like?

It feels too good, and yet, I know it should not. None of this should feel good. I should push her away. Command her to stop. But instead my eyes are drawn to her face, to her beauty and her fire, to her complete lack of fear. I could crush her head with my hand, and yet, she is more concerned for my well-being than her own.

"Just lie down," she orders as she drops into a squat next to the bed. She prods the sore flesh on my side, and I clench my teeth.

"Your work?" I ask.

"What?"

"You said I was going to ruin your work."

"Uh … yeah."

Another prod sends hot agony through me, and I suck in a breath. "And what work is that? Torturing me?"

"I'm trying to help you."

"By stabbing me with your tiny sword?" I hold up the needle I pulled from her hand, and she frowns.

"I was closing your wound."

"By making more wounds?" *Am I teasing her?*

"I was sew— Wait. You're speaking English? How?" She stands and looks at me like I've done something impossible.

"The same way as you. With my mouth." Her expression pinches in annoyance, so I add, "I learned it. Now, explain what you were doing to me with your sewing sword." I cannot tell if I am being playful or mean, but both are out of character for me. Perhaps I have lost more blood than I thought?

"I was stitching your wound closed." She makes a sewing gesture with her hands, and I nearly smile.

"Ah, a seamstress of the flesh." I give her a wink and offer the needle back.

She doesn't take it, but her cheeks burn a brighter shade of red. "Do you really not know what stitches are?"

"It is much more fun to pretend I do not." I *am* teasing her.

Her lips betray a smile, and she shakes her head, sending another strange flutter through my chest. "Is it safe to say you aren't mad I kept you alive?"

My stomach drops as the reality of my situation comes rushing back with sickening speed. The joy I was feeling disappears, and I am left with a hollow pit in my chest. She saved my life, but she also cost me my throne. I should not be enjoying light conversation; I should be determining if she is a threat. My claws bite into my palms. I need to know why she is here. Who sent her? What is her purpose?

"How did you gain access to my cell?" I ask, my tone both commanding and sharp. To my surprise, her expression hardens into a look of disgust.

"So you *are* pissed I saved you."

"How did you gain access to my cell?" I repeat more firmly.

Her brows raise. "Wow, from charming to charmingly aggressive in ten seconds flat. You know, I'm almost impressed." She waits for me to respond, but I hold steady until she breaks. "For fuck's sake, ok. The guards opened your cell after you passed out. I asked them to help since I couldn't without sedating you—at least not legally—but they just stood there like a couple of sentient paperweights. So, I took action."

"The guards let you in?"

She shifts her weight, but her expression remains hard. "They didn't fling open the doors and wave me in like some long-awaited messiah, no."

Some of her words are unfamiliar, but it is clear she is being sarcastic. Possibly trying to hide guilt or deception? Yet her face shows no signs of deceit. Strange. This must be a defense mechanism of some sort. Perhaps she is more wary of me than I thought?

"And neither guard tried to stop you?" I ask, softening my tone.

"Obviously not."

I glance at the closed door. "Why is the door shut?"

"I don't know, maybe because they shut it behind me?"

"Is it locked?"

She tilts her head forward, purses her lips, and stares at me through long lashes. "What is this? Twenty questions?" When I don't respond, she sucks her teeth and folds her arms over her chest. "No, they didn't ask me to help you. No, they didn't try to stop me. Yes, they shut the door and locked it. And yes, I'm your only hope of staying alive." She lets out a heavy breath. "You know, you were a lot more fun before you started interrogating me."

"Why did they lock you in here?"

"This might come as a shock, but they didn't give me an explanation."

I run a hand down my face, trying to process the information she's provided. Under normal circumstances, the guards would never allow someone to break Gaius's laws—it is their job to enforce them—but according to this nurse, they just stepped aside and let her in. If what she says is true, it reveals something far more sinister than incompetence.

A weight settles in my chest. It seems my fears were not unfounded.

My eyes flick back to hers, and a tightness grips my spine. Her expression is cold and too similar to the stony features of Xelora. It is strange. Eerie even. And so achingly familiar.

"Did you know my contract stated I was not to receive medical treatment?" I ask, pleased that my English is already improving.

She bites her lip, and her expression softens. "The head nurse mentioned it. Said I couldn't help you even if you were sedated, but I took a chance and assumed you didn't want to die. Did I get that wrong?"

Somehow, I do not think she knows who I am. But my mind is foggy from the pain and blood loss, and it is clear I cannot trust my own judgement. I feel distracted. Distant.

"Why?" I ask plainly.

"Why what?"

"Why did you enter my cell? I assume you are aware of the consequences, so why did you do it?"

She picks absentmindedly at the dried blood between her fingers, but her eyes stay fixed on mine. "As I already said, I assumed you didn't want to die, so I decided to help."

Gods, she is difficult. "What I am asking is why *you* chose to risk your job—and possibly your freedom—for me." Gaius takes his laws very seriously, and I doubt her transgression will be easily forgiven. In the best possible scenario, she will lose her job, but there is a risk of far greater consequences.

She stares at me for a long moment, as if she is trying to work out some complex question in her mind. "I don't know." *Lie.* "I wouldn't have been able to live with myself if I let you die."

I wait, hoping she will elaborate. She does not.

"Why are you lying to me?" I ask.

Her brows furrow. "I'm not." I bobble my head, and her lips pull back in a sneer. "I'm sorry, are you mocking me right now?"

Wait, what? "No, I am not mocking you."

"Then what the hell was that?" She mimics my head bobble with a rude expression.

"It is a gesture of uncertainty."

"Oh..." she says slowly. "Sorry, you just ... well, you're speaking English and it's kinda hard to remember you're an alien." She twirls a finger next to her head, and I assume she is referencing my horns.

"Do you know who I am?" I ask. If she does, her actions will make much more sense.

She throws her hands up. "I don't know. I was told your name is Vexar. Is that wrong?"

I cock my head. "Did Gaius send you?"

"Who?"

I shake my head, dismissing the question. The name did not spark any familiarity on her face, and I believe her. She does not know who I am. Gaius did not send her. *What am I missing?*

"You risked your job and possibly your freedom to save my life because ... it was the right thing to do?" Humans aren't known for their self-sacrificing behavior, are they?

"I did it because the alternative was worse."

"The alternative?"

Her eyes narrow before she shrugs. "Maybe it was the wrong choice, but at least it was *mine*."

She has stopped lying, but her words are cryptic, and it is clear I cannot trust her. My vow may be broken, but my discernment is not.

"Thank you for saving my life," I say, bringing the questions to an end.

She lets out a humorless huff. "I— Uh... Well, that was a quick 180."

"Are you aware that your speech is very unclear?"

"Are you aware that you're a bit of a twat?"

That was an insult, but I am not sure what it means, so I ignore it. "Well, thank you anyway. For saving me."

"So you aren't mad?"

"No."

"I hate to break it to you, but you *sound* mad."

I let out a low, rumbling breath and gaze at the sharp ripples in the stone above me. *Where is my control? My calm facade?*

"I am not mad at you, I—" I stop myself before I reveal more than necessary. "I am in pain," I say awkwardly. She raises a brow, and somehow, that small action has me scrambling to take my words back. "The pain is fine, and I am not mad, I am grateful. Thank you."

Why do I keep saying 'thank you'? This human is confounding my sense of reason and testing my self-control. If I did not know better, I might assume she had some sort of dangerous pheromone that was affecting my mind.

"Well..." she trails off, cupping her elbow in one hand and tapping her lush lips with the other. "You're welcome."

A warmth spreads over my skin, and I quickly avert my eyes.

Discipline and control.

My wound needs to be closed. I should focus on that.

8

VELADOO

VEXAR

"WHERE IS THE thread?" I ask as I work to reposition myself until I can better see the wound spanning my torso. Now that the bleeding has slowed, the depth and severity of the gash is clear, and the sight has my stomach in knots.

"Why? Are you planning on sewing yourself up?" she asks, moving closer.

"I am." I have no desire to hand my fate over to this ... vexing stranger. "Now, can you find the thread for me?"

"No."

My eyes slowly track up her body. "Did you just tell me, 'no'?"

"Uh, yeah."

The absolute nerve...

"Fine," I growl as I push myself to a sitting position and start searching for the thread. My breath turns ragged as the pain intensifies, but I do not stop. I can handle pain. It is nothing new. The white sheet is stained with large patches of dark red that make identifying objects harder than it should be.

"You've got to be fucking kidding me." She reaches for the side of the bed and scoops up a handful of small packets.

Is that the thread? Why would they put it in packets?

I reach for them, but she draws back.

"Really?" I ask, raising a brow.

"Are you a doctor?"

"No. Are you?"

She scowls, and my heart thuds wildly, as if I am enjoying her ire. But that makes no sense.

"If you sew yourself up, you'll do a shit job and either give yourself an infection or a hernia."

"What do you care if I give myself an infection or a hernia?" Whatever a hernia is.

"Just to be clear, you, a guy who couldn't even control his own bleeding, wants to sew himself up? Instead of accepting help from me? Someone who knows what they're doing?"

"Yes," I answer.

"Right. Ok." She tosses the packets onto my chest and folds her arms. "I can tell you have some sort of complex going on, so we'll just do this the hard way." She turns, walks to the far side of the cell, and sinks to the ground.

A "complex"?

With her legs crossed, she gestures towards me. "Well, go on, Nurse Vexar. You have what you need."

The only people who have ever treated me this way are my brothers, and I am not sure how to handle it coming from someone else. She's obstinate and argumentative and the exact opposite of everyone I have ever met. Half of me finds her infuriating, while the other half is intrigued. Captivated even. I almost want to push her further and see what she does, but I resist the odd temptation.

Working to ignore her, I rip open a thread packet and am surprised to find a needle with the thread already attached. It takes me a few tries to get a hold of the small needle, but I manage. All the while, the nurse sits, picking dried blood off her hands and occasionally flashing me impatient glances.

"Am I boring you?" I ask.

She shrugs. "Just waiting for the interesting part."

With the needle in hand, I grip both sides of my wound and start to sew. Sweat beads on my brow as bolts of pain ricochet through me, but I do not stop. *Never stop. Never slow.* By the time I've driven the needle through my flesh for the fourth time, I realize my error. I failed to tie a knot in the first stitch, and now, with every pull and release of the thread, the wound opens and closes.

I have no idea what I am doing.

I glance over and find the nurse watching me with a quiet intensity that makes my skin tighten and neck burn.

"Have you never seen someone sew themselves up?" I ask.

She stands and approaches. "Not like this, no." Her voice is soft and caressing—a shocking contrast to her earlier tone. She adjusts the light next to the bed and squats down, gazing up at me. "I get it, you're a big tough warrior, but you don't have to do this yourself. You *can* accept help."

"I am fine," I insist, not meeting her gaze.

Her hand reaches out and rests on mine. The intimacy is startling, but I do not flinch away. Wide, dark eyes bore into me with a kindness and depth that cracks the stone around my resolve, and I feel myself already giving in to her.

"Let me help. Please."

I want to refuse, but my body moves on its own, offering her the needle before I have a chance to consider my actions. Something about her makes me want to trust her. Some urge in the back of my mind. A pull deep in my gut.

With gentle movements, she takes the needle and reaches

for something on the edge of the bed. Her fingers brush my side, and I tense as my nerves fire all at the same time.

"Sorry," she says, glancing up, "you were laying on the needle-driver."

I hope I have not made a horrible mistake by accepting her help, but my vow is already broken, and it is too late to choose honor over survival. Dying here would leave a power vacuum and cause irreparable damage to the empire. Beyond that, I am quite certain of the cause of my peril, and it is a crime I cannot allow to go unpunished. I may not be able to retain my throne, but I can still retain some semblance of order in this empire.

After a few waves of the sani-light, she picks up a pair of long tweezers in one hand and a clamp-like instrument in the other. With an apologetic smile, she says, "I wish I had something to help with the pain, but I don't. So, just tell me if you need a break. And if you feel like you're gonna pass out, tell me."

I nod, still uneasy about accepting her help but willing to trust my instincts. I just wish I knew what she was getting out of this. Motives are as important as actions, and hers make no sense. She risked her freedom for a stranger. Why?

She must notice my apprehension, because she pats my shoulder and says, "Don't worry, you're in good hands. Just don't move, yeah?"

The needle dives into my flesh, sucking the air from my lungs.

"Are you intentionally making this painful?" I grunt.

"Surprisingly, no. But this is going to suck for a bit, and there's not much I can do about it."

Somehow, despite my obvious pain, she seems entirely unaffected. Calm even.

My muscles tense as I struggle to lie still, and when I look down, there is a pleased smile curling her lips.

"Are you enjoying this?"

She shrugs. "I'm just glad you finally pulled your head out of your ass. You butchering this would have been the real torture." She pauses. "For me, that is."

I watch her, transfixed by the relaxed contours of her familiar face. "Why are you helping me?"

"Because you need it," she says, and I feel the truth in her words.

"I DO NOT KNOW YOUR NAME," I say, still unable to take my eyes off her face as she focuses on her careful dance of thread and steel.

"Amara."

"Amara," I repeat back, enjoying the way the sound rolls off my tongue. "I like it. Is that a common human name?"

"There aren't any names that are common for *all* humanity. We're too ... separated."

"By what?"

"Different cultures and languages and stuff."

Of course. Her people have many languages. "How many languages do your people have?" I ask, wishing I already knew the answer.

"A lot," she says slowly as her face scrunches like she's just realized something. "How is it that, out of thousands of human languages, you just happen to speak English? Not French or Spanish or whatever else?"

"I do speak Spanish."

"Of course you do," she mutters.

"Mandarin too," I add. "Like I said, I know many languages."

"Let me guess, you're also an accomplished marksman and you compose symphonies in your free time."

"I do not understand." I know what her words mean, but it feels like I am missing her meaning.

She shakes her head, a ghost of a smile on her lips.

"That was sarcasm, yes?" I ask.

She laughs. "Yeah, it was. So where are you from?" Her hands still, and she looks up at me with concern. "You're not from *here*, right? From Calidus?"

"No one is from here." How does she not know that? "I am from Vhorath," I say.

"Oh, right. Forgot I knew that."

"How did you know I am from Vhorath?" I thought she did not know anything about me.

"They told me when I was looking for your sedative—before I knew you didn't have one." Her hands settle on the edge of the bed. "You keep acting like I should know more about you, but then you get weirded out by the things I do know. So what's going on? Are you a criminal or something?"

I bite back a laugh. "I am not a criminal, no."

She resumes stitching with a hum. "Well, what's life like on Vhorath?"

"We all speak the same language and function under the same government. We value family and community, but above all else, we value honor. Our biggest exports are weapons, wood, and produce."

"Wood?"

"We have very large trees."

"Huh. Alien trees." There's a sharp pain as she tugs on something in my side. "For some reason, I never considered what other planets would be like. Beyond this one, obviously." She pauses and wets her lips. "What do you miss most about it? Home, I mean."

"That is a very personal question."

Her eyes narrow. "Uh, not really." When I don't respond, she adds, "There's no one here to judge you but me. Sure, I might be a bit of an asshole, but I'm not going to be a dick about your heartfelt answer."

"The *veladoo* orchards."

"*Veladoo*? Is that, like, a fruit?"

I take in the color of her lips—the exact color of ripe veladoo. "Yes. My favorite fruit."

Our conversation continues, discussing our homes and the things we miss the most. She tells me about lush, green forests and something called "moss". Her expression brightens as she tells me about tall mountains, covered in snow, and how humans slide down them for fun. It sounds like a strange activity, but also very enjoyable. The one thing she does not talk about is family or friends. I wonder if that is why she is here.

A short while later, we take a break. She perches on the table with a cup of water clutched in her small hands.

"You know, you're different than I thought you'd be," she says, kicking her legs in the open air.

"As you thought I would be?"

"After our conversation through the door, I made some assumptions."

"And what assumptions were those?"

She laughs. "Honestly? I thought you'd be a bit of an idiot Casanova."

I frown in confusion.

"Sorry. I keep forgetting about the cultural barrier—your English is really good by the way." She pauses, glancing away in thought. "I guess I assumed you'd be a meat head— Nope, that won't work. Uh ... I thought you'd have more muscle than brain. You know?"

"What would have given you that impression?" I do not

remember all of our earlier conversation, but I doubt I would give off such an impression in any state. *Except this woman seems to draw out the least polished version of me at every turn.*

She raises a brow. "For starters, making cocky and suggestive remarks when you're about to die is relatively rare. For most people at least."

What did I say to her?

Keeping my surprise from my face, I ask, "And how are you so familiar with what people are capable of when they are close to death?"

She sets down the water and moves back to the side of the bed where she kneels to resume stitching. "I was a corpsman," she says before adding, "a combat medic in the—"

"*You* were in the military? In combat?"

She scoffs, and it is clear I have made an error. "You're surprised," she says coolly.

I can feel the trap closing around me, but I fall into it anyway. "I am just surprised—" My words are cut short by a particularly painful jab of her needle, and when she meets my gaze again, there is a ruthless threat in her eyes that makes me swoon. She is fire and fury in a very deceiving package. "I am no longer surprised," I grunt. Whoever this woman is, she defies my expectations at every turn.

She smirks, clearly satisfied with bringing me to heel, and continues. "As I was saying, I was a medic—we call them corpsmen in the Navy... Uh, Earth Navy? Whatever. What I'm trying to say is that I've seen my fair share of tough-guys with serious injuries and your reaction was ... surprising." Her eyes meet mine, and something strange happens.

For a heart-stopping moment, the cell around us melts away until the only thing that exists is her. The tug in my gut grows, and it is clear something inside me has shifted.

Words fall out of my mouth with little thought. "You are magnificent," I say.

Her lips press together, holding back a smile. "You've lost a lot of blood. Let's save the flirting for later, yeah?"

9

THE EMPIRE

AMARA

WELL FUCK. NOW I've done it. I didn't mean to flirt with him, but evidently I just couldn't resist, and now I've gone and confused the guy. Ok, maybe not 'confused', but I'm definitely leading him on. Is he stunning? Yeah. Is he fun to talk to? Yeah. Is he easily the most captivating person I've ever met? Yeah. But I still can't let him distract me from the reason I'm here in the first place.

I finish another set of knots and clip the thread, trying to ignore the sensation of Vexar's eyes burning into my face. My only hope is that he's still delirious from blood loss and this will all blow over soon. Honestly, he might not even be staring anymore. It could just be in my head. I should check.

My eyes pop up and lock with his. *Oh shit.* I drop my gaze back to my hands as my heart threatens to beat out of my chest. He's definitely eye-fucking me, and instead of feeling weirded out, I'm ... I'm a little turned on.

What the hell is wrong with me? I shouldn't be turned on; I should be wary as hell. But I'm not. For some weird reason, I feel completely safe around this giant murder machine. Like really safe. Even though I shouldn't. Obviously.

Nothing about my situation is 'safe' right now. I'm basically standing at the base of my own gallows waiting for the guards to tie the noose, and all I can think about is how safe and horny I feel with this guy. *Ugh, why is being human so weird?*

I wipe my brow with my forearm and reposition the light, trying to keep my focus on my task. I'm making decent progress, but we still have a ways to go, and I'd like to finish this before the guards come back. The big bastard might be determined, but if I hadn't pushed him to let me help, I'm sure he'd still be stabbing himself repeatedly with nothing to show for it.

Needing to steady my hands, I rest the side of my palm on Vexar's side. He sucks in a sharp breath, and every visible muscle in his body tenses.

"Do you need a break?" I ask, forcing myself to look away from his chiseled abs. A part of me feels guilty for looking at him like that, but I can't help it. He's shirtless, and it would be impossible not to admire the obvious lethality of his body—every hard-earned ridge and valley, every scar—it's impressive as hell.

"I am fine. Please continue."

"Are you sure? You seem..." Overstimulated? Nervous? All of the above?

"The pain is fine."

So why is he so jumpy?

"Wait," I grin, "are you ticklish?"

He snaps a quick, "No," and I can't help but laugh.

"Don't worry, I won't tell the other gladiators about your secret weakness." I glance up, still laughing, and his impossibly green eyes meet mine. For a moment, everything seems to stop. Then it feels like I'm being dropped out of a fucking plane. My stomach jumps, heart rattles in my chest, and every nerve in my body stands at attention. It's so overwhelming, I have to drop my head between my arms and bite back a moan as waves of what can only be described as painful euphoria rush through me.

"Are you alright?" he asks, his voice coming out in that deep rumble that only increases the thrashing of my heart.

Whatever doubts I had about Vexar being the cause of my sudden 'heart-problems' are quickly evaporating, and I don't know what that means. It's weird, that's for sure, but it probably doesn't matter. I'm not going to live long enough for any heart problems to really be an issue.

I palm the medical shears still stuck between my boobs and say, "Yeah, I'm good." I just wish this weird reaction was less distracting. My body is *ramped* up.

A thought occurs to me, and I start to ask, "Does your species have ph—" Nope. If I ask about his pheromones, he's going to assume I'm lusting after him. *I mean, I sort of am, but still.*

Changing the topic, I nod to his wound and ask, "How did this happen?"

He considers me for a moment, like he's trying to decide how to answer. "The fight was over before I noticed the blood. I do not recall being struck."

"Are you trying to impress me or something?"

"No, I am being honest. The fight was very fast. That is how I fight best, fast." He smiles, showing a hint of fang, and I can't look away. The sharp lines of his jaw and the curve of his soft lips have me in a chokehold.

"Do you do all things with such speed?" I ask, realizing the innuendo a little too late. I almost slap a hand to my mouth, but Vexar interrupts my shame.

"Some things are good fast, but..." he trails off as his eyes run down my body and back up, before he quickly looks away. He clears his throat and presses a hand to his chest. "Sorry."

Fuck me...

Sweat beads on the back of my neck, trailing down my skin like a caress that does nothing to cool the fire in my veins.

I need to get a hold of myself. There's a reason I'm here, and it's not so I can eye-fuck this handsome alien. Time to change the subject. "So, what brought you to this dusty hellscape?" I ask casually as I start in on the next stitch.

Really, Amara? That's what you're gonna go with? Dusty hellscape? I press my eyes closed, wishing I was better at flirting and simultaneously hating myself for wishing that. I'm an enslaved nurse who's going to be dead in a few hours, and he's a wounded gladiator. Whatever *this* is, can't happen.

"You mean, Calidus?" he says, a sly grin curling his lips.

Shit. He knows I'm trying to flirt.

"Yup," I say, keeping my eyes low as I throw the first knot of the suture with more force than I need to.

"It is a requirement ... of sorts."

"A requirement?" That piques my interest.

Out of the corner of my eye, I see his hand brush over his chest before he scratches the short scruff on his chin. "It is complicated."

"Oh, come on. You can't tempt me with a backstory and then hold out at the last second. Do you know how long it's been since I've seen a TV or read a book?"

"Why is that?"

I point the forceps at him. "Don't try to change the subject."

"Fine," he relents, "if you must know, it is ... I am not sure of the word." He pauses. "The direct translation would be 'obligation'. Yes. An ancient obligation for some members of my family. My path has always led here."

"And ...?" I prompt. It's clear he's hesitant, but I hold my ground and he breaks.

"It demands that any King or Queen of Vhorath prove themselves in battle before taking the throne. It is a right of passage."

I laugh. "Right. King Vexar."

"I am serious," he says, his tone matching his words.

King.

The heat in my blood turns to ice. *Not a slave. Not a gladiator. A king.* I slowly set down the needle-driver and forceps. "King? As in, *you* are a king?"

A pained look crosses his face. "Not exactly. I am still a prince." He goes silent for a long moment. "Does that bother you?"

"You being a king ... or, sorry, a prince?" I ask, my voice grating through the seized muscles in my throat.

He nods, and my thoughts start firing at a million miles a second. He's a king. Not a slave. Not some guy fighting for a better life. He's someone in power. *Does he know I'm a slave? He has to, right?* Then again, he did call this my "job". Unless he's playing dumb...

My stomach drops, and whatever feeling of safety I had is overridden by rational thought. He might not seem like a monster, but what do I know? I've known him for an hour, max.

And yet, my gut is telling me he isn't lying. That he isn't a monster. I mean, he did sound really sincere when he called this my "job." And why would he say that if he already knew? What would be the point? And why would a king or prince opt out of medical care?

So either he's lying to me and is just really, really good at playing dumb. Or he has no idea that I'm a slave, and despite being a prince, he was left to die in his cell...

A sickening feeling creeps up my spine. None of this feels right.

"What's your ... uh ... kingdom?" I ask, trying to keep my voice calm and failing.

His brow furrows. "The Vhorathi Empire."

Empire. Not kingdom. I clench my hands together and watch my knuckles go white. "Where is this empire?"

The lines between his brows deepen, but he still looks so damn kind. So gentle and sincere. Like he thinks I might have hit my head or something. "Here, Amara. The Vhorathi Empire is here."

Nausea rises in my throat as I remember the woman the Magistrate brought. The 'Queen'. But no matter how hard I think about it, I just can't imagine Vexar being related to that woman. His eyes are too kind. Too gentle. Too trustworthy. Maybe I'm being foolish, but I've always trusted my gut, and my gut is rarely wrong.

"You're really a prince to this ... empire? You're not just messing with me?" I ask.

"Why would I lie about that?" he asks earnestly. Then he points to the large, scrolling tattoo that covers most of his chest, and when I show no sign of recognition, he deflates a bit. "It is my family lineage."

At this point, it's clear he thinks I'm some sort of idiot, but I think that's a good thing. If he knew why I was here, he wouldn't be surprised that I don't know any of this. He would expect it. Slaves aren't usually given history lessons, right?

"So Calidus is part of the Vhorathi Empire?" I ask, still needing extra confirmation.

"Yes."

Over the next few minutes, I learn there are hundreds of star systems in this empire, there are no other royal families nearby, and he has never been to the Coliseum before.

"How do you not know any of this? You *live* here," he asks.

A part of me wants to tell him, but the other part isn't interested in what will happen once he knows about my situation. The last thing I want is pity ... or to learn that he really is a monster and I read him all wrong. So instead of answering, I deflect.

"I guess this explains why you were so pissed when I wouldn't help you find the thread. Let me guess, you're used to people doing whatever you tell them to, right?"

He scoffs. "I was *asking* for your help."

"Your version of 'asking' kinda sucks."

His lips pinch, no longer amused by my snark. "You could have just said my title bothers you."

Shit. I went too far. I shake my head. "Sorry. It's not that. Really. I'm just ... surprised."

He eyes me suspiciously before grunting a sound of acceptance and brushing a hand over his chest again.

10

INCONGRUITIES

AMARA

"SO WHY DID you come *here* to complete your Obligation?" I ask, as I pass Vexar a cup of water and lean my hip against the table. As much as I would've preferred to keep suturing, my hands were tired and needed a rest.

Outside, the afternoon winds have begun to churn, kicking up sand and casting an eerie orange glow over Vexar's face. He's even more stunning right now, and that just seems to irritate me further.

"That is the purpose of the Coliseum," he says before draining the cup and handing it back. "It was originally built as a temple for the rulers of the empire to test their worthiness. Obviously, its use has expanded, but it still serves its original purpose."

I refill the cup for myself and take a sip, watching Vexar carefully. I still can't decide if I trust him or not. My gut says I should, but logic tells me something completely different. Almost every person I've come in contact with on this planet—who wasn't a nurse—was aware of, and in support of, the slave trade. It's hard to believe any future ruler of this place would be unaware of what's happening.

"Just to clarify, you're expected to prove your worthiness by killing gladiators? Here?" I ask. Seems a bit ... barbaric for a society capable of traversing star systems. Then again, it's not like I've seen much in the way of empathy out here.

"No ruler of Vhorath has ever led without being tested in battle first. It is important for us to uphold our traditions, and the Coliseum allows us to do that without risking real conflict. It is an honor to fight here."

I swallow a mouthful of dirt-flavored water and try to keep my voice steady. "So you practice manufactured war to prove you're worthy of a crown? And that's honorable?" Vexar's expression tightens, and I suddenly feel guilty for my lack of a filter. "I didn't mean to—" To what? Insinuate that his 'ancient obligation' is essentially just manufactured war? Obligated murder? Because it is.

"You are not wrong." He scrubs a hand over his face. "The reality of the Coliseum was not what I expected." He pauses and grimaces. "It is pointlessly cruel and archaic."

My brows shoot up. I was expecting him to defend his 'obligation', not agree with me. And he looks ... pained. No, that's not it. He doesn't *look* pained; it's like he's radiating sadness or something. Like his ache is infecting me. I feel it tightening my chest.

Trying to shrug off the strange sensation, I ask, "Do you want to talk about it?"

He's silent for a long moment. "The more I think about it, the more certain I am that this"—he gestures to the room around us —"does not fulfill the original intention of the law. It is a misalignment of values that I am shocked my predecessors allowed to continue.

"Before my people were a unified tribe, battles were a fact of daily survival. There was no need for a formal rite of passage; it just happened naturally. Once the tribes unified beneath a single leader and the constant battles stopped, we needed a way to keep our traditions alive. But *this*? *This* is what they chose?"

He runs a hand over his braided hair, and his expression darkens. "I was told fighting here would be heroic. I was told *this* is how we avoid unnecessary bloodshed while upholding our traditions. But that"—he points at the door—"did not align with tradition. It was a farce. A deadly, horrible farce."

I have to work to keep my expression neutral as the shock of his words rolls through me.

"My fight today did not feel like an act of valor. My opponent was not a normal gladiator. He looked ... gods, I think he was a hybrid. Like he was made rather than born." He pauses and looks away. "He had no chance of surviving that. Of surviving *me*."

His clear distress over what he did in the arena has turned my world on its head. How is this guy the next in line for the throne? It just doesn't make sense. His morals clearly don't align with the brutality of this place, and yet, he's supposed to rule over the millions of people who come here weekly to cheer for blood?

"Does anyone else in your family feel this way?" I ask.

"No."

That sinking feeling in my spine returns, and it's harder to shake this time. My eyes flick to the strange wound in his side, and I have to swallow down the wrongness of it all.

"Have you ever taken a life? Before today?" I ask.

"No."

I climb onto the table and sit facing him. As strange as it seems, I swear I can feel his emotion—that familiar weight of guilt and disgust that comes after doing something you know can't take back. It sparks distant memories that feel more like someone else's life than mine.

My hands press into my thighs. "No one told you what it would be like, did they?"

"They did, but they were wrong." The bed creaks as he raises a hand to rub his eyes. "They were cheering for his death," he whispers darkly.

Wind howls past the window as the sandstorm continues to rage outside.

"That's the worst part, isn't it? The incongruities? How none of it seems to make any sense?" That's where the true horror of warfare lies. Where expectation is crushed beneath the strangeness of reality. Beneath the rawness of death and despair, and the cruelty of others.

"Yes," he whispers.

He took a life in the most disturbing setting possible. Even worse, he wasn't fighting a war or trying to protect anyone. He was killing for killing's sake. He took a life while thousands cheered him on, and it's clear that being in that arena was not a choice he would have made on his own. At least not if he knew what it actually meant. Despite our many differences, this is something we have in common.

My eyes fall to my feet. "I wish I could tell you it gets easier, but it doesn't. The killing, I mean. But that's probably a good thing, you know? There are people who can kill without a second thought, and I sometimes wonder if that would be easier? But then I remember that killing should never be easy." I shake my head. "I don't know. I'm not in that business anymore, but I do know that you should try to talk about it. If you hold in that pain, it's going to get worse."

"I chose to be here, and I have to live with the consequences of those choices." He swallows and rubs his palm over his chest as if he's trying to rub away an ache, before adding, "I don't know why I told you all that."

Our eyes meet, and a look of confusion flits across his face before it's replaced by shock. His left hand grips his chest violently, and I watch in horror as his claws sink into his skin.

11

OR SOMETHING

AMARA

"**S**TOP!" I SHOUT, as I jump off the table and rush towards Vexar, desperate to stop him from mauling himself.

With all the strength I can muster, I pull at his hand, trying to wrench it back. It's like fighting a brick wall. My thrumming heart becomes a deafening roar. Electricity bursts over my skin. Animalistic fear grips me. Our eyes lock. And just as quickly as the chaos started, it stops. His hand gives under the pressure of my own, the bolts of electricity stop, and my heart calms.

"What the fuck," I say breathlessly.

His gaze falls to his chest, where five pin-pricks of blood well like red blossoms in a field of golden grain. "I'm sorry," he whispers.

I drop his hand and step back. "Are you going to tell me what just happened?"

"Everything is fine," he grunts.

"Are you sure, because it looked like you were trying to rip your heart out after confessing some heavy shit."

"I was not trying to rip my heart out."

"Then what were you doing?"

No answer.

I let out a ragged breath and turn towards the window. A gust of sand-filled air hits me, cooling my sweat-damp skin and covering me in a thin layer of grit. I close my eyes and press my palms into the table.

I've dealt with plenty of intense, fucked-up situations, and never once have I felt the way I did a few seconds ago. It was like my body was on fire and I was ... terrified. Terrified that he was hurting himself. Terrified that I wouldn't be able to stop him. Like some bone-deep instinct to protect.

Fuck. I don't know.

The urge to trust him is so strong and seemingly out of place, considering everything that just happened, and yet, it's exactly what I want to do.

He's not at all what I expected a future king would be, and a part of me can't stop wondering if he might be able to help me. Vexar has power. If anyone can do something to actually stop the slave trade, it would be him. I just need to know if he's the kind of person who would rather fix his problems or ignore them.

I lift my head and stare at the wall of orange sand outside the window. "If you win your fights, what happens next?"

It takes him a long time to answer, but he eventually says, "I become king."

"And if that happens, do you plan on changing how the Obligation is done?"

"Yes," he says firmly.

I turn and point at his chest. "Let me clean that up."

"Just to confirm, we aren't going to be talking about this?" I ask, as I dab the blood from his chest with a clean square of gauze.

"What is there to discuss?"

"I dunno, maybe why you just mauled yourself?"

He grunts and turns his face away from me, clearly uninterested in the topic.

I was convinced he was trying to claw his heart out, but honestly, the gouges he left are pretty shallow, and that makes me think he isn't lying. At the same time, I was putting my entire body weight into his arm, and it didn't move. At all. It felt like he was really digging those claws in. Or maybe his arm was locked in place? Or—

I let out a choked laugh as I realize why his arm didn't move. "Holy shit, you're scary strong."

The tension breaks, and he lets out a laugh of his own that quickly turns into a groan.

"Sorry," I say with a wince, "didn't mean to make you laugh."

He shakes his head reassuringly. "It is fine."

Ready to get back to work, I move into position and run the sani-light over everything. "You know, I'm still a little shocked you haven't passed out again."

"Why would I pass out?"

"The pain," I say as I open a fresh suture packet.

"I am used to pain. It does not bother me so much anymore."

I glance at the scar that runs down his forearm. "Is that because of all the scars?"

He grunts in confirmation but doesn't elaborate. Sometimes scars are just painful memories, and if that's the case with him, he has a lot of painful memories.

"You good if I keep stitching?" I ask.

He nods, and I get back to work. But seconds later, he's squirming and breathing like he just ran a marathon.

"You sure you're ok?" I ask with a raised brow.

"Have you ever taken a life?"

I reel back, surprised by the question and the lack of preamble. "Well, that came out of nowhere..." I'm not sure if I should even answer that. "Why do you want to know?" I ask.

"I am curious."

I click my tongue. "So are you in pain, or not?" He doesn't answer, but he's stopped squirming, so he must be ok. With a sigh, I give him an answer. "I have."

"In combat?"

"Yeah, I'm not big on casual murder." I start on the next suture, and Vexar doesn't react at all to the forceps or the needle. *Maybe it's not the pain making him restless?*

"Was that the worst part? Of being a warrior, I mean?"

I want to joke about his sudden shift in perspective—from being surprised I was in the military to now calling me a "warrior"—but I resist. He's probably just looking for camaraderie, and if I'm being honest, I sort of want to give him that.

"No," I finally say. "It wasn't the worst part." It was certainly in the top three, though. "Maybe that makes me a bad person, but when someone's trying to kill you, you don't have much choice in how you respond."

"That does not make you a bad person." He pauses, and I feel his eyes dance over my skin before he asks, "What was war like?"

"That's a big question."

"I have time."

My toes rub along the inside of my shoes as I shift my weight. "It was different than I thought it would be. There was a lot more waiting around, I guess. We'd spend weeks doing nothing and then suddenly, we'd be fighting for our lives. After a while, the waiting got harder. Everyone was on edge, just knowing how quickly things could shift from calm to chaotic.

We'd be sitting on the side of a mountain, or in an empty house, or in the back of a truck, and guys would be praying for the next bullet to fly, just so we weren't stuck in limbo anymore.

"It sucked, but it gave me a real appreciation for camaraderie and gallows humor." I let out a hollow laugh. "Honestly, if it weren't for the jokes, I don't think any of us would have come out of it sane. We got through it together." And that's why being here is so impossible. I'm alone. No one has my back, and at the end of a really messed-up day, there's no one to joke about it with. "I dunno. It was all just so surreal. Like we were living in a really weird, really fucked up dream."

"What made it so surreal?" he asks, genuinely curious.

I rest my elbows on the edge of the mattress for some added stability while I continue working. "The war I fought in wasn't a normal war. At least not in the way most human warfare had been fought up to that point. We weren't on a battlefield; we were in cities and villages. There were always civilians around. We'd be in the middle of a firefight, look over into a house, and see some guy watching TV."

"That sounds very unsafe."

"No kidding. We'd be walking down the street in full battle-rattle while people were out buying groceries."

"And the enemy would attack with civilians around?"

This is easily my least favorite thing to talk about.

"Yeah," I take a breath, "the enemy was desperate, and desperate people do some really, really fucked up things."

He gives me a long look. "That seems to be something most species have in common." A few moments later, he adds, "I have a question. You were a medic, but you speak like a warrior. Why?"

My cheeks heat, not because he said I "speak like a warrior", but because it's clear he's genuinely interested. I don't think I realized how much I missed this kind of interaction. "I was in the Navy," I say, "which is just one branch of my country's military. The Navy trains its own corpsmen, or medics, and they're really good at it." I squint and ask, "Am I confusing you with the terms?"

"Corpsman or medic is fine." He smiles softly. "My memory was not wounded, just my flank."

"Right," I say with a chuckle. The guy knows a bunch of languages. A few new terms aren't going to trip him up. "The Marines—the branch of our military that focuses on taking the fight to the enemy—doesn't train their own medics. Which makes sense," I say with a shrug. "Those folks are about as far from healers as you can get. So, the Navy sends its corpsman to keep the Marines alive. And since the Marines bring the fight to the enemy, being efficient with resources is important. Having someone who only serves as a medic and doesn't carry a gun isn't efficient. So, corpsmen who deploy with the Marines are trained like a Marine and fight like a Marine. At least until someone gets hurt, then we become 'Doc'."

"'Doc'? Is that a title?"

"It's more like a term of endearment and respect."

"Doc," he says, like he's trying the word on for size. "I like the term." The muscles in his side bulge as he shifts a bit. "Thank you for sharing that with me."

I'M FAIRLY confident that if Vexar knew what was actually going on here, he'd want to stop it. Everything about him screams, "Good guy". Maybe I'm being too optimistic, but I think his heart is in the right place, and I think I have to tell him. If not for myself, then at least for the other nurses who might still be stuck here after the Magistrate is dead.

My heart pounds and palms sweat as I search for the best

way to start the conversation. Do I just come out and say I'm a slave? That this isn't just some job that pays the bills? Or do I like, slowly work into the subject?

Fuck. And what if he already knows? *God, I hope he doesn't know. I really hope he doesn't know.*

The more I think, the more my anxiety builds. Just the thought of saying the words out loud has me—

Vexar's hand flies to his chest as he says, "What is wrong?"

I jerk back, surprised by his sudden movement. "Jesus! What was that for?"

"Something is wrong. Tell me."

I glance around, confused. "What are you talking about?"

"Tell me what is frightening you," he says more firmly. His eyes are intense and focused, like he's waiting for me to say there's a xenomorph about to burst out of my chest. The muscles in his jaw tick, and he adds, "Your heart rate has risen. It is too fast."

I drop the needle-driver and have to grab it as it swings from the thread embedded in his side. "How do you know what my heart's doing?" I ask. "Do you have super hearing, or x-ray vision, or something?"

"Or something," he says flatly.

"What the hell does that mean?" I quickly clip the thread and toss the shears to the side, waiting impatiently for an explanation.

His face hardens. "Tell me what you are scared of," he orders. The thunderous roll of his voice vibrates through me, and my body reacts in the worst way possible, with a shiver and a wave of lustful heat.

Frustrated, I growl, "You can't just demand things from people and expect them to give you whatever you want!"

A wildly inhuman sound vibrates through his chest—like the bellow of an alligator—and his eyes narrow with a heated ferocity that feels like a challenge. Like he's testing me. And the need to hold my ground wins out over everything else.

I lock on to those impossibly green eyes, eyes the color of grass in early spring, and I give no quarter. In seconds, I start to regret my choice. My skin prickles. Breath quickens. And the longer I look, the harder it is to look away. There's an entire universe in those eyes, a million questions swirling, and a sense that I might already know the answers to them all.

To my surprise, he looks away first. I sink my fingers into the side of the mattress, trying to keep myself rooted to the planet while it feels like I might float away. I don't know what it is about Vexar that makes me feel this way. It's this strange feeling of rightness I can't shake. This heavy pull towards him. A feeling like I want to hold on and never let go. Like I could curl into his arms and sleep forever.

"You are safe with me," he says, breaking the weighted silence. "I will never let anyone harm you."

I glance up, confused and about to ask what he means, when he shifts uncomfortably and my gaze catches on his tented pants. A surprised, "Oh," escapes me, and I force myself to blink and look away. But it's too late. He already knows I know, and there's no going back.

With a groan of embarrassment, he reaches down and adjusts himself. Right in front of me. My cheeks burn as I tilt my head back and stare wide-eyed at the ceiling. Salacious thoughts take over my mind, and a liquid heat curls between my thighs, persistent and overwhelming.

"I am sorry," he rumbles in that deep voice that does everything but cool the persistent desire building in me.

His fingers brush over mine, still clutched to the side of the bed, and the resulting full-body chills have me squeezing my legs together at a reckless speed. The bare skin of my knees drags over the unforgiving floor, and a sharp stab of pain burns up my right thigh.

There's a flash of movement that almost knocks me over, but Vexar catches my shoulder and steadies me. He's sitting up—damn, he moves fast—expression tense with concern. "What happened?" he asks, his voice almost frantic.

12

HAIL MARY

AMARA

A S IF ONLY just noticing that his hand is on my shoulder, he pulls it back and glances around awkwardly.

"Everything's fine," I say, shaking my head and trying to hold back the rush of adrenaline and emotion. I can't tell if I want to cry or fuck or fight, but the past few minutes have gotten me so wound-up I think I might shatter. "You need to lay back down," I say, as I go to push his shoulder again, but the second my hand touches his skin, my body buzzes like I touched a fucking light-socket. I pull my arm to my chest, nearly in a panic.

Noticing my reaction, his face softens, and he starts to reach for me again.

"Stop moving!" I shout. "You're going to tear your stitches!" I'm starting to crack, and I don't know how to stop it. My heart is pounding so hard my ears hurt. My skin feels like it's covered in Icy Hot. I'm aroused past the point of reason. And every time I look at Vexar, I just want to curl up in his arms and sob.

"You're hurt," he whispers.

I shake my head, "I'm fine," and push on his shoulder again, trying to ignore the way my body reacts to the contact. But no matter how hard I push, he doesn't budge. It's infuriating. Like pushing on the side of a building, and—

Wait. I didn't say anything about my knee. "How do you know I'm—"

"Let me see," he interrupts as he swings his legs over the side of the bed, caging me between his muscular thighs.

My breath catches at the decidedly inappropriate position we're in, and I slowly bring my eyes up to his. From this angle, he looks even more dangerous than before. Dangerous, massive, and impossibly beautiful.

"Let me see," he whispers, "please."

I stand, and his eyes rake down my body until they land on my knee, where a superficial cut has started to bleed.

"See? I'm fine," I say, motioning to my leg. He reaches down and squeezes the sore flesh, making me wince. "Hey," I say, trying and failing to pull away.

"How long have you been bleeding?" he asks, hand still on my leg and eyes burning with a furious intensity.

"I'm fine, really."

He glances up. "Why is there so much blood?"

"It's not all *my* blood. It's mostly yours." I point at the floor where the blood I couldn't mop up still sits in the deep pockets of eroded stone. "You made a bit of a mess."

He lets go of my knee with a frustrated grunt. "Zar'vok, Amara," he growls. He looks mad. Honestly mad. I open my mouth to speak, but he cuts me off. "Gauze and water," he says, his voice calm but unwavering. I blink in confusion until he repeats himself. "I need gauze and water."

I frown. "Are we really doing this again?"

"I am *asking*."

"I get that you *think* you're 'asking', but you're really 'demanding'."

He drags a hand down his face, but I swear the corners of his eyes crease with the hint of a smile. I almost smile too. "Can you please hand me some gauze and water so I do not have to stand?" he asks. "I would like to bandage your knee."

I blink a few times. *He's joking, right?*

In response to my shocked expression, he lowers his head so we're eye-level, reminding me of our height difference. I'm standing, he's sitting, and he still has to bow his head. "Please let me help. It is the least I can do," he says gently.

A bit curious, I hand him the partial cup of water and a fresh roll of gauze.

"Your foot," he says, spreading his thighs and patting the small triangle of mattress between them.

I hesitate, but he pats the bed again, and I relent.

He dips a piece of gauze into the water and slides his free hand under my calf. An almost imperceptible gasp sucks through my lips at the contact, and an absolute disaster of confused emotion floods me. I swallow. *I'm just touch-starved, and he's touching me. That's it. That's all this is. He has a life of his own, and I'm a dead girl. I'm totally fine with that.*

His eyes flick up to mine, and for a moment I swear I could sink into their depths and live there forever... *Or not. Probably not.*

Fuck, what is wrong with me?

With gentle, almost affectionate touches, he clears away the mixture of our blood and rubs his thumb in a small circle on my calf. I press my eyes closed, willing myself to stay calm.

"How did this happen?" he asks, as he starts to wrap my knee.

"The floor is sharp."

He smooths the last piece of gauze into place before lowering my foot to the ground and meeting my gaze.

The hair on the back of my neck lifts.

His eyes are black. *Completely* black, no color or white at all.

I step back, surprised by the sudden change. I've never seen anyone's eyes do that.

"Amara?" he asks, brows drawn in confusion.

There's a dangerous venom behind those eyes, but it's not frightening. If anything, it feels like it's drawing me in. Begging me to—

Trust him, something whispers in the back of my mind.

"Why do you look like you want to murder someone?" I ask, noting the fact that I said "someone" and not "me".

"The only thing I want to murder is this floor." He lets out a huff of frustration before rubbing his hand over the back of his neck.

I cock my head. "You want to murder the floor?" Is this a mistranslation or something?

"It *hurt* you," he says, the darkness in his eyes slowly contracting as his gaze runs back up my body, "right after I promised I would not let anything harm you."

Ignoring the implications of that, I ask, "Why did they go black?"

"What do you mean?"

"Your eyes. Why did they go ... black?" I can't think of a better way to phrase it.

His lips part, but no sound comes out, and it occurs to me then that he doesn't know it happened at all.

I frown. "How did you not notice? Does your vision not change?" It should, right?

He glances away with a strained expression and runs a hand over his chest again. "It has never happened before."

"Well—" I stop, unsure of what to say. "Is it normal?" Because if it isn't, we should probably figure that out.

With a concerned look, he asks, "Are you frightened of me?"

I consider his question and decide to answer honestly. "No. I probably should be, but I'm not."

He hums. "That is good. And I apologize for my body's earlier reaction. I did not mean to make you uncomfortable."

"It's fine," I say, brushing the hair back from my face. I swear, this has to be some sort of karmic punishment for past misdeeds. He's unreasonably attractive, and now that I know him better, the attraction is only getting stronger. It's distracting, and if I can't find a way to shut it down, leaving this cell and walking to my death is going to be impossible. Right now, I don't feel like a rage-filled killer; I feel like a yearning teenager, and that's not the mindset I need.

He tilts his chin down and asks, "How is your knee? Does it hurt?"

"Uh, it's fine. Thanks." Clearing my throat, I ask, "Do you want a few minutes to compose yourself, or ...?"

"I am afraid a few minutes will not make any difference." He looks at me through long, dark lashes, and a pained smile crosses his face. His meaning is clear, and it sends a new rush of heat between my legs. His boner is 100% because of me.

Damnit.

I rock back on my heels. "So what do you want to do? I don't want to make this weird, but I'm not done stitching you up, and I'd rather not leave you like this."

"Are you able to ignore my body's relentless pursuit of your attention?" he asks in an earnest tone that only increases my desire to jump on his lap and find out exactly what sort of monster he's hiding in those pants.

No, no, no! Bad thoughts.

But I can't stop thinking them. Every time he looks at me, I get this feeling that he wants to protect and ravage me at the same time. And I *want* him to.

Nope. No. I am not going there. I should not go there.

But it's more than just the way he's looking at me. It's that deep pull in my gut; the fluttering in my chest; the way I can't stop myself from looking at him. It's the way he takes all of my snarky comments and pointed jabs and seems to enjoy them. It's the way he wrapped my knee. It's how he's curious and gentle when I know he's strong enough to rip my limbs off. It's his deep introspection on what he did in the arena, and his willingness to voice his regrets. It's the way he listens and actually *hears* me. It's all of that, and somehow more.

Then again, I am about to die, and this could just be a natural reaction to that. People get horny and weird after any brush with death, right?

"I'll be fine," I answer, sounding anything but confident.

With a nod, he pulls a pillow from the bed and holds it out. "Please," he says, "for your knees." The gesture stirs up even more complicated emotions, and when I don't take it, he lowers it to the ground, maintaining eye contact and barely hiding a grunt of pain.

The thrumming in my chest increases.

After another grunt, he's lying back down and staring at me expectantly. "Is this position good for you?"

This is going to be harder than I thought.

THE STORM STILL RAGES OUTSIDE, but it's clear the sun is setting, and exhaustion has begun to take hold. My arms ache, and with the frequent breaks and ongoing conversation, a procedure I thought would take an hour has stretched into nearly three. Turns out, giant aliens with 20-inch-long jagged wounds take a lot longer to stitch than I thought, and now I have to wonder if the guards are going to come for me tonight or if they're just gonna leave me in here.

"When do they normally bring you dinner?" I ask, standing to take a quick drink and grab another suture packet.

"I do not know. This is my first night."

"Right." Forgot about that. I rip open the packet and clumsily drop the contents on Vexar's abdomen. Without a thought, I grab the little spool and watch his entire body tense. "Shit, sorry."

"Do not be," he says. "This is new to me, and I am still ... adjusting."

"What's new? Getting stitches?" I ask as I lower myself back to my knees, grateful for the soft pillow.

"No," he says lightly, "having physical contact with a female who is not a member of my immediate family."

I glance up, confused. "What do you mean?"

"I have never touched or been touched by a female before. Besides my mother and sisters—in a platonic way of course," he adds.

A memory of Solta saying something about Vexar not touching people of the opposite sex comes rushing back. But Vexar didn't say anything about it, and neither did the guards; they just said we didn't have sedatives... That sinking feeling in my spine returns before it's overruled by a darker realization. *That's why he wanted to stitch himself up.* Oh my god, I fucking violated him.

"I'm so sorry. I shouldn't have— You were bleeding. And you couldn't give consent. Not that that's a— But then I pressured you to—"

He cups my chin with his massive hand, interrupting my incoherent apology. My skin burns with a fiery anticipation. Stomach tightens and flutters. His lips part, and suddenly I'm standing on the edge of a cliff, knowing there's no way to keep myself from falling off.

I'm completely fucked.

"Please," he says, his voice deep and calm. "You have done nothing wrong. I have already told you that."

He releases my chin, and it takes a moment before I can think straight. The spot where he touched me pulses with heat.

"I should have..." I whisper, trailing off as I realize I don't know what to say.

"Should have what? Let me die?" He shakes his head as if the idea is absurd. "I am *glad* you saved my life. And you did not pressure me into anything. I needed your help, and you gave it. You did everything right." He takes a breath. "I am perfectly capable of determining my own boundaries and ensuring they are not crossed."

"But you were unconscious."

"And I am still grateful." His soft gaze seems to crack something open in me, and suddenly I don't want to leave this cell at all. I don't want to die just to kill a tyrant. I want to stay right here, safe and comfortable.

I tense and drop my head. Fuck me, this is bad. This is so fucking bad. I can't lose my nerve. I've already made it past the point of no return, and if I lose my nerve now, this will all have been for nothing. At some point, I'm going to be dragged out of here, and when that happens, I need to be ready.

Trying to calm myself back down, I ask, "Did you, uh, not touch women out of choice? Or ...?"

"It is a vow I had to take."

"And that's why you opted out of medical care?"

"Yes."

I nod. "So it's a serious vow..." I whisper, almost to myself. "Are you going to be in trouble because of"—I motion between us—"this?"

"I do not think so," he says gently. "Not now."

"That's good." I glance down, uncertain of what else to say. The cell is getting steadily darker, and with that darkness comes the inescapable knowledge that either I have a few minutes left in here, or a whole night. Chewing on the inside of my cheek, I ask, "Do you think they're going to leave me in here all night? Or do you think they'll come for me soon?" I don't know why I'm asking him, there's no way he knows more about the routines of this place than I do.

His jaw tightens. "Come for you?"

"The guards, I mean. Do you know when the guards will come?"

He grunts, and his eyes flash black before returning to their normal green. "I will not let them take you. Whatever happens, I —" His chest vibrates with that strange sound that I feel more than hear before he turns his gaze to the ceiling. "You saved my life. I will ensure you do not face repercussions for your actions."

The desire to believe him is overwhelming, but it's just another fantasy. He's making promises without having any idea of what he's actually promising. I'm a *criminal*. Criminals don't survive this place. And even if Vexar is who he claims to be, he's still locked in a cell, just like me.

I've been trying to avoid thinking too hard about the strangeness of his situation, but I don't think I can keep ignoring it anymore. His injury is unlike any I've seen come out of the arena; he doesn't seem to know that this place is run by slave labor; he's obviously more empathetic than he's supposed to be; and ... fuck. I just get the feeling that he isn't supposed to leave here alive. It's a weird, instinctual feeling—more than a gut feeling—and it's impossible to shake.

At the same time, I desperately want him to survive. Not only have I grown fond of him, but he might be the only person here who has the ability to save the other nurses. Sure, I might be able to kill the Magistrate, but that's as far as I'll get. The second that bastard's bleeding out, the guards will make sure I'm right behind him. But Vexar has a much better chance of survival. He might just be my Hail Mary.

I clear my throat and take a deep breath, knowing that what I'm about to say will kick off a series of events entirely out of my control. Meeting his gaze, I ask, "Even if those repercussions are my immediate execution?"

He stiffens. Brows drop. And a ghost of rage crosses his face. "What do you mean?"

The tension drains from me.

He doesn't know.

13

MAKE HIM BLEED

VEXAR

I SIT UP, gritting my teeth against the pain as I try to remain calm, but the rapid hammering of Amara's heart has me on edge. Wide brown eyes lock on mine. Fear pulses in the air between us. But she is not afraid of *me*.

"Who wants to execute you?" I ask.

She doesn't answer, but I need to know. I need to know *who*. I feel like little more than an arrow, waiting to be aimed. I feel dangerous. Deadly. Entirely out of control and very unlike myself. When I learned about the *Zhyrrak*, a loss of control was never mentioned. It was always said to be the opposite. And yet I feel less in control now than I ever have before.

Realizing I may be overwhelming her, I adjust my tone and say gently, "I am sorry. Please, tell me what you meant."

She takes a deep breath and shifts slightly, gripping her hands together and resting them on the edge of the bed. "I never told you how I got here," she whispers. Her eyes are glassy and distant, and her anxiety is palpable. It lingers in the air like electricity, tingling across my tongue and drying my mouth.

"How did you get here?" I ask.

She swallows. "I was on Earth, staying in a little apartment while I figured out what to do after leaving the military, and one night, I went to bed and woke up ... on a ship. A spaceship."

My blood chills as her words sink in.

"The ship was full of people—or aliens? No one was there because they wanted to be."

My claws bite into my palms, but the pain is so distant I hardly notice.

"They took them ... uh, us. And sold—" She chokes on the words as her eyes well with tears. "We were..."

She cannot say it, but she does not have to. My mind spins, thoughts colliding and clashing in a swirl of utter chaos.

They *took* her.

"Vok, Amara," I say, sliding a hand over my mouth. "You are not here by choice?"

"No." Her eyes drift over my face, and I can feel her gauging my response. "I was sold to the Coliseum and I can't leave."

The metallic taste of blood coats my tongue. I must have bitten it. Both my hearts pound violently, twin hammers against an anvil. How could this have happened? There are laws to prevent this; laws that should have protected her. But they *took* her. *Sold* her. How? Who?

"What did they look like?" I ask, fearing her answer. "The people who took you."

Her eyes drop to the edge of the mattress as her hands squeeze together. "They were humanoid. Grayish skin."

No.

"Slim bodies, and big, dark eyes."

No.

"That's all I really remember."

I want to scream. To rage. To tear something apart.

The Senate promised the rumors were unfounded, but they were wrong. They missed something.

It takes all of my willpower to tamp down the rage that

threatens to split me in two as I look at the pain etched on Amara's face. An all-consuming need to hunt the Tusku traders responsible for this roars to life. Dark thoughts follow. Violent thoughts.

Is Gaius keeping her as a slave? He must be.

I lean forward and grip my thighs, resisting the urge to reach for her hands. "And you believe you will be executed for helping me? Is that what you meant?" I ask, working to keep my tone even and controlled despite the fire burning beneath my skin. She has done nothing wrong, and yet she faces death? My rage continues to build despite my attempts to calm it. It is out of control. A creature of its own making. Violent and limitless.

End them, something whispers in the back of my mind.

"I broke the Magistrate's laws by helping you, and I didn't do it quietly," she says, picking at the dried blood on her hands.

I need to do something. Anything. I swing my legs over the edge of the bed. Amara stares up at me from where she's knelt on the floor. A tearing sound rends the air as I remove the corner of the bedsheet. I hardly register the pain as I reach for the cup of water on the table. My entire being is focused on her. On her pain. Her fear.

"Give me your hands," I say gently as I wet the fabric.

"Why?" she asks, even as she offers them.

I place her right hand on my thigh and cradle her left in my palm. "You were picking at the dried blood. It looks uncomfortable." I begin to wipe her hands, and somehow, the simple act seems to calm some of my rage. "Why did you not correct me when I said I thought you would lose your *job*?" The fabric turns a light pink that deepens with each stroke.

"I don't know."

"Were you going to let me think you were here by choice?"

Her hand tightens on my thigh, and I force my breathing to remain steady.

"I didn't know if I could trust you," she says. "I was told everyone knows we're slaves, and that if I escaped, the people who live here would skin me alive for sport." She speaks almost casually, but a muscle in her jaw tenses with every pause. "I thought all of the gladiators were in the same position as the nurses: slaves. But then you told me who you were, and I ... well, I don't know. I thought you had to know I was a slave."

"And you still chose to save my life?"

"That was before I knew who you were," she says in a small voice. She is uncomfortable with that truth, but she told me anyway. This is good.

"Who told you everyone knows?" I ask, dragging the scrap of cloth between her soft fingers.

"The Magistrate. But I didn't just take his word for it. All the guards know. Solta knows. The people who come through here to bet on the gladiators know. None of them care. And a while back, the Magistrate brought someone here on a tour or something." She pauses and takes a deep breath. "He kept calling her 'my Queen' and made us bow to her. She knew, so I thought everyone must know."

Queen. It takes everything in me to keep my face neutral and unaffected by that sickening detail. She can't possibly mean my mother.

Amara's eyes flick up to mine, searching for a reaction.

Who else would Gaius call 'my Queen'?

No. It is a ridiculous accusation. Impossible. My mother may not have been a kind ruler, but she was an honorable one. She only visited this place once. For her own Obligation.

"You must have misunderstood," I say.

Amara looks at me long and hard, her lips downturned in an apologetic frown as if she knows what I am thinking. "I don't think I did," she says.

"Well, you must have, because no one who carries the title of

'Queen' would know anything about this ... this slave trade." She may think she knows what is going on here, but her claims are wrong. *She* is wrong.

"Vexar, the slave trade is *real*," she says, as if that is what I am disagreeing with. "The other people on that ship didn't end up here, so they had to have gone somewhere. I ... I don't know how long I was on the ship, but I think I was one of the last people released. I don't know where everyone else was taken, but it wasn't here."

I feel sick.

"Well," I say, "if they are not here, I am certain they were taken outside the bounds of the empire." I take a deep breath and start to clean her other hand. "Why were you so eager to risk your life to save mine? Was it because of what the Magistrate told you? Because you had no hope?"

"In part."

She is still holding back her true reasoning, but she has already told me what I need to know. Gaius backed her into a corner and used her desperation against her. He knew she would enter my cell. He manipulated her to get to me. He *used* her.

Another wave of rage begins to crest. Gaius will burn for this.

End him.

"Did you know?" I ask. "Before you entered my cell, did you know your actions would result in your death?"

"Yeah," she says plainly, as if her life is worth nothing.

I release her hand, not trusting myself to be gentle anymore. My gaze drops to the bandage on her knee, and my voice comes out deep and deadly. "Why would you do that?"

She gets to her feet and wipes her damp hand on the skirt of her dress.

"Why?" I repeat.

An angry flush creeps over her cheeks as she glares at me, displeased with my tone. "I did what I had to do."

I shake my head. "No more half-truths," I growl. "Tell me why."

She leans forward aggressively and shouts, "Because it was the only choice I could make that was mine!" Her chest heaves before she points at the door and adds, "And because that fucker needs to pay for what he's done."

The air between us stills. Sand whispers over the dunes outside. Amara's sweat-damp skin glistens in the low light.

She didn't choose death; she chose revenge and an end to her imprisonment.

It is a choice I would expect from any warrior, so I do not know why I am so shocked. Amara is a warrior. A fully blooded warrior. It would be wise for me to remember that. She might look harmless, but that is far from the truth.

"So you entered my cell to take back your control?" I ask.

Her nostrils flare. "And to make that bastard bleed."

14

PEOPLE OF HONOR

AMARA

VEXAR RUBS A hand over his mouth in disbelief. "You did all of this for a chance to kill Gaius? I mean, the Magistrate?"

"His name is Gaius?" I ask. It seems strange for him to have a name at all. After all this time, he's become more of a mythological monster in my mind, and giving him a real name feels too humanizing.

Vexar nods, but there's a hollow look behind his eyes, like he's watching something beautiful burn.

"Don't look at me like that," I say, turning towards the window and running a hand through my hair. "He should die for what he's done... For what he's *doing.*"

"And how is saving me going to accomplish that? How is your death going to fix anything? Hmm? Tell me what your big plan is here."

I slowly turn back to face him, running the tip of my tongue over the sharp edge of my teeth while holding back a humorless smile. "You'd be dead right now if it weren't for my 'big plan', so maybe consider that before trying to judge me." I cross my arms over my chest and curl my toes in my shoes. "Obviously, you think I'm some sort of idiot who ran into this blind, but I'm not." I glance at my feet. "I know the odds—I'm not stupid—and I wasn't planning on doing any of this today. At least not until I saw you bleeding."

Vexar doesn't say anything, but I swear I can feel his sorrow.

My gaze returns to the window, where the raging storm has become a sea of swirling dark. Sand whips by in random gusts, making a tinkling sound as it brushes against the stone. It reminds me of the sound of corn snow falling on ice in the winter, and it sparks a longing for a past I'll never return to. I clench my jaw until the blood roaring in my ears drowns out the sound.

"After I first got here, I tried to escape. When that failed, I was taken to the Magistrate's office." I glance over my shoulder. "It was just the two of us. No guards. And that was the only time I've been close enough to do anything." I press my eyes closed. "But instead of killing him, I sat there like a good little slave. I don't know if what I've done will land me back in his office, but if it doesn't, at least my death won't have been for nothing."

Vexar makes a pained wheezing sound behind me.

I rub my thumb and forefinger over my brow, still feeling like my explanation is incomplete. "He took everything from me, and I can't watch that happen to anyone else." My voice cracks, but I don't stop. "I can't watch another woman show up here, traumatized and completely fucked up. I can't." Tears burn the corners of my eyes, but I wipe them away quickly.

The thought of the Magistrate living happily while the rest of us suffer fills me with anger. I turn back to Vexar, ready to face his judgment. Even if he doesn't understand, I know I made the right call. "I can't just look the other way," I say. "I can't continue on like this. And right now, I have an advantage. He doesn't see me as a threat, and I'm not going to throw that away, I'm gonna to use it."

"You don't have to do this," he whispers.

I shake my head, feeling the cold burn of my rage grow. "You don't get it. I *want* to kill him. I want it to be *my* face he sees as he's gasping for breath at the end. *My* face he sees before he's dragged to the deepest pits of hell. I want him to know that a human slave he thought was nothing more than property is the reason his life is ending, and if I need to follow him into death to do that, then I'll go with a fucking smile."

Vexar drops his face into his hands.

My nostrils flare. "I get it. You don't understand." And how could he? He's the heir to an empire. A prince who's never experienced true desperation. "But at a certain point, when you have nothing left to lose—"

"You have everything to lose," he interrupts, raising his face out of his hands.

I laugh, and it sounds hollow and sick. "Like what? Another 50 years of setting bones and wrapping wounds in a dungeon? Another 50 years of being at the mercy of a bunch of psychopathic guards? Another 50 years of traumatic flashbacks and watching young women get trapped in this hell with me? That's not a life, Vexar. That's a drawn-out death sentence."

He extends an arm towards me, and for some reason, I don't pull back. The pads of his fingers trace over the back of my hand, and the sensation pulls me from my rage so fast I don't know how to process it.

"Please," he whispers as he gently grips my wrist and draws me towards him. His calloused palm dwarfs my hand as he carefully unfurls my fingers. "You have your life, your future, your ... heart," he whispers, as he picks up the damp square of cloth and resumes dragging it over my blood-stained hand. "That is enough to lose."

"None of those things are *mine* anymore, Vexar."

He makes another pained sound. "This should not have

been your path. You are—" His hand stills, and he shakes his head. "My blood should not stain your hands."

"I didn't do this for you," I whisper, knowing it's a lie.

"When the guards come, I will not let them take you," Vexar says, breaking the silence.

I glance up from the side of the bed, feeling a new weight settle between my shoulders. He can't save me from this, and I get the feeling that when he figures that out, it's going to break him.

With a sigh, I ask, "And how are you going to do that?"

"When they come, I will demand you stay here, with me, until I finish my fights."

I drop my gaze back to his side and finish throwing the knot I was working on. "I don't think they're gonna go for that. I'm a *criminal*, remember? Besides, staying here with you won't get me any closer to where I need to be."

He grunts a sound of disapproval. "What if I ensure Gaius is brought to justice through the proper channels? Would that change your mind?"

Would that change my mind? I don't know. If I thought he could actually follow through, maybe, but he's injured, and he still has more fights. And if that sinking feeling in my spine is correct, surviving this place won't be as easy as he thinks.

With a sigh, I ask, "Why didn't you hire a male nurse to be on standby for you?"

"You didn't answer my question."

"I know. Just ... humor me, please."

"Because I should not have needed medical care at all,"

"Sure. Ok," I agree. "But in the event that you were injured, what was the plan?"

"I should not have been—"

"Jesus! Ok. I get it. You're a really great fighter, and you weren't supposed to get hurt."

He looks at me like I've slapped him in the face, but there's a flicker of something else there too. Interest? Curiosity? I look away when I finally recognize it. *Lust.*

Fucking hell. Is that why he wants to keep me alive?

I shake off the fluttering in my stomach and press onward. "What I'm trying to say is that you're next in line for the throne of an empire. Don't you think it's a little risky to not have a backup plan?"

He scoffs as if it's the most absurd thing he's ever heard. "My people are a people of honor. It would have been dishonorable for me to bend the rules for little more than a safety net."

"So there was no other way to ensure you didn't die from an injury?" I ask, as I set down my tools and rub my temples.

"There was another way, but it would have been more dishonorable than bending the rules."

"And that was ...?"

"A proposal. Had I accepted it, my vow would have been nullified, and I could have received medical care."

"A proposal? Like, for marriage?"

He thinks for a moment before saying, "Pairing. Mates. Yes."

A surprising surge of jealousy hits me at the thought of him 'mating' with someone, and I nearly groan. This is getting ridiculous. I can't keep having these thoughts.

Returning my focus to the conversation, I ask, "And you didn't accept the proposal, even though it would've gotten you medical care?"

He looks at my mouth for a moment before answering. "She was a poor match, selected by my government. It was expected that I would agree to that proposal, but I could not. Her family has long sought control over the empire, and I am certain a pairing with her would have ended in my death."

That sinking feeling deepens as I study his expression. He seems entirely unaware of the implications of what he's just said, and I can't figure out why. He's smart. That much is clear. But it's like he has a giant blind spot.

Brows furrowed, I ask, "And that doesn't make you even a little concerned?"

"What are you insinuating?"

I throw my hands up. "I just think it's strange that any empire would let its soon-to-be emperor bleed out for no reason. Don't you?"

"We are a people of honor. If I had died here, it would have been an honorable death."

I still can't tell if my observations are completely off-base, or if his honor-tinted glasses are so thick he can't see what's right in front of him. Either way, I'm more certain now than I was before that he isn't supposed to leave here alive.

———

"I NEED you to explain your arrangement with Gaius," Vexar says, interrupting my questions about his family. After learning about his refused marriage proposal, I was curious and kept probing him about his family and his culture. Turns out, him turning down that proposal was a *big* deal, and I'm sort of impressed that he was willing to do it. I assumed he was more of a 'by the rules' kinda guy, but maybe I'm wrong.

I push the hair out of my face with the back of my hand and ask, "What do you want to know?"

"All details regarding your contract and the events that preceded your arrival here."

My stomach drops a bit, and I set down my tools. "Why do

you want to know?" This is the last topic I want to talk about, so unless he has a good reason, I'm not revisiting it.

"I want to help you, and to do that, I need to understand your situation."

"Help me ... how?"

"By getting you out of here and ensuring Gaius faces consequences for his actions."

With the quickly darkening sky outside, the warm glow of the cell's lamp has begun to cast long shadows on the walls. I stare at the dark void cast by Vexar's horns and shift on the soft pillow beneath my knees. I don't know how to respond. He's so dead-set on keeping me alive.

My eyes lock on his. "Why do you care so much if I make it out of here alive?"

The muscles in his jaw tick. "You saved my life, and I"—he sighs—"admire your ferocity." He brushes a hand over his chest before adding, "I also believe in what you are fighting for."

"And having this information will help?"

"It will. Greatly."

Even if he can't save me, it's probably good he knows what's going on.

"Alright," I say, trying to steel myself for what I know is going to be a painful conversation. Immediately, my hands start to shake, and my heart rate soars.

"Are you well?" Vexar asks, his accent thicker than normal.

"Yeah," I say, rubbing my eyes. "It's just not my favorite topic." My skin turns to melted ice, and I blow out a heavy breath. *I can do this.* "They ... uh, the people on the ship. The aliens." My lungs tighten. *"Fuck..."* Images of the box flash through my mind, and my teeth grind together as I try to keep myself in the present. "There was a document. I think." The sharp metallic scent of the ship burns my nose. I swallow and try to focus on the pattern of the deep red stains covering the bedsheet in front of me. "They showed it to me, but I couldn't read it. Different language, I think." If I tilt my head a little, that stain kind of looks like a cloud. "They were talking so fast. Said I had to bleed? I didn't..." I close my eyes, willing away the intense surge of fear. *It's over. You're safe.* "They—"

The dam breaks, adrenaline surges, and I fold in on myself, wrapping my arms around my torso like I might be able to hold myself together.

"Amara?" Vexar whispers.

Something touches my shoulder, and I flinch back.

"Don't," I rasp. I don't want him to touch me. I don't want him to look at me, or talk to me, or even acknowledge me right now. I drop my head into my lap, gripping my hair tight enough to hurt. I hate that my body does this. I fucking *hate* it so much. There's no easy way out. No 'emergency eject' button. I just have to sit in it and wait for it to pass.

I shake as my nervous system reacts to the past like it's still happening. Like I've just been ripped out of that fucking box. The smell of death and shit and sour bodies surrounds me, but I'm still here. The memory hasn't pulled me under. Not fully.

The air around me shifts, and I can feel the radiating heat of Vexar's legs as he drops them on either side of me. I want to tell him to lay back down, but I think his nearness is actually helping.

"I am sorry," he whispers. He doesn't touch me again. He just sits there. Inches away. Breathing steadily. Waiting.

After a few agonizing moments, my head clears enough that I can finish what I started. Keeping my face in my lap, I say, "I couldn't read the contract. They pricked my thumb and pressed it to something. I don't know what happened after that." When the words are out, I feel marginally better, and after maybe a minute, I'm able to sit up again. I feel shaky and horrible, but at this point, I'm used to it.

I look up at Vexar, expecting pity, but there's no pity on his face. He looks calm, hands folded in his lap, blood oozing down his side, and a soft expression on his face.

"Do you have any idea what the contract said?" he asks.

I roll my shoulders and wipe my eyes with the backs of my hands. "I asked Solta to get me a copy. She said she couldn't and that I wouldn't be able to read it anyway. When I asked if she could tell me what it said, she told me I'd have to work five years to pay off my debt, and then I'd be free. But that's a lie. There is no debt, and no one leaves here alive."

His brows dip, and he leans forward enough that I can smell the warm scent of his skin. "Why do you believe that?"

"All the other nurses were told the same thing, and most of them have been here for a lot longer than five years. Some of them have been here for most of their lives."

Vexar rubs a hand down his face, but his calm expression doesn't change. I want to thank him for not trying to coddle me. For not looking at me like I'm broken. But I don't.

"You should lay back down," I say.

15

CANDY LAND

AMARA

’M NEARING THE end of Vexar’s wound where it curves up towards his groin, and I have maybe ten minutes before I’m going to have to figure out how to handle that. It shouldn’t be an issue, but with Vexar, the thought of having my hands so close to his groin is nerve-wracking. Which is insane. I’ve always been able to handle medical procedures just fine, no matter the location or the person. I mean, I spent eight years of my life treating dudes whose primary medical concerns were STIs. Needless to say, I’ve seen a lot of dicks in my time. But with Vexar, things feel different, and I can’t seem to find that place of mental-detachment.

“Do you have family?” he asks, propping his head up by tucking his hand underneath the pillow.

“Why do you ask?”

“You do not like answering questions, do you?”

I’m about to scoff when I realize he’s sort of right. “I guess I’m just not used to talking about myself.” Over the past year, I’ve had to be guarded, and it’s kept me alive and mostly sane.

He hums. “When you leave here, will you want to go home?”

I tighten my grip on the needle driver and start in on the

next suture. "You do realize that I'm probably not leaving here, right?"

"You are leaving here," he states firmly.

It's clear fighting him on this is pointless, so I let it go and say, "I haven't really had a chance to think that far ahead."

"Do you have any family to go back to? Friends? A mate?"

"I don't know." The only real family I have is Marta, and she was 84 when I was taken. Her health seemed good at the time, but at that age, things can change quickly.

"What do you mean?"

"My grandmother. She's my only family, and she was old when I last saw her. I don't know if she's still alive."

He shifts beneath me, and I almost stab him with the needle. "How long was your journey here?"

I don't have a way to answer that, so I just shrug. There wasn't a way to tell time in that box. No lights or windows. No clocks.

He studies my face before asking, "Do you have parents?"

"Of course I have parents, I wasn't born in a lab."

He looks entirely unimpressed, and for some reason, it's hilarious. A smile breaks my face and suddenly, I'm laughing. To my surprise, he grins and his chest starts to shake as he winces in pain from the suppressed laughter.

When I catch my breath, I apologize for making him laugh. It's clear laughing is painful.

"I am fine. Do not worry about me," he says.

"It's hard not to worry when you hide your pain so well."

His expression turns darkly curious, like he's trying to look inside my head and see what I'm thinking.

Feeling exposed, I drop my eyes back to his side and clear my throat. "I do have parents, just not anymore," I say lightly. "I never knew my dad, and my mom died when I was fifteen."

"I am sorry," he says.

I wave the forceps in a dismissive motion. "It's fine. It was a while ago. Besides, my grandmother is one hell of a woman. She filled the shoes of both parents easily." I smile, thinking about Marta. "You and her would get along," I say glibly. But it's true. I think they would.

"Tell me about her."

And I do. I tell him the story of the time she picked me up from school with a dead deer in the back of the truck because some tourist hit it with their car. According to her, "You should never let good meat go to waste". I tell him about the time I started a fire in the microwave, and Marta casually put it out by tossing a handful of sand onto the flames.

"I still don't know why she had a pocket full of sand," I say with a laugh.

When I tell him the story about Marta chasing a raccoon away from our chicken coup in the dead of winter, barefoot, with nothing but a brick, he looks shocked.

"Are they dangerous?" he asks, referring to the raccoon.

"Sometimes. They're small and adorable, but they can be vicious when they want to be. And they have claws."

A grin splits his face as he nods towards me. "Reminds me of someone."

My cheeks heat, and I drop my gaze back to what I'm doing. I've finally reached the point of his wound that I've been dreading, and I still don't have a plan. I set everything down and take a moment to think. From my position on the floor, I can't really reach without contorting my arms and hovering an elbow over his groin. As far as plans go, that's not one I'm comfortable with. But the alternative is to sit on the edge of the bed, and that just feels so ... intimate. Then again, what choice do I have?

With a mental shove, I force myself to my feet. "Are you ok if I sit on the edge of the bed? I ... uh, I can't reach from down there."

He nods and shifts to the side, making room for me.

A bead of sweat drips down my spine as my stomach tightens. Nothing about this feels purely medical anymore, and I don't know how to handle that. The heat in his gaze is suffocating, but for some reason, I have no desire to extinguish it.

Holding my breath, I lower myself onto the mattress. My hip presses against his thigh, and a ripple goes through his body, muscles tensing and relaxing in a strange sequential motion. It's easily one of the most alien things I've seen him do, and for a moment, I can't stop staring, wondering if it might happen again.

"Are you ok?" he asks, dragging my attention back up to his face. The green of his eyes is gone, taken over by a shimmering black.

"Uh, yeah," I whisper, "are you?"

Silently, and without breaking eye contact, he takes my right hand and guides it to his abdomen. That small action sends my mind reeling as the sensation of tightening flesh creeps over my entire body, all the way up to my jaw.

Right. Ok. He's fine with me touching him now. Good to know.

With fumbling hands, I adjust the lamp and open a fresh suture packet. My heart thrums in my throat, pounding against each breath as I lean over his hip and start to stitch.

His skin is warm and soft. Thinner here than on his ribs. It should be painful, but he isn't flinching or tensing at all, and now it's clear his earlier reactions to my touch had nothing to do with the pain.

His gaze runs like fingers over my flesh, tracing the lines of my face, my neck, and down my body. The heated weight of his attention burns my skin and has me nearly panting. My nipples harden beneath my dress. Stomach tightens. Vexar's chest rises and falls with short, hungry breaths as his left hand indents the skin of his uninjured hip, pressing down with every plunge of my needle. The atmosphere of restrained need is so thick I can hardly see, and by the time I tie off the last suture, my mouth is dry and I'm glistening with sweat.

"I'm done," I say breathlessly as I stand to put away the equipment.

Before I can take a step, Vexar's hand catches my stomach, holding me in place. The heat of his touch ripples out, curling around my sides.

"I ... I have to get a bandage," I stutter out.

His fingers retreat slowly, trailing over my hip with a molten promise that weakens my knees. I know if I let myself look at his face, I won't be able to look away.

What started as a quiet tug in my gut has become a gravitational force that's sapping away my resolve and begging for my surrender. And I want to surrender. I want to give in and let myself believe that there's still good in this world—that after everything, I can still find joy, and comfort, and pleasure. But the logical part of me is pushing back. It says I'm imagining his desire. That he's too good to be true. That I need to stay focused. That if I give in to this, it will only make what comes next harder.

He can't save me. I have to remember that. I have to remember why I'm here.

Vexar watches me through the dim light as I get a bandage, lay it over his side, and start taping it in place. When I let go, the tape peels back. His skin is damp with sweat and hot to the touch.

"Shit." I prop my hip on the edge of the bed and press my hand to his forehead. "Do you feel like you have a fever?"

His left hand wraps around mine, warm and strong, and he guides my palm down to his chest, holding it over his heart. "I do not have an infection, if that is what you are asking," he rumbles.

A deep yearning burns in his black eyes, like he's struggling to stop himself from grabbing my face and kissing me. I suck in a breath as his right hand ghosts over the skin of my knee, and any doubt I had about his desire evaporates.

I spin out of his grip before I do something I can't take back. "Uh, the tape won't stick," I say, moving to grab a roll of wrap from the med-bag. "I, uh, have to wrap it … uh, the bandage, on you. Can you sit?"

Vexar pushes himself up, letting his legs drop over the side of the bed. His lips part, his head cocks, and he watches me with those dark, curious eyes.

Doing my best to ignore the ache between my legs and the growing bulge between his, I step up to the edge of the bed, directly between his thighs, and press the end of the wrap over the bandage. "Can you hold it there?" I ask.

His fingers brush over mine, and before I can pull back, his chest vibrates with an inaudible rumble. I don't know what that sound means, but it sends a jolt right through me.

I step back, off-balance and breathing so much harder than I should be. My body's on fire and I don't know how to stop it.

Sure, I think Vexar's extremely attractive and nearly irresistible, but *this* can't happen. I don't need a distraction, I need revenge. Besides, he's not even human, and I doubt we're even compatible. And yet, I can't seem to resist his pull. He's drawing me in like I'm starved, and he's the best buffet I've ever seen. I don't get it. I thought I was the one with the experience, but right now he's playing 4D chess and I'm playing fucking Candy Land.

Catching my breath, I unroll the wrap and try to focus. Vexar's torso is massive. There's no way for me to pass the wrap around his waist without hugging him, and I'm definitely not doing that. I doubt I'd be able to reach around him anyway. He's a fucking mountain.

Feeling a bit like a child, I climb onto the bed and walk over the mattress behind him, pulling the wrap across his back and passing it under his arm. He lets out a chuckle as I repeat my circles. I want to chew him out for laughing at me, but at this point, if I open my mouth, there's no telling what will come out.

When I reach the end of the roll, it's clear I'll have to step between his legs again to secure it in place. Trying to ignore the fluttering in my stomach, I step forward, bringing my face within inches of his. His warm, spicy scent surrounds me as I dip my fingers beneath the wrap, tucking the loose end under.

"Stay," he whispers, almost too quiet to hear.

Slowly, I meet his gaze.

Let me lose myself in you, his eyes seem to say.

Calloused fingers run up my wrist. I'd forgotten I was still touching him. With soft movements, he guides my hand to his chest as I lose myself in the depthless, midnight oceans of his eyes. There's a hopeful caution in those eyes as he releases my hand. He wants to know if I'll stay, and, against my better judgment, I press my palm more firmly to his skin, letting my eyes fall shut as I soak in the delicious feeling of being this close.

"Your heart beats faster when you touch me," he says as his hand slides back over mine.

And he's right, my heart fucking roars when I touch him.

16

MARCH OF ENTROPY

VEXAR

I HOLD AMARA'S hand to my chest, where, just beneath the surface, one of my hearts beats in perfect synchrony with hers. It is a strange sensation, having two heartbeats when I have only ever had one. Strange and beautiful.

When I was young, I spent many afternoons dreaming that I might someday forge a *Zhyrrak* bond. That I might find the one person my heart would awaken for. It was a silly dream. An impossible one. But I was young and full of hope, and somehow, that hope was not nearly as foolish as I was told.

Amara's eyes open, and I drink in her beauty. She looks so much like the Goddess Xelora that if her skin were any paler, I might mistake her for the statue I kneel before every morning. Small round nose, full lips that turn down at the corners, and an uncanny depth in her eyes.

Stunning.

Darkness has consumed the desert outside, but the winds still howl, pummeling the Coliseum with sand, slowly reclaiming bits of the structure and returning it to the barren wilds beyond. It is the never-ending march of entropy. The unseen hand that constantly moves us all towards predictable chaos.

These cycles have always been and always will be. They are resolute and reliable. And perhaps that is the way of all things, coming and going in dependable waves of chaos and reorganization. A pattern that only exists if you know what to look for. Amara is chaos, and instinct tells me to trust her the way I trust these cycles.

"My people have two hearts," I say slowly. "One here," I move her hand to the left, "and the other, here," I move her hand to the right. "But this heart is meant to be dormant. Under normal circumstances, it should only beat a handful of times each day."

"But yours is..." Her eyes flick up to mine. "Is there something wrong? Did you lose too much blood?"

"There is nothing wrong."

"Then why is it beating like that?" Her posture straightens. "It's getting faster. Is that normal?"

"It is matching yours."

Her mouth pinches, and her brows furrow. "Why would it do that?"

"Because you are the second half of my soul."

She rips her hand from beneath mine and glares at me with unbridled irritation. "Fucking hell, Vexar. Really? The second half of your soul?"

"I... Do you not feel—"

"Feel what? Whatever weird alien wizardry you're up to?" She shakes her hands out and takes another step back. "No, yeah. I feel it. I feel like my heart is going to break out of my chest. Like I'm losing my fucking mind!"

"Alien wizardry?" I ask.

"Yeah! Wizardry! Like you've put me under some sort of spell, or are dowsing me with alien pheromones. Wooing me with those perfect green eyes, and your witty but somehow poetic banter, and those deceptively gentle hands, and ... and that fucking body!" She presses her palms over her eyes and starts to pace. "Oh my god!"

My heart warms at her many compliments.

"I can't believe this!" she shouts, throwing her hands up. "You're trying to *scam* me, aren't you?" She glances at me and shakes her head. "*Soul mates. Kings.* Jesus fuck. How did I fall for that?"

I press my lips together, but I cannot hide my smile.

"Why are you smiling?" she shouts, her voice reaching a much higher pitch than usual.

"Amara, I am not 'dousing you in pheromones' or trying to 'scam you'. I am not doing anything."

"What the hell is that supposed to mean? Are you trying to say that I'm doing this? Because—"

"No," I say, shaking my head while a laugh plays at the edge of my teeth, "*fate* did this."

"Fate?" Her face drops into an unamused expression. "You want me to believe that 'fate' is making your pants tent?"

I scrub a hand over my face. This is not going well, but she is all fire, and I love it.

Pressing my palms into my knees, I lean towards her, ignoring the pain in my side. "Do you really think the only thing happening here is me being aroused by you?"

"I..." she says, trailing off and biting her lower lip before throwing her hands up again. "I don't know!"

"Let me show you something. Please." I wave my hand, inviting her back towards me, but she stays firmly in place.

"How about you just tell me."

"Right. Of course." I bring a hand to my chest and start tapping out the beat of my bonded heart. "This," I say, tapping out the beats, "is my heartbeat—my *bonded* heartbeat. Tap out your own."

"I know it's beating! I fucking felt it!"

When I continue tapping, she reluctantly raises her fingers to her neck, eyes burning with anger. A few seconds later, that anger turns to confusion.

She has finally realized I am tapping out *her* heartbeats. Not mine.

"You feel it?" I ask.

Her cheeks flush, and she shakes her head. "No," she warns, "you said you could *hear* my heart."

"*I* never said that. *You* suggested that as a possibility, and I did not correct you." I point at my chest. "This is how I knew."

She makes a grunting sound and throws her hands up again. "You just have an answer for everything, don't you? Fucking infuriating." For a moment, she just stares at me. Then her jaw sets, and she steps forward as if she can't control herself. "Ok. Just for fun, let's pretend I believe you. Why is my heart beating in your chest?"

"We are linked. Bonded by the Zhyrrak."

She scoffs. "Zhyrrak? Is this another word for your weird alien magic?"

"It is not magic. It is physiology. We are bonded. Or, we are meant to be bonded."

"Why?" she asks.

"Why are we bonded, or why is it not magic?"

"I don't know! Both?"

"I do not know why it chose us," I answer honestly. "But the bond is science, not magic. It has something to do with our heart's electromagnetic frequencies, and, evidently, a long-dormant gene within my DNA." I frown. "And possibly yours as well." I hadn't really considered that she might carry the gene, but it certainly makes sense. From what I understand, humans and Vhorathis have common ancestry. Albeit, very ancient common ancestry, but still.

She tilts her head before stepping back between my legs. The ease of her movements and her willingness to be so close is a confession of sorts that calms my nerves.

Her eyes ask permission, and I grant it with a slight raise of my chin. A moment later, her hand returns to my chest. Warmth and desire spread beneath her palm as I sink my fingers into my thighs, fighting the urge to touch her. The urge I've been fighting almost all day.

"So you're not doing this?" she asks with a look of confused wonder.

"No, I cannot control my bonded heart. It follows yours."

"And this is real," she says, more as a statement than a question.

"It is."

She's silent for a long while, and I feel her mind working frantically. Then she asks, "Is that why my heart's been acting so weird? Like the beginning of a panic-attack without the panic?"

"If the weirdness is a recent development, then yes."

She looks unimpressed again. "Obviously, it's a recent development, or I wouldn't have—" She huffs. "You know what? Never mind." She drops her hand from my chest, and it lands on my thigh. I do not think she is even aware of what she is doing, and it feels like another confession. "So what does this all mean? If I have a panic attack, are you going to pass out? Or if you start running around, is my heart going to explode?" Her eyes lose their ferocity as she asks, "And what happens when the guards come and I'm executed?"

Ice creeps through my veins at the reminder of our situation. This feeling of being out of control is not one I enjoy. I need information and options. If I could just speak to Gaius... No, that will not solve the problem. He *is* the problem. He is the reason I am wounded, and Amara's life is in danger.

If the guards do come for her, I have very few options, and I do not like any of them. The bond has changed our situation—my vow no longer matters—and if I want to take my rightful place as the head of this empire, I cannot kill Gaius's guards, and I cannot let Amara kill Gaius. I need time to think. Time to plan. But for now, I need to focus on her and our bond. The sun has set, and no guards have come. It is unlikely they will come before morning—Gaius wants as much assurance of my failure as possible—and if they do come, I will not let them take her, even if my actions cost me my throne. She is more important than any title. She is the heartbeat of my people, a beacon of hope for a future once thought impossible.

I grip both of Amara's hands in mine, feeling the soft warmth of her skin. "Your heart will not explode. I will not pass out if you do. And you will not be dying today. Or tomorrow. Or the day after that. You will be old and gray when your time comes. I promise."

Her eyes drop to the bandage on my side, and a look of disappointment crosses her face. "I really want to believe you, but trust has to be built. You get that, right?"

I do not make idle promises. Ever. She *will* leave here alive. "What I said is true. No matter what happens, you will not die here. You are the future. *My* future. Even if you do not trust me now, at least let me prove myself to you. Please." Inside this cell, we have only words. There is no test or action I can take that would show her I am worthy of her trust, and it only complicates our situation further. I do not think bonds like this were meant to be forged in a cage.

Her eyes squint. "You're serious, aren't you?"

"Very." There's a lingering question on her face, so I wait.

"I'm sorry, this is just a lot. Humans don't do this. We ... we get to know each other over a long period of time and…" She shakes her head. "I guess, I just don't get it. What does this mean? Like, if we do survive, what then? We spend time together and figure out if we actually like each other, or if we're just trauma-bonded, or what?"

There is only one way for me to answer this, and I do not like it. My thoughts trail down to the bandage on her knee, and my chest tightens. I cannot tell her.

"The choice is yours," I say. "You will be free of this place, and you can decide your own fate." I hate the lie as it leaves my mouth, but I continue anyway. "If you would like, I can take you home. To Earth. Or, you could come with me. Back to my home and my people." I stare at our hands, her small fingers curled around my palms, and a deep fear grips my gut. I cannot take her back to Earth, not until I know how long she was on that Tusku ship for. Years may have passed without her knowledge, and there might be nothing left for her to return to.

"And if I go with you?" she asks quietly.

My eyes pop up. "Whatever you desire."

She releases my hands and steps back. "I need to think." She paces across the room a few times before stopping to face me. "This is crazy, you know that, right?"

"I suppose, for you, it must feel that way." Her culture has no reference for this. "But for me, this is a life-long wish come true."

I feel her heart stutter in my chest. "Oh." Her eyes move frantically as if she is searching for something. "And this is something you want? With me?"

"More than anything."

She barks out a humorless laugh and quickly covers her mouth as she turns her back to me.

I stand, uncertain if I should approach or not. A second later, my decision is made. I step up behind her and am almost surprised by her size. The top of her head barely reaches my chest. Hesitantly, I place a hand on her shoulder, and she turns her head to stare at it. My fears melt when she does not try to pull away. If anything, she seems to relax.

"What if I still don't believe you?" she asks, focus still trained on my hand.

"Which part?"

My hand slides down her arm as she spins to face me and slowly tilts her head back, eyes scanning up my body until they lock on mine. "Fucking hell," she whispers. "You ... uh"—her throat works down a swallow—"are bigger than I thought."

"Which part do you still not believe?" I ask again, resisting the urge to do more than just hold her elbow. I want to touch all of her. I want her to touch all of me.

"All of it," she says.

I take a step back and hold out my hand between us, palm up. She moves towards me, sliding her hand into mine like it's the most natural thing in the world. And it does feel that way. Natural and easy.

"Can I show you something else?" I ask.

"Something else?" Her brows rise with a taunting, irreverent expression that sends a throbbing heat between my legs. Gods, if this is what she does to me with a single look, I will be forever at her mercy.

"I did not mean ... *that*," I cough out.

"Uh huh," she says, her expression far lighter than it had been before. She is teasing me. This is good.

I guide us back to the bed, where I sit on the edge and pull her towards me. The way her breath catches as I press her palms back to my chest is a pleasure I doubt I will ever forget.

"What's up with you wanting me to touch your chest all the time?" she asks. "I mean, it's a nice chest, but I don't need to be touching it *all* the time, just like, some of the time."

I press her hands more firmly to my skin, holding back a laugh as her teeth latch onto her bottom lip.

"I will always want your hands on me," I whisper. Her eyes go wide, but I do not give her a chance to respond. "I am not certain this will work, but I have a theory. Do you trust me?" She stays silent, so I continue. "Close your eyes and clear your mind. Then, focus on me—on the space between us."

"Really? We're meditating now?"

"Trust me. Please."

Reluctantly, she closes her eyes, and I can't deny I am impressed by her endless fight.

"Keep focusing on me and the space between us. Maybe imagine opening a door and seeing me on the other side?" I wait a few moments, wondering if she is actually trying or just playing along, when a surge of emotion floods the space between us. The ghost of connection I felt before turns into something formidable and all-encompassing. Wave after wave of emotion crashes into me—fear, pain, confusion, desire, rage, relief—and for a moment, I am lost in her torrents.

Discipline and control.

I do not know what else to do, so I work to calm the deluge. Sweat beads on my brow, but my efforts prevail, and her raging river slows to a manageable, trickling stream.

Her mind is an expanse of chaos, and the one emotion that burns the brightest also sinks a blade into my heart. It is the evidence of my failure, and seeing how deeply it has scarred her is a pain beyond words. But she is here. She is alive. And she is stronger than I thought possible, carrying an immense burden without losing her kindness or humor. It is a miracle. *She* is a miracle.

And I am a monster.

I take a deep breath before allowing some of my emotions to slip into the space between us, grateful for the years I spent developing control over my mind. Some things, I am not yet ready to share.

She finds me quickly, slipping between my body and soul like a set of phantom hands. It is ... uncomfortable, and more intimidating than I anticipated. While she may have felt some of my emotions before, this is different. It is deeply intimate.

Her hand jerks beneath mine, and I *feel* her surprise.

"Oh my god," she whispers. "Is that ... you?"

She opens her eyes, and I ask, "Do you believe me now?"

17

PERMANENT

AMARA

"DO YOU BELIEVE me now?" Vexar asks.

I have no idea how to answer that. Whatever's going on here isn't just some party trick—like tapping out my heartbeats—I can *feel* his emotions. As much as I want to scoff and berate him for trying to fool me, I can't. He isn't trying to fool me. This is *real*.

Fucking hell, this is real.

The foundation of my reality begins to shake as it has so many times over the past year. Let's just say being abducted by aliens can really do a number on your sense of what's real. My human understanding of the universe has been smashed over the head so many times, I don't trust myself to know the difference between fact and fiction anymore. At least not out here. Everything's just so much stranger than I thought possible. Maybe I just need to accept that some things are beyond my understanding. Like this. This is beyond my understanding.

"I'm not sure what I believe," I say.

He rubs his thumbs over the backs of my hands as his two hearts thud against my palms, one of them mirroring my pulse.

He's nervous. And hopeful. And I can *feel* that. Not in the same way I feel my own emotions, more like having a stray thought slip through the back of my mind. But it's still there. And I've never experienced anything quite like it. I feel strangely whole.

"You're so ... calm," I say.

"I have had a lot of practice controlling my emotions."

I hum, but it's a quiet, thoughtful sound. "Just for the sake of confirmation or whatever, can you tell me what you're feeling right now?" An echo of anxiety passes through the back of my mind, but it's small in comparison to everything else I'm feeling from him.

"Curiosity, excitement, and ... desire," he says, glancing down to where my hands are still pressed to his chest.

I don't think I've ever felt so vulnerable, but the strange part is, it doesn't feel scary. It feels good. But the urge to devour him is nearing the level of inescapable compulsion, and I'm not sure how to handle it. My eyes keep locking on his mouth, and each time it gets harder to look away.

"So this is part of the ... bond?" I choke out, clenching my legs together. "Being able to feel each other's emotions?"

"I believe it is called a tether, although I know very little about it. And yes, it is part of the bond."

Bond. Tether. It all sounds very ... permanent. Very ensnaring.

I drop my hands from his chest and brush the hair back from my face. "If you don't know anything about these *tethers*, how did you know we had one?"

"You've been noticing my emotions all day, as I have been noticing yours." His head tilts as he waits for me to agree with him, but I honestly don't know what he means. "When I was telling you about my experience in the arena, you knew what I was feeling despite me doing everything in my power to hide it. No one can read me when I do not want them to, and yet, you did."

My mouth drops open as I think back to that moment. His face was blank, but it was like his sadness was infecting me. I blow out a breath through pinched lips. "I still don't get what this all means..."

"That we are paired. Mates."

I frown. "Didn't you say a 'mate' is the equivalent of 'marriage' for you? I'm a human. And a slave. And I broke your vow. And you're a king." I cut myself off before I start sounding whiny or insecure. I'm neither of those things, but I am a realist. The one thing I know to be true is that my life is not some happy fairytale with godmothers and ball gowns. There's no Prince Charming or magical love that will solve all my problems, and it's more likely I'll have my heels sliced off than wear glass slippers to a ball.

Vexar reaches for my hand, but I pull back. He grimaces and says, "None of that matters now. You are mine, and I am yours."

Nope. "No." I point a finger at him. "I don't belong to you. Besides, isn't your government supposed to choose your mate?"

He runs a hand down his face. "You have a lot of fight for someone so small."

My mouth drops open. "And you've got a lot of confidence for someone so wounded!"

He doesn't look amused, and I have to admit it isn't my best work.

"I will have white hair long before I should," he mumbles in what I assume is Vhorathi. Fortunately, my translator makes quick work of it.

"The fuck did you just say?" Even while I'm verbally sparring with him, my body is betraying me—prickling and tingling beneath his gaze and with the deep vibrations of his voice. Worse than that, I'm enjoying arguing with him. Like, a lot. *I'm so fucked.*

"Amara, that rule does not apply to us. To *this*. Our bond

supersedes any chosen mate, and any outdated rule." The muscles in his jaw tick. "If you choose to accept the bond, it will be binding in every sense of the word. No one will separate us, and I will not let any harm come to you." He shakes his head. "That did not come out right. Even if you do not accept the bond, I will not let any harm come to you."

Binding. He said, "binding". One more word that tightens my chest and sparks a perverse sort of interest. Would it really be so bad to just—

Oh god, I'm considering this. I'm considering going along with this. The urge to just say 'fuck it' and kiss him is almost too much to bear. Except at some point, this fantasy *is* going to fall apart, and he'll realize he can't save me. What happens then?

That annoying voice in the back of my head chimes in with another, **Trust him.**

Even if I went along with all of this and he managed to get us out of here alive, what then? I'd be *tethered* to a stranger for the rest of my life? I don't know if that's something I should even be considering. Then again, I sort of want to. I mean, what do I have to lose?

Breathing gets hard, like sucking air through a straw.

Would it really be so bad being stuck with Vexar forever? He's handsome, kind, thoughtful, and introspective. He's great. *But I don't know him.* At least, not really. It feels like I do, but I'm smarter than that.

Then again, maybe this is a chance to do something greater. Something bigger. A chance to be a team with someone again. And damn if that isn't the most tempting part of all of this.

I take a steadying breath and ask the most important question I have, "Will you help me stop Gaius?" He already said he would, but now that I can feel his emotions, any promise he makes will hold a lot more weight. It's the one thing I need to know before letting myself have this.

His expression turns serious, and he says, "I will."

And I believe him.

18

WOVEN

VEXAR

"I WILL," I answer. I have already told her as much, but she is slow to trust, and I cannot blame her for that.

"Ok," she says, nodding her head like she is coming to terms with everything. "You said it's permanent? The bond?"

Everything I know about the Zhyrrak is mired in conflicting information, and none of it is aligning with the actual experience. It is difficult to be certain of anything.

I glance down at the bandage around her knee and resist the urge to give her my honest assessment of our situation. If she panics, it will be nearly impossible to ensure her safety. And considering the conflicting information I have, there is every chance the *sasi-temwá* is just another myth inflated over time. All I know is that she should have a choice in this. Even if that choice is mostly an illusion.

"If you accept it, it will be permanent," I say.

"Right," she says slowly.

"You must choose for yourself. I will support your decision, no matter what it is."

Her face relaxes further. "I get to choose," she says on an exhale.

"You get to choose."

"And I don't have to choose now?"

"No."

She shifts, and the edge of her dress brushes the inside of my thigh. I suck in a breath.

Her expression turns curious, and she presses her hand to my cheek in an unexpectedly tender touch. "I still don't know how to process all of this," she whispers. Small fingers trace the contours of my cheek, down the length of my nose, and over my lips. "It's like being in a dream. A very beautiful dream." Her gaze is penetrating, diving into my very soul. "A dream I don't want to wake up from."

No one has ever looked at me this way. No one has ever touched me this way. I spent years of my life alone, having no idea I was missing anything at all. But I was. I was missing *her*, and I cannot go back to that island of isolation I once called home.

I brush her hair back from her face. "Then do not wake up. Stay with me," I whisper, almost like a prayer.

Trust her, a voice says from the depths of my soul.

"I'm so comfortable with you, and I don't get it. It's almost like," she pauses and takes a breath, "I don't know. Like being around you is giving me a piece of myself back."

"Zhyrrak bonds are strong."

"Zhyrrak," she says. "What does that mean? My translator doesn't know the word."

My hands are resting on her hips, but I do not remember putting them there.

"It means two hearts beating as one. And it has not happened in a very, very long time."

"Why not?" she asks.

"No one really knows."

She pulls my face closer to hers, and her eyes drop to my

mouth. My stomach tenses. I can feel her intention. I know what she wants, and I want to give it to her. But I...

"I have never kissed anyone," I confess.

Her eyes flick between mine, and it's clear her vacillating indecision is gone. "Do you want to?"

"Yes." I wet my lips.

"And you trust me?"

"Yes."

She gives me a small smile as her eyes search my face and then close. Her breath ghosts over my mouth, and the soft contours of her lips brush mine.

For a moment, I am lost. The sensation is overwhelming. My lips tingle and heat. The pads of my fingers dig into the soft flesh of her hips. Then she does it again, lips parting and caressing mine.

Cautiously, I emulate her movements, and the entire universe narrows down to a single point. I do it again, and desire floods our connection.

Her fingers grasp at my neck, and she breaks the kiss, pressing her forehead to mine and leaving enough room between us to suck in a ragged breath. A haze of pleasure clouds my mind.

"Holy shit," she gasps. Her hands tremble against my skin. Heart thuds wildly in my chest. And I feel her slipping between my cracks, into every corner of my being like a warm, sensual flood. Whatever barriers I built between us shatter.

"Zar'vok," I say, my voice deep and heavy. "I feel you every-where." I grip her waist and pull her against me as her mouth returns mine.

The tip of her tongue brushes the seam of my lips. Heat pulses down my spine. I match her stroke with one of my own, and she opens for me, beckoning me in. She tastes better than any fantasy. Like chaos and fire.

What began as a slow exploration becomes unguarded and carnal. Her fingers knit into my hair, her hips press against the insides of my thighs, and she moans. The sound is unlike any I have ever heard. It is a confession, a plea, and an endorsement all at once.

I break the kiss for the barest of moments. "That sound," I say, staring down into her eyes, seeing the fire burning behind them.

More.

My mouth crashes back into hers as I wrap an arm around her back, desperate to keep her here. Her tongue plunges into my mouth. Fire burns my veins. I want to capture her, devour her.

More.

Instinct begins to drive me. My hand reaches for the nape of her neck, and I tilt her head back so I can deepen the kiss. She moves with me, yielding to my touch in a way that is both shameless and trusting.

It is addictive. *She* is addictive.

"Fuck. Why are you so good at this?" she moans before returning her mouth to mine and letting her hands explore my chest.

I am a good fighter and a good student. This is not so different. Matching strike for strike. Anticipating your opponent. Finding their weakness and exploiting it. Moving, lunging, dodging, dancing together. But it is so much better than fighting could ever be.

Her fingers continue down my chest, and when they reach my abdomen, a deep, uncontrollable rumble rolls through me. Her body quivers in response. The power we wield over each other is indescribable. I cannot tell if it is the bond or just ... us, but it is clear she could control me with a single drag of her finger, flick of her tongue, or whispered word in my ear.

"What's happening?" she asks, lips swollen and the color of ripe veladoo.

I trace the line of those lips and then the curve of her jaw with my thumb. "Our hearts made a choice," I say, before following the path of my thumb with my mouth, tasting her skin and nearly falling apart at how perfect every inch of her is, how it feels like every part of me was carefully crafted for the singular purpose of loving her.

She has done the impossible. She has awoken the ancient miracle of my people, and I will worship her accordingly. I kiss and lick down her neck, tasting the salt on her skin and feeling her pulse beneath my tongue. The Zhyrrak chose her. It chose *us*. Amara is my mate, my destiny, my Queen.

When my lips return to hers, I feel a shift. A deep acceptance. Her hands slide down my arms. A rumble vibrates my chest. Then a pleasure unlike any I have ever known overtakes me, and a single word fills my mind.

Mine.

Her hand presses over my heart.

She has accepted our bond. There is no question.

I feel her soul weaving itself into mine, rebuilding me from the ground up, threading us together, and flooding me with a power that feels as ancient and as raw as the stone beneath us.

This is what my ancestors sang about.

This is why they were mighty warriors.

This is how I will protect my Queen.

19

FOREVER

AMARA

THE INTENSE, MAGNETIC pull between us has won the battle against my rational mind, and I've forgotten all sense of reason or self-preservation.

"What's happening?" I ask, my voice breathy and unguarded.

His thumb ghosts over my lips before tracing the line of my jaw, sending bolts of euphoria dancing over my skin. "Our hearts made a choice," he whispers. He follows the path of his thumb with his mouth, patiently kissing and licking down my neck until I'm out of breath and trembling.

Is it supposed to feel this good? I don't remember anything ever feeling this good.

When his mouth returns to mine, the kiss is claiming and greedy and achingly familiar, like I've always known how he would taste, how his lips would feel on mine, or how the firm planes of his muscles would tighten and ripple against my body. It's like a dream I've already had, and it feels so ... right.

He pulls me closer, tighter, harder. Every touch becomes a delicious promise, and I want it all. I want his gentle but deadly hands, his wild kiss, his impossible confidence, his steady calm.

I want *him* for as long as I can have him. Maybe that's only an hour, or a day, but I want whatever I can get. I don't want this to end. I don't want to lose this feeling of wholeness.

My hands slide down his arms, and a deep rumble vibrates his chest. He tastes like my undoing. Like aching lust and hidden violence. I should want to take this slow, but I can't. Not when I have no idea how much time we have.

Whatever's happening between us is pure magic, and I can't die before I've gotten a chance to sink into him and this over-whelming feeling of rightness. As much as I wanted to deny it, now that I'm here, in his arms, it's clear I can't go back. I can't ever be without this. Without *him*. In his grip, I feel freer than I have in years. Free and safe.

I *know* this is where I'm supposed to be.

I want this.

I press a hand to his chest, feeling the quick thud of *my* heart beneath his skin. We're already so deeply entwined. Threaded together in a way that shouldn't be possible.

What he called a "tether" isn't a tether at all, it's a thread. It's not a trap, it's a connection. It's not binding, it's … freeing. And as strange as that sounds, it's exactly how this feels.

A singular word plays on repeat in my mind, "*Yes,*" and a surge of some indescribable sensation overtakes me. I gasp. Emotions bubble up in its wake. Unfamiliar and beautiful. They're *his* emotions, but they're stronger now, clearer. Like bright pops of color in a landscape of gray. And beneath the gratitude and excitement, there's something raw and powerful. Like the air before a storm. Crackling with potential energy. And it feels good. So. Fucking. Good.

I open my eyes and realize I've been crying. I didn't even notice.

I move to wipe the tears away, but Vexar catches my hand.

"Leave them," he says, "they are the messengers of fate."

With a look of pure reverence, he kisses the pads of my fingers before pressing his lips back to mine.

The thread of our connection flourishes and grows until he's spilling into me. I feel him deeply. His confidence is like a salve to my fear. The clenching tightness in my chest loosens, the lingering headache dissipates, and I feel hope.

Maybe we can survive this.

I *want* to survive this.

I run my fingers along the contours of his jaw, over the coarse stubble of his beard, feeling the way his muscles move beneath his skin.

"I am so glad I found you," he whispers before nudging my nose with his own. He grabs my hips and lifts me easily, guiding my legs until I'm straddling his lap. It feels so natural to let him pick me up—to give him control of my body like this. Everything right now feels second-nature. No fumbling limbs or awkward movements, just grace and certainty.

"You're going to tear your stitches," I say, running a thumb down the side of his neck, over a long scar that runs from the base of his ear to the top of his shoulder. He has so many scars, and each one sparks a new curiosity. He may have never killed before today, but it's clear he's experienced enough violence to last a lifetime.

"The stitches are fine," he says, dragging his calloused hands over my bare thighs. "The pain is nearly gone. Besides, I needed to see your face."

Sitting in his lap has brought me almost eye-level with him. Almost.

I hum. "You are freakishly tall."

"Maybe you are just very short."

Rude. "I'm above average height."

"For a goblin."

My eyes nearly burst out of my skull. "How do you even know what a gob—"

He silences me with a kiss, and by the time he pulls back, I've forgotten everything I was going to say.

"Gods, you are beautiful," he says, gripping my chin and studying me as if he can read every tick of my face like words on a page. "The past few hours have been impossible. Every time your fingers brushed my skin—" He sucks in a breath. "I think I have found my greatest weakness."

The past few hours? "How long have you known about this?"

He pushes my hair over my shoulder and stares curiously at my neck before dragging a finger down the side of it. "From the moment I dug my claws into my chest."

"That's why you did that?"

Still focused on my neck, he says, "It was a surprising experience, having a second heart suddenly beating in my chest."

"Why didn't you tell me sooner?"

His eyes meet mine, and they narrow. "Would you have wanted to know sooner?"

I consider his question. "I guess not." I would have likely pushed back a lot harder had he said all this a few hours ago. "So, just to confirm," I say between little gasps as he starts to kiss my neck again, "you weren't freaked out because you realized you were bonded to me, right?"

He leans back, brow furrowed, and takes my face in both hands. "Amara, if I could have chosen anyone in the universe, I would still have chosen you. You are the most astonishing creature I have ever met."

I swallow around the lump in my throat, suddenly feeling far more vulnerable than I did a moment ago. The urge to run starts to grow in my gut, but the urge to stay overpowers it.

"What are you thinking?" he asks.

I blow out a breath between pinched lips. "It's just really

hard to believe you when you say things like that," I admit. "It freaks me out."

He nods slowly, clearly trying to wrap his head around what I'm saying. "It makes you uncomfortable when I admit that I am entranced by you?"

I rub my thumbs down the sides of his thick neck, trying to formulate a response. "It freaks me out because you don't know anything about me. When you're making these big claims, I can't help but think you must be lying or trying to manipulate me."

His shock lights up the back of my mind. "I do not say these things lightly. Who you are is as clear to me as the brown of your eyes." His hands hold my face, keeping my eyes trained on him. "You are a fearless protector and warrior. You would willingly walk into death for a chance to save others from the fate you have suffered. That is your essence, and that is why I respect you the way I do." His voice is rough with emotion, and I feel my walls starting to crack again. The honesty in our connection is unmistakable, and there's no way for me to deny he's speaking his truth.

For a moment, I just sit there, shocked. Then my mouth collides with his in a desperate, hungry kiss. Somehow, he sees me. This entire time I thought I had shown him nothing but my worst parts—my anger, fear, avoidance, and frustration—but that isn't what he saw.

A clarity washes over me. I have nothing to lose and everything to gain. If we survive this, and if he keeps his promise to me, I will have gained a future I never thought possible. I will live to fight another day, and I won't be alone.

His hands slide to my waist, fingers digging into the fabric of my dress as I sink deeper in his lap, sliding forward until the bulge in his pants presses between my legs.

Fuck I need this.

He groans, rocking his hips up into me. But a second later,

he's lifting me and pushing me back. "You do crazy things to me," he rasps, "and I do not want to lose control."

"Just let go," I beg, knowing how desperate I sound and not caring. I'm done policing myself and trying to be reasonable. The hottest man—alien?—I've ever seen is between my thighs, and his desire is boiling through the back of my mind, blending with my own.

"I do not want to lose control ... yet," he says. Then he winks.

I groan, letting my head fall back. "If you don't plan on losing control, then you can't wink like that. It does things."

He growls. He fucking growls. And goosebumps break out over my skin. "Now I know two of your weaknesses," he whispers before dragging his teeth down my neck.

My entire body is buzzing. Alive with a thousand bees. I press my hands against his chest, trying to get some space. "You can't tease me like this," I pant. "I'll combust, or have a heart attack or something."

"I am not teasing, I am taking my time." His fingers dig into my hips, holding me close and ratcheting up my need even higher. The strength in those hands is too much to ignore, and my horny brain conjures images of riding them a thousand different ways. This poor alien has no idea what sort of Pandora's box he's opened.

"This feels a lot like teasing," I say, even as I try to remind myself that he's never done any of this. He might be a quick learner, but this is all new to him. He might not even know what he's doing to me right now. I just need to calm down and let him set the pace.

A cool breeze filters in through the window, brushing over my sweat-damp skin, and I sigh at the sensation.

Vexar's eyes soften, as if he's just remembered something. "I never thought I would find you."

My stomach tightens with the anticipation of another heavy confession.

"You are the only one who could have done this." He taps his chest with one hand, and I feel a sudden, deep ache that scares me. The way he's looking at me feels like he's memorizing my face, like he doesn't plan on sticking around.

After all of this, if he leaves me here, I will fucking shatter.

I press my forehead to his and whisper, "Don't leave me here." It's a silly wish. More of a prayer than anything. A prayer that he will keep his promise and get us out of here alive.

"I will never leave you," he whispers.

"Please—" I start, before his thumb lands on my lips. I feel desperate. Terrified. And so vulnerable. I've just given Vexar the keys to my own destruction, and I hardly know him.

"I am yours," he says in that commanding tone that makes my heart skip. "Forever." I can feel his vulnerability even though his expression is hard and nearly regal. "Are you mine?" he asks.

Without thought, I nod and immediately think, '*Fuck, why did I do that?*' But my heart is thrumming louder than it ever has before.

Forever. He said, "forever".

Instead of overthinking, I grab onto the 'now'. Our hands become frantic and shameless, roaming over each other with abandon.

He feels like the embodiment of power itself, and it's intoxicating. I trace the contours of his chest until I graze a nipple and gasp. Looking down, I expect to find Vexar's hand doing the same to me, but his hands are nowhere near my breasts.

What did I just feel?

Confused, I run my finger over his nipple again and ... there it is. An unmistakable jolt of pleasure.

"Holy shit," I whisper, before flicking my finger one more time and shivering at the sensation that I don't feel on my skin, but somewhere ... else. "I can feel that." I shake my head, trying to find the right words. "It's like I can feel your pleasure."

Vexar quirks a brow, and in a motion that tells me he doesn't plan on teasing forever, he pulls my hips forward until the hard contour of his erection presses between my legs. Shockwaves of pleasure roll through me, and he lets out a deep, guttural, "Vok."

Pure. Alien. Wizardry.

20

WHAT NEXT?

VEXAR

AMARA'S HIPS GRIND into my lap, sending arcing jolts of pleasure through me as a voice in the back of my mind begs me to 'let go'. To relinquish my control. To take what is 'mine'. The possessive nature of these urges is disquieting, and resisting them is like holding back the sea with my bare hands. It is a dangerous game. Every moment pushing me closer to the breaking point, spreading my control a little thinner, loosening my grip on reality.

Take her.

There is a darkness lurking in my depths. Something new to me but ancient. At first, I thought it was the bond itself, but now I am not so sure. It feels ... dangerous. Like it should not be there.

I should stop her. I should tell her I cannot control myself. But the words will not surface. And maybe I do not want them to. If not for the uncomfortable darkness vying for my surrender, I would sink willingly into this bliss. But instead, I am grasping for restraint.

No training, exercise, or knowledge could have prepared me

for the onslaught of emotion and sensation overtaking me. It is inconceivable. Perfect. Terrifying. Everything.

More.

Her hands move to the hem of her dress, and I know she is asking me to take it off. No words are needed, but I ask anyway. "Can I take off your dress?"

This is dangerous.

I watch her deft fingers work the laces free until the front of her dress parts and a pair of metal scissors clatters to the floor. My eyes track the falling object, confused as to why she was keeping scissors in her dress.

"What were—" My words cut off as the sight before me steals my attention. I am speechless.

"Touch me," she says, bringing my hand to one of her breasts.

"*Vok'talja*," I rasp as I run my fingers over the soft curve of flesh before brushing my thumb over the firm peak of a pink nipple. Her head falls back as I gently roll her nipple between my fingers, feeling the pulses of pleasure as they roll through her body and into mine.

"You feel so good," she says in a breathy moan, fraying my sanity.

It is an exquisite agony. Being so close to her, touching her, feeling her pleasure, knowing there is nothing more than a layer of leather between us. Both torment and bliss.

Let go.

I do not listen to the voice. I will not. My control is what keeps me safe. It is what ensures I do not act rashly or purely on emotion. Without my control, I fear I would become a savage beast. But I need to taste her skin. Feel her pleasure. It is all I can think about—calming my raging desire by sating hers.

Moving with pure instinct, I lift her hips until she is on her knees and I can wrap my mouth around one of her nipples. The taste of her skin explodes over my tongue, and I nearly sink my teeth into her. She is earth and salt and fire. My blood buzzes for more. For *her*.

When I flick my tongue, she lets out a whimper and grips the back of my neck. I smile at the reaction and teasingly graze my fangs over her flesh. The rolling pleasure I feel through our connection is remarkable. It is as if the pleasure comes from a body part I did not know I had. There is so much more to the Zhyrrak than I was ever told. It is remarkable.

"You taste like home," I rumble as I grip the hem of her dress and start to pull it over her head. Pain shoots up my side with the movement, but the sight of Amara, fully bare, makes me quickly forget the discomfort. I run my fingers down her abdomen and watch enrapt as small bumps rise on her skin in the wake of my touch. At the apex of her thighs, there is a patch of dark fur that I drag my claws through. "Gods, I love your body."

Her fingers trail over my shoulders with the lightest touch. "More," she whispers, before kissing the side of my neck and licking her way up to my ear.

I tremble when she drags her teeth over my earlobe, and my cock strains painfully against my leathers.

She moves to lower herself back into my lap, but I stop her. The thin grasp I have on my control is quickly waning.

Take her.

Gripping her hips, I stand, spin, and lay her on the bed. More pain stabs through me, but I ignore it.

"You're going to hurt yourself," she protests as she props herself on her elbows and watches me stand. Her tongue flicks out to wet her lips, and my knees go weak.

I take a step back, breathing deeply, drinking in the sight of her, and working to cage the darkness in me.

"I am not as breakable as you seem to think," I pant.

She gives me a lopsided grin. "I never said you were breakable."

Her body is a flawless feast for my eyes—every curve, every dimple, every rise and fall is absolute perfection. Her unwrapped knee is still stained with my blood; dark hair a mess of tangles and waves; pale skin flush with arousal. She is the most beautiful creature I have ever seen—laid bare in the middle of this nightmare like a shining beacon of light.

I have no idea how we ended up here. Somehow, in the worst moment of my life, the gods sent me a beacon. "You are perfect," is all I can say.

"Then why are you still up there?"

"I am admiring you," I answer, unwilling to share the truth of my distance.

She bites her bottom lip while her eyes dance over me. "How does all of this feel so right?" she asks, kicking off her shoes. "I don't even know you, but I ... it's hard to explain. You're just... Fuck." Her words are fractured and confused, but I understand her meaning.

Unable to resist the pull any longer, I climb onto the bed and lie by her side. For some reason, I still feel hesitant to touch her, but she smiles, and my apprehension melts. "We wouldn't be bonded if we weren't made for each other," I say, running my fingers down her exposed stomach and watching a shudder roll beneath her skin.

"Why do you say that?" she asks, turning on her side to face me.

I ghost a thumb over her lips. "Because your lips are the color of my favorite food, you smell like my favorite place, you look like the Goddess of War, and I have never seen someone more beautiful or fierce than you."

Her eyes go wide, and I kiss away her surprise, needing her mouth on mine, but I am forced to pull back when her hand slides down to the waistband of my leathers. I catch her hand and guide it back to my chest. I cannot lose control with her, and if I remove the last layer between us, I will.

"Shit. I'm sorry. This is all moving too fast, isn't it?" She looks troubled as she tries to sit.

"No," I say, wrapping an arm around her waist and pulling her back down with me. "I just want to learn your body first. I want to give you pleasure. I want to know you."

"And you don't want me to do the same with you?"

"You have worked hard enough today. Let me do this for you," I nearly beg. It is not the best excuse, but it is better than saying, "There is a darkness inside me that wants to do horrible things, and I do not want it to harm you."

She pauses for a beat and raises a single brow. "Do you know what you're doing?" The question is playful but honest. I know very little about pleasuring a female, and if it weren't for my brother Steinarr, I would be completely lost. Fortunately, Steinarr has taken his vow far less seriously than the rest of my siblings and enjoys sharing more details than he probably should. But that is not my only source of knowledge.

"Did you forget I can feel your pleasure?" I ask, as I throw a leg over her body and pin her hands above her head.

She lets out a puff of air. "Well, it certainly seems like you know what you're doing." Her eyes trace a path down my body with hungry intent, and I love it. Others have looked at me this way before, and it always felt ... uncomfortable. But not with her.

Vok, this is going to be impossible.

I lower my face to her neck, running my tongue over her thudding pulse. "I will need you to guide me." I nip her ear. "To tell me what I am doing right. But first, I would like to tell you the story of the Zhyrrak." It is important for her to know. To give her context. Explain why she feels the way she does.

"Story time? Now?" she asks, exasperated.

"I am capable of completing more than one task at a time."

She lets out a moan as I capture her nipple between my teeth. "A man who can multitask? How did I win this lottery?"

Working to recall the story of the Zhyrrak I learned from my father's books—the more romanticized version—I release her hands and run the tips of my claws down her ribcage. "My ancestors were mighty warriors. Fearsome even. It is said they got their strength from love—from the Zhyrrak bonds they had with their mates." I press my lips above her heart. "Their power and skill in battle were unmatched, and when they fought, they were demons." I nip at the thin skin beneath one of her breasts, and she lets out a surprised gasp. "It is said that when two parts of one soul find each other, their heart's electromagnetic fields resonate at the same frequency. When the fields interact, they strengthen and amplify, creating a bond that threads their souls together." I run my tongue between her breasts, tasting the salt on her skin. "It is also said that only the Vhorathi have the ability to forge such bonds."

"But I'm not Vhorathi."

"It seems the gods have chosen to ignore that fact." I grip her chin with my thumb and forefinger and ask, "Why did you accept the bond?" I was not expecting her to accept it so quickly, and it seems odd, especially considering her reluctance to believe my admiration of her.

"I'm not sure."

My stomach drops as my thoughts turn to her bandaged knee. "Is this what you want?"

"Yes. But I want something else too."

"And what is that?" I ask warily, praying this is not the moment I discover she was sent here for some nefarious purpose.

Her hands run up my arms in a soothing motion. "I need you

to promise that for as long as this lasts, it will be a partnership. You don't get to order me around, or keep me in the dark, or make decisions that will affect me without talking to me first. We have to be open with each other and trust each other's judgment. Is that something you can agree to?"

I let out a held breath. "Yes, I can agree to that." But the moment the words leave my lips, the sting of guilt burns my tongue. There are some things I cannot share with her. Not yet. I just hope she will be able to forgive me when she learns this.

I kiss her hard and deep, pouring all of my hope into the movement of my lips against hers. A bruising, painful hope for our future. And she returns that hope without restraint, whipping up a new wave of frenzy between us. A hot, powerful, desperate, frenzy.

Her legs slip around my lower back, and I can feel her aching need like it is a physical object hanging between us.

She needs you.

"You will teach me?" I ask between kisses, knowing she understands my meaning.

She nods and drags her blunt nails down my arm.

"Tell me what you need."

Her eyes lock on mine, and she grins. "Touch me. Explore me. Do your worst."

"Good human," I rumble playfully.

Her lips pinch together, and her eyes turn towards the ceiling. "Well, fuck."

"What?"

"I think you just unlocked a new kink."

I kiss her neck. "Kink?"

"Something you like in a sexual context, but maybe not in other contexts."

I sit and stare at her, holding her legs around my waist. "You like it when I call you, 'human'?"

Her cheeks flush. "Uh … I guess so. Specifically, you saying, 'good human'." She lets out a husky laugh and gently slaps my forearm. "Ok. Enough talking, more … mouth stuff."

Taking my time, I caress, lick, and nip every inch of her, making note of each gasp, moan, and beat of her heart. I learn her body as I go, memorizing the things that bring her pleasure. When I reach the base of her abdomen, the smell of her arousal floods my entire system, and I nearly roar with the over-whelming urge to rip off my leathers and bury myself in my mate.

My mate. The thought is as surprising as it is arousing.

Ignoring the incessant throb in my cock, I lift one of her ankles and kiss the length of her leg, from calf to thigh, getting drunk off the taste of her skin and the tempting sounds she makes.

Just before I reach the crease where her leg meets her center, I stop. "How am I doing?" I ask.

She looks at me with shameless desire before letting her legs fall open, inviting me in. "You're a natural. Like a penguin on ice."

I do not know what a penguin is, but the sight of her glis-tening sex urges me forward, drawing my full attention. *I need to taste her.* That is what she wants. I know it as clearly as I know my own name. It is a pure knowing. Instinct in its most un-evolved form.

"You want me to kiss you. Here," I whisper as I run the backs of my fingers over her swollen mound.

"Fucking hell," she whimpers, pushing her hips towards my hand. I brush over her again, and she nods quickly. "Yeah … that's exactly what I want."

My mouth quirks up in a grin. I can feel her pulse thudding between her legs as she watches me with wide eyes. Her breasts rise and fall with each hungry gasp. Her fingers dig into the mess of sheets around her.

I run my fingers through the arousal dripping from her and watch in pure awe as she bucks against my hand. She is all fire and fury and need. And I am lost in a haze of disbelief. She is real. This is real. I bring my fingers to my mouth, sucking her arousal from them and watching her watch me.

A bright red flush creeps down her neck. "Fuck… Ok." She gasps. "Yup. This is … uh … wow."

"What next?" I ask playfully.

"Now you continue what you started." She pulls her feet towards her hips, opening herself further to me. "Now you kiss me." Her eyes flick down between her legs.

As I lower myself, it becomes clear my shoulders are too broad to fit between her thighs. I grip the backs of her knees and position her legs over my shoulders, feeling pleased with my solution.

"And now?" I ask, working hard to avoid smiling. It is clear she knows I am teasing her. Her eyes are full of indignation that sends a nearly painful throb through my cock. *Gods, I really do enjoy her ire.*

"Now you use that clever tongue of yours," she manages.

Tongue. That makes sense.

When my mouth is less than a breath away, I ask, "Here?"

"You're such an asshole!" she pants. "Please lick me before I grab those fucking horns and—"

I interrupt her with a long swipe of my tongue, and she cries out a broken and exquisite sound.

I think I love this woman.

21

A NEW FEAR

AMARA

THE SIGHT OF Vexar's horns rising between my thighs is the most erotic thing I've ever seen, and I add it to the growing list of things about him that are both new and strangely familiar. The deep rumble of his voice, the reverence in his gaze, the feeling of his rough hands on my skin; all of it seems to spark some distant familiarity. Like I've already lived this in a dream.

What started as a clumsy exploration is no longer clumsy. My eyes roll back as his hand digs into my hip, holding me tightly. Tension builds and flutters as he moves—finding what makes me moan but never lingering long enough to push me over the edge.

I knit my fingers into his hair and manage to ask, "Are you trying to tease me?"

He responds by slowing his pace further.

"Fuuuck." He's not a tease, he's a jerk. A big, beautiful jerk. And somehow, he's my perfect match. He's not intimidated by me, or overly sensitive to my snark, and damn, he's good with his mouth.

I'm nearing combustion at his gentle exploration, but no matter how much I roll my hips, or how hard I pull on his horns —*holy shit, I'm pulling on his horns*—he keeps his languid pace. I think he's intentionally avoiding my clit, and nothing I do earns me anything more than a gentle flick. My body is coiled like a spring—muscles tense, sweat glistening, breath heavy and narrow.

"Please," I beg, "just a little higher."

He laughs. He fucking laughs!

Ok. So he knows exactly what he's doing.

"Is this payback for the pain I put you through?" I groan. He flicks his tongue over my clit, and I shout, "Please!" I've become nothing more than a needy, pliant beggar, but at this point, I'll beg shamelessly if it means I get some sort of release from this carnal torture.

He flicks his tongue again, making my vision blur.

"Holyfuckingshit," I moan.

"I love feeling your pleasure," he growls. "I could live down here, tasting you and feeling your ecstasy build."

Fuck. I forgot he can feel my pleasure. Which means he can also feel the edge he's been holding me on... *Why does that make this so much hotter?*

The warm pads of his fingers press into my hips, and suddenly he's dragging me to the edge of the bed. He drops to his knees like he's about to pray, and the altar's my cunt. *How the hell did I end up here?*

His molten gaze heats my skin as he spreads my thighs, exposing me fully and gazing down at my bare sex like he hasn't just had his mouth all over it.

"What do you call this?" he asks, pressing a finger against my clit and rubbing gentle circles over it.

"My"—gasp—"clit."

His eyes flick up. "I like this ... clit."

"Yeah, me too," I manage.

"And just to confirm, if I continue what I am doing," he says, still rubbing, "you will reach a point of ... heightened pleasure?"

Oh. Right. He's asking if humans can orgasm. Why didn't I consider that we might be different in that way? "Yeah," I say. "We call it orgasming, or climaxing, or coming, or ... uh, we have a lot of terms for it."

He nods, brows furrowed, taking this lesson very seriously. "The same is true for me." His head tilts. "And human males have a"—he glances away, looking for the right word—"penis?"

"They do."

"And it is expected that this penis penetrates"—he moves his finger down slightly, but doesn't press into me—"here?"

I'm shaking, but I manage to say, "Yup."

"I understand," he says. His long arm pulls a limp pillow off the bed, and he uses it to prop my head up. "I would like to see your face when you ... orgasming."

"Just 'orgasm'," I say, trying not to chuckle.

He smiles. "When you orgasm." The way his black eyes are lit up with excitement, and the soft smile that curls his lips, make him look like a completely different person. There's no careful facade or calculated expression. He's completely bare, and my heart swells.

I don't want to die.

Holding my gaze, he loops his arms around my thighs, locking me in place.

"Do not look away," he orders in a commanding tone that shatters the moment of vulnerability and sends a pulse of lust and defiance through me.

"This is some king shi—"

He interrupts me with a flick of his tongue, and I howl. I'm throbbing, swollen, and so sensitive I think I might pass out, and he's fucking smiling. The combination of black eyes and that nearly sadistic smile sends a pleased shiver down my spine. Then he proceeds with focused purpose.

"Mmf ... fuck," I groan as his tempo increases and his arms tighten around my hips. I feel trapped in the best way possible. The mixture of danger and pleasure is building a wild tension in my body. I know he won't hurt me, but it's clear he's the deadliest person I've ever met, and he's eating me out like I'm the only meal he's ever had.

His mouth wraps over my clit, and he pulses his tongue until I'm seeing stars. Every second stretches into a lifetime as my pleasure builds.

Slowly, I sink deeper into his gaze, like I'm being hypnotized. Those fathomless black depths speaking to me. Beckoning me higher until I'm balanced on a tightrope, just a gentle breeze away from falling into the depths of release below. A shudder rolls through me, and I start to lose myself in the building tension.

Then he stops.

I force my eyes open, confused and angry. "What the—"

"You closed your eyes," he says with a satisfied smirk.

My mouth drops open. "You're serious?" He raises a brow, and I shake my head in disbelief. "You're unbelievable, you know that?" But even as I say the words, I'm inwardly smiling, loving our weird little dynamic.

"You will keep them open?" he asks, his accent thicker than it has been all day. I give him a reluctant nod, and he says, "Good, human."

Pressing my lips together, I suck in a deep breath, trying to calm the heat burning my skin. "I'm going to regret telling you that, aren't I?"

He grins. "Maybe."

I go to jab him with my toe, but before I can even really move my foot, it's in his hand.

How in the hell...?

I'm still blinking away my surprise when he tosses my leg back over his shoulder, and with a grunting laugh, dives back between my legs. A few seconds later, I feel the tip of a finger and gasp. I'm expecting claws, but I don't feel any, and when I glance at his other hand on my thigh, the claws are gone, replaced by dark, blunt nails.

He raises a single brow as his finger barely presses into me, and I answer the question he doesn't have to ask.

"Yes," I moan.

The darkness in his eyes seems to swirl as he slowly works into me, the decadent fullness racking my body with impossible pleasure.

Oh. My. God.

I didn't know I had the ability to feel this much.

"Fuck... " The building pressure of my looming release hits an impossible peak.

"Give me your pleasure, Amara," he growls.

And I shatter.

Endless, pulsating waves of pure ecstasy consume me. My eyes are still open, but my vision's gone black. I'm in an uncontrolled free-fall, tumbling and crashing through every peak and valley as Vexar's strong hands anchor me in place.

I don't know how long we're like this—him holding me steady, pushing my body to its limits, and me riding an endless climax—but eventually I come back to reality and my vision returns. I find Vexar, face flushed and forehead glistening as he laps lazily between my legs.

"Gods, that was beautiful," he moans before climbing onto the bed, pulling me with him as he flops onto his back.

"You are really, really good at that," I say, burying my face against his chest and inhaling the scent of his sweat-damp skin. *Fuck, this feels good.* I haven't felt this safe or cared for in a long time. "Your claws disappeared," I add, still in a haze of endorphins as I run a hand over the ripples of his abs, and towards the top of his pants.

He catches my hand and presses a kiss to my fingers. "They did," he says.

"How?"

"They are not natural. Nano-material. Good for fighting, not so good for love-making."

I hum a sound of understanding and turn my face towards his. "I want to give you what you gave me." Even if he won't let me ride him, at least let me hear him moan. Let me watch him fall apart in my hands.

"You already did," he says.

I mouth a silent, 'oh', and grin as I press a kiss to his skin. I think the big, bad alien came in his pants. *Fuck, that's hot.*

"Do you need to clean up?" I ask.

He shakes his head.

Huh. He didn't make a mess. Despite my confusion, I decide not to dig into that further. It's probably a conversation for a different time.

My fingers find another scar, and I trace the line of raised skin from his collarbone to his armpit. "What's this from?" I ask gently.

He stiffens. "It is a story best saved for another time."

Duh, because he already said he didn't want to talk about it.

Feeling like an asshole, I quickly say, "Then tell me something else."

"Like what?"

"I don't know." I reposition myself so my head is resting on his upper abdomen and my knee is tucked between his thighs. "Tell me a secret. One you've never told anyone."

Flashes of emotion cross our connection. Anxiety. Then curiosity. Then what I think is hope.

"You changed me," he says, as one of his hands slides up my neck and tangles in my hair. "The bond changed me."

"Wait, already? How?"

He lets out a humorless laugh. "I feel ... different. Like I could defeat an entire army to keep you safe. I feel stronger, more connected, and much more protective." He rubs his fingers over my scalp. "I also have a new fear."

"What's that?" I ask with caution.

"Losing you..."

My heart stumbles over itself, caught between the shock of his confession and the deep ache it brings. Neither of us should feel this way. We don't know each other. And yet, I believe him, and I can't deny that I feel the same way. Somehow, I *know* he's going to do everything in his power to keep me safe, but that knowledge sparks a new fear. A fear I knew would come.

"I don't want to die," I whisper, and I mean it. Before I walked into this cell, I had one option to regain some control and find a small bit of purpose in this nightmare. But now? Now there's hope. And that is so much more terrifying than morbid resignation.

His grip around me tightens, and his lips press into the top of my head. "I will never let any harm come to you. Ever. If you need me, I will be there. If you are sad, I will bring you joy. If you are fearful, I will vanquish the darkness. I am yours, and I will fight for you, or with you, no matter the enemy."

A dam of emotion breaks in my chest, and I sob. It comes out of nowhere. Ugly, racking sobs that shake my entire body. I haven't cried in so long that I forgot how much it hurts. My throat aches. Head throbs. But I can't stop.

Instead of shying away from my tears, Vexar holds me tighter, letting me bury my wet face against his warm skin while tracing soothing circles over my back.

When my crying slows, the deep, rolling waves of his breath and the warm scent of his skin coax me to the edge of sleep.

"Sleep, Amara," he purrs. "Sleep."

22

NOT THE KING THEY WANTED

VEXAR

SHE DOESN'T WANT to die.

As Amara sleeps, her words echo in my mind, increasing the ugly weight of my guilt.

Her ability to trust has been eroded into something sharp and brittle, and I feel those jagged points with every doubtful glance and word. She has experienced the very worst sentient beings have to offer, and I dread what will happen when she learns of my complicity in the horrors she faced.

The scent of her hair fills my nose as the shadow in my depths begs for vengeance. It repeats the same phrase, again and again, even as I try to silence it.

End them. End them.

Gaius placed Amara in my cell. That much is clear. And Amara is convinced he will execute her for saving my life. While I do not doubt he will try, he will not succeed. No act of the gods or force of nature could tear her from my grasp. There is no price I would not pay, nor sacrifice I would not make.

She is my Queen. My mate. Chosen by the gods themselves to bring hope to my people and shine a light into the dark places

I once ignored. And yet, there is also a darkness in our bond. One I am beginning to fear.

The Zhyrrak is not what I thought it would be. A new violence lurks beneath my surface. A rage that sears my heart at the very thought of Amara being harmed.

If she is ever truly in danger, what will I become? A monster? A demon? A thoughtless killer?

An inner turmoil stretches through me. A mix of apprehension and dark curiosity. Until now, I had never considered how much damage I could do with my bare hands, but as I lay here, holding my Queen, I know the scale of destruction I am capable of has no bounds. No limits. And that is terrifying.

Is there anything more dangerous than a Vhorathi with no limits? A *King* with no limits?

The true danger of a Zhyrrak-bonded warrior is so much greater than I was ever told. While I do feel stronger, the threat of my increased physicality pales in comparison to the threat of my restructured priorities and the shadow that has awoken in my depths. It feels like *Talrath* incarnate—a demon with a singular purpose—and I know I will not be able to keep it caged forever. Worse than that, I fear it is the reason my ancestors were so deadly. Perhaps that is why the stories are all so vague: the truth was too horrible to share.

I wish I understood what this all meant, but I know so little, and with each passing moment, it seems I know a little less. My eyes lock on the outline of the cell door, just barely visible in the dim light. The only thing I am certain of is that getting Amara out of here will not be easy.

She is not on Calidus by choice, and that complicates our situation. She is bound by a contract I have no power to nullify. Securing her freedom will require Gaius's agreement, and if my suspicions are correct, the only thing he plans on agreeing to is my death. While killing him would be the easy option, it would ultimately cause more problems than it solved. It would leave my Obligation incomplete and Amara's contract intact. A challenge to my throne is one thing, but I am not willing to risk Amara being tied to an incomplete contract. She would become a fugitive, and nowhere would be safe for her.

No. If we are to leave this place alive and free, it cannot be achieved through brute force. We must be smarter than our enemies. We must plan carefully. And, we must ensure that Gaius's actions are seen by many.

I trace the line where Amara's hip meets her abdomen and watch the subtle quiver of muscle beneath her pale skin. In sleep, her emotions flow unbidden through our tether. Wordless cries echo through my mind as her dreams oscillate between unimaginable terror and steady unease. I hate what has been done to her and the scars it has left behind, but I think I hate myself more.

I failed her. I failed to see what was right in front of me.

I knew about Gaius's insane laws—I saw the fights where 'criminals' were 'brought to justice'—and yet I refused to see the truth until Amara told me she was not here by choice.

Gaius is not putting 'criminals' to death; he is murdering slaves for sport and using his ridiculous laws to do it legally.

I was a fool.

When I first heard the rumors, I scoffed. The idea of the Tusku selling sentient beings was absurd. Impossible. But the rumors kept coming until I could no longer disregard them. And yet, I failed to prove they were true.

I wish I had pushed back against Marius harder. He was so content to believe the Senate. So fearful of disobeying them. I recall the words he spoke to me so clearly. "If the *Lysaer* and her government have determined this investigation is pointless, we must accept that. Do not ruin your reputation for this."

At the time, I accepted his wisdom, but looking back, I fear that was a mistake.

I grit my teeth and force down the wave of regret that threatens to overtake me.

Emotion serves no purpose. Do not let it control you.

What happened cannot be changed. I must focus on the future, not the past.

Needing to remind myself that she is here now, I gently pull Amara closer, feeling her warm skin as it presses to mine and the way her breath skates up my neck.

There is a flicker of something panicked in our connection, and she wakes in a storm of flying limbs. Shrieks perforate the silence. Hooked fingers claw at me. Glassy eyes, wide and unseeing, search for something that is not there.

A nightmare.

"It is ok," I say, gently redirecting her attempted strikes so she does not hurt herself. "You are safe."

I repeat the words until her limbs fall and her eyes go wide with recognition.

Then she cries. For the second time in as many hours, her body shakes as she expels what feels like a lifetime of pent-up pain. It is nearly unbearable, knowing there is nothing I can do to fix it. So I hold her and let her pain become my own. I accept every festering fear and absorb every limitless sorrow until her anguish blends with mine.

My muscles tense as if preparing for a fight, but there is no enemy here. Not anymore. The damage is in the past, and only the echoes of it remain.

"You are safe," I say, uncertain of who my words are for. Her or me.

The Zhyrrak brought us together so I could be her safe harbor in the violent storms of life, but I fear that I am the violent storm.

When her sobs turn into silent tears, she whispers, "I'm sorry."

I roll onto my back, pulling her with me until her head rests on my chest. "Do not apologize to me. Ever."

"I hit you," she whispers.

I shake my head and pull her arm over my body. "The only way you could harm me is by denying me your heart."

She lies so still while her mind pulses with a mixture of embarrassment and frustration.

"I am so sorry," I whisper. She pulls back to look at me, sensing the burden in my voice. "What were you dreaming about?" I ask, hoping to distract her from the increasing concern in her eyes.

With a sigh, she lies back down and pulls the blood-stained sheet up to her waist. There's a long moment of silence before she answers. "The ship that brought me here," she says quietly. "The box they kept me in. I go back every night, and I can't make it stop."

I close my eyes and breathe through the bubbling rage. Through our tether, I can nearly see the cramped space she was trapped in, and a sick understanding takes root. She was not just brought here; she was tortured. Her rage, her fear, her chaos, it all makes sense.

They put her in a box.

For that alone, there is nowhere those Tusku traders could hide where I will not find them. I will hunt them to the ends of the galaxy and bury them in the heart of a star. It is what I should have done long ago.

"Do you want to talk about it?" I ask in a steady voice.

She's silent again for a long while, her cheek pressed against my chest, face turned away from mine.

"It was so dark, and then suddenly, it wasn't. There was a window or something at the end of the box, but it just looked like a blinding square of light. I don't know... That light scared me more than anything else had at that point." I feel her jaw working as she tries to find her words. "They took them, the others ... one by one." Another pause. "I had to listen to it all. I *heard* it all."

My throat tightens. The silence between us stretches. Wind whips by the small window in whistling, howling gusts as if it is lamenting her pain.

"That's what I dream about most—the screams. And this crashing metal sound that happened after they took someone." She shudders slightly. "I wasn't sure how long I'd be able to take it. How long I'd stay ... *me*." She pauses, and I feel her eyelashes flutter. "Sometimes, jets of ice-cold water would shoot through the box to ... wash things away, and"—she inhales deeply as her fingers dig into the ribs of my uninjured side—"I just kept wondering how much longer I could lay there before I'd try to suck in a breath of it."

Every word feels like a blade that digs a little deeper into my heart, but I listen anyway. I let that blade bury itself in me, knowing my pain pales in comparison to hers.

End them, the dark voice whispers.

"Everything hurt. All the time. My skin. My joints. My fucking hair. And I kept hearing voices. Languages maybe? Sounds I didn't recognize. For a while, I thought the sounds were all in my head, but when that light came on, I saw." She swallows thickly. "There were so many boxes. Like a living morgue. That's what I dream about most. The light. The boxes. The screams. All of it."

End them.

Her story is worse than I had imagined. I knew she had been taken, but the brutality of it is unthinkable.

"That should not have happened to you," I say, my voice rough with emotion. "I am sorry."

She angles her face towards mine, the dim light of Calidus's moon dancing over her skin. "Your eyes..." she says quietly. "Why do they go black?"

I clear my throat. "I think it happens when you're in danger."

"But I'm not in danger."

"You were."

She nods slowly. "You know this isn't something you can save me from, right?"

I bite back the tears that threaten to spill and work to keep my shadow buried deep. It wants out. It wants ... destruction? Absolution? Vengeance? Maybe all of them.

End them. Save her.

Her thumb brushes over my lips. "Hey, it's ok. I'm ok."

My fingers weave themselves into her hair as I turn her mouth towards mine, letting her kiss pull me from the depths of my guilt and into the warmth of her embrace.

Emotion serves no purpose. Do not let it control you.

But the pain refuses to let go. It *wants* out.

When our lips part, I see the concern in her eyes. "What's wrong?" she asks.

"I am fine," I lie, even though I know she can see through it.

"No, you're not." She sits up, pulling the sheet with her to cover herself. It is the first time she has been shy about her body, and it feels like a slap in the face. Our fragile trust is already breaking.

"Is that ... guilt?" she asks. "Why do you feel guilty?" When I fail to answer, her expression turns cold. "I get it, this is new and really fucking weird, but you agreed to not keep shit from me."

As terrified as I am of losing her, my word is stronger than my axe, and I do not intend to break it. I will do the hard thing and be honest.

23

CHOOSE

AMARA

REPEATED SURGES OF intense guilt flow from Vexar into our connection. I don't know where the guilt is coming from, but I'll be damned if I let him brush me off.

He sits up and pulls a leg towards his chest, wrapping his elbow around his knee before scrubbing a hand over his face. "I am sorry—"

"No," I interrupt. "I don't need a fucking apology, I need honesty. You're hiding something, and I..." I let out a grunt of frustration. "Fuck, Vexar!" I can handle a lot of things, but his cagey guilt is *not* one of them. Especially right now. "If you want me to trust you at all, you need to open your fucking mouth and talk."

His eyes stay fixed on mine, nervous but surprisingly steady. "I knew," he says slowly. "I knew about the slave-ships."

A stillness hangs between us for what feels like an eternity as my brain repeats his words over and over. But no matter how many times I hear them, the meaning doesn't change. *He knew about the slave-ships.*

"Well, fuck," I whisper, rubbing my hands over my eyes. "That's, ugh... Wow." He knew about the slave-ships. A heavy pain climbs up my spine and settles behind my heart as the implications of this settle in. "Did you know I was a slave when you met me?"

"No," he says quickly. He's watching me carefully, trying to gauge my response, but even I don't know how I feel right now. Then there's a tickle at the back of my mind. Like he's trying to poke around in there. Trying to figure me out. It feels like a violation, and a fresh rush of anger boils through me.

"No," I say, pointing a finger at him. "You don't get to dig around in my head." After I say it, I realize I have no idea how to shut him out, or if it's even possible. I try anyway, focusing on that strange sensation at the back of my mind as I imagine closing a door. And then ... silence.

He opens his mouth like he might say something, but closes it again.

I think it worked.

Clutching my hands in my lap to keep them from shaking, I say, "Explain."

"There were rumors about the ships," he says slowly. "At first, I did not believe them. But when they continued, I realized there might be some truth there. Marius and I launched an investigation into the rumors. We had some preliminary findings—nothing firm—but that was as far as we were allowed to take it."

Allowed. That sinking feeling grips my spine again as a cold clarity takes root.

"Who's Marius?" I ask. The name's familiar, but my mind is so scattered I can't recall why.

"My advisor and oldest friend."

Right. He mentioned him earlier when I asked about his home. "The guy who helped raise you, right?"

He nods.

Instead of pushing forward and barking out questions, I take my time and think. He wasn't "allowed" to continue his investigation. He also doesn't believe his mother was here, while I'm fairly certain she was.

"Amara, I—"

"What do you mean by 'investigate'?" I interrupt.

His gaze drops. "We searched financial records, ship-design specifications, transaction logs, everything we could, but we found very little evidence to prove the rumors were true. When I asked to send an inquisitor to confirm our findings, the Senate and my mother denied the request. I was told the rumors had already been proven false."

As much as I want to rage at what feels like an excuse for doing nothing, something far more important has taken over my thoughts. *His mother denied the request...*

The rest of my lingering frustration melts away, and all I'm left with is a hollow pit in my stomach.

With a heavy heart, I ask the question I really don't want the answer to. "You didn't believe the rumors were false, did you?"

"I..." He trails off, and his eyes drop to his hands. His answer is clear, but he doesn't want to say it, and that makes it hurt so much more.

"Want to try that again?" I ask.

"I do not know."

I really thought Vexar was some bastion of honor and goodness, but he's just as fucked up and fallible as I am.

I shake my head, disappointed that he won't admit the truth. "If you believed what you were told by your mother and the Senate, why the guilt?" I raise my brows. "Why did you say you *knew* about the ships if you thought they were just rumors?"

His gaze drops to the bed between us, and my disappointment grows.

I try a different tactic. "Let me guess, you knew you were

being fed a pile of shit and instead of pushing back, you just ... looked the other way. And now you're feeling guilty because you want to fuck someone who suffered because of your inaction. Am I close?"

"I trusted the Senate's investigation. But even if I had not, what would you have had me do?"

Is he fucking serious?

The longer I stare at him, the clearer it becomes that he's completely serious. He thinks that because the Senate said 'no', he couldn't do anything. I rub my hand over my mouth, confused and unsure.

This empire profits from slavery and barbarism, while Vexar clearly disagrees with those things. He didn't know about the slavery, but he did know about the barbarism, and instead of pushing back, he just went along with it. He feels guilty that he didn't follow through on the rumors of the slave-ships, but he also didn't think he had another option. How is it that the guy who's supposed to become king ends up feeling functionally powerless?

"You're supposed to be next in line for the throne, right?"

"Yes," he says, looking confused.

"But you didn't feel like you could push back against your own government?"

He looks at me like I'm an idiot. "The Senate's word is law. I cannot break the law."

"So you let countless people get sold into slavery so you didn't have to break the law?"

He shakes his head. "It is not that simple."

"It *is* that simple," I say. "Tell me, if there were a law that said it was illegal to save babies from burning buildings, and you saw a baby in a burning building, what would you do?"

"What kind of question is that?"

"Answer me," I say forcefully. "Would you let the baby burn because the law said you had to?"

I watch his mind spin, searching for an answer. Everything I know about him makes it very clear that his heart is in the right place, but it seems rules matter to him more than his own morality, and if that's the case, I've tied myself to a very dangerous person. Someone who would sacrifice anything for the sake of law and order.

"Why was the law made? Who is it meant to protect?" he finally asks.

God dammit.

"That," I say, pointing at him. "That's the fucking problem." My calm burns away in an explosion of anger. "I thought you were better than that. I thought you were something different, but your head's so far up your own ass that you think being a good person is the same fucking thing as being an obedient one. But it's not the same thing." I suck down a deep breath, trying to keep my voice from shaking. "Following unjust laws doesn't mean your actions are free from consequences, Vexar! You can't just brush away atrocities by saying, 'I was following the law.' That's ... fuck! That's the kind of shit the worst people in human history did." I drag my fingers through my hair. "Are you really willing to divorce your own morality to follow some fucked up ruling? Because if that's who you are, I need to know right the fuck now."

Hurt etches deep lines into his face, but he stays silent.

I let out a heavy breath. "I *know* you don't agree with everything your people do. I *know* you don't agree with slavery. I *know* you didn't want to kill anyone in the arena. I can *feel* you're fucking heart! But if you can't use that pain, that regret, that horror to drive your actions, then you're no different from Gaius or any other monster out there."

"I am not a monster," he says.

I'm about to keep yelling when clarity hits me like a baseball bat to the ovaries. Every time he asked if I was afraid of him. The deep hurt over killing his opponent in the arena. The proposal he refused to accept. His desire to stop those slave-ships. The deep wound in his side. The lack of medical care.

Someone realized that Vexar isn't the monster they needed him to be, and because of that, they don't want him to be king. There's no way an empire supported by slavery would allow someone like Vexar to rise to power. They wouldn't be able to trust him.

My gut was right. He was never meant to leave here alive.

Even if we survive this place, what then? What chance do we have at stopping Gaius or those ships?

A better chance than if you were dead, a quiet voice says in the back of my mind. And it's right. A small chance is better than no chance. I have to try.

I meet his gaze, feeling completely sure for the first time in a long while. "Maybe you don't see it, but it's clear to me that you aren't the person they wanted you to be. You aren't the *king* they wanted. You're better. You have a heart and you want to do the right thing, but if you don't wake the fuck up and figure that out, none of this will matter. We'll both die here, and whatever chance we have of fixing this massive shit-fest will die with us. The system you were raised in is broken and homicidal, and if you aren't willing to disobey it, then you might as well feed us both to the fucking wolves."

I need him to make a choice. I need to know if he would rather die, showing obeisance to the power structures he was raised to protect, or live, and help me tear them all down.

A few seconds later, he shakes his head. "It is not broken. It is flawed, yes, but not broken."

Hope disappears like a flame below the waves.

"Really? That's what you took away from that?" At a

complete loss on what to do, I crawl to the other side of the bed and curl up facing the wall.

"Amara," he whispers.

I pull the sheet over me. "I'll be over here until you either decide you're done defending the boot on your neck, or until the guards come and execute us both."

24

WHAT SHALL WE BUILD NEXT?

VEXAR

AMARA HASN'T MOVED. Only the curve of her spine is visible in the dim light, partially covered by the tattered sheet pulled around her. A large tattoo colors the skin between her shoulders. A tattoo I did not know was there. I want to drag my fingers over it. I want to go to her, hold her, but I know she would refuse me.

She thinks I am too … obedient, that I am blinded by the laws that have held my people together for generations. But she does not know my people. She does not know our laws or our ways.

I drag a claw over the bed frame and watch a flake of metal drift into the shadows below. "Why do you think this system is broken?" I ask.

She sighs, but does not move. "It allows slavery on a large scale. It forces its future rulers to compete in a bloodsport to prove they're willing to do anything to obtain power. And it's convinced you that obedience is more important than actual honor."

"It has convinced me of no such thing."

Sheets rustle behind me. "You couldn't tell me if you would let the baby burn, Vexar."

I say nothing.

"You know how I would have answered? I would have said, 'Fuck the law, if someone needs help, no matter who they are or what the cost is to me, I'll help them.' And the fucked up part about all of this is that I'm pretty sure you would do the same. Or you would want to at least. But the second I mentioned a 'law', you couldn't give me a straight answer." She pauses. "Because you value the law more than anything else."

Breathing becomes a challenge as I ask, "Why do you say my people have allowed slavery?"

"Your mother told you the rumors were false, right?"

My chest tightens. "She did."

"And *she* told you to drop your investigation?"

Another flake of metal falls. "Initially, yes."

"And *she* was the head of your empire at the time?"

I fold my hands in my lap and stare at the wall across from me. "Yes."

The bed shifts. Amara moves closer. "You said no one with the title of 'Queen' would have known about the slave trade, but you were wrong." There's a beat of silence as her cool hand slides over my shoulder in a comforting caress. "Your mother knew."

No. "She believed the rumors were spread to sow dissent. That is why she told me to drop the investigation."

Amara takes her hand off my shoulder, and for the barest of moments, I feel her apprehension and sadness through our connection. It is a slip that she fixes quickly, closing me out again like a threat. Perhaps I am a threat.

"I told you I saw a woman here with Gaius," she says, her voice heavy and slow, "and that Gaius called her, 'my Queen'. She was tall. Not as tall as you, but close. She was thin and looked ... older. Had long white hair pulled back into a braid. Pale skin. And she was wearing a ring. A big ring. Black with a symbol carved on top, like a couple of x's and dots."

"No," I say, shaking my head. "You are mistaken."

"I'm just telling you what I saw."

I stand, heart racing and stomach knotting.

Jagged stone presses into my bare feet.

My mother.

"Vexar," Amara pleads.

I step away from the bed. Amara's words are tree sap in the summer. Cloying. Penetrating. Impossible to shake. She should not know what my mother looked like. She should not know about my family sigil.

A barrage of questions overwhelms me. Suspicion spreads. Was Amara sent here to break me? To destroy my mind? Is that why Gaius allowed her into my cell? Gods. Was it a mistake to trust her? Panic settles into my bones. I have made a mistake. I should not have trusted her so easily. She has deceived me. She is trying to make me betray my family, my people.

"Open the tether," I command, spinning to face her.

She flinches back at the volume of my voice.

"Open it!" I yell.

Her expression goes cold, and a moment later, I feel her. But her presence is not passive. The dark eyes of Xelora burn into me as she boldly sifts through my mind, searching, prying, digging. She is invading me. Manipulating me.

"Stop!" I growl as the tendrils of her mind dig their roots into the very foundation of my existence.

There is a flicker of fear behind her eyes, and something inside me shatters.

Stop.

My rage breaks beneath a tsunami of guilt as my hand covers my mouth. I turn away.

What am I doing?

I need to move. Need to cool the fire raging beneath my surface. Need to regain my control. Need to think.

My ears roar.

She speaks again, but this time I cannot hear her. Words no longer register. My heart crashes against my ribcage as terror curls in my gut. *My mother...*

Discipline and control.

Thoughts race. I glance back at Amara. At her wary eyes. At her concern. *What have I done?* There is no deceit in her, no desire to control. I want to scream. To run. To break something.

My mother knew.

Memories surface. Moment after moment, coming into question. Lesson after lesson, turning to doubt.

My mother knew. She was here. She *lied*.

I thought she was honorable, but she *lied*. She lied to me, to the Senate, to our people. And for what? What reason could she have had? Was she protecting Gaius? Did someone force her? No. I scrub my hands over my face. That is impossible. My mother could not be forced; she was monolithic and uncompromising, made of iron and heartwood.

They put her in a box, the voice whispers.

Rage surges. Burning ice courses through my veins. I squat down, gripping my head and panting with the effort of holding back the surge of darkness that threatens to consume me.

She *put her in a box*.

My mother allowed it to happen. She *knew*. So many lies.

My fingers dig into the scar that runs from the bottom of my ear to the top of my shoulder. I wish I could tear it out of my flesh. How many falsehoods did she etch into my skin? How many lies parade as truths? Did my mother lie about the Zhyrrak? Or was she just as lost as I am? I cannot know. I will never know. She is gone, and I will never get the answers I need.

I feel the cold weight of the blade she placed in my hand that day as if it were still there. The sun-warmed sand beneath my feet, diffusing the scent of sweat into the air. Leaves rustling in the cool breeze overhead. My mother's steady footfalls as she stalked a circle around me, daring me to strike. I was young, barely the height of her shoulder, but I was already scarred. Already fearless. Already a warrior.

Xelora's eyes found me that day. She watched from the shadows with a look of confusion as my mother began to speak.

"You are a prince of Vhorath," my mother said, swinging her blade lazily at her side. "Dreaming of impossible things is for fools, not kings."

Her blade nicked my forearm. I did not flinch. I focused. Even as blood streaked my arm and settled into my palm. Even as the grip of my blade grew slick. I was a warrior, and Xelora was watching.

Never stop. Never slow.

"The Zhyrrak is dead, but you are not," my mother continued. "You are meant to be king of a vast empire, and you will not allow your *heart* to dictate your rule." She spat the word 'heart' like it was a curse. "Discipline and control, Vexar."

I dodged her next strike, but not her next words.

"You will not give in to petty emotions or love. Emotion serves no purpose, and you will not let it control you. You will learn these lessons and obey them. You will become the king we *need*. Strong. Imperious. Honorable. You will lead our people and you will be feared."

Xelora reached out towards me, a pleading look in her eyes. But she could not save me then any more than she can save me now.

I did not want to be feared. I wanted to tell my mother, "No", but my focus slipped, her words became permanent, and Xelora disappeared as my blood pooled in the sand. And yet, even now, Xelora's eyes burn into my back as she waits for me to choose.

My mother lied. While I cannot know if she lied about the Zhyrrak, it is clear she lied about many things, and the realization chips away a little more of my resolve. She lied about the slave trade and the Tusku ships. About her relationship with Gaius. About the Obligation and the brutality of it. About her health. About my father.

A sickening feeling washes over me. Is Amara right? Am I not the king they wanted me to be? My mother always wanted me to be feared, and yet, I am not. I refused to do the things she asked of me. I refused to play her games and paint myself as a monster.

The ache in my side grows. Is it possible that my mother ...? I swallow the lump in my throat. No. She would not. But Gaius would. Gaius *did*.

A new terror surfaces. Is there more I have missed? More I have ignored? I cannot afford any more errors. The gods have entrusted me with something precious, and I cannot allow it to be destroyed. I must protect her.

My eyes catch on Amara's pale feet, dangling so close to the floor that has already harmed her once, and my focus shifts. I drop to my knees and slide forward until my legs are beneath her feet, guarding them from the stone below. I do not meet her gaze or touch her. I just allow myself to be a barrier. She may not need my protection, but I give it anyway, and in return, her surprise turns to gratitude. She is glad I am here. Glad I have not turned from her.

"I am sorry," I whisper.

Her fingers ghost over my jaw, and I tremble as our connection broadens. There is no condemnation or fear in her heart. Only openness. An embrace of my entire being. The light. The dark. The kind and the cruel. The mistakes and the victories.

She cradles the back of my neck as my hands find her hips, and my cheek settles on her thighs.

Time slows. Sand whispers over the dunes outside. Stone crumbles beneath my knees. The thread between us tightens. And a new, darker reality consumes the old. A reality where I have far fewer allies than I thought.

I am not sure how much time passes, but I am not alone. Amara is here—the only person who exists outside the structures of everything I have ever known; outside my mother's lies. And yet, my first reaction was to distrust Amara's words. To distrust the one person who cannot lie to me.

"I am sorry," I whisper again as I run my thumbs over her soft skin.

Her emotions slip through me, unguarded and unfiltered. I feel every thought, every fear, every desire as it moves through her mind. With her, I do not have to guess; the truth is clear.

"You don't have to apologize to me," she says as her fingers slide through my hair and over my scalp.

"I do." I take a breath. "I yelled at you. I failed you. And I do not want you to fear me."

"You think I'm scared of you?"

The image of her terror as I demanded she 'let me in' flashes through my mind and sends a stabbing pain through my heart. "I saw the fear in your eyes."

"I wasn't scared of *you*. I was scared of the way you were looking at me. It was like you didn't see me at all. Like you were looking at an enemy."

Needing to see her face, I lean back and lift my head from her lap.

The dark eyes of Xelora burn into me. Watchful. Expectant. Then Amara speaks. "I don't want to be your enemy, but I will be if that's what it takes to finish Gaius and free everyone in bondage here." Her expression is hard and domineering. "If it were up to me, I wouldn't stop with the Coliseum. But it's not up to me." She tilts her head to the side. "It's up to you."

This version of Amara is new to me. She is powerful. Radiating a strength and determination I have not seen from her yet.

"Tell me," she says, "if we survive this place, what do you plan to do next?"

As I stare up at her from my kneeling position on the floor, everything seems to fall into place.

Amara is not some traumatized woman who needs a protector. She is the trickling stream, the quiet, unassuming rivulet that cuts its way through mountains, waiting to become a violent flood. The Zhyrrak brought us together so I can be her raging storm, not her safe harbor; so I can fill her basins and let her torrents cleanse the places that a storm cannot.

She is Xelora. My Goddess of War. My Queen, and she is asking if I will fight with her.

The wind outside has stopped, as if even the gods are holding their breath, waiting for my answer. After all these years, I still remember her face. It is clear now that this path was carved for me many years ago. My choice has been made for a long while; I just did not know it until now.

The words form and burn through me with a purpose unlike any I have felt before. "I failed you once, but I will not fail you again. I will be your avenging tempest, your warrior, your champion, your army. I will hunt the monsters who caged you to the ends of the galaxy, carving a scar through this empire until every person in bondage has been freed, every slave-ship has been shredded, and every enslaver has been fed to the void of space. And when we stand over the shattered wreckage, I will ask you, my Queen, 'What shall I burn next?'"

Amara's palm finds my chest where the steady, determined march of her heart thuds beneath my skin. "No," she says, "what shall we *build* next?"

25

TRUST HIM

AMARA

THE FIRST SLIVER of morning light creeps over the stone wall as I drag my fingers through Vexar's hair. He wakes slowly, a sleepy smile curling his lips and warming my body.

"Hey," I whisper, staring down at his beautiful face still nestled in my lap.

Last night changed things. A lot. He listened to me, even when I was telling him things he didn't want to hear. Maybe a part of him already knew everything I was saying was true. Maybe he just wasn't ready to face it until I forced him to. Either way, I feel confident he's on my team now. Does that mean I think he's fully broken out of his cultural cage? No, but at least he's willing to consider there's a cage at all. For now, that's enough.

His eyes flick to the window where the sky has become a soft painting of muted colors—oranges, pinks, yellows, and dusty blues. "It is morning," he says. His brow furrows as he sits up. "Did you not sleep?"

"I'll sleep when we get out of here." After our conversation, I tried to sleep, but the nightmares wouldn't stop. Then my fist discovered just how hard Vexar's face really is, and I gave up. "Is your face ok?" I ask.

He rubs a hand over his jaw with a wistful smile. "You punch well, but I am more concerned about your hand." Warm fingers gently rub over my swollen knuckles. "Does it hurt?"

"Not really, but I think you're made out of actual stone."

He grins and presses a kiss to the new bruises. "I will have to be faster in the future."

"You were asleep. I'm pretty sure your reaction time doesn't matter when you're asleep."

"I can do many things when I am asleep," he says with a wicked smile.

My eyes roll. "Alright, alright. Enough flirting. Let me check your stitches."

"I am fine," he says with a wave of his hand. "The pain is nearly gone."

"Nope." I point to the wall and say, "I'm checking them."

He groans, but scoots over and props himself against the wall anyway. "Really, I am fine."

"I'm sure you are," I say as I straddle his right leg to get access to his torso.

A grin spreads across his face as his eyes track down to the apex of my thighs, and I remember that I'm still naked. For a moment, I consider pulling the sheet around me, but that just seems silly, so I sit my bare ass down on his leather-clad thigh. When I was in my twenties, and as strong as I've ever been, I walked around like I was a cave troll. Now, despite feeling a bit frail and soft, I'm more proud of my body than I've ever been. It's gotten me through thirty-something years of shit, and I'll be forever indebted to it.

As I lean forward to loosen the bandage, Vexar lets out a deep rumble that sends a pulse of heat through me. When I glance up, he's smirking.

"Stop that, I'm trying to focus," I say as I peel back the bandage and—

Huh?

Confused, I lean over and glance at his other side.

"What? Did you forget where my wound is?" he jokes.

The joke falls flat as I pull the bandage down further and stare at the nearly healed line of pink, raised skin. "No, it's just..." I tilt my head, not sure how to verbalize my confusion. "It just healed a lot faster than it should've."

"That's a good thing, right?"

"Well, yeah... But why?" What I'm looking at is not the same injury I stitched up yesterday. This wound is nearly closed, and most of the discoloration and bruising are gone.

"What do you mean, 'why'?" he asks.

"Why did it heal so fast? It looks like this happened over a week ago, not yesterday." I glance up at him. "Is that normal for you?"

He reaches down and pulls back the bandage himself before grunting in surprise. "I thought you were exaggerating." He looks slightly rattled as he says, "Maybe it is the Zhyrrak?"

"Can it do that?"

He rests his head against the wall and looks up at the ceiling. "I do not know, but the moment we get to our ship, I will be searching for a reference manual."

I rest my full weight on his thigh while examining his face. "You're really just as confused about this bond stuff as I am, aren't you?"

"I was told two very different versions of what Zhyrrak bonds are, and neither version matches up with reality." He gives my thigh a comforting squeeze. "I wish I had more answers for you."

"What are the two versions?" I ask.

"One of the stories said the bond made warriors more obedient, more deadly, and gave them superior control over their emotions." His mouth pinches before he continues. "The other story said that the warrior's power was rooted in love and the need to protect their mate. There are similarities between the versions, but neither makes much sense now, and neither mentioned..." He trails off, shaking his head with a troubled look in his eyes.

The first version sounds like propaganda to me, but I keep that thought to myself and smooth the bandage back in place. The contradicting versions of the Zhyrrak aren't really important right now, and if we make it out of here, there will be plenty of time to unpack all the bullshit he's been told.

Fucking empires.

"Well, Zhyrrak or not, you're going to have a nasty scar," I say lightly.

He laughs and looks at me like I've just said the most absurd thing he's ever heard.

I wait for an explanation, but he doesn't offer one. "Alright, I'll admit, I missed the joke. So are you gonna clue me in, or ...?"

"It is just funny that you are so concerned about adding a new scar to my collection." He gently cups my cheek. "I will be glad to look at this one; it is a far better memory than the rest."

My eyes flick to the scar that runs the length of his neck, the one he keeps absentmindedly touching, and his face tightens. It's clear he isn't ready to talk about those yet, and I get the feeling their origin is darker than I'd originally thought.

"What's the new one a reminder of?" I ask, trying to keep the conversation light.

"The day I met you."

He strokes my cheeks with his thumbs, and all of the sudden, my mouth is on his. The hunger in our kiss is unmistakable, and the last clear thought I have is, **Trust him.**

26

I OBEY

VEXAR

GRATITUDE BECOMES MY entire existence as I focus on the taste of Amara's mouth and the rhythm of her tongue. She does not hate me. After everything, she still does not hate me. I do not understand why, but I have never been more grateful for the opportunity to prove myself.

Her fingers grip my neck, thighs tighten around my leg, and I can feel the heat of her desire.

Gods, I want to hear her moan.

I lift my leg, pressing my thigh against her bare sex as I tense my muscles until she gives me what I desire. A wanton moan.

I am already hard for her, aching for her, and yet I cannot give myself to her. The darkness in me has begun its fight for dominance again, and I do not know how to shut it out. How to make it stop. It is louder and more persistent now. Less willing to be buried. And yet, it has been mostly silent all night. So why now? Why does it insist on pestering me when I want to forget about the weight of responsibility and just enjoy this new experience?

Let go.

Mindlessly, I reach to untie the laces at the waist of my leathers. As the knots loosen, Amara sinks her teeth into my bottom lip. The mix of pain and pleasure jolts me enough that I realize where my hands are. With a rush of fear, I release the laces and grip Amara's lower back.

Gods, I almost lost control.

That was close. Too close.

Her hips grind against my thigh as I begin to fall deeper beneath her spell, losing parts of my rational mind to the rhythm of her breath. She feels so good. Every inch of her. I drag my claws over her bare skin, nearly growling as those little bumps rise in the wake of my touch.

Let go.

I ignore the voice.

She raises herself onto her knees, and my face follows hers. "You're like a drug," she says, her voice shaky and eager.

"Good."

My bonded heart flutters as she groans, "Stop weaponizing your wink."

Did I wink? How did I not know I winked? I work to keep the surprise from my face. There is a disconnect between my mind, words, and actions. A blur between myself and the shadow. It is slowly gaining control.

She kisses me again, and I growl into her mouth, feeling her need grow into a desperate, hungry thing. I want more of her. *All* of her. Her wild passion. Her unburdened honesty. Her anger and rage. Her sorrow and pain. Her light and dark. All of it.

Let go.

I lift her hips and roll us away from the wall, pulling her beneath me. Our eyes lock, and the absolute ferality in her gaze knocks the air from my lungs.

She wants me.

Now.

Her desperation mixes with my own, building and consuming as it grows. I was not prepared for this.

I strain to speak as I wrestle with my own control. *I cannot risk harming her.* "Amara, we will have plenty of time to mate when we are off this planet."

Now, the voice repeats.

"What if we don't make it off this planet?" she asks, eyes flicking between mine.

I stare into the simmering fear behind her strong expression, and the shadow creeps up my throat before I can fight it back. My voice comes out as a deep rumble that vibrates everything around us. "We will survive this, *mek Lysaer*. There is nothing that could take you from me." I lower my mouth to her ear, and in a whisper that drips with danger, I add, "I am a very different monster than I was before."

"Fuck," she groans, rolling her hips in search of friction and finding me just out of reach. "Scary Vexar is my new favorite."

Our tether floods with a combination of lust and raw power. My hips lower between her legs. Our combined need is too much. It is blinding. Heady. Irrepressible. The shadow is all-consuming. It demands I give in to her. It demands I cede control. It demands. It demands. It demands. And I want to. More than anything.

I grab her jaw and kiss her deeply, using more force than I should. Instead of flinching back, she leans into me, moaning and pulling me closer, begging for more.

Mine.

Every twitch of her muscles and sound from her lips drags me further from my control. My body burns. Hearts thrum. Vision broadens. A rumble shakes the room. *It came from me.*

A sliver of reason snaps back into place. I cannot take her like this, not with this darkness roiling through me. My hands feel like weapons against her flesh. But my body is moving on its own. I am little more than a passenger, a spectator of my own actions.

"I can't lose you," she moans as my hand slides down her stomach, dipping between her thighs.

"I know."

She is so warm and wet. My cock throbs.

Take her pleasure.

I slip a finger into her and she cries out, rocking her hips against my hand. Her nails dig into my shoulders. She shudders. I feel like an animal. Possessive. Protective. Ravenous.

Mine. The voice of my shadow is deafening.

"I don't want to wait any longer... I need you now," she moans.

Her words, mixed with her clenching heat, pull me deeper until I am little more than a creature of need.

Let go.

I push against the darkness, gritting my teeth. "Amara, tell me exactly what you want, or I will take it all." My words are raw and merciless. They hardly sound like my own. And her body responds in the worst way possible, clenching around my fingers as a mewl escapes her lips. "Tell. Me," I demand. My body is tense and vibrating. Every muscle coiled tight enough to shatter.

"Let me give you what you gave me," she says. There is no fear in her despite the darkness raging through me. She sees my shadow—there is no way she does not—and yet does not recoil.

Claim her.

No!

I pull back quickly and stand, raking a hand down my face and adjusting myself to relieve the pressure behind my leathers.

"Vok," I whisper, rubbing a hand over my mouth and stepping back from the bed. I was so close to putting her in danger. Too close.

"What's wrong?" she asks.

Let go!

It won't stop. I cannot make it stop. I trained for so long to have superior control over myself, and the Zhyrrak has stripped me of it in less than a day.

So many lies.

Let go.

I do not want to hurt her!

I think I am losing my mind. My hands grip the sides of my face. I cannot live like this, in the middle of this battle between myself and whatever ... whatever this darkness is. This voice that I cannot drown out. This unyielding hunger.

"Are you ok?" she asks, pushing herself up. She is concerned but not scared. She should be scared.

"Why are you not scared of me?" I ask.

She looks confused as she scoots closer to the edge of the bed. "I'm not scared of you, Vexar. I thought we just—"

I shake my head and take another step back. "I do not want to hurt you."

She pinches her lips for a moment, watching me. Then a gentle confidence takes over her face as she tilts her head and says, "You won't." Keeping her eyes locked on mine, she leans back onto her elbows and lets her legs fall open, baring herself to me.

Take her pleasure.

My body moves on its own, closing the distance between us in a single stride. I grip her hips and drag her to the edge of the bed with more force than I should. The lustful whine she makes sounds like the creaking of trees in a strong wind. Like shifting ice on a dark night. It is the sound of nature's power.

"Look at me," I demand as I lower myself to my knees in front of Amara's glistening sex. "I need your pleasure." I do not know what is driving me, but I know this is the only way to calm myself. To regain control.

The smile that curls her lips is the most wicked thing I have ever seen. "Then take it," she says, raising a single brow.

I toss her legs over my shoulders, and this time, I do not tease her. With my arms locked around her thighs and my hands pressed against her stomach, I use what her body has taught me, and I show no mercy.

Her first climax comes fast. Screaming, writhing, animalistic pleasure. I release one of her legs and press my fingers into her, growling as she pulses, gripping me and pulling me deeper. Begging for more.

Her taste, her smell, her sounds, her pleasure rolling through me, all help to clear the blurring line between myself and the shadow.

I devour her until her face is red and my shadow is little more than a ghost at the edge of my mind.

"Please, I ... can't," she whimpers, hands wrapped tightly around my horns and hips grinding against my face. I had no idea how much I would enjoy my mate's desperation. To feel her tugging me closer while begging me to stop. The push and pull warring in her mind.

"Your words and your actions ask for two different things, *mek Lysaer*."

Her face screws up in confusion as she lets go of my horns, looking at her hands like they might belong to someone else.

"Do you want me to stop?" I ask.

She shakes her head rapidly. "No."

My pride swells. "Good human."

I dive back in, feeling her pleasure wash over me, clearing away the remaining darkness. None of this makes sense. The shadow begs me to claim her, but relents when I have done nothing more than give her pleasure? I do not know what it wants, and the longer it lurks within me, the more confused I become.

When her voice grows hoarse and she starts to flinch at my touch, I slow my movements, waiting for her heart to calm and her breathing to return to normal.

"Holy shit," she pants, as she pushes herself up and lets her legs hang over the edge of the bed on either side of my body. Pink cheeks and hooded eyes greet me.

I press a kiss to her bandaged knee and run my hand down her calf.

"That was … fuck. That was life-altering." Her palms grip my face, and she pulls my mouth to hers with surprising force. When she breaks the kiss, her eyes run hungrily over my body. "God damn you're beautiful. You look like a statue." Her teeth drag over her bottom lip, and she whispers, "A beautiful fucking statue." With a finger pressed to the underside of my jaw, she says, "Now stand."

I obey, not entirely sure what is happening.

She looks up at me from her perch on the bed, head tilted back, face perfectly level with my hips.

"Good alien," she says with a quirk of her lips.

Zar'vok. The muscles around my spine tighten, and I think I am beginning to understand why she enjoys that so much.

Cool fingers slide down my abdomen, over the medical wrap, and to the sensitive skin just above my leathers. Her eyes go wide when they catch on the head of my already weeping cock, trapped between my waistband and stomach, and she licks her lips with pure, carnal desire.

"Vok'talja," I curse under my breath as understanding dawns. She is going to be my undoing, of that much I am certain.

"Just tell me if you want me to stop," she says gently.

"Never."

My head is spinning. Heart racing. Her hands are on the laces of my leathers. My erection springs free. Her eyelids flutter.

The urge to touch her is overwhelming, but I give her what I have never given anyone—complete control over my body. I am terrified and captivated. Drunk on the way she looks at me.

Her searing gaze narrows in on the appendage above my erection, and her curiosity builds. I assumed our species' anatomical differences were nearly non-existent, but her expression tells me something different.

"It is my *virga*," I say, carefully watching her reaction.

Her eyes flick to my face. "*Virga*?"

"A sensory and sexual organ."

"What's it for?"

"Pleasure."

Her pupils expand. "For me, or for you?"

"Both. It seeks out the electrical impulses of nerve endings and—"

Amara gently touches the writhing appendage. It sucks onto the end of her finger, and her lips form a silent, 'oh'. "I think I'm going to enjoy that," she says.

In an attempt to remain calm, I start speaking. "I have little control over what it doe—"

Shockwaves of pleasure surge through me and cut off my speech as Amara wraps her hand around my cock. I grit my teeth and tense to avoid climaxing right then. It is too much. Too good. I want more and less at the same time. My vision narrows, and I hiss out a breath.

Her hand looks small but feels massive as she strokes me from crown to root. The combination of vulnerability and pleasure tugs at my very soul. I have never been so exposed. So vulnerable. Entirely at the whim of another. My legs shake, and I have to steady myself with a hand on her shoulder.

She flashes me a pleased smile and raises a second hand to join the first. A roaring fire consumes my skin. I am coming undone. Breaking at the seams. Falling apart in her hands. My hips buck involuntarily as my virga latches onto the space between her knuckles.

I move to meet her strokes, every second building a blissful tension as I reach the space between torment and rapture.

Is it supposed to feel *this* good?

A flash of pink is all the warning I get before her small, soft tongue swirls over the head of my cock, sweeping up the beads of precum she has coaxed from me. Throbbing, pulsating euphoria forces an urgent cry from my lungs.

Smoldering eyes meet mine as she wraps her perfect lips around the head of my cock, and takes me into her mouth.

Gods.

I whimper, unable to speak in the throes of near ecstasy. She swirls her tongue. Hollows her cheeks. Moves with abandon. I have never experienced anything—

I have to slow her pace.

Knitting my fingers into her hair, I try to slow her speed, but it does nothing to calm the building pressure. I am too close. Her hands work the base of my shaft, moving in tandem with her mouth. The sight of her rosy cheeks and stretched lips imprints into the marrow of my bones. A sight I will never forget.

Tension builds in my groin, squeezing through my center.

"Zet naklá," I beg, *"zarpulá."* I am completely at her mercy, praying she does not stop. Oh gods, do not let her stop.

My hand loosens in her hair as the pleasure builds past the point I thought possible. Fear begins to grip me. It is too much. Too good.

She plunges forward, taking more of me into her mouth until I doubt she can breathe. Her eyes do not leave mine. I am falling into their depths. She swallows around me, squeezing me with the back of her throat, and she moans.

I break. My muscles tremble. A whimper escapes me. And

the pleasure takes over. Wave after wave of my pulsing release hits her throat, and I watch in absolute astonishment as she gulps it down with hungry abandon.

The moment her lips release me, I am little more than a trembling mess, ready to collapse. But her tongue flicks out, and, still holding my gaze, she carefully laps up my length, cleaning away the evidence of the power she wields over me.

I sink to my knees and take her face in my hands, kissing her like it is the last thing I will ever do, tasting myself on her tongue and groaning at the shocking intimacy of it.

"*Tir'rek tak ennivegit, a vek verla jahv'nek*," I whisper, holding her face and speaking the words of my ancestors. Words that have not been spoken for generations. Words that barely convey the truth that burns in my chest.

Her eyes bounce back and forth between mine, the question in them clear.

27

NOT A PRIZE

AMARA

VEXAR'S BLACK EYES swirl with some shimmering emotion that I can't quite name. Something between rapture and devastation. Then he translates the words he spoke. "I am yours eternally, and open to you always."

Our connection seems to vibrate with the unspoken significance of what he said, and yet, I have no idea what that significance is. "There's more to those words, isn't there?" I say.

He presses a kiss to my lips, steps out of his pants, and pulls me onto the bed with him, curling around me like a giant shield. His breath warms the back of my ear as he says, "They are words that have not been spoken in a very, very long time."

"What language is it?" I ask.

"Ancient Vhorathi. The language of my ancestors."

"It's beautiful," I whisper, as I press my lips to his forearm.

"Would you like to learn it?"

"Someday." With a little effort, I wriggle around until I'm facing him. Rays of morning light spear through the cell, backlighting Vexar's warm, golden skin. I trail a finger down the muscles of his shoulder, over the line where shadow meets light, and ask, "Why did you say you were afraid you'd hurt me?"

"It is difficult to explain."

"Try."

He sighs, like he doesn't want to tell me. "When you accepted the bond, something came with it. Something that was not there before." He takes a deep breath. "It feels dangerous, and I do not want it to hurt you."

I brush a stray lock of hair from his face, confident he would never hurt me. "Tell me more."

"It *speaks* to me."

"Speaks?" I ask gently, trying to hide my surprise.

"It is hard to explain. I hear it, but not with my ears. At first, I thought they were my own thoughts, but they are not. The voice is distinctly *not mine*. And it demands things."

"What kinds of things?"

He groans and buries his face in my neck, tickling my ear with the rough stubble on his cheek.

I wrap my arms around his head and whisper, "Whatever it is, you can tell me."

With his voice muffled against my skin, he says, "It urges me to let go. It wants me to give up my control. Give in to my baser instincts. Dangerous instincts." I feel his lips press to the spot just below my ear. "I will not let it hurt you."

"What do you think it wants you to do?"

"Seek revenge for you? Mate you? Claim you? I am not sure."

I have to stifle a laugh. Fortunately, Vexar doesn't notice. His *darkness*, or whatever the hell he's calling it, just wants to rail me and kill my enemies? Doesn't sound so bad. But he's clearly not comfortable with it, so I bite my tongue and avoid making him feel worse.

"The Zhyrrak was something your people evolved to have, yeah?" I ask. He hums an agreement. "Then it doesn't make any sense that it would be dangerous to me."

"And yet, I *know* it is dangerous."

I slide my fingers through his hair, massaging his head as I go. "If your ancestors all turned into dangerous monsters who harmed their partners, there probably wouldn't be very many Vhorathis left. Evolution isn't perfect, but if a mutation is deadly, it doesn't last."

He pulls his face back and frowns. "Obviously. But if this darkness is part of the bond, why does it feel so violent? What if it is not part of the bond at all? What if it's a part of me?"

A memory of seeing two pigs mating flashes through my mind, and a surge of anxiety follows. "Vhorathis don't have sexual rages or anything, right? Like, you don't go into a mating frenzy?"

"No, we do not."

I let out a silent sigh of relief, and then feel silly for trying to hide it. He knows what I'm feeling. *It's probably going to take a while to get used to that.*

"Well," I say, "maybe it feels so intense because you're denying it? I'm not an expert or anything, but when I try to hide an aspect of myself, especially if it's a need, it only gets louder and more persistent. Maybe this 'darkness' is just an unmet need? Or maybe it's a lizard brain thing, just trying to get you to procreate?"

"Lizard brain?"

"Uh... Like your animal brain—the part of you that hasn't really evolved. The instinctual part." He grumbles, so I add, "It's not a bad thing. Maybe you should consider giving in to it? Just to see what happens?"

He cranes his head back and looks at me like I've completely lost the plot. "It is trying to strip me of my control and push me out of my own mind. I will not willingly hand myself over to some ... some *shadow* that craves violence."

I sigh and give his arm a light squeeze. It's clear he's going to have to work this one out on his own.

"You don't have to do anything you don't want to. Just know that whatever this *darkness* is, I can't feel it at all." Every part of him is gentle and protective. Not dangerous. "I don't think it wants to hurt either of us."

"Maybe," he says before burrowing his face back into my hair and sniffing the side of my neck.

"Did you just sniff me?"

"Yes," he mumbles, "your scent is soothing."

CHUNKS OF STONE crumble beneath the rounded edge of the medical shears as I slowly work another groove into the window's ledge. The muted colors of the morning sky have morphed with the rising sun, turning brighter and more vibrant, begging for my attention, but I'm focused. We don't know how long we have, and I want to get this done sooner rather than later.

"Are you going to tell me about your plan yet?" I ask Vexar while I deepen the groove I'm working on.

"I am still thinking," he says. He's been as still as a statue since I got up. Eyes closed, head leaned against the wall, legs outstretched, and hands folded in his lap. He looks peaceful, but beneath his surface, I can feel the rapid pace of his thoughts as their emotional echoes dart across the back of my mind.

I tuck my crossed legs in a little tighter and rock side to side, trying to bring back circulation to my butt. This table is not the most comfortable place to sit. "Well," I say, "we don't have a lot of time. The sun's all the way up." Puffs of orange fill the air and are sucked out the window as I blow away the accumulated dust.

"We have until midday. The fights won't begin until then."

I resume scratching. "Oh? I didn't realize you'd gotten a schedule from the guards already." He huffs at my sarcasm, and

I add, "Really, though, why are you so confident in this timeline?"

"They bring food to the gladiators in the morning, yes?"

"They do."

"Then we have time."

My face scrunches as I try to figure out how he came to that conclusion, but I come up with nothing. "I hope you're as clever as you think you are."

"I am," he says with complete confidence.

Alright.

Once I've finished the final groove in my rudimentary design, I blow away the dust and admire my handiwork. It's a messy pictogram, but Roveen is smart. If she finds it, I'm certain she'll figure it out.

I wipe my hands on my bare thighs, drop the shears on the table, and spin around to face Vexar. From my perch, I'm almost taller than him, and I get the sudden urge to inspect his horns in the daylight. They're so strange. But there are more important things to address right now.

"Can we talk about something that's been bothering me?" I ask, folding my hands in my lap.

Vexar opens one of his eyes and says, "What is that?"

"What sort of weapons were you using in the arena yesterday?"

His other eye opens, and he lets out a knowing sigh. "Not the same kind of weapon that injured me."

"Wait, what?"

"I was not injured in my fight," he says. "I already told you that."

"Great, yeah. That's super helpful." His eyes flick down my naked body, and the urge to smack him becomes overwhelming. "Oh my god! Focus for five seconds." I swear, a few hours ago the guy was groveling in front of me, swearing to tear down the world in my honor, and now he can't even focus on an important conversation because my tits are out. *Huh. Maybe that actually tracks...*

"Sorry," he says, shaking his head like he's trying to clear his thoughts. He pulls his knees towards his chest and drapes his elbows over them. His movement draws my attention downward, and I fall into the same trap he just did. *Fuck.*

Ripping my gaze back up, I nod at the bandage around his torso and ask, "If you weren't injured in your fight, how did that happen?"

He raises his hands in a placating gesture. "This took a while to work out. I have not been intentionally keeping it from you."

"I never suggested you were."

With a nod, he lowers his hands. "I have reason to believe Gaius had me shot. My injury is consistent with a pulse-round, and pulse-weapons are not allowed on this planet, much less inside the arena. The only way for that weapon to have ended up here is if Gaius approved it."

Well, there goes my calm. "For fuck's sake! How long have you known they were trying to kill you?"

"By 'they', do you mean Gaius?" he asks. My face drops, and he continues in a more serious tone. "Gaius is the only person trying to kill me, Amara."

"Then why didn't—" I cut myself off as a tickle in the back of my mind draws my attention to the question I should have asked a while ago. "Is it normal for future kings to die during the—" I wave my hands in the air, trying to find the word he used.

"Obligation?" he supplies.

"That."

He bobbles his head. "The goal of the Obligation is to ensure the next leader is both fearless and willing to die for their people. If it were without risk, the purpose would be null. So yes, it can be deadly."

I stare, blinking slowly as my mind works through everything. "So is it normal to also refuse medical care?"

"It is," he says.

Huh... My mind spins as I scratch my forehead. "So Gaius is the *only* person who wants you dead?"

"The only person with the means to make it happen, yes."

"And you don't have any concerns that everything else going on might point to a bigger conspiracy? Like, maybe your Senate wanting you dead?" I raise my brows and lean forward.

"My Senate?" There's a serious air to his tone, but his expression hasn't changed. "Why would they want me dead?"

This is going to suck.

"Well, from where I'm sitting, it seems like they all know about the slave trade and were clearly trying to keep you from sticking your nose in it. If they have vested interests in keeping the trade going, it would be a pretty bad call to let you become king. I mean, you've already shown them you wanted to end the trade. It would make sense that they might not want you to be king at all."

He frowns, but there's something else there. A flicker of fear he can't hide from me. And yet, he waves his hand and says, "No. I doubt the Senate would be part of such a thing."

It's clear he's reached his daily limit of discovering betrayals, so I take a different tactic. "Maybe I'm overreacting, but will you just keep it in mind as a possibility while planning our way out of this? If they aren't involved, great. But if they are, I'd prefer we don't die because we failed to consider it."

He gives me a brief nod. *One battle at a time, I guess.*

"Back to Gaius," I say. "You knew he was trying to kill you?"

Vexar shrugs, distracted, but he does answer me. "When I discovered I was injured, I suspected he might be responsible."

"And why do you think Gaius wants you dead?"

He links his fingers together, elbows still caught on the outside of his knees. "He has long sought control over the trade routes surrounding Calidus, and before my mother died, she promised him a contract that would give him temporary control over those trade routes, but she never delivered. From what I understand, at least."

He knew Gaius and his mother spoke, and he still didn't want to believe she was here? *Damn.* Denial is one hell of a drug.

With a serious expression, he continues. "Gaius knows I will not give him power over those routes, but my sister, Aelrith, who is next in line for the throne," he sucks in a breath, "is more easily persuaded."

"So you think he shot you and left you to die over trade routes?"

"He did not leave me to die. He sent me you."

I laugh, but quickly stop when Vexar's expression doesn't soften. "I'm sorry, what?"

"If I am not mistaken, he planned on you entering my cell. He knew if I was injured and a nurse helped me, I would either leave in a body bag or with indisputable evidence of my broken vow." He pats a hand over the bandage covering his stitches— the ones he got from me, a *female* nurse. "If everyone believes I chose my life over my vow, there will be no investigation into my death. It will be seen as a natural consequence of my moral failings."

I'm stunned silent for a second before I say, "Holy shit."

"Yes, holy shit."

I don't know why it didn't occur to me that Gaius himself would have a reason to want Vexar dead, but it makes sense. It also explains why the guards didn't try to stop me. They knew.

"Wait, how did he know I would do it? Enter your cell, I mean."

"He did not *know*, but it is clear why you were selected for the task." I stare at him blankly, and he gives me a disappointed frown. "You cannot tell me you have never done something against your own self-interest to save a life."

"Well, yeah, but not here—" I pause, and an annoyed huff escapes me. "Fucking Thoratliums."

"Thoratliums?" he asks with a lopsided grin, clearly no longer fixated on the issue of the Senate.

I wave my hand dismissively. "Ok, he wants everyone to know you broke your vow so they don't come digging and find out he's a treasonous sack of shit? And then he plans to ... what? Kill you in the arena?"

Vexar nods and stretches one of his legs out. "I believe that is the plan, yes."

My muscles tense with a strange kind of rage, and I swear, if Gaius were within arm's reach right now, I'd rip out his jugular with my fucking teeth. Vexar, clearly noticing my rage, appraises me with a hungry look that does nothing to cool the fire beneath my skin.

"Don't look at me like that when I'm angry," I snap. "It's ..." I let out a groan and drop my head into my hands, looking up through a curtain of hair. "Why are you so calm about this? He's about to ruin your reputation and kill us both."

"He is not about to do either of those things."

I straighten, and Vexar's eyes catch on my very exposed breasts. I snap my fingers to get his attention. "Hey, sexy alien." When he looks back up, I say, "If we both survive this, you can look at my tits whenever you want, but right now, I need you to focus. Why can't Gaius ruin our lives and kill us?"

"My reputation will be fine. As I said before, our bond supersedes any vow or rule about mate determination. My people *will* rally behind us—*behind you*—once they know what you have done. You have done the impossible and ensured

Gaius's plan will fail. Now all we must do is survive and clear our contracts."

"But I broke your vow."

"My people will forgive that when they learn that you have awoken the ancient miracle of my people."

"Ancient m...miracle?" I stutter out.

"The Zhyrrak bond," he says plainly.

Well, that's something we'll have to dig into at some point.

Pushing my hair back from my face, I ask, "Why are you so confident he'll let us leave here alive? We know he's committed treason, so aren't we a massive liability to him?" If I were in Gaius's shoes, I would definitely not let us leave here alive.

"He doesn't know about our bond," Vexar says thoughtfully.

"Ok ...?"

"So, he won't see us leaving as a risk. Not a large risk anyway. From his perspective, he has already won. Even if I survive the arena, my vow is broken and my throne is lost. He will be confident that anything I do after that point will be seen as little more than a desperate attempt to regain power. No one would believe me. I would have lost all credibility. All we need to do is ensure that Gaius is in a position where letting us leave has a more favorable outcome than killing us."

"And how do we do that?"

With a sly grin, Vexar says, "Visibility. If there are millions of eyes on us, any action he takes will be heavily scrutinized. He will be forced to maintain the illusion that everything is normal, or risk implicating himself in a serious crime." He scratches the short stubble on his chin. "When I win my fights and claim my prize, we will leave as conspicuously as possible and avoid ever being at his mercy."

"Your *prize*?"

"You. You will be my prize," he says simply.

My eyes feel like they're bulging out of my skull. "First, I'm not anyone's *prize*; I'm a person. Second, I can't tell if you're delusional or just really bad at explaining things. Gaius doesn't want you alive. What's stopping him from doing what he already did and just shooting you?"

Vexar smiles. "He wants his fights. That is how he makes his money, and the fights of a future ruler bring in a shocking sum. He will not do anything that might jeopardize his income unless he sees a larger risk at play."

"Ok. Then what's stopping him from putting you in the arena with a monster that'll definitely kill you?" That's what I would do. "And on top of that, how are you planning on getting me in the arena, too? And how the hell are we supposed to *leave*?"

He nods gently and waves a hand, beckoning me to him. "Come here."

Without shoes on, I'm not risking stepping on the floor, so my plan is to jump the gap. But, before I can even stand, Vexar's arms wrap around my waist, and he lifts me onto his lap with ease.

"Show off," I say.

He smiles and takes my hands in his. "Do you remember when I told you that I am a very different monster than I was before?"

AN HOUR LATER, I finally understand why Vexar is meant to rule an empire. He's smart, and it's clear he has an excellent understanding of how to manipulate people. Honestly, it's a little scary. Scary and sexy. *Is it wrong to find Scary-Vexar so hot?*

"And you think he'll agree to that?" I ask.

Vexar gives me a dark, devious grin, flashing his long canines. "It is a deal he thinks he cannot lose."

I'll give him this, Vexar's thought through everything, and despite the numerous variables, his plan is simple and solid. On top of that, he listened to my thoughts, concerns, and recommendations, and adjusted things accordingly. For the first time, I feel confident that we might actually survive this, and that realization stirs up a hornet's nest of emotion.

Noticing the change in me, his demeanor shifts. His eyes soften, and he takes my face in his hands. "I know it is hard for you to trust, but please, trust me when I say we will survive this." When I don't respond, he adds, "Tell me where these tears are coming from, *mek Lysaer*."

I'm crying? How did I not notice I was crying?

I quickly wipe my eyes. "Why do you keep calling me, '*mek Lysaer*'?" My translator says it means, 'warrior first', which I don't get. "Is that like a pet name or something?"

He shakes his head. "Do not avoid my question."

I groan. "Fine. I knew you wanted to keep us alive, but without a firm plan, I didn't think it was possible."

"Amara," he says in that deep rumble that makes my heart pound, "my word is stronger than my axe. I have said it already, but I will say it again. We will not die here. Not you. Not me. Neither of us will die here. We will leave this place and live out very long, very happy lives. Do you understand?"

His pupils expand until there is nothing but black in his eyes, and I find myself getting lost in them. I wasn't expecting to feel like this, but I guess I was holding onto more doubt than I knew.

"Do you understand?" he repeats, after I fail to answer.

I nod, my vision still blurred. "It's a good plan."

He kisses me and brushes his thumb under my eye, wiping up another escaped tear. "I have just as much brain as muscle, remember?"

I laugh through my brimming tears at the fact that he

remembered my earlier dig. "You know, I meant that as a compli—"

The sound of something metal in the hallway pulls our attention, and before I can register what's happening, I'm on the bed and Vexar's on the other side of the room, standing between me and the cell door, fully naked, looking like some sort of imposing god.

28

PROMISE

VEXAR

THERE'S SOMEONE IN the hall.

I move Amara off my lap and onto the bed before crossing the cell and positioning myself in front of the door. There are no voices, just footsteps. I pray this is a food delivery and not the guards, but I mentally prepare myself for the worst.

Gods, I do not want to leave her side. But I have to. There is no other option.

Discipline and control.

A small slot in the door falls open with a clang, revealing a glimpse of the darkened passageway beyond. I slap my palm against the door. "I need to speak with a guard," I say in Vhorathi.

Bolts of fear flash through the back of my mind. I turn and find Amara, wide-eyed and shaking. "What is wrong?" I ask.

There is no response. No recognition in her eyes. Her heart pounds in my chest, and I am torn between comforting her and trying to communicate with whoever is in the hall.

Before I can make a choice, an intense instinctual urge pushes me to focus on our connection. So I do.

Chaos. That is what I find. Amara's panicked chaos.

Something else pushes me now, urging me to calm her racing heart and organize the mayhem. I think it is my shadow, and despite how wary I am of it, I listen. My breathing slows, and I focus on settling the panic within Amara's mind. In less than a second, her heart rate steadies, and familiarity ghosts across her eyes.

Did the shadow do that? Or me?

Footsteps. Metal rattling over stone. Something sliding. No time to think.

I turn back to the door. Drop to my knees. Peer through the small opening. Shadows move in the dim light beyond. *Are they ignoring me?*

My fist impacts the door in another attempt to gain their attention. The metal frame shakes violently, raining stone-dust from the ceiling and creating a sonorous bang. I glance down at my fist in confusion. *I barely used any force...*

Shaking off the wrongness of how the door reacted, I repeat, "I need to speak with a guard."

Nothing but the sounds of shuffling.

Do they not understand me?

I repeat the phrase in seven different common languages before I receive a response.

"What do you want?" a slick, musical voice says in *Temátu*.

Strange. What is a *Tèmtárh* doing here? **What is a human doing here?** A knot forms in my throat as my thoughts travel back to Amara—the human who was taken from Earth despite a very stringent treaty.

I rake a hand down my face. "I need to speak with a guard," I repeat.

"Why?" the Tèmtárh asks.

"I would like a meeting with the Magistrate before my next fight." While my Temátu is not what it should be, the Tèmtárh seems to understand. "Can you deliver a message to the Magistrate?"

"Yes."

"Tell him I would like to expedite my fights and complete them all today. Tell him I am willing to renegotiate my contract."

Two metal meal-trays slide onto the shelf jutting out from the slot in the door, and the Tèmtárh and their cart continue down the hallway. I call after them. "When will the guards return?"

"Later," they say.

When the hallway is silent, I stand and face Amara. Her eyes are still glassy, but her heart is steady, and the panic is gone.

"Did it work?" she asks.

I close the distance between us and cup her face in my hands. "Are you ok?"

"Yeah," she says casually, "the sound of the meal-slot just freaked me out."

Her emotions feel almost too steady, and I am not sure what to make of that. "Are you sure?" I ask. She nods, and I decide to trust her and answer her question. "I am not sure if it worked, but we will know soon. Are you hungry?"

AMARA SITS cross-legged on the bed, the bloodied sheet draped over her lap while she devours her food with surprising intensity. I pick at my food with far less enthusiasm. My mind is spinning, testing every assumption I have made about our next steps, looking for holes in our plan or errors in my reasoning.

"How many languages did you try?" she asks.

"Seven."

She takes another bite off her tray. "You really weren't exaggerating when you said you know a lot of languages, huh?" I hum and she asks, "What was that last language you used?"

"Tematú. It is the language of the Tèmtárhs."

"Tèmtárhs... Do they have antenna?" She holds up her fingers above her head and wiggles them.

Unable to avoid grinning, I say, "Yes, they have antenna. And yes, I know the word."

"I think Roveen is a Tèmtárh. That language ... I'm pretty sure it's the same one she speaks." Her eyes go wide with excitement. "Wait, can you help me translate a message to add to my pictogram?" She points at the window where her carving is waiting.

"Of course." I push a slice of graying meat across my tray. "I suppose we should have thought of that before you did all that work."

She shrugs. "Sometimes you don't think about the things you need until after you need them." She gives me an appreciative smile, and we dive headfirst into coming up with a suitable phrase. It's ingenious really, leaving a carving that is likely to only be found by other nurses or gladiators. Hopefully, Roveen does find it. It will make our return much easier.

"Why aren't you eating?" Amara asks, after we've updated her message to Roveen.

I glance at the questionable food and feel my stomach churn. "I am not sure I would consider this *food*."

She smiles playfully. "I think it's great."

"You will eat anything, won't you?"

Her eyes flick down below my waist, and her brows raise suggestively.

"Not what I meant," I say.

"Still funny." Another piece of graying meat disappears into her mouth. "And no, I'm not too picky anymore. Enough time in the military, or here, will do that to you."

I hum a sound of understanding. "You should put your dress back on. I do not know when Gaius will want to meet, and the guards should not see you like this." Our plan hinges on discretion.

She glances at the crumpled, stained garment on the floor, and an almost imperceptible shudder rolls through her. "I will. In a bit."

Her reaction is painful to witness. That pile of fabric has become a symbol of her bondage, and I wish there was something I could do to protect her from it. Unfortunately, she will have to wear it. The illusion must be maintained.

Gods, this plan is foolish...

I push my tray to the side, no longer interested in it. The caloric injections I received will last another day or two, even if my stomach feels painfully empty.

Amara looks at my unfinished meal like I've lost my mind. "Are you really not going to eat that?" When I shake my head, she proceeds to clear my leftovers with a hum of satisfaction. "I feel so much better," she says, as she leans back and kicks a leg out, readjusting the sheet in the process and revealing a strangely shaped blotch of blood on the white fabric.

"Is that ...?" I ask, turning my head to get a better view of the stain. "Did you write on the sheet in blood?"

She glances down to where I am looking and shrugs. "Yeah. I didn't have anything else to write with, and I needed to keep track of your heart rate."

Sure enough, the smudges appear to be a series of base-10 numerals. Side-eyeing the ominous smears, I ask, "Where did you learn that trick?"

"Navy." When she notices my raised brows, she elaborates. "We would write triage information, like the time a tourniquet was placed, on casualties' bodies so—"

"In blood?" I blurt out, accidentally interrupting her.

"Well, no, you're supposed to use a permanent marker, but when shit hits the fan, you use whatever you've got. Last deployment, some shitlicker shot my marker, and while blood doesn't have much staying power, it works in a pinch. Or at least until you can get someone else's marker."

I swallow back my surprise. "You were shot?"

"Not that day."

"You just said…"

"My armor—and I guess my marker—caught that round."

I shake my head. "So you were shot another time?"

She lifts her arm and points to a scar beneath her bicep that I had not noticed before. "Just a little," she says with a wink.

It takes me a moment before I can find my words. "What happened?"

Her brows knit together like she doesn't understand my question. "I was shot."

"By who?"

"An asshole with a death wish."

I narrow my eyes. "And what happened to this asshole with a death wish?"

She nudges me with her toe and smiles. "You can't hunt him down and kill him if that's what you're asking," she says, clearly meaning the man is already dead.

Every conversation with Amara seems to further dispel the illusion that she is defenseless, and the more I learn about her past, the clearer her true disposition becomes. She is more like one of my warriors than one of my sisters. I have heard rumors about some humans being violent, but I did not expect Amara to be one of them. I wonder how many humans are like her. She is caring and gentle, but behind her dark brown eyes, I can see the violence there. I can feel it simmering beneath her surface.

"You ok?" she asks.

I smile. "Just nervous." Everything about our plan has me on edge, but this is the only way to ensure I do not lose my throne or my ability to stop the Tusku slave-ships. "Are you ready for today?" I ask.

She blows a breath between pinched lips, puffing out her cheeks. "As ready as I can be."

Sliding fully onto the bed, I grip her feet and pull her towards me, wrapping her legs around my torso and my arms around her waist. "I need you to promise me something."

"What's that?"

"When you see Gaius, do not anger him. Do not let him see you as a threat."

She scoffs like my request is ridiculous, but it is not. She is fire, and fury, and war incarnate, and it is clear she does not know this about herself. I am certain she could kill Gaius, but there are too many guards. She would not survive what happened after he was dead.

My hand moves to her chin, and a deep thunder vibrates my chest. "Amara, do not give them a reason to kill you."

Her discerning gaze digs through me, and her expression morphs to one of concern. "Hey," she coos, placing her hands on either side of my face, "it's ok. I'll be fine, I promise."

Her words do little to soothe me or my shadow. The darkness in me would rather tear this galaxy apart than let her out of my sight. The instinct to protect is overwhelming. "Promise me you will follow the plan and do only what we discussed. Promise me you will not risk your life."

She nods. "I promise."

29

DISCO BALL

AMARA

"**A**ND YOU'RE SURE it'll fit in your greaves?" I ask as I turn and walk across the cell again, already sweating in the heat of mid-morning. The skin beneath my arms burns from the scratchy fabric of the bed-sheet I'm wearing as a toga, but every time I look at my nurse's uniform, I can't bring myself to put it on.

"I am certain," Vexar answers.

"And Marius? You're sure he can get the ship to us?"

"Yes. He is the only person with access."

I scratch my forehead. "And you trust him?"

"With my life."

We've been over this plenty of times, but I need a final rehearsal. Some training you can't unlearn.

I run through my mental checklist one last time. The message for Roveen has been updated. We've practiced our 'mission-abort' signal, and we have an escape plan if needed—sort of. We both know our individual objectives and our mission objective. We've covered priorities, capabilities, time-frames, weather, and pretty much everything else we could think of. And Vexar has drilled into me the rules of engagement—no killing, no fighting, no snarky comments. I swear, it's like he thinks I'm some sort of feral gremlin.

My teeth work over my bottom lip as my brain tries to find any remaining gaps in our plan. "And you're certain you can win?"

"As certain as I am that there is air in my lungs."

A sharp pain shoots through my lip, and I hiss. My fingers come back from my mouth bloody. I bit myself. "Shit."

Vexar's already standing, cupping my face and tilting my head to get a better look at the damage.

"It's fine," I say, as he examines me. "I'm just nervous."

He nods and rubs his thumb gently over my lower lip. "We are almost there."

My eyes trace the sharp rise of his cheekbones and the deep shadows they cast. His unearthly beauty is hard to look away from. I drag a finger down the scar that bisects the right side of his face, trying to remind myself that he might not be happy about killing, but I'm pretty sure he's good at it. If nothing else, I think I can trust him to survive.

His body goes rigid, and my hand stills on his cheek. "They're coming," he says.

I don't get a chance to ask him how he knows because his mouth is already on mine, kissing me with a desperation that makes my chest ache and the pain in my lip fade. This is it. This is goodbye.

I pull back just enough to whisper, "Don't lose."

His brows dip in a look of pure determination, and he says, "I will never leave you," before descending on my mouth again like it's the last thing we will ever do.

I'm nearly in tears when he breaks away and says, "I am with you until the very end."

"Until the very end," I whisper back.

The screech of metal fills the room, and a flash of bright

light follows. My body jolts. Heart leaps into my throat. Adrenaline pours into my system.

"Stand back!" a voice yells, but the sound is distant. Miles away.

I drop into a squat and grip my knees to my chest. *Everything's ok. You're ok.* I have to calm down. I can't have a flashback right now. *Just breathe. Breath.* I suck down heavy gulps of air, feeling my chest tighten with each inhale. It's not working. Fog clouds my vision. The sharp smell of metal fills my nose. *No, no, no.*

There's a tug at the back of my mind, and the cell rushes back into focus. I nearly vomit from the rapid change as I fall forward onto my hands and knees, gasping for breath. *Fucking hell.*

I turn my eyes up to Vexar's looming form, standing between me and the guards. Somehow, he pulled me out of a flashback. I don't know how he did it, but that was definitely him.

I shake my head, trying to clear the remnants of the adrenaline dump. My mouth is dry. Limbs heavy. Stomach roiling. But I'm here. Fully present and in control. Time to get up.

The guards say something else, but Vexar's ominous growl drowns it out. A fresh pulse of fear chills me. I scramble to my feet, grabbing the edge of the table for stability while trying to gauge Vexar's state of mind. If his eyes are black, we're completely fucked.

"Vexar, you must come with me," someone says as I urge my body to cooperate and move.

Vexar responds in a calm but commanding tone. "Close the door and give us a moment."

Calm. He's calm. *Holy shit.* I grab my chest where my heart is rattling against my ribcage. He's still in control. His eyes aren't black. He's just being intentionally intimidating.

God damn, he's good at being scary.

"I h-have to t-take you now," the voice says, and I finally recognize who it is. The lizard. The traitorous bastard who duped me and locked me in here.

Waves of raw, primal energy radiate from Vexar, and I'm shocked the lizard hasn't turned tail and run. Either he has balls of steel, or the threat of not getting Vexar out of this cell is more terrifying than Vexar himself. My stomach drops at that thought, but I shake it off. *There's no way.*

"Amara," Vexar says, his voice gentle but stern, "dress."

Shit. I'm still wearing a bed sheet.

Regretting waiting until the last second, I grab my nurse's uniform and throw it over my head, dropping the toga in the process. Thankfully, I'm already wearing shoes.

"Vexar," the lizard warns.

"Give. Her. A. Minute," Vexar growls loud enough that dust falls from the ceiling. *Why is scary-Vexar so hot?* And why am I even capable of thinking about that right now?

Fully dressed, I step up behind my hulking alien.

He spins to face me, and I almost touch him before remembering our plan and clasping my hands behind my back.

"Trust me," he mouths silently, before turning and walking out the door.

***

I'M IMMEDIATELY BROUGHT to an upper level of the Coliseum by a guard wearing a breather mask that covers his entire face. I expected to be left in Vexar's cell—at least until his meeting with Gaius was over—but that's not what's happening, and I don't know what that means. Vexar was nearly certain I would be left in there until he'd finished his negotiations. Then again, we knew there would be variables. This must just be one of them.

Sempre gumby, and all that.

We reach a door, and the guard shoves me through it with a grunt. The force is so unexpected that I almost fall and have to run a few steps to catch myself. "Dick," I mutter as he slams the door shut behind me.

I'm hit with an overwhelming scent—something between jasmine and eucalyptus—and a thick, wet heat that settles in my lungs. My eyes go wide as I take in the room.

"For fuck's sake," I mumble.

The room is circular and grotesquely opulent, unlike anything I've seen in the Coliseum. Floor-to-ceiling mirrors wrapped in gold filigree cover the curved walls. A strange chandelier hangs from the ceiling, dripping with thousands of tiny, reflective beads that tinkle as they spin and collide. And, at the center of it all, there's a steaming pool of water, surrounded by smooth stones.

It's a bathroom. I'm in a fucking bathroom.

I shake my head at the wrongness. There's no way Vexar's had time to strike a deal with Gaius. It's been like five minutes. So why am I in a bathroom?

My crimes should land me in the arena. That's the penalty for breaking a law. When I was pulled from Vexar's cell, I assumed I was being taken directly to a weapons room or something. That's where I should be. But I'm not. I'm in a bathroom, and I'm pretty sure I don't need to be clean to die.

I bite my lip and wince as my teeth find the raw spot I bit earlier. I don't like how far things have already deviated from the plan, but I can still feel Vexar's calm confidence, and that helps settle my nerves. Unless things go completely FUBAR, I'm not giving him the signal. If we fuck this up, we lose our chance at fixing things, and I can't live with that.

Steeling myself, I step further into the room and nearly jump out of my skin as a hundred different angles of my face turn to look at me. *Holy fucking mirrors.*

I move towards the wall and frown at the nearly unrecognizable woman staring back. Pale skin. An unkempt mess of dark hair that reaches my mid-back. Deep, bruise-like circles beneath my eyes. Good god, I knew this place was taking a toll on me, but I didn't think the physical evidence would be so ... shocking. I look sick. And hungry. I squeeze one of my nonexistent biceps and frown. A lifetime of work gone in a single year. Fuck this place.

The distant sound of voices pulls my attention as a mirror on the opposite side of the room swings inward. Two beautiful, towering women with dark blue skin slink through the doorway, their feet silent on the smooth tile floor. The women's slender frames and long legs carry them to me in just a few strides. I'm expecting some sort of conversation, but instead, the taller one reaches out and grabs the shoulder of my uniform.

"Whoa," I say, brushing her hand away. "What's thi—" The other woman grabs at my dress next, clearly ignoring my protests. I duck out of her grip and step back. "What the hell?"

The taller one pulls her hands to her chest, making herself appear smaller, and whispers, "Please." Her eyes are wide with the kind of terror I know all too well, and my ears start to ring as I take in the rest of her appearance. There's a deep purple bruise on her arm and another on her neck. She's favoring one of her legs. And she's missing a finger on her right hand.

"Fucking hell," I mumble, rubbing my forehead.

It's clear they're both terrified, and I don't want them to face repercussions for my failure to comply. More than that, I don't want to give Gaius another reason to be the sadistic fuck he clearly is. So, I nod and say, "It's fine. Do what you came to do."

As they disrobe me, the muscles in my jaw tense so hard my teeth start to ache. None of this is ok, and I hate it. Somehow, I got the golden ticket out of here while these women have to stay in hell. I want to tell them that I'll come back for them, that they just need to hang on a little longer, but I can't. I can't say anything. I just have to hope they're still alive at that point.

My thoughts wander to Roveen, and I feel sick. I don't want to leave her behind. She's going to think I'm dead, and unless she finds my message, she'll have no idea what happened. This isn't how I thought I would feel about leaving. I expected relief and excitement, but all I feel is dread. Dread and a deep fear that if today doesn't go perfectly, no one will be leaving this place at all.

Before I'm led into the bath, I remove the bandage from my knee and set it on a nearby stone. When I'm in the pool, I double-check that we're alone and whisper, "Do either of you know why I'm here?"

They answer me with wide eyes that quickly dart away. Clearly, they aren't supposed to talk. So, while they work on my hair, I focus on channeling my anger towards the two people responsible for all of this. Gaius and Vexar's mother. Gaius's retribution *will* come at my hand, and when that day comes, Gaius will know the devil has come to collect his fucking soul. As far as Vexar's mother goes, she's already dead, and all she left behind is her legacy. A legacy that I'll make sure is burned to the ground.

These women may not have a Prince Charming, but they have *me*. And I'll stop at nothing until I see them freed.

A few minutes later, I'm left standing naked, confused, and clean as the two women exit the room. They took my uniform, but they left the bandage. Carefully, I re-wrap my knee and wait with my arms crossed and a scowl on my face. It feels like an eternity, but eventually another woman enters with what looks like a garment bag draped over one of her four arms. Her pale gray skin glistens in the low light under a beaded dress that hugs her wide, muscled torso and leaves nothing to the imagination.

Quite the outfit.

She stalks forward and proceeds to appraise me like livestock, inspecting every inch of my naked body, lifting my arms, tugging my hair, and then staring at the bandage on my knee. I can't read her expression, but when she reaches for the dirty gauze, I take a step back.

"Leave it," I say loudly.

She doesn't reply, but she also doesn't reach for it again.

A few minutes later, I'm dressed in an outfit that is uncomfortably similar to the one she's wearing. A beaded top and skirt. Revealing and impractical. The last thing she does is wrap a thin, gossamer skirt high around my waist. If the extra layer is meant to add additional coverage, it's failing miserably.

"What about shoes?" I ask before she leaves.

She turns, face unreadable, and shakes her head.

Fuck.

For the past year, I've been going through a pair of shoes a month because of the shit floors here, and now I'm supposed to go barefoot? This is clearly intentional, and whoever made the call to rob me of my shoes is a dick. My feet are going to be destroyed if I have to walk around like this.

Trying to shake off the surge of anxiety, I pace and come to terms with my situation. I don't have any control over what happens to my feet, so there's no point in freaking out about it. I just have to embrace the suck, keep my head down, and survive.

As I pace, my reflection catches my attention, and I let out a deep groan. I look like a disco ball. A mostly-naked disco ball. This was not part of our risk assessment. Even in the dim light of the bathroom, I sparkle and glint like a giant "Shoot Here" sign.

At this point, it's clear we aren't the only ones with a plan, and I don't like that at all.

30

NOT PROPERTY

VEXAR

I GRIP MY flank in mock pain as I follow the Palatian guard through the snaking passageways. Sparks of concern flood my connection with Amara, sending anxiety tickling down the back of my neck. I cannot tell if she is in danger, or just ... uncomfortable.

Gods, this is foolish. I should never have let her out of my sight. My knuckles crack as I clench my fists, working to keep myself calm. She has not opened and closed our tether yet. I need to trust that she is fine and that she can handle herself.

Gaius's office is more suffocating than I remember—the endless array of artifacts now seems less like a curious collection and more like a museum of Gaius's own insecurities. Every new item, another attempt at filling a void he is incapable of filling any other way. A part of me almost feels bad for the monster—he did not need to become what he is now—but that does not make me want to kill him any less.

"Vexar, what a lovely surprise," Gaius croons.

Instead of responding, I inspect a shelf of old security devices and give one of them a gentle shove. *He really does have a broad collection.* With I sigh, I turn and face the stout usurper. He is sitting behind his stone desk, staring at my shirtless chest with an expression of pinched annoyance.

"Apologies for the lack of clothing, I was not given access to my personal effects," I say as I gingerly lower myself into one of the stone chairs without invitation. Gaius's face contorts further as he tries to process my continuing disrespect. This is a delicate dance. If I push him too far, I will get nothing from this meeting. But if I am too respectful, I risk losing the air of a soon-to-be-deposed prince. Leaning back comfortably, I ask, "Do you want to explain why a nurse was allowed into my cell, Gaius?"

His jaw tightens. "While you are under contract here, you will refer to me as Magistrate."

I wait a beat and dip my head politely. "Apologies, Magistrate. Can you explain why a *female* nurse was allowed into my cell?"

A shadow of a smile crinkles his eyes before he quickly hides it with a frown. He is clearly pleased with himself. "The nurse chose to disregard a direct order. I apologize for the situation and my delayed reaction, but my guards failed to notify me until this morning." *Lie.* "I *would* launch an investigation, but as we are both aware, you are needed on Vhorath by the end of the week, and that is not a sufficient amount of time to complete an investigation." *Another lie.* "Is it safe to assume this is why you requested a meeting?"

I suck my teeth and say, "It is."

Unfazed by my clear frustration, he leans over the desk and picks up a decanter of water, pouring me a glass before gesturing to it. "Please."

Keeping my eyes on him, I take the glass and tip the water to my closed mouth. I doubt he would try to poison me, but it is not worth the risk.

Seemingly gratified, he continues. "If you agree, I would like us to forgo the formal investigation and discuss the issue like old friends."

I twirl the glass and watch the water dance. "Why?"

"I am sure you would rather not draw excess attention to the issue at hand?"

He is right. If I were in the position he believes me to be in, I would be less than eager to parade my broken vow for little more than an explanation. I nod in agreement.

"Excellent. I would like to hear *your* side of the story first." He leans forward eagerly, watching me the way a child watches a wild animal behind a wall of glass. It is unsettling, as if he no longer sees me as a threat. "Let us start from your return to your cell, yes?"

I clear my throat and let a pained expression cross my face as the action shakes my ribs. The flicker of glee behind Gaius's dark eyes is clear. I have convinced him that I will be easy to kill. That is good.

"I was wounded during my fight," I explain, keeping my knowledge of his involvement out of the conversation. "I was bleeding and knew I could not receive medical treatment." I offer him a humorless smile and set the glass on his desk. His expression remains passive, but his eyes never leave my hands. It is clear he still views me as a physical threat, but he is too calm, as if he is not sitting across from a man who could destroy his entire life.

I continue explaining the events that followed my injury, telling him the relevant details up to the point of Amara arriving outside my cell door. All the while, he listens with rapt attention, showing no signs of concern. He should be fearful that his treasonous plan will come to light. He should be anxiously hanging on to my every word, praying I have not figured him out. But instead, his only anxiety is what I am doing with my hands.

I have missed something.

"Then, I fell unconscious from blood loss," I say.

"And after that?"

"When I woke up, I had been stitched together, and there was a *female* nurse in my cell."

"And what happened after you discovered the nurse?" he asks. I open my mouth, ready to tell an edited version of the events following my discovery of Amara, but he stops me with a raised hand. "And do not tell me you did not *have* her. My guards informed me of her nakedness."

Outwardly, I show nothing. Inwardly, I feel a wave of terror. I should have ensured Amara was dressed before the guards came. That was a mistake on my part.

Keeping my face calm, I give a casual shrug. "I looked, yes. She broke my vow, so I made her pay penance." I flick my hand nonchalantly while my stomach tightens with discomfort. Then I tell him how terrified she was of me when I woke up. I laugh, adding to the callous nature of my story. It is painful, but necessary.

When I have finished, I say, "I would like to see that she is properly punished for her actions upon my return to Vhorath. If you will allow me to take her, that is."

He smiles knowingly, unsurprised by my request. "That is something that can be discussed. But first, I would like to ensure the matter of her transgression has been fully resolved. At least as far as it pertains to this establishment."

We spend a short while discussing how this was allowed to happen before I ask, "Will the guards who failed to prevent her entry be punished?"

He gives me a pensive look and folds his hands over his stomach. "In time."

"What about restitution for the damages I have suffered?"

"Is your life not payment enough?" His confidence is out of place and confusing. I feel off balance. I assumed I had the upper hand when I entered this meeting, but now I am not so sure. As a test, I remain silent, not providing him with an answer. It takes only a few seconds before he's shifting uncomfortably and says, "That is all I can offer you."

With a sigh, I say, "I will take that into consideration when I write my report."

To my surprise, the mention of a formal report sparks no fear in Gaius.

"Can we consider the matter closed?" he asks.

"For now."

"Excellent. On to the next order of business, then. You mentioned taking the nurse with you." He pulls a paper scroll from beneath his desk, unfurling it before him with a ridiculous flourish of his hand. "You also mentioned a renegotiation of your contract to ... Elex." *That must be the Temtárh I spoke to.* He pushes the scroll towards me. "This is a revised contract that includes the verbiage required for you to take the nurse."

Ice floods my veins. *He knew I would want to take her with me.*

I raise a single brow, allowing some of my surprise to leak through, as I say, "That was rather forward."

"It is just good business. Now, I'll leave the choice up to you. You can either complete your current contract, as planned, and leave the nurse behind, or you can stamp this revised contract." His lip curls dangerously. "It requires an extra fight, of course."

"And why would I agree to that?"

"I cannot allow my property to leave without suitable compensation."

Property. That word heats my blood and sends the shadow in my depths scrambling for purchase. Gaius knew I would want to save Amara's life. He was confident enough to have a revised contract drafted before I even spoke to him. Had I not bonded with her, I still would have negotiated for her freedom—it is in my nature—but Gaius does not know that. He does not know me. I am a very private person, and beyond my immediate family, there are few who know me well enough to foretell my actions.

What am I missing?

With my throat tight and heart racing, I scan through the contract. It is exactly as expected. Gaius gets what he wants—my very public shaming and multiple chances to end my life. And I get what I want—expedited fights and Amara.

"It says here that the nurse's contract will be transferred to me? Not cleared?" I ask.

"Correct. She will be your property to do with as you please."

Property. There's that word again. I want to strangle Gaius, but I resist the urge and continue reading. When I reach the section discussing my failure, I pause. The terms are fine, but the phrasing is ... oddly familiar.

My stomach drops as I realize why.

Amara was right. It is not just Gaius.

Willing my voice to remain disinterested, I ask, "And if I do not agree to this, what will happen to the nurse?"

"She will be given the opportunity to fight in the arena, just like every other criminal."

"So you will kill her," I say.

"Oh no, I will not kill her. But she will die, yes."

I lean back and scratch the scruff on my chin as if contemplating my choices. "Three fights?" I ask. "While wounded? All today?"

"Those are the terms."

I smile humorlessly. "Rather steep terms."

He tilts his head in a subtle shrug, showing his indifference to my protest. I do not want to sign this contract, not now that I know there is a third party involved, but I have no other choice. Amara is in the care of Gaius's guards. If I kill him, I cannot ensure her safety. If I do not sign, she will be executed. There is only one option.

I plunge a fang into my thumb and leave a bloody print on the bottom of the scroll. "It would be wrong of me not to offer her justice," I say, handing the contract back to Gaius with a pained grunt. "She saved my life. If nothing else, she deserves a trial."

He takes the scroll and uses an ink pad, not blood, to stamp his print next to mine. It is still legally binding, but it feels like a slight. A slight I am forced to ignore.

I spend the next few minutes ensuring Gaius creates electronic copies of the relevant documents and sends them to my ship. A paper trail will be necessary when he inevitably claims Amara abandoned her contract.

By the time we are done, Gaius looks annoyed as he waves his hand to dismiss me. "The guards will escort you to the preparation chamber."

I rise slowly from the chair, still playing the part of an injured gladiator. But instead of leaving, I turn towards the wall of artifacts and drag my finger over a dusty shelf. "Tell me, Magistrate, when was the last time you spoke to my sister?" I glance over my shoulder just in time to watch Gaius's face contort with alarm.

Truthfully, I should have realized it sooner. Gaius is not known to be clever, but my sister certainly is, and her ambition knows no bounds. The betrayal is painful, but not in the way I would have thought. It feels like a rebuke against my own judgment. A confirmation that Amara is more right than I care to admit. That I have been blinded for too long, refusing to see the uncomfortable truths in front of me.

Gaius stutters out a few incoherent words before turning in his chair to file away the stamped contract behind him.

Hands in my pockets, I duck through the doorway and offer Gaius one last nerve-wracking thought. "Oh, if you do speak with Aelrith, let her know her eldest brother says hello."

31

GILDED?

AMARA

THE DOOR BURSTS open, and I suck in a breath as a guard marches towards me. I think it's the same guard from earlier. Breather mask covering his face, humanoid shape, long sleeves, and gloves. Probably the same guy. Without a word, he grabs my upper arm and tugs me into motion.

Doors and empty hallways flash past my periphery as I'm dragged through the Coliseum at a pace I can hardly match. I try to remember the turns we're taking, but the pain in my feet is too distracting.

So much for playing amateur cartographer. Sorry, Vexar. If we do have to bail before this is all over, I'm just gonna have to hope my way out of here.

A raised section of the floor catches the ball of my foot, and I stumble. Pain radiates across my sole and up my calf. The guard doesn't slow down. Every step turns into a test of mind over body. My feet throb. Each new bolt of pain makes me feel a little more helpless and a little more angry. Eventually, that feeling grows past my ability to contain it.

I don't like feeling helpless. I don't *do* helpless.

Letting my rage take over, I sit back in my hips, using my bodyweight to pull against the guard's grasp, forcing him to stop. My feet dig into the stone as his fingers dig into my arm. Blinding pain shoots through my body, but I don't give a shit. Fuck him.

"Move," he orders with a tug that almost knocks me over.

"Find me some shoes!"

He grunts and keeps pulling. My shoulder feels like it's going to pop out of its socket. I bite back another expletive as my feet slide and a knife-like pain burns through my left heel. In that moment, my resistance slips, and with one hard pull, the guard gets me moving again.

"Move," he says again.

My heart pounds as I prepare to unleash a volley of insults, but then we stop. I flinch, expecting the guard to strike me, but he just releases my arm. With caution, I open my eyes. The guard isn't even looking at me. And there's a door. I blink a few times. This must be our destination.

Standing still makes the pain in my feet worse, and I can't resist checking the damage. I glance down and—

Fuck... My head drops as I stare at my bloodied feet.

At least I don't have to worry about that mental map Vexar wanted me to keep. There's a physical trail of my blood leading back to the bathroom. I rub my hands over my face in frustration.

Today's going great. Really. Fucking. Great.

The sound of the door opening and the smell of food pull my attention up, and the room tilts on its axis.

The Magistrate.

I knew this was going to happen, but my body seizes up anyway. Black spots appear on the edge of my vision. My stomach churns, and sweat slicks my palms.

I've spent months imagining what I would do in this exact moment, and now that I'm here, I'm frozen.

Gaius's lips curl in a menacing smile, and my stupor breaks. I recoil, only to be met by the unyielding frame of the guard behind me. My eyes search for something. Anything. A weapon, an escape route, I don't know. I'm a wild animal caught in a trap.

"Amara," Gaius purrs. My breath catches. He's holding out a paunchy hand like he expects me to touch it. Bile rises in my throat. "Do not be rude. Take my hand," he orders.

I'm shoved from behind and stumble through the door, unbalanced and unable to avoid the grasp of cold skin around my wrist. Vexar's words echo in the back of my mind. *"He will want to know why you saved me. He will want to meet you. Use your time wisely."* Fighting every instinct I have, I let Gaius pull me towards a long table as a definitive 'thunk' marks the closing of the door behind me.

I can do this. I can do this.

"Sit," Gaius says.

My legs shake as I collapse into the oversized chair. I feel like a child in a room built for giants. Everything's too big. The massive table, the oversized trays of food, the vaulted ceilings, the tall windows that span the length of the wall, and the endless desert that stretches out beyond them.

I wipe my sweaty palms down my legs and stare at the monster that's haunted my every waking moment for the past year. I frown as my terror morphs into confusion. The image I've built of Gaius is so different from reality. He's not large, or imposing, or scary at all. Nothing like my memory. He's about my height—maybe five feet seven inches? He moves with a slow wobble, his cheeks are ruddy, and the horns I remember being intimidating now just look pathetic. They remind me of Vexar's horns, just a lot smaller, and ... weirdly shiny?

I narrow my eyes and catch a flash of golden light as he

settles in the chair at the far end of the table. *Oh my god.* I have to press my lips together to hold back a laugh. *Did he gild his horns?* He definitely gilded his horns. *Holy shit, how am I supposed to not make a joke about that?* This fucker gilded his horns. Oh god, it's comedy gold. If he were in grade school, he'd be ripped to shreds in seconds.

A sudden surge of glee hits me as I realize I'll be able to share all of my bad jokes with Vexar tonight. I won't be locked in a room by myself.

"I have good news, my dear Amara," Gaius says. "Vexar has agreed to be your champion!" He flourishes his hands wildly, as if he's revealing some sort of prize, and my eyes go wide. He's like a bad TV show host. How in the hell was I ever scared of this guy? *Probably because he has the power to have me killed. Duh.*

"Champion?" I ask.

"Indeed!"

I raise a brow, confused by his over-excited demeanor. "What does that mean?"

"He will fight, and if he wins, he will take ownership of you. Is that not grand?"

Be calm. Don't let him get to you. Yeah, no. That's not working. "Ownership?" I growl.

"He asked to take you back to Vhorath so you can stand trial for your crimes. A very noble gesture to be sure. And *if* he wins, your contract will be transferred to him."

I swallow down my rage and remind myself that this was part of the plan. Right now, I need to be a gracious idiot, not a pissed off killer. I drop my eyes to the table like a fawning idiot and say, "Well, I guess that is good news."

"Indeed." He grins, and the tip of a sharp canine appears between his cracked lips. A second later, my brain catches up. *Holy shit, Gaius is Vhorathi.* I hadn't even considered that he could be the same species as Vexar. They're so ... different. Then again, there's a pretty wide range of appearances in humans too. He takes a swig from his goblet and wipes his mouth on his sleeve. "Truthfully, I wasn't expecting him to agree to the revised contract at all, but I suppose that is the folly of those who are more noble than intelligent."

This fucking asshole. 'More noble than intelligent'? Really? With extreme effort, I keep my face calm, press my hands into my lap, and launch my first question. "Can I ask what would have happened if the gladiator didn't volunteer to be my champion?"

To my surprise, Gaius doesn't hold back. He gives me an overly long explanation about the importance of law and order, maintaining balance in the galaxy, and the honor of a good death. I listen carefully, nodding with interest, and smiling when appropriate. My translator does a good enough job, but I make a point to look confused when he speaks in metaphors or uses more complicated terms.

Everything about Gaius screams insecurity, so I'm hoping Vexar's right and my gracious-idiot performance will get him to open up. So far, it seems to be working. Sure, he's burying the truth beneath a layer of pageantry and virtue signaling, but the information's still there. He's confirmed that he kills slaves in the arena—although he's calling them "criminals". Real slick.

"You see, the criminals are given a chance to earn their freedom back. Although it rarely works out that way." He lowers his voice conspiratorially and leans forward. "You would be surprised by how many criminals walk these halls, *undiscovered*." Then he shrugs. "Or maybe not."

I pretend not to notice the dig. "Well, I feel like a very lucky girl."

He smiles and gestures to the food. "Please, enjoy this meal. I had it prepared for you!"

There's no way in hell I'm eating any of this, but I play along and randomly spoon things onto my plate. The next few minutes flash by as I ask frivolous questions and pretend to be interested while pushing food around and shifting my throbbing feet on the floor. *At least there's tile in here, I guess.*

To my surprise, Gaius hasn't asked me a single question. Vexar was convinced he would be curious about me, but so far, he's shown zero interest. Which is weird. If he didn't bring me here to get information, what's the point?

Then I remember he's an egotistical psychopath. Maybe I'm just a captive audience here to listen to him ramble. It's weird, but I've seen weirder. Once, I went on a date with a guy who would ask me questions, interrupt me mid-answer, and then answer the question himself. Needless to say, that date didn't last very long.

I prop my chin on my hand and lean forward. "It sounds like running this place and keeping it staffed must be very taxing." Vexar coached me on manipulation tactics earlier, and this was one of them. He said you can get everything you need without ever asking a real question. It makes sense. If you ask someone a question, they might get defensive. If you make an incorrect claim, they'll want to correct you. And if you inflate their ego, they'll probably elaborate.

Gaius looks flattered as he takes a bite of something and chases it down with a sloppy gulp from his goblet. He tries to set his goblet down, but it lands on something and nearly topples over, sending a splash of drink onto his hand. Instead of using a napkin, he wipes his hand on the tablecloth.

Is he drunk?

With a grin, he says, "It really is a challenge, but it's a challenge I am particularly suited for." He scratches his forehead, just underneath a gilded horn, before rolling into a lengthy explanation of his long-standing relationship with the Tusku— the species that runs the slave-ships. He claims to have helped the Tusku build their operations to an "economically beneficial scale", and now the Tusku return the favor by supplying him with "workers" at a discount. I knew this conversation was going to suck, but it's hitting harder than I expected.

"So the Tusku had the original idea for the operation?" I ask innocently, as a bead of sweat rolls down my spine.

Gaius takes the bait. "No, no. That was me. I was the one who developed the system, including the ordering process. It's a clever system, really. Anyone in need of a worker can place a request—with their desired profile, of course—and delivery occurs within sixty days."

Anyone in need of a worker...

"Of course, the Tusku are very good at screening candidates and ensuring the selected workers have the aptitude to fulfill the job requirements." He takes another swig and refills his goblet. *Definitely drunk.* "For example, the nurses here, including you," he adds with a smirk, "were selected for their ability to handle a high level of violence, trauma, and isolation."

I nearly choke on my own tongue, but he doesn't stop speaking, and with every new word, I'm left feeling a little more violated. The Tusku spied on me for months. They knew everything about me. They *chose* me for this because of my history and lack of personal connections.

I guess they missed the part about me being a vengeful bitch.

Gaius continues. "The transport ships are another particularly clever bit of engineering I assisted with. They are designed to put the cargo through a myriad of physical and emotional stressors." He leans forward and whispers, "It helps to weed out the weaker ones before they reach their final destination. You see, if they arrive too damaged for work, it is clear they were never a good fit to begin with. Now, the ships themselves..."

He keeps speaking, but the roaring in my ears drowns him out. *They put me in a box to see if I would break?* My entire body vibrates. I'm not sure if it's the rage or the pain or the overwhelming disgust. Probably all three.

Does he really think I didn't break? That despite everything, I'm still fine and normal? Because I'm not. That box fucking shattered me, and when I pulled myself back together, everything soft, everything kind and forgiving was gone. That ship didn't make me into a better slave; it just sanded me down until I was little more than my sharpest parts.

I press my hands against the table to keep them from shaking. Something cool pricks my palm.

A knife.

I almost laugh. *This fucking idiot gave me a knife?*

There's a silent shift of power in the room that Gaius is oblivious to. He's given me a weapon, there are no guards present, and he's drunk. The stupid bastard. He's just like every other toxic male in the universe, refusing to believe a woman could be a threat. Going on, and on, about how brilliant he is. How he did all the smart things that no one else could possibly do. And yet, he's sitting across from someone who was trained to kill, and he has no fucking idea. Granted, most of my training was focused on keeping people alive, but my second deployment was a shitshow, and I am well-practiced in taking out pieces of shit like him.

With cautious movements, I pull the knife into my lap. Fortunately, he's so engrossed in his own story, I doubt he'd notice if I stood up and took a shit on his plate.

"That is very interesting," I say, as I slide the knife along my thigh, blade side up, and tuck it between my waistband and hip. My sweat-damp skin clings to the metal, and I casually adjust my top. "It's remarkable that you were able to develop such a robust system," I say, hoping he'll continue to elaborate.

He does, and I can't deny I'm impressed by how effective Vexar's techniques are. I don't think I'm exactly *good* at this manipulation thing, but Gaius is eagerly spilling his secrets. Then again, he thinks he's talking to a dead girl, so ... it could just be that.

When he pauses, I ask my last 'question'. "The gladiators must be a remarkable challenge to procure."

He looks up for a moment, as if considering this. "Sometimes, yes. But I don't rely solely on the Tusku for that. Some of our gladiators are looking for a way to expunge their debt, others have criminal charges and choose the Coliseum over prison." He picks something out of his teeth with a fork and continues to ramble, but I have everything I need.

I push the food around my plate, considering whether using the knife is a good idea. It's probably not, but I'm going to hang onto it anyway. You never know when you might need a weapon.

"Vexar, on the other hand," Gaius says, pulling my attention back, "has proven that royal blood alone does not make one fit to lead. He is weak-minded, foolish, and unable to consider the consequences of his own choices. A creature like him could never lead an empire. It is absurd to even think such a thing."

My fork falls to my plate with a clatter. *How did we get back to the subject of Vexar?*

"I warned him, before he stamped his contract, that he needed to accept the mate chosen for him, but he chose pride over security." Gaius flicks his hand dismissively and mumbles, "Wanting to prove himself. Ridiculous. What an excellent example of how pride can be one's downfall. Although, considering what a horrible king he would be, it is probably for the best..."

His words seep through me, cold and slow. A glacier peeling back my skin. I feel raw and dangerous.

He's still speaking. "I suppose you can't expect someone like him to be fit to lead. Just look at him ..."

I'm too angry to focus on his words anymore. This pathetic

shit-stain of a weasel is trying to tear down the strongest man I've ever met. My fingers move to my hip, tracing the outline of the blade beneath my skirt. The cool metal is a thousand degrees warmer than the ice in my veins. I promised Vexar I wouldn't do anything stupid, but this isn't stupid. This is the only correct choice right now.

"It is a good thing he will not survive the day," Gaius says, as he continues to drone on.

I press my aching, bloodied feet into the floor, focusing on the pain. I can't tip my hand. I need Gaius to see me as meek. Harmless.

He pauses his diatribe and stares at me, clearly waiting for me to speak. It's the first time he's asked me a question, and I have no idea what he said.

I clear my throat. "So who should lead the Vhorathi Empire?" I ask, hoping the topic of conversation hasn't strayed too far from Vexar and his throne.

Gaius points a finger at me. "That is the right question."

I stare into his dark, dead eyes, waiting for a name. I want to know who this fucker is rooting for.

"Well," Gaius says, setting down his goblet and standing. "It is almost time for the fights to begin."

Of course he won't give me a name. He's a weak creature who was given power when he should have been given a short rope and a long drop.

He starts walking towards me, and I note the more pronounced wobble of his gait. My mind clears. I can end this all right now. He doesn't see me as a threat, he's drunk, and the guard is on the other side of the door. The *only* guard. I can take one guard. Then I just have to open and close my connection with Vexar, and he'll find me, and we can leave. He won't have to risk his life in the arena. He won't end up with extra blood on his hands or guilt in his heart. We'll be free and safe.

It's been a long time since I practiced fighting with a knife, but I *know* I can do this. I stand and push the chair back, keeping my body angled so my right hand is shielded from Gaius's view. Cool metal slips into my palm. I grip the blade underhanded, letting the spine sit flush against my forearm. Hidden. Ready.

"My dear Amara," Gaius says, reaching for my hand, "it has been an honor—"

I move, letting muscle memory take over as I slash the back of his hand in a right-to-left motion. Blood hits my skin. I'm already moving for my next strike, extending my elbow, aiming the blade's tip at Gaius's jugular.

One jab. That's all I need.

Time seems to slow as the blade moves towards his neck, and then, everything stops. Pressure rolls down my arm, a loud crack splits the air, and I'm thrown backwards by what feels like an explosion. I hit the ground. Air erupts from my lungs. Muscles cramp. Skin burns. That wasn't an explosion.

Shit, shit, shit! I have to get up.

I scramble to my feet. *Where's the knife?* I dropped the fucking knife!

Something impacts my ribs. Not an impact, an electric shock. Hot agony turns my muscles to stone. Then it's over. I'm on my back. Gasping. *Need to move.*

"Stop her!" Gaius shouts.

I try to get up. Someone grabs my hair. *I need the knife. Where's the fucking knife?* The second my hair is released, I roll, but the tip of what looks like a cattle-prod slams into my gut, pinning me in place. Pain consumes me. Every muscle contracts violently. My skin crawls and burns. Eyes shake. *It's too much.* The tile floor squeaks beneath my skin. *He's not going to stop.* Helplessness spreads as the shock continues for far too long.

Then it's over. I suck down lungfuls of air, trying to get my bearings.

"Get her out of here!"

I'm dazed, but I know what I need to do. I spot the cattle-prod only a foot away, clutched in the loose hand of the guard. The guard who thinks I'm too weak to be a threat. I get to my knees and lunge for it, but I'm too slow. *Shit.* The guard kicks me in the ribs and gives me one more jab for good measure.

As electricity rips through me, I see Gaius shuffle past my field of view. His face is a mess of fear and panic as he grips his hand, leaving a trail of crimson in his wake.

When I can finally suck in a breath, I laugh. I've never heard such a sick sound come out of me before. It's the resigned sound of someone who knows they're already dead. Ragged and absolutely mad. Maybe it's the beating, or the lingering rage, or the year I've spent in captivity, but seeing Gaius bleed is one of the greatest joys I've ever experienced.

32

EVEN THE GUARDS

AMARA

THE GUARD DOESN'T give me a chance to keep fighting. He grips my hair and drags me back through the door as I try to break his grip. It's no use. We reach the hall, and the stone cuts into my legs as I scramble for traction. My scalp burns. We come to an abrupt stop a few feet away, and he shoves my head forward. Stars burst behind my eyes.

"Get up!" The order is booming and sends a terrifying chill through me.

Reality zooms back into focus.

What the hell did I just do? Fuck, fuck, fuck. He's gonna kill me.

Still seeing stars, I get to my feet, squeezing the muscles in my thighs and abdomen like a fighter-pilot, trying desperately to keep from passing out. Trying to stay focused. Trying to stay alive. Spots cloud my vision. Everything hurts. I wobble, but before I fall, rough, angry hands dig into my arms, and something solid slams into my back. I wheeze. A sharp pain radiates through my torso. It's a knee. The guard has his knee pressed to my stomach, and he's holding me against the wall.

My eyes tear up as I try to take a breath, but can't.

"You should not have done that," he growls, and my heart breaks. *I know that voice.*

The tears fall as cold metal seals around my wrists, digging into my flesh. Then I'm on the ground, released into a puddle of shaking regret with my hands raised in the universal sign for 'stop'.

"Yuxta," I choke out, "please."

He makes a hissing sound from behind his mask before he grips the chain between my hands, pulls me to my feet, and starts marching me down the hall. After a few minutes of silence, Yuxta stops and turns to me. "Why would you do that?" he asks, his voice low and dangerous, even through the translator.

"I..."

"You are lucky he wants you alive, or I would have had to—" he cuts himself off and tenses. "Do what you are told, and you might survive."

My mouth opens and closes a few times as I search for words. Is Yuxta warning me because he doesn't want me to die? Or ...? Then it clicks. "Workers." *All* workers. That's what Gaius said. My tears fall more freely as I ask, "Are you here because you want to be, Yuxta?"

He grunts, grabs the chain between my hands, and we continue down the hall.

Even the guards.

I lose track of everything as my mind fumbles with this new reality. I wouldn't have thought it possible before—that enslaved guards would be willing to commit such violence against other enslaved people—but after hearing Gaius's explanation, it seems plausible. Willingness to commit callous acts of violence is definitely a trait the Tusku could screen for, and as much as I want to believe they missed the mark on Yuxta, I'm not so sure anymore.

A whisper pulls my attention back to him, and if not for my translator, I doubt I would have heard him at all. "I am sorry," he says, "but they are watching."

My mouth opens to ask what he means, but before I get a chance to speak, he's opened another door, and my focus fixates on what lies beyond. Darkness. Complete darkness. A small, dark space, just big enough for a person.

I panic. It's the box all over again. I try to dart away, but Yuxta's grip is bulletproof.

"Please. Please don't—" I beg, hoping he'll listen to me.

With a shove, my hope turns to horror.

I collide with something metal and unforgiving. The darkness swallows me whole. Pain radiates through my shoulder, and I slide to the floor as the last sliver of light disappears with a dull thud.

33

THE ONLY WAY OUT

VEXAR

AMARA IS SUFFERING. Alive, but suffering.

If she does not survive the day, I do not know what I will do. It will break me. Every hope burned in a single breath. I want to find her. Make sure she is safe. But I cannot. If I leave the preparation chamber, the trail of death left in my wake would seal her fate long before I could reach her.

The only way out now is through. I just pray I am right about Gaius, and that he will bring her to the arena.

"Ten minutes," a voice echoes through the darkened room.

Discipline and control.

I pound a fist into the sore flesh of my flank, testing the pain. It is manageable. Amara is right, I am healing quickly. Very quickly. With a strip of leather secured over the bandage, I trade out my pants in favor of a pteruges skirt—the leather pleats only cover from hip to thigh, but the added mobility is worth the loss of protection.

By the time I've finished lacing up my leather vambraces and greaves, my shadow is clawing at my throat, as if it senses the coming violence. So much has changed in the past day, and as time marches forward, I find I recognize myself a little less with each passing moment. I look at my hands. Their appearance has not changed, and yet they are impossibly different. The hands of a stranger. Able to shake a solid steel door with little more than a knock. Every inch of me feels different. Like I've become a weapon.

I did not want to tell Amara how much I have changed. I do not want to scare her. But I was not exaggerating when I said I am a very different monster than I was before. I doubt there is a gladiator on this planet who could kill me now, and that truth is more terrifying than I expected.

Sheathing my axe, I step towards the portcullis.

"Ready?" the guard asks, his clawed hand resting on the opening wheel.

I nod.

The portcullis shudders and begins to rise. A thin line of afternoon sun reaches my feet and expands upwards, slowly climbing my body and warming my skin.

I take a deep breath, and in the calm before the carnage, I focus on Amara. The steady thud of her heart in my chest. The trust in her mind. The memory of her lips. The bright timbre of her laugh. She is scared, yes, but her fear is balanced with her rage. *My unstoppable Queen.*

I allow myself a single moment to sink into her bliss before I bury our connection in the deepest recesses of my mind, locking away the part of me that is capable of tenderness and love. Locking away the fear that grips me. Locking away her ability to see my darkness.

Then I enter the arena.

Sharp, deadly spires cast deep shadows across the killing-floor. Sand grips my feet with every step. Sweat beads on my brow. I glance up, and too many eyes stare back, waiting to receive their share of the blood.

The darkness in me rises, and I let out a feral roar, channeling the injustice and rage in my heart. The crowd responds with a roar of their own. It is so loud that the sand beneath me shakes until grains of dust dance unnaturally over its surface. This time, I absorb the energy rather than reject it. It is frenetic.

A voice booms over the cacophony, and the crowd settles.

Gaius, in his finest dress, glints in the sunlight at the edge of his viewing box like a decorated sack of shit. He holds a microphone in a bandaged hand and waves to the crowd. Strange. I do not recall his hand being injured earlier.

"Today is a momentous day!" he says. "I introduce our first Gladiator, Prince of the Vhorathi Empire, Fury of Solira, Vanquisher of Verdoon, Vexar Valdís!" Gaius waits for the crowd to calm before continuing. "Today, Vexar does not fight for his own glory; he fights for the freedom of his dearest love! A love that defies both reason and honor, but a love that is true." The crowd breaks out in a whispered frenzy as I grit my teeth. "Behold, Amara! The courtesan that stole our dear prince's heart!"

I try to steady my breathing. I knew he would put her on display, I knew he would turn this into a spectacle—I tried to prepare myself for it—but the fire that pulses through my veins is beyond anything I had expected. Rage consumes me. My vision broadens. Fists turn to stone.

He called Amara, a courtesan.

He called *my Queen* a courtesan.

I watch, muscles tense and shaking, as a chain beside Gaius raises, and my sense of self is consumed in a sea of wrath.

34

A DEADLY PROMISE

AMARA

THE GROUND BENEATH me jolts, and my stomach drops. *I'm moving.* Or ... the closet I'm in is moving.

Ok, so, probably not a closet. Maybe an elevator? A very dark, very small elevator?

A circle of light appears above me, growing larger by the second, accompanied by a distant, heavy thunder. Holding my breath, I stand and wince at the pain in my feet. My legs are shaking, but I'm standing.

"You can do this," I whisper to myself.

The expanding circle of light reaches me, and I'm thrust into heat and light and sound. Immediate sensory overload. I blink rapidly, trying to force my eyes to adjust, but as my surroundings come into focus, I sort of wish I were blind. Vertigo nearly knocks me down as I take in the open space. So much open space.

I'm above the arena. And there are millions of eyes. So. Many. Eyes. A sea of thousands of alien faces. Screaming and pointing. A shiver rolls over my skin. It's not thunder, it's the crowd. I swallow and then notice the bars. I'm surrounded by bars. Why are there—

My stomach drops. *It's a cage.* I'm in a fucking cage.

Ok. Everything's ok. I'm ok.

I swallow down the anxiety and drop my eyes to my feet, but the sight there isn't any better. Dark stains pattern the metal beneath me, barely covered by my new, brighter contributions. Clearly, I'm not the first person to bleed in here. I pinch my eyes shut and grip the bars, willing myself to stay calm.

"If Vexar can defeat all three opponents, Amara will be his!" Gaius's voice booms. The sound of his voice drowns my terror in a furious rage.

Just focus on your breath, Amara. In for four... I turn and make eye contact with Gaius. *Hold for four...* He's standing in front of a throne. *Out for four...* Gripping a microphone. *Hold for four...* And gesturing at me. I repeat the box breathing as I take in his fresh robes and bandaged hand.

No matter what happens, at least I made him bleed.

"But if he fails," Gaius continues as he walks up to my cage and gives it a push, sending me swinging, "she will be my gift to all of you!"

Gift to the crowd?

"You fucking dick!" My arm shoots through the bars of the cage, fingers hooked and ready to do damage, but the cuffs pull tight, stopping my hand and nearly flaying the skin from my wrist. I claw at open air, hoping the swinging of the cage will bring me close enough to rip out an eye. It doesn't.

The volume of the crowd rises further, and I think they're cheering *for* me—or at least for something unexpected to happen—and I can't help but think that's a good thing.

Gaius keeps speaking, but my focus is pulled down to the arena by a tug at the back of my mind.

My eyes lock on Vexar like he's a lighthouse in a storm, and despite the distance, I know he's staring back. My mind quiets, heart calms, and the arena seems to fade away. He's impossibly beautiful in the sun—all sharp angles and rippling muscle under a layer of warm, golden skin. His expression is stern, and there's an unmistakable promise in the hardened lines of his face. It gives me hope.

His gaze drops as he squats down and gathers a handful of sand, methodically rubbing it between his palms in a way that feels almost ritualistic. I rest my forehead against the bars and focus on our connection, wanting to feel him. But there's nothing there. I blink a few times, confused, and try again. Nothing. The connection's still open, but his end is silent.

Maybe he's just really focused.

With calm, practiced movements, Vexar stands and pulls an axe from the sheath on his back. A small grin pushes through my discomfort. The axe suits him.

"And now, I introduce our first contender!" Gaius says.

There's a rattling sound and a metal gate thing—like the kind you'd see in a castle—begins to rise at the far end of the arena. My grip tightens on the bars as I wait for some horrible creature to crawl out of the shadows, but to my surprise, it's an average-looking bipedal male carrying a sword and shield. I think he's a Sikut? But from here, I can't be sure.

The crowd reacts with gasps and whispers, and it feels like they all know something I don't.

"Nonus," Gaius shouts, "our most beloved gladiator!"

Beloved... Shit.

Something flashes across the back of my mind. The emotion is foggy and hard to discern, but I think it's resignation? Or maybe cold resolve? Then it disappears, leaving nothing but a barren void between us again. I shift nervously, wishing I knew if the disconnection was intentional or if something's wrong.

Nonus, the very average-looking gladiator, raises his sword towards the crowd like a salute before fixing his gaze on Vexar, who's been stalking him this whole time. I haven't seen this side of Vexar yet. He seems like an entirely different person.

A horn sounds from somewhere. I jump at the noise. Nonus takes a single step forward. And Vexar explodes into kinetic action.

My jaw drops as their massive forms clash.

Sand kicks up around them in sweeps of glittering orange. Vexar moves like a shadow—smooth and swift, always one step ahead of Nonus's attacks—his long braid swinging behind him with each graceful movement. The blur of strikes is impossible to follow. My eyes just can't keep up. But I spot a trail of blood on Nonus's arm while Vexar appears unscathed.

I've never seen anything like it. Vexar is a storm in flesh. Beautiful and terrifying.

Nonus blocks the attacks, but Vexar doesn't stop his torrent. While I've seen my fair share of violence, this is something completely different. It's intimate and brutal.

Without warning, Vexar's axe lands on Nonus's back with a sickening thud. Horror flares through me, but I quickly douse it. Vexar is trading his peace for my safety, and I won't shy away from that sacrifice. He didn't have to do this. He could have run. But he didn't. He's doing this for me. For *us*. For every person the Tusku have taken.

Strengthening my resolve and my spine, I watch Nonus crumple.

Silence descends on the arena as Vexar removes his axe from Nonus's back. Bloodied and glorious, my champion turns to face me. At this distance, I can't see his eyes, but I know they're two dark pits of rage. He's still for a long moment before his head tilts back and he lets out a roar that can only be described as a deadly promise. All the hair on my body stands on end, and a single word flashes across the back of my mind. *Xelora.*

I've never seen anyone look so savage or unstoppable, and as his roar ends, the crowd responds with one of their own. The Vexar I'm watching right now is not the same man who lamented about the incongruity of death and celebration. He said he was a very different monster than he was before, and now I think I understand what he meant.

Gaius's previously buoyant demeanor is gone. He notices me watching him and plasters a confident smile on his face. With a raise of his goblet, he says, "To the show." I spit through the bars, and he laughs. "Like a feral *jhyrata*. So feisty, but so helpless."

I let out a frustrated growl and slam my hands against the bars. I need to break his smug face. To feel his blood on my hands. To watch the terror in his eyes. "Fuck you!" I snarl.

There's another shuddering sound from the arena, and Gaius smiles. It's the gate again. *They haven't even removed Nonus's body, and he's already starting the next fight?*

Feeling out of breath, I turn back to the arena, shielding my eyes from the sun. Vexar is pacing, watching the gate and the darkened passageway beyond. Something moves in those shadows, and I watch in terror as a walking fever-dream enters the arena. That's not a gladiator, that's a fifteen-foot-tall killing machine shaped like an oversized praying mantis.

And Gaius is laughing.

35

THE MANTA

VEXAR

THE RAGE INSIDE me dies at the sight of the Manta, a flame slowly flickering out.

I let my axe slide through my grip until the head rests in the sand near my feet. I do not want to do this. This creature is not sentient, it is not a gladiator, it is just an animal trying to survive. When I signed the revised contract, I knew there would be no guarantee of who I would fight, but this? This is not what I imagined.

My eyes flick up to the only true monster in this place, Gaius. He has kept his power for far too long, and I can only hope my actions today are the first steps towards removing that power.

I scrub a hand over my face and lift my axe as I come to terms with what I must do. I cannot save this beast. Only one of us can leave here alive, and it must be me.

Amara's heart pounds in my chest. *I wish I could tell her not to worry.* Sweat drips into my eyes. Sand permeates my boots and sticks to my feet. The horn sounds. And nothing happens. The Manta just watches me with large, curious eyes. It has no idea why it is here or what it is supposed to do. I am not prey, this is not its territory, and it has no reason to attack.

There's a cracking sound—most likely an electric pulse delivered to the Manta's collar—and the creature bursts into action.

I dash to the side, narrowly avoiding its thrusting arm while positioning myself to strike. I swing horizontally. My axe powers through carapace, sinew, and bone, until the end of a twitching leg lies in the dusty sand between us.

The Manta stares at the detached extremity before letting out a shriek that vibrates my chest.

I am sorry.

Biting back the sob that threatens to escape me, I dart between the Manta's legs and let my axe drag along the length of its belly. A rush of green, metallic gore spills as the Manta frantically stomps, trying to spear me with its legs. But I am already clear.

End it, the dark voice inside me whispers.

Rage begins to burn in my chest as my shadow claws for dominance. '*I do not need you,*' I think as I try to shove it down. All I need is for this poor beast to die quickly.

I run towards the Manta's hind-quarters, jump, plant a foot on its upper leg, and swing. One of the beast's arms catches my bicep, tearing flesh but not slowing my forward momentum. One heart beat. Two. My axe slams into the creature's shoulder with a sharp crack that rings in my ears. Sand flies as I impact the ground and roll to my feet. I turn, ready to strike again, but the fight is over. The Manta is dead. Its body lies in two pieces, arranged horribly in a growing pool of its own blood.

"Vok!" I throw my axe to the ground with a growl of frustration and cover my face with my hands. Sand crunches between my teeth. Blood runs down my arm and drips from my elbow. Rage burns through my chest, and I drop to my knees, praying that I can be forgiven for this. "Vaeryth, god of love and connection, forgive me," I whisper.

The Manta did not need to die. I did not want to kill it. But the horrible truth is that my shadow did.

I stare at the corpse, struggling to look away. I did not just kill it, I mutilated it. *Was this really what my ancestors coveted?* I grab another handful of sand and aggressively rub it between my palms, focusing on the sensation of abrading skin. I feel like little more than a killing machine. A vengeful monster. The exact thing I feared I would become.

The portcullis rattles its warning cry again, distracting me from thought as my shadow creeps back up my spine. My eyes flick to Amara, and a rush of fresh savagery pulses through me. I bite back a scream. It is all too much. The death. The malice. The loss of control. The burning need to protect. The desire to let it all consume me. To be rid of this turmoil.

The ground shakes with a heavy thud. Then another. And another.

My eyes narrow on the clawed, gray foot that emerges from the open portcullis. The creature that follows is at least three times my height, maybe more. It walks on two legs while its long arms drag by its sides, carving deep furrows in the sand with its claws. A mass of coiled muscle sits between the beast's shoulders, twitching and betraying the power of those long limbs.

Let go, the voice begs. I resist, but the shadow presses forward anyway, sending tendrils of rage through me until any hint of mercy I once had is gone. I have no pity. No kindness. Only violent brutality and a deep desire to return to my Queen. Images of her in that cage flash through my mind, as if the shadow is reminding me of my purpose.

I bend and retrieve my axe, feeling the smooth wood meld with my hand while my focus stays on the beast. A bony, skull-like face, stained with blood and shielded by a crown of antlers, turns towards me. It is static and expressionless. Impossible to read. Black, lidless eyes ruin my ability to track its gaze. I have seen this creature before, in the storybooks of my childhood. It is a myth turned monster—a lab-born creature, I am sure—and unlike the Manta, this beast's murderous intent is clear in every snap of its jaws and tilt of its head. It wants to kill me. So I must kill it first.

"For our final fight, I introduce a creature that stalks the shadows and haunts only the darkest dreams. A beast that cannot be caged by the confines of time or space. The Skugga!"

The horn sounds, and I cling to my last sliver of restraint. I will not allow myself to be consumed by this darkness.

Discipline and control.

The Skugga bursts towards me with alarming speed. I jump and ready my axe to strike from above, but the creature is already gone. *It is faster than I thought.* By the time I land, it is already charging again. I dive to the side. Scramble to my feet. But before I can get my bearings, I am forced to duck again. This time, I am too slow. A clawed hand drags over my already injured shoulder. Searing pain spreads down my arm as I dance back. Blood spills into my hand, slicking my grip. I shake my head at the familiarity of the situation and risk a glance at my Queen. At my Xelora.

Never stop. Never slow.

A long tongue flicks out from between bony jaws, and the Skugga begins to lick my blood from its claws, shuddering in delight. I seize the opportunity and charge, but the beast antici-pates this and jumps, copying my move from earlier. *It is learning.*

Anxiety fills me, but I push it down and watch the beast's shadow pass overhead. When it reaches the apex of its arc, I launch myself backwards and roll. My timing is good. The Skugga lands directly in front of me as I push off the ground and swing. My axe connects with the back of its leg, releasing a thin ribbon of blood, and I laugh.

The demon does bleed.

The Skugga turns, but I'm already in the air, swinging my axe towards the creature's head, ready to end this fight.

But I have made an error. A horrible error. Everything happens in slow motion, like watching a kinetic dart descend towards a planet at relativistic speed. I cannot change the trajectory or result; all I can do is brace for the inevitable as the Skugga's powerful arm barrels towards me.

My muscles tense just before impact. Then it hits. Bones rattle. Pain spreads. The arena spins around me. I try to control my fall. No use. I hit the ground. Try to roll. But I tumble instead, and my vision blots out. *I have to get up. Have to move.* Pain becomes my entire existence as I push myself to my feet. *Where is the beast?* I glance up as something blocks the sun, and a second later, I am slammed into the sand with impossible force. A sharp metallic taste coats the inside of my mouth. And pressure, unimaginable pressure, pushes down on my chest.

The Skugga has me trapped beneath its foot.

My fingers dig into the furry flesh, and I push with every ounce of strength I have.

Nothing. No movement. Can't breathe.

Let go.

I am running out of options.

Axe. I need my axe.

A glint of metal catches my eye, more than an arm's length away. I claw at the sand, desperate to feel the smooth wood in my palm, but I cannot reach it. It is too far. I am failing her again. My Queen. They will rip her apart. They will...

I want to scream, but without air, I can't even clear the blood from my throat. I am trapped. There is no winning this. No getting free. Blood pounds beneath my skin. My head feels like it might burst. Hot sand glides between my fingers as I try again and again to reach the one thing that will save me.

But there is no use.

My eyes burn as I turn them upwards, towards the expanse of unfamiliar faces, searching for the woman whose heart is a panicked bird in my chest.

36

HE KNOWS

AMARA

MY BREATH HITCHES as a twenty-foot monster comes crashing into the arena.

That's not a gladiator... It doesn't even have a face. Just a skull on a body.

Gaius's voice cracks through the speakers. "For our final fight, I introduce a creature ..." I lose focus until he shouts the final word, "... Skugga."

Skugga.

The vibration of the creature's colossal steps rolls through the metal bars I cling to as Vexar stares the creature down. Somehow, he seems unfazed. Maybe even calm?

My tongue roams the chalky roof of my mouth. Teeth dig into my cheek. This is wrong. Everything about today has been wrong. The bath. The brutalized women. The disco-ball outfit. The conversation with Gaius. Yuxta's admission. This fucking monster.

I turn towards Gaius, a perverted grin splitting his face, and I feel the sharp points of some invisible trap closing in around me. My pulse quickens.

"What the hell is that?" I shout. "What did you do?" The roar of the crowd is so loud I can't hear my own voice, but Gaius stands and stalks towards me anyway.

He leans forward, less than a foot away from the cage, and shouts to be heard, "You should not have tried to kill me, little *jhyra*."

I don't know what a *'jhyra'* is, but the pet name sours my entire body anyway. My vision broadens, and an inhuman growl vibrates my chest. I want to pummel his face in until that sick smirk is gone and he's drowning in his own blood.

Gaius laughs. "Right there," he says, pointing at me. "That is how I knew."

What? He turns before I can ask what he means, so I shout after him. He ignores me.

How he knew, what? I search my mind for an explanation, but the horn blares, and my focus is pulled back to the arena just in time to see Vexar jump. He clears the massive creature in a single leap, and I swear the man is defying gravity. *I just need to trust him.*

Then everything falls apart. The Skugga's claws dig into Vexar's already injured shoulder. Gaius's laughter hits an impossible volume. And understanding slams into me like a gunshot to the spine.

He knows.

My blood goes cold as my pulse thunders in my ears.

Gaius knows about the bond. That's why Vexar's fighting monsters instead of gladiators. The feeling of being powerless to stop the nightmare unfolding before me reaches a point of complete hysteria. I've never felt like this before. Terrified, desperate, and powerless. And for some reason, my first instinct is to beg.

"Please!" I shout at Gaius. "Stop this!" There's no way Vexar can kill that thing. It's the size of a fucking school bus.

Gaius ignores me.

My skin is damp ice. I can't calm my breathing. I scream as the Skugga's massive arm slams into Vexar, knocking him out of the air and sending him tumbling across the arena like a ragdoll. My hands grip the bars of the cage. Metal digs into flesh. And I wait for him to get up. But he's not moving.

"Get up!" I scream, shaking the bars. "Get the fuck up!"

He stands, and for a split second, I feel hope. But that hope is ripped away as Vexar is pinned beneath a giant, hairy foot.

I choke out another cry. "Stop!" No one can hear me. The crowd is so loud it hurts. I turn to Gaius. "Stop! Please!" Nothing. My voice cracks with the effort. Vocal chords feel like they're ripping as I scream again and again and again. I pull on the cage door, plant my feet on each side of it, using every ounce of strength I have, desperate to get to Vexar. Desperate to do something. But the door won't move.

I slam my hands against the bars, again and again, screaming his name. But I'm trapped. Vexar can't hear me. Tears pour down my face.

He's going to die.

Help him.

'I can't,' I think as I drop to my knees and find the empty, silent thread still holding us together. It feels like picking up a dead bird, body limp and head lolling. I sob and pour all of my love, my strength, my energy, everything I have left into that thin thread. The silence I get back threatens to kill me—to stop my heart right here on the floor of the blood-stained cage.

Through the tears, I watch Vexar turn his face towards me, neck muscles straining with the effort, face bright red with a maze of bulging blood vessels.

"Please," I sob.

How can a storm like him fall? It shouldn't be possible. It can't be possible. I can't... I can't do this again. I can't lose everything. I can't lose *him*.

Then fight back.

"This wasn't supposed to happen!" I roar to whatever god might be listening. After everything, after all of the pain and the misery, I thought there was hope. I slam my fist into the floor of the cage and scream, "Give him back!" Something inside me shifts. My sorrow melts beneath a fire of desperate rage. A thousand knives dig into my very soul, holding me steady, keeping me angry. He will not die today. Not like this. He will not leave me. He will keep his promise, and he will get the fuck up.

I scream, not into the arena, but into our connection. *"Get up, you fucking asshole! You made me a promise and you're gonna keep it!"* He can't hear me, but I keep screaming anyway. *"Vexar!"* I'm so angry he made me trust him. *"You can't make me love you and then just leave! Fight back!"* Longing, sorrow, love, fear, anger, frustration, rage, and a thousand other emotions fill me, and in my mind I shatter that silent space between us with a final roar, *"Get up!"*

Vexar's eyes lock on mine, the distance between us shrinks, and a bolt of brutal electricity punches through me. My heart slams into my ribs, trying to rip out of my body, as I collapse.

37

TALRATH INCARNATE

VEXAR

IT IS A hallucination. A beautiful hallucination. Amara's voice fills my mind as the arena spins around me and the cold fingers of death grip my heart. I want to see her before the end. Hot sand burns my back. Blood pools in my throat. I keep searching the stands for my Queen, but I cannot find her. There are too many faces.

"Vexar!" I hear again, her voice like a soothing hand to the ache that is my entire existence. *"You can't make me love you and then just leave! Fight back!"*

Love. She loves me. I want to tell her I love her, too. I want to say that I am sorry, but I cannot speak. Cannot breathe. The pain spreads, burning across my chest and back as I keep searching, praying my eyes will find hers before I am truly lost.

LET GO.

A tsunami of emotion slams into me. My eyes go wide. Amara's voice pulses through me as my gaze finally lands on her. *"Get up!"* she screams.

My shadow pushes forward, and in the split second it takes for me to process Amara's words, I decide to let go. To let the shadow consume me. To give up my control to whatever savage beast the Zhyrrak has conjured. It is the only option I have. Ice-cold fire spreads through my veins. Both my hearts slam against my ribcage, again and again in perfect synchrony as a tempest takes my place and rage becomes my god.

My hands are moving, claws digging into the gargantuan foot, sinking deep and holding strong. My muscles creak, bones threaten to snap, but the foot moves. In the echo of the creature's deafening shriek, I am freed.

I roll away, sucking in air and sand, each breath like a lungfull of glass.

End them.

I am no longer a Vhorathi. I am something different. A monster with a singular purpose. Talrath incarnate. Smooth wood slides into my palm. I stalk towards the Skugga. A spray of blood bursts from my mouth, and I roar, "I am going to end you!"

The beast limps back, confused by the sudden shift in dynamic, and a dark laugh shakes my chest.

Out of the corner of my eye, I spot the disembodied foot of the Manta. There's a tug at the back of my mind, and instead of fighting it, I move with it, bending like grass in the wind. In the span of a single heartbeat, something strange happens. I feel the cool embrace of shadow around my logical mind, and then there is no separation. No difference between me and it. We become one until I am no longer watching from some distant place in my own mind; I am standing astride the darkness.

Logical thought crescendos in a symphony of intelligent, chaotic aggression.

The Skugga's footfalls thud against the ground. Time slows. A million thoughts flick through my mind, and I see the fight play out. I *know* what to do.

I dash forward, grab the Manta's severed foot, and launch it at the Skugga's face before it reaches me. With a swing of its long arm, the Skugga bats the flying appendage away, giving me an opening. I meet the beast with an upwards slash, carving muscle from bone along the creature's hip, and in the shower of gore, I hear it scream.

I spin out of the strike zone, sheath my axe, and dash to Nonus's corpse. Fighting is not about brute strength; it is about strategy. Strategy and the will to do what is necessary. With as much speed as I can muster, I sprint back to the Manta's corpse with Nonus's sword in hand.

Gaius left no time to clear the dead, and that will be his undoing.

I smile as I drag the flat of Nonus's blade up my bleeding arm. With a roar of effort, I launch the bloodied sword at the beast's face, grab a handful of mud created by the Manta's pooling blood, and charge. As expected, the beast is distracted by the bloody sword and doesn't register my charge until it is too late.

I jump and climb. The claws of my free hand dig through flesh and fur as I launch myself upwards. The surprised beast flails, swinging wildly in an attempt to swat me off, but those long arms are clumsy at such a close range. It can no longer bat me away.

I reach its bony head and shove the handful of mud into the creature's eye sockets. It bucks as I lock my legs around its neck and slide my hands around its jaws. With a roar of effort, I wrench the beast's mouth open, not stopping until I hear the crack of bone and the tearing of flesh. A gargled shriek breaks through. It thrashes. I fall, landing hard on my back. But I do not stop. I get to my feet. Ragged gasps shake my chest. The creature is digging at its eyes, trying to clear the mud, but only blinding itself further.

Somehow, it is still not dead. Its jaw hangs loosely from tendrils of torn flesh. Blood runs down its chest. But it does not die. I unsheathe my axe and start to swing, enraged by its resistance. *Why won't you die?* Rage turns my vision red, and by the time I stop swinging, the Skugga is little more than a pile of meat, and the arena is silent.

Heaving, bloodied, and furious, I turn towards Gaius, axe still clutched in my hand.

Amara is on her knees, gripping the bars of that barbaric cage, eyes wide and locked on me. *My Queen.* My body moves on pure instinct. I sheath my axe and march towards the wall of the arena, directly beneath the Magistrate's box, and I climb. Stone crumbles beneath my fingers. Rage curls in my gut. And by the time I reach the first landing, the crowd has already dispersed, clearing the way for the crazed gladiator. Clearing the way for *me.*

"Stop!" Gaius orders over the loudspeaker.

I do not.

Gaius lets out a nervous laugh and continues to speak.

I claim the next level, and the next, ignoring Gaius's words while ruining the walls of his precious arena.

A line of guards with pulse-sticks waits for me at the front of Gaius's box. The fools. I am the monster their parents warned them about, and I have come for my Queen. I pull myself up the final wall and release a deep, rumbling growl. Some of the guards scatter, their instinct for self-preservation winning out over their loyalty, but some remain.

Crackling electricity breaks the air, and I backhand the guard wielding the pulse-stick. He careens off the landing, and the remaining guards retreat in a flurry of panicked shouts.

To my surprise, Gaius remains by this throne, standing in place as if fleeing is not an option. I offer him a toothy snarl, and he responds with a growing puddle of piss between his perfectly polished shoes.

Ignoring the coward, I turn towards Amara. The bars of her

cage give way beneath my hands like warm wax, bending back and snapping with satisfying ease. For a moment, we just stare at each other. Then she launches herself through the opening, impacting my chest with a gasp, and wrapping her legs around my waist.

I hold onto her. My arms shake, but I do not let go. Her wide, damp eyes search my face. Trails of salt streak her cheeks. And a thousand words hang unsaid in the air between us.

"Are you ok?" she rasps, her voice cracking and frayed.

"Fine," I answer as I scan over her. Her hands are shackled, skin mottled with bruises and cuts, and her feet are bare and bloody. I lower her to the ground and inspect her shackles, searching for a way to release them. But I am distracted by the blood. Her hands are covered in it.

"Where are you injured?" I ask, scanning her body frantically.

"I'm fine," she insists. "It's not all mine." Her eyes flick behind me, and I understand. *She* is the reason for Gaius's bandaged hand.

I pull her against my chest again, working hard to keep the fear from my voice. "Are you ok?"

She nods, and before I can say anything else, Gaius clears his throat expectantly.

I growl, turning to face the pseudo-king of this shit planet while pulling Amara tight against my side. He is still standing in a puddle of his own piss, gripping his microphone in a shaking hand like it might protect him from me. His lips part, but before he can say a word, I wrap my fingers around a bar of the cage, wrench it free, and throw. The metal projectile impales the microphone, knocking it out of Gaius's grip and pinning it to the stone wall behind him. Shrill feedback pulses, then silence.

Gaius stares at his empty hand in confusion. Then horror. And like a fearful child, he runs.

Amara's entire body tenses against my side. Her weight shifts. And I feel the urge roll through her. *She is going to chase him.*

I move quickly, wrapping an arm around her waist and pulling her back into my chest. "Not today," I whisper into her ear.

She spins to face me, and it takes a moment to process what I am seeing. Two black eyes stare up at me. My knees hit the stone as I drop to be level with her. "Amara," I whisper, staring into the void-like darkness of her eyes, "breathe."

38

ON OUR OWN

AMARA

"**B**REATHE," VEXAR WHISPERS.

I shake my head, pulling against his grip as I watch Gaius disappear into the shadowy passageway. I don't want to breathe; I want to tear out Gaius's jugular. He was *laughing* while Vexar was dying, and I would really, really like to return the favor. *He can't have gotten that far. If I could just...*

Vexar turns my face back to his, sliding his thumbs over my cheeks. There's a deep, calming reverence in his gaze that I want to sink into.

But Gaius is so close.

"Stay with me," Vexar whispers.

But I...

Choose, a voice whispers in the back of my mind.

Can I even do that? I can hardly think straight. The rage is too much. I need to finish what I've started. I need to end Gaius.

Can you live without him?

The question is loud and commanding, and my answer is clear. *I can't.* I can't live without Vexar. Slowly, my fury melts, dripping down my spine and slipping away in the wind.

"We will come back for him. I promise," Vexar says.

I let out a heavy breath and nod. "Ok."

Vexar looks at me with a combination of gratitude and admiration and kisses me. He tastes like pain and sweat and joy, and I don't want to let go.

"We need to get out of here," he says against my mouth.

I suck in a sharp breath. "Did you get it?"

He releases me and reaches down to his grieves, pulling out a small, black device that looks a lot like a cellphone. It takes a considerable amount of effort not to pump my fist with excitement. While it's great we have a way to call Marius, we aren't out of danger yet, and I need to remember that.

Vexar stands and starts tapping on the small screen as I try to regain my situational awareness. My brain is still fuzzy, but I push through it. First things first. We need cover. I spin around, taking in the skybox we're in.

"We need to move," I say, planting a hand on Vexar's chest and guiding him back against one of the only two walls available. The box is shaped like a fat piece of pizza, with the crust facing the arena, and a passageway where you'd take your first bite—if you aren't a complete psycho, that is. The walls start about halfway back from the crust, and they end at the tip where the passageway is. Also, there's no roof. No matter where you stand, you can see about 300 degrees of a sniper's wet dream, and I'm dressed like a fucking disco ball. *Awesome.*

My fingers dig into the leather strap secured over the bandage wrapped around Vexar's ribs. "I've got a question for ya," I say as I use both hands to toss the leather strap over my shoulder. The metal cuffs burn my skin, but I ignore the pain and start working the bandage free. "If you were trying to kill someone at a distance without anyone seeing you, how would you do it?"

"What?" His eyes flick down to mine in confusion.

"Don't stop what you're doing, just answer me. I need to know what I'm looking for here. Do y'all have sniper rifles? Like, am I looking for people or robots or what?"

"Reflected light or movement. No robots."

Alright. Same as Earth. Cool.

My eyes flick between all the high points around the arena while I finish unwrapping the bandage so I can use it on his shoulder. When the bandage is free, I glance down at his exposed ribs and groan. A deep purple bruise has started to form, and it looks bad. Really fucking bad. I watch his face as I press my fingers into the bruise. No reaction. Ok...

Prioritize and execute.

I start packing the wounds on his shoulder with the gauze that somehow made it out of the fight mostly clean, and ask, "Is it working?"

"Patience," he says, still focused on the screen.

Right, yeah. Patience. I've got a shit ton of that.

About two minutes later, the wounds are packed, and I use the leather strap to secure it all in place. It looks ridiculous, but the bleeding has slowed, so I'm considering it a win.

My hair whips against my face, stinging my skin and pulling my attention to the weather. "The dust storms are rolling in," I warn. Our safety hinges on being in the public eye, and if we don't hurry, we're going to lose that safety net. I glance down at the stands. "And people are starting to leave."

"I know," Vexar says.

With Vexar as patched up as I can get him, I turn my full attention to our surroundings. We're in the worst place imaginable right now, and there's nowhere else to go.

"How much longer?" I ask, shifting nervously and trying to ignore the burning pain in my feet.

"Marius?" Vexar says. He's holding the device to his ear like a cellphone. *It must be working.* There's a beat of silence, and Vexar starts speaking quickly in Vhorathi. My translator tries to keep up, but the wind must be interfering with the microphone because it's missing every other word.

Sand swirls around us as my eyes flick between sectors, praying I don't see a flash of light. Hopefully, this storm moves faster than the crowd. The last thing we need is an empty arena while we're still sitting in the open.

Movement at the back of the box catches my eye, and three guards step out carrying guns. Not cattle-prods. Guns.

Fuck...

I jab Vexar with my elbow.

He says something else into the holoCom and shoves the device in my hands. "Work with Marius. Get the ship here."

"But I—"

"Amara," he says sternly, not taking his eyes off the guards.

I raise the device to my ear as Vexar takes a few threatening steps towards the three newcomers. They don't raise their weapons, and Vexar doesn't take out his axe. Yet.

"Marius?" I ask, hoping he speaks English.

"You must be Amara," Marius says. I let out a sigh of relief. I don't think my translator works with phones ... or holoComs, or whatever.

"I am." I press my back against the wall as Vexar unsheathes his axe and rounds the raised dais, where Gaius's throne sits. "Are you working on getting the ship here?"

There's a moment of silence before Marius says, "Sure."

"Well, the sooner the better. We have company."

"I am aware."

Vexar takes a few more cautious steps, drawing the attention of all three guards. The wind roars past my ears, but I can still see at least 300 yards. The storm hasn't hidden us yet.

"What do you need from me?" I ask.

"Tell me about your bond with Vexar."

I frown. "I don't think now's the best time for a story," I say, sliding along the wall while keeping my eyes bouncing between all the potential hazards. So far, none of the guards have made a move, but I can feel the tension. We're one spark away from this all going to shit.

"Indulge me," Marius says calmly.

Fine. "He was wounded. Gaius set the whole thing up. I entered—"

"No," he interrupts. "You misunderstand me. I want to know about the bond." There's a sharp inhale before he continues. "How did he realize you had bonded? Did you accept it? Did you complete the blood exchange?"

"Blood exchange?" I ask.

"Yes, did you exchange blood?"

"Why would we—" I cut myself short as a chill runs down my spine. *How does Marius know about the bond?* I clear my throat and consider my next words carefully. "What exactly did Vexar tell you?" My eyes catch on the metal bar that's still pinning Gaius's microphone to the wall, and I start inching towards it.

Marius doesn't respond.

Vexar was talking to Marius for less than a minute. There's no way he had time to talk about our bond.

"Marius?" I ask, breaking the silence.

"Did Vexar tell you he made a small fortune off investments in the very company that landed you in your ... current line of work?"

My mouth goes dry as I realize what's happening. Marius is trying to drive a wedge between me and Vexar.

He's not on our side.

I take a few more steps towards the metal bar. It's about two feet away now. Almost close enough to reach if my hands weren't shackled together and trying to hold the holoCom to my ear. "You're not working on getting the ship here, are you?"

There's a heavy sigh before Marius says, "Unfortunately, I've been locked out of the onboard systems."

Vexar said Marius was the *only* person with that access, so why is he locked out? Is he lying?

I creep closer to the metal bar, moving slowly to avoid drawing attention. There's a haze of sand in the air now, clouding my view of my arena. It's good. In this weather, I doubt a sniper could get a clean shot. *Unless they have thermal scopes.* Shaking off that terrifying thought, I pin the holoCom between my shoulder and ear and extend my hand towards the bar.

"How about you stop reaching for that weapon and just go with the guards, yes? It would make our lives so much easier," Marius says coolly.

I drop my hands and spin in a circle. *He's fucking watching us?*

Focusing on keeping my voice calm, I ask, "So, did you decide to take a trip to the desert, or are you more of an 'experience it from home' kinda guy?"

My eyes scan for a camera, but I don't see anything obvious. Then again, Yuxta did say, "They are watching."

I need to get Vexar's attention.

There's a chuckle on the other end of the line as the guards raise their weapons. But their fingers aren't on the triggers. *They're waiting for something...*

Oh, fuck me. They're waiting on Marius, aren't they?

I try to think back to everything Vexar told me about his oldest friend and advisor. He took care of Vexar and his siblings when they were little. He helped guide Vexar's training for the arena. He—

God damnit.

Marius helped Vexar investigate the Tusku slave-ships. I was right. It's not just Gaius.

"Why do you want him dead?" I ask, as I grip the holoCom too tightly.

"It's nothing personal."

"Are you sure about that? Cause it's starting to *feel* a little personal." I need to keep Marius talking. If he's the one ordering those guards, I need to distract him while I figure out how to tell Vexar what's going on.

"Trust me, this is much more than a personal matter."

"Oh, great. I feel so much better, thank you…" I suck down a deep breath and regret it as the hot, sandy air burns my throat. Holding back a cough, I ask, "Do you still want to know about the bond?" With shaky hands, I reach down and start to unwrap the gauze from my knee.

"Is someone trying to strike a deal?" Marius asks slyly.

"Sure," I answer, parroting his earlier response as I wrap the gauze over my mouth and nose.

"Then yes, tell me everything, and we can go from there."

Everything. "Alright," I say slowly, as my brain works over-time trying to decide what I should and shouldn't reveal. "For starters, he can feel my heartbeat in his chest."

"Obviously."

"And my emo—" Wait. Did Vexar actually hear me when I screamed at him through our connection earlier? I feel like he did.

"And?" Marius prompts.

Shit. Focus. "Uh, he can feel my pleasure. When he makes me come …" I continue describing, in great detail, the most uncom-fortable things I can think of while mentally screaming Vexar's name into the space between us. A few seconds later, Vexar's eyes flick to mine. *Holy shit. I think it worked.* "As far as connec-tions go, it's pretty powerful. I've never come so hard …" I keep rambling out loud, while I shout internally at Vexar, saying, *"Marius is not a friend! We have to go. No ship."*

"What about your shade? Has that made an appearance?" Marius asks.

"My shade?" I parrot. I'm still not certain if Vexar can hear me, so I repeat myself a few more times, praying for another sign of acknowledgement.

Marius hums and then asks, "Have his eyes gone black?"

"Black? No. Should they?" I'm not sure why I'm keeping this piece of information from Marius, but I'm running on gut instinct here, and it feels like he really cares about this detail. I keep talking to Vexar through our connection, adding, *Marius is watching. He's going to kill us. We need to go.*

Vexar finally looks at me, his eyes narrowed with confusion. *He definitely heard me.*

"He's not sending the ship. We're on our own," I tell Vexar.

Marius makes a non-committal sound. "So he has not exhibited any ... violent tendencies? Beyond the incident in the arena?"

"No. He's been a perfect gentleman. You on the other ha—"

A loud crack splits the air. Gunshot. My body reacts automatically, and I drop to the ground. If Marius is the one calling the shots, it's clear he's done talking.

Vexar lunges towards the guards, sweeping one of them off the edge of the box with his axe. I tuck the holoCom between my boobs as another crack pierces the air. With as much speed as I can muster, I crawl along the wall, scramble to my knees, and wrap my fingers around the metal bar. With a heaving tug, the bar pops free, and the microphone drops. Wielding my improvised weapon, I turn towards the melee.

Vexar's moving on the second guard, but the third has turned towards me. I tighten my grip, wincing as the cuffs dig into my flexed forearms.

The guard steps forward, weapon raised, but he doesn't shoot.

Idiot.

I take a short step before lunging and swinging. The bar impacts the guard at his knees. I take another step, bringing myself nearly chest-to-chest with the guy, and slam my elbow into the barrel of his gun, pushing it away. It goes off. Heat sears the back of my arm. I swing again, aiming higher. There's a nasty crack as the bar hits his head and he crumples.

I say a silent "Thank you" to Gunny Biggs for all the hours he spent kicking my ass. Who woulda thought I'd need to whack someone with a stick one day?

Something grabs me from behind, and I spin, already swinging, but a massive hand stops the bar.

"Holy fuck," I pant as I recognize the hand and let go.

Vexar drops the bar, and it clatters to the stone as I glance around us. Two of the guards lay in bloody pools, but the third is missing. Where did the third— *Oh, right.* He was launched over the edge and is probably somewhere in the stands below.

"What do you mean, 'there is no ship'?" Vexar asks, grabbing my chin and staring down at me.

"Marius isn't who you think he is, and he isn't calling your ship."

Vexar's brows drop, and he gives me a hard, uncertain look.

"There's no time. Please, just trust me. We need to go." My eyes dart between Vexar and the shadowy passageway that could be hiding more guards. "If we go now, we can still use the crowd as cover."

The muscles in his jaw tick. Then he sweeps me off my feet, sets my ass in the crook of his left arm, and takes off towards the edge of the box. He jumps from the box onto the nearby staircase and somehow manages to keep me from falling. I toss my cuffed hands around his neck, and I hang on for dear life as he bounds down the stairs. This is not a normal way to be carried, and it's terrifying. Sure, he's holding onto my thighs, but I'm literally just sitting on his forearm.

We hit the first level of stadium-style seating, and through the sandy haze, a crowd appears. I expect Vexar to slow, but he doesn't. He barrels onward, propelling us into the densest part of the throng as people dive out of the way. Shouts of terror spill from the trembling faces around us, and I watch in horror as the crowd surges forward like a wave, condensing and colliding in a dangerous, writhing mass.

"Vexar, someone's going to get killed," I shout over the noise.

They're terrified of him, and who can blame them? They just saw him brutally kill a monster, and now he's charging through them, carrying an axe, covered in blood, and looking absolutely deranged.

"Vexar!" I shout, as someone in front of us is swallowed up by the horde.

"Hold this." He shoves his axe into my hands. It's awkward and impossibly heavy. My arms shake as I do everything in my power not to drop it. A second later, Vexar pulls someone up from the ground. It's the person who fell.

A furry face and yellow eyes lock on Vexar, and instead of terror, I see gratitude. They exchange a few words, and when the badger-like alien is walking on their own, I hand the axe back to Vexar and shout, "Put this away." He doesn't need it right now, and it's just freaking people out.

He listens to me, but his expression stays static. He looks like a statue, and it's starting to worry me. On top of that, his eyes are still black, and our connection's empty. I press my forehead into his cheek and whisper, "It's ok. We're ok."

As the visibility gets worse, the crowd seems to calm, and so do I. I might be dressed like a fishing lure, but in this storm, we're just as invisible as everyone else.

"Do you still have the holoCom?" he asks.

I pull the device from my top and hold it out, staring wide-eyed at the illuminated screen. I guess Marius didn't end the call.

Vexar takes the device like it weighs more than I do, and slowly raises it to his ear. "Marius," he says coldly. There's a long pause, and his expression hardens. "Is it true?" he asks. A moment later, the holoCom turns to dust in his hand.

39

ALL I NEED

AMARA

"THE GATE IS there," Vexar says, pointing at nothing but a wall of orange haze. The storm is thick and punishing, like being sandblasted in a convection oven.

I pull down the strip of gauze covering my mouth and shout, "Where?"

He shakes his head and reaches for my hand before remembering I'm still cuffed and offering me his arm instead. I grip his elbow and follow.

I'm not sure how he knows where the dockyard is—I can't see more than a few feet right now—but he's confident, and I'm learning to trust that. We also haven't run into any more guards. I want to say it's because of the storm, but the sinking feeling in my spine suggests something different.

We follow a long fence line, trudging through shin-deep sand drifts that tug at my torn feet and leave me cursing under my breath with every step. Shit burns. Bad. But I don't complain.

After what feels like an eternity, we stop, and Vexar points to my ear. "Your translator. We need to remove it. It may have a tracking device."

I hadn't even considered that, but the thought is terrifying. It would also explain how I was found after my first escape attempt.

"Do it," I say loudly so he can hear me over the wind.

His hand runs up the side of my neck, coaxing a shiver from me despite the heat. Then there's a crunching sound and a sharp pain. I massage the sore cartilage as he launches the device into the hazy abyss.

When he looks back at me, his face pales. "I hurt you."

My fingers come away from my ear, tacky with blood. It's not too bad, so I wipe my hand on my thigh and nod at his shoulder. "My ear isn't the priority right—"

"*You* are my priority. Always," he interrupts before turning his attention to the fence.

Three-inch diameter metal rods reach vertically into the haze above us, separating us from the dockyard beyond. Climbing it isn't an option. I'm about to ask what the plan is when Vexar wraps his hands around two of the bars and bends them outwards with ease. My jaw drops. I know he bent the bars of the cage earlier, but those bars were tiny in comparison. This ... this shouldn't even be possible.

Scratching my forehead, I ask, "Uh, is that a new skill, or ...?"

"New," he says, waving me through the gap.

Gripping his arm, I let him guide me in a zigzagging pattern that makes no sense until I look up. "Holy shit," I whisper. Massive shapes loom like foggy shadows in the swirling sand. They're ships. Giant ships.

We stop a moment later, and Vexar says, "In. Quickly."

Confused, I look around. Then I notice the ramp. But the ramp doesn't seem to go anywhere; it just goes up into ... nothing. *Weird.*

He gives me a gentle nudge, and I start up the ramp. Cold metal presses into my bare feet. I freeze. That familiar metallic scent burns my nose. Heart races. Panic takes over. *No, no, no.* I start backing down the ramp. *Need to get away.* Something stops me. I spin, ready to dart past the obstacle, but it's not an obstacle; it's Vexar. He's knelt at the base of the ramp, staring up at me with sad eyes. His hands grip my waist. I try to move, but he's too strong.

"Amara," he says gently. "It is not safe out here. We have to get on this ship."

My head shakes, mouth moves, but no sound comes out. I can't do this. I can't get on another spaceship. I should have known this would be a problem. He's going to have to leave me here. Every cell in my body *knows* if I get on that ship, I'll die. It will be the end of me.

"I am sorry," he says, and then his hands tighten around my waist, sending a fresh surge of panic through me. I know what's about to happen. He's going to pick me up. He's going to force me on that ship.

"No!" I scream. I try to push him away, but my hand hits his wounded shoulder, and he flinches. I freeze, watching as he tries to hide the pain, but he can't. It's written all over his face. As clear as anything I've ever seen. His bright green eyes tense, lips press together in a tight line, and a deep furrow digs between his brows.

What the fuck am I doing?

The panic vanishes, embarrassment hits, and then purpose takes over. I narrow my focus on his shoulder, at the blood dripping from his elbow, and I let everything else disappear. If I don't stop that bleeding, he might lose consciousness, and I'll have no way of getting him out of danger. We have to move. Now.

"Up the ramp," I order.

Vexar looks confused, but I shake my head and lead the way, ignoring the intense roar of blood in my ears. I'm shaking and ready to vomit, but I keep moving. Cold metal burns my skin, desperate to drag me back to that box, but I just keep focusing on Vexar. On his injury. On the way he tried to hide his pain so I wouldn't feel guilty.

We reach the top of the ramp, and I start pulling at the buckles on his axe-holder-thing.

"Amara," he whispers.

I shake my head. "No. If you're going to fly us—"

"Amara," he interrupts.

I let out a frustrated growl. "Unless you want me to be completely fucking useless for the rest of the day, you're going to stop looking at me like that and let me do my god damned job."

He looks conflicted, but after a moment, he glances down and says, "Your hands are still shackled."

***

ONCE MY HANDS ARE FREE, I manage to convince Vexar to sit in one of the two bucket seats on the bridge. He put up quite the fight, insisting that he take care of my feet first, but I'm not the one who has to fly us out of here.

"Are you ok?" he asks, watching my shaking hands.

"I'm fine." Or close enough. The ship is less ... ship-like ... than I expected, and if it weren't for that faint metallic scent and the cold metal deck beneath my feet, I might be able to forget it's a ship at all. My adrenaline's still pumping, and every sound keeps making me jump, but I'm focused on getting Vexar stable enough to fly. That's all I can do right now.

The ship's med-kit is well-stocked but confusing. Most of the items are things I've never seen before, and everything's labeled in Vhorathi. After some digging, I manage to find a couple of pre-loaded syringes that look a lot like morphine shots. I hold them up. "Are any of these for pain?"

He grabs one of the syringes, flicks off the cap, and jams it into his thigh. "Vok," he groans, letting his head fall back as the automatic plunger releases the drug into his system.

I raise my brows. "I was going to ask if those might interfere with your ability to fly, but I guess we'll just, uh ... worry about that later."

A whisper of our connection flits through the back of my mind before quickly disappearing again.

With a sigh, I stand from my crouched position and ask, "Why can't I feel you anymore? Are you blocking me out?"

He makes a pained grunt and looks at the display that's showing an image of what I assume is outside. It's just a wall of orange that shifts as gusts of wind shake the ship beneath our feet.

The bridge is simple. An oval-shaped room, two bucket seats, a display that curves along the forward bulkhead, and a control panel that spans the length of the display. The control panel looks like a long piece of glass, but when Vexar touches it, symbols appear. And then there's Vexar, leaned back in the port-side bucket seat, covered in the evidence of the war he just fought for us. It's clear his mind is no less affected than his body, and my heart breaks for him. Today was a complete shit-show. Our plan might have gotten us out alive, but in the process, everything else seemed to fall apart.

I rub the back of my arm over my eyes, abrading my skin with the grit that covers my entire body. I don't know what to say. I don't know if there's anything I can say.

"Come here, please," Vexar whispers. His hand wraps around the back of my thigh, tugging me closer as he appraises me with a distant longing, like I'm a million miles away and never coming back.

"I'm right here," I whisper.

He nods, but it's clear he doesn't fully believe it.

"Don't we need to get out of here?" I ask.

"We have time."

With that, I place my hands on the sides of his neck and climb onto his lap, hoping the closeness will help ease some of his anguish. It feels a bit odd at first, like I'm sitting in the lap of a stranger, but the feeling fades the moment his hands find my hips. It's hard to remember how new this is, especially when it feels like I've always known him.

"Talk to me, please," I say, pushing the sweat-soaked hair from his face.

His expression doesn't change, but his eyes shift uncomfortably. "I did not want to do it," he whispers. "That manta was innocent... It did not know why it was there, or what it was meant to do. It was just an animal." He closes his eyes. "And I butchered it."

A lump forms in my throat. "I'm so sorry."

In a voice so quiet I almost miss it, he asks, "Do you think I am a monster?"

My eyes close as I try to hold back the sadness his question brings before I shake my head and say, "No. Never."

"You saw what I did to the Skugga."

I blow out a breath and rest my forehead against his, right between his horns. "Do you want an honest answer, or a nice one?"

"Honest."

"What happened with the Skugga was ... bad—maybe the most savage thing I've ever seen. But it wasn't evil. And it doesn't mean you're a monster." His eyes lock on mine, green instead of black, as I stroke the sides of his face. "I've seen monsters. *Real* monsters." Memories from my past push forward, but I fight them back, trying to stay present. "You are nothing like them. Nothing." My voice cracks, but I keep going.

"What you did today was motivated by love, not hate or fear or greed. You did it because you had no other choice. Because this was the only way to help a lot of people who *need* your help." People like Roveen and those women from the bath. "Real monsters commit atrocities for personal gain, or out of fear, or because they don't believe other people have value unless those people are useful to them. You are the furthest thing from a monster, Vexar."

He's silent for a long moment before saying, "But I *wanted* the violence. I *craved* it."

"Why?" I ask. His brow furrows and he shifts uncomfortably, not understanding what I'm asking. "Why did you crave the violence? Was it because you hated those other gladiators, or was it because you"—I take a steadying breath—"was it because you wanted to protect me?"

His eyes say a thousand words in a single second. There's a deep sadness there, but also a heavy truth that scares me a little. A truth that he would do more to protect me than he's willing to admit.

I press a gentle kiss to his cheek. "If there's one thing I know to be true, it's that the violence we're capable of in the name of love is so much greater than the violence born of hate."

"So you do not fear me?" he whispers.

"No," I answer, "the only way you could make me fear you is by denying me your honesty." The corners of his eyes crinkle as he notices my choice of words. Then I add, "So please, don't hide from me. Don't shut me out."

"That is all you need? Honesty?" he asks.

"That's all I need."

Seeming to accept this, he nods, and a moment later our connection bursts open. His emotions flow through the back of my mind like a gentle wave, washing away the uncomfortable feeling of detachment. He's full of shame and sorrow, but now he doesn't have to carry it alone.

We sit in silence, just holding each other and breathing deeply, until I fear we've been here for too long.

I lean back. "We should probably get out of here. And I need to patch your shoulder."

He frowns. "I have something I need to tell you first."

I feel the distressing sadness that accompanies those words, and anxiety tightens my gut. "Ok," I say slowly.

"My sister, Aelrith, was working with Gaius..."

40

WOULDN'T CHANGE ANYTHING

VEXAR

"I S THAT IT?" Amara asks.

"For now," I say as I start up the autopilot system and release the controls.

On the view-screen, Calidus shrinks behind us, a textured sphere of oranges and browns losing its detail as we head into the darkness of space.

Amara rubs her eyes and leans back in her seat. "It went faster than I thought it would." Her face, lit by the cool glow of the view-screen, scrunches. "Wait, we're in space, right?" I nod, and she lifts one of her arms into the air before letting it fall to her lap. "Then why is there still gravity? Shouldn't we be floating or something?"

"This ship has a gravity generator."

"That's a real thing?"

"Yes. As I understand it, the generator bends space-time by exploiting the thing that gives particles mass." She raises a single brow, and I shrug. "I do not fully understand it myself. The technology was stolen, so I doubt even our engineers really understand it."

"Stolen? From who?"

"The Tusku," I answer. "It is how we obtained most of our technology. They tried to invade our planet a long while ago, but they were overconfident and unaware of our own capabilities. It took less than a year—a Vhorathi year—for my ancestors to take control of multiple Tusku ships and turn their weapons against them."

"You didn't have weapons of your own?"

"Nothing like what the Tusku had. They had been engineering stars for longer than our people had language."

"And you still managed to overpower them?"

I shrug and narrowly avoid wincing as the action makes my shoulder burn with a fresh intensity. "The Tusku might be technologically advanced, but that has made them overconfident and soft. We allowed our warriors to be captured and imprisoned on their ships, and then we took their ships from the inside."

"That's ... wow. That's impressive." She bites her lip and asks, "What did the Tusku want?"

"I do not know."

She hums and her eyes flick from the view-screen to my shoulder. "It's weird that no one's come after us," she says as she unclips her harness and pulls the medical bag from beneath her seat.

"It is," I agree.

After learning that both Gaius and Marius are aware of our bond, my mind has been mulling over the strangeness of our escape. It feels like we are still missing something. My sister. Gaius. Marius? They must all be working together, and that does not bode well for us.

When I told Amara about my sister's probable involvement, she was concerned, and I cannot blame her. At this point, it is clear that returning to Vhorath would be unwise. For all we know, my sister has already claimed my throne. The thought is disquieting. Aelrith is dangerous, not just to us, but to everyone. I cannot allow her to rule the empire.

Amara hoists the medical bag into her lap and starts digging through it. "I still don't know how Gaius figured it out. Our bond, I mean."

"Your eyes," I muse.

"Eyes?"

"They went black. Like mine."

She looks up with her hands still in the bag. "Did you see them go black?" I nod, and she tenses. "When?"

"After I got you out of that cage and Gaius ran away. You wanted to chase him, and your eyes went black. Not fully, but I could no longer see the brown."

She grimaces and scratches her hairline. "Shit, I guess I shouldn't have tried to stab him..." With a sigh, she adds, "I thought maybe he figured it out because I got murderously protective over you." I frown, and she holds up a hand, palm out. "In my defense, he was saying some *wild* shit."

"Is that why his hand was bandaged and you are covered in his blood?" I ask, glancing at the cuts and scrapes that cover her exposed skin. The sight of her injuries sends a confusing mixture of guilt and rage through me. It is clear what happened, and I do not like it. It makes me feel violent.

She hums and goes back to digging through the medical bag before stopping and growling in frustration. "I was so close!" Her hands cover her face, and she shakes her head. "Inches away from his fucking jugular, and then"—she drops her hands —"I got shocked or something."

I secure the flight controls and unclip my harness. "Gaius wears an electron shield generator. That is why you could not kill him—not with a solid-state weapon anyway."

She rubs her nose and looks away. "Do you think that's how Marius found out? Gaius told him?"

The mention of Marius sends a fresh ache through my heart, but I manage to answer anyway. "Most likely, yes."

She proceeds to fill me in on the details of her conversation with Marius, including everything she did not tell me earlier. With each new word, a little more of my foundation crumbles away.

"He was really interested in it," she says before returning her focus to the medical bag.

I wish I knew what all this means, but we do not have enough information to come to any real conclusion. As much as I want to use the comms to contact home and get answers, we cannot. Not until we are a safe distance from Calidus. This ship was built for stealth, not war, so until we are out of range of Calidus's sensors, we must stay quiet.

With an array of items set in her lap, Amara lowers the medical kit to the ground. "He asked if we'd exchanged blood. Do you know what that means?"

"Maybe." I scrub a hand over my face and stare at the viewscreen where distant stars have begun to appear as faint pinpricks of light. "But I am not sure of much anymore."

"Tell me what you do know, and we can go from there." There is no recrimination in her tone, no distrust, only a desire to understand, and I love her for it. She knows I am just as lost as she is, and her acceptance of that gives me hope.

I lean towards her, expecting to take her hands in mine, but she dodges my grip and reaches for my shoulder instead. Her fingers dig under the leather strap, and I do my best to compartmentalize the pain.

"On Vhorath, there is a ritual of sorts," I explain, hoping "ritual" is the correct term. "It is done when two people choose to be together—like marriage—and they call it a blood-binding. While it is symbolic now, its origin stems from the Zhyrrak bonds." I bite back a hiss as she starts removing the packed gauze. It is hideously painful. "From what I have been told, it was originally used to make a bond permanent. To make it stronger." Unable to resist, I glance down at her knee where an angry, pink cut stands proudly against her pale skin. A testament to the power of fate.

She follows my gaze, and I feel her burst of surprise as she drops her hands to her lap, fists full of bloody gauze. "Are you saying we already did it? The blood-exchange? By accident?"

I glance away. "Maybe." Then I sigh. "Yes. I believe we did."

"But, is it supposed to be literal? Like actually swapping blood?"

"Yes."

She balls up the soiled gauze and sets it to the side. "Well, that's a surprising custom."

"Is that your only concern?" I ask as I stare at her in confusion.

She shrugs and picks up the bottle of liquid wound cleaner. "That, and our blood swap—or whatever it's called—is incomplete. I got some of yours, but you didn't get any of mine."

I hum, surprised by how little concern she has. "Can I ask you something?" She nods. "If you did not think our bond was permanent, would you feel differently about ... us?"

Her lips press together before she says, "No. It wouldn't change anything for me."

41

HOME

AMARA

I HISS OUT an expletive as Vexar rinses my feet with whatever torture-fluid is in that damn spray bottle. "Is it supposed to sting this bad?" I ask.

Vexar's face pulls into a confused expression. "It does not sting."

"Maybe not for you, but for the rest of us mortals, it sucks."

He narrows his eyes. "I am mortal."

I pat the side of his face with a smile. "Keep telling yourself that big-guy."

To my surprise, he laughs. It's the first time he's laughed since we left the cell.

Over the past hour, I've come to terms with being on a ship again, and my nervous system has settled down considerably. Sure, the metal decking beneath my feet is still freaking me out, but beyond that, I think I'm doing ok. And, after getting a better look at Vexar's shoulder, I'm feeling must less stressed. The lacerations are deep, but they're clean and were relatively easy to patch up with the regen-tape. Roveen was right, the stuff is pretty great. I'm still concerned about his ribs, but there isn't much I can do about that. His pain tolerance is too high for me to get an accurate read on what might be wrong.

"Is there any way to get an X-ray of your chest?" I ask.

He smooths another piece of regen-tape over the bottom of my foot and asks, "X-ray?"

"Like an image. Of your ribs. To make sure nothing's seriously wrong."

Lifting my feet, he carefully inspects his handiwork. "Everything is fine, but if you are worried, we can have one done on Vhorath." He pauses and frowns. "Or when we get to wherever we are going."

"Where are we going?" I ask.

"There is a planet with a rocky moon on the outskirts of this star system. It has no atmosphere, but it is tidally locked. We can land there and remain hidden until we have a plan." He's pretending to be calm and confident, but I can feel his fear and disappointment. He wanted to go home so badly.

"Well," I say lightly, "with any luck, we can go home soon."

His eyes flick up to mine and he stares at me with a quiet intensity, as if I've just anchored myself to him in a way no one else ever has. "Home?" he asks. "As in, Vhorath?"

As casually as I can, I say, "Yeah, home."

Without a word, he lowers my feet to the deck, drops the roll of regen-tape, and stands. Black eyes full of intense desire prickle my skin as he leans over me, gripping the back of my chair. The material creaks beneath his hands. With a subtle raise of my chin, he moves, scooping me into his arms and carrying me off the bridge. I tighten my legs around his waist and kiss up his neck, tasting the salt on his skin and feeling his pulse against my lips.

We reach a small, empty room lined with gray tile, and he lowers me to the ground, eyes still swirling black.

With careful hands, he works the beaded top over my head,

avoiding the raw skin on my elbows and back. His fingers trail down my sides, and with a pull of his claws, he releases the skirts from my waist. The fabric pools around my feet. Beads scatter. And Vexar drops to his knees before me.

He's focused and reverent as his eyes roam my skin, finding every scrape and bruise, examining each of them as if he's taking inventory of the harm done to me. My throat tightens as he begins to kiss each one. When he reaches the raised cut on my knee, he pauses. His eyes meet mine, and he guides my hands to his shoulders before lifting my leg and pressing a sorrowful kiss over the cut that sealed our bond.

This entire time, he's been struggling with the knowledge that a simple accident may have trapped me in something I didn't understand and hadn't agreed to. He was terrified to tell me because there wasn't any way to reverse it. He knew I would panic and feel trapped, and he was right. If he had told me when it happened, I would have wanted to run. But not anymore. That small cut is a symbol of how little control we had over our bond and how perfectly it worked out anyway.

He traces the circular burn marks on my stomach, courtesy of the cattle-prod, and a wave of guilt leaves him. With his hands on my lower back, he lets out a heavy exhale and hugs my stomach to the side of his face. The muscles of his neck relax beneath my hands. His right horn presses against the curve of my ribs, curling up around my breast as if it were sculpted to fit exactly there. And then his guilt turns to gratitude. An over-whelming gratitude that blurs my vision.

This is the most vulnerable I've seen him—knelt before me, face pressed to my skin, eyes closed, and a deep calm in his mind. He's always so stoic, and seeing him this way feels like I'm being let in on a deep secret. A truth he shares with no one else.

Eventually, his eyes meet mine and he stands. In slow move-ments, I undress him. The sound of creaking leather and short breaths surrounds us. My fingers trail over his skin, feeling the raised lines of tendons, blood vessels, and scars. He tenses and shudders, fists clenching at his sides and eyes following my every movement.

When the last of his armor falls away, he leans down and pulls me into a kiss that is both passionate and claiming. I love the way he kisses me. The heady desperation of it. The heat of his mouth, the rough feel of his hands, the desire that clouds his emotions, and the intense look in his eyes when he breaks away. It's like he can't get enough of me. Like he's consumed by the idea of me.

Water begins to rain from overhead, it drips off the end of his nose, catches on his eyelashes, and all I can think is that he's the most beautiful man I've ever seen. Every perfect imperfection. Every crease and scar. His life story written on his skin.

A pleasant, woody smell perfumes the air as he lathers a bar of soap between his hands. He drags his fingers through my hair, and a wanton moan escapes my lips. I've never had a lover wash me before, and it's ... fuck. It's nice. My back presses against his abdomen as he rubs my scalp in soft, caressing motions.

His strong hands begin to move down my body, rubbing gentle circles over my skin before dipping between my legs. My knees go weak but he holds me steady. The heat of his breath ghosts over my ear. His lips press to my neck. Then he's on his knees again, spinning me to face him and running his hands down my legs as ripples of murky water disappear between the tiles at my feet.

42

NO MORE SECRETS

VEXAR

AMARA IS THE only person in the galaxy who will ever see me kneel before them. Her skin flushes as I work my hands down her legs, mesmerized by the soft feel of her body and the way she grips my shoulders like I am the only stable thing in the world.

Somehow, she was not gravely injured today, and I have never felt more grateful for anything. When I saw the blood on her hands, the terror was too much. I feared that after everything I had done, after everything we had survived, it still might not be enough. But she is safe. She is here. We are together. And there are no secrets left between us.

I gaze up at her face, and all I can think is how much I already love this woman. She has seen my darkest shadows, seen the monster that lurks within, yet she does not recoil. If anything, she draws closer. The more I reveal to her, the more she leans in.

The scent of veladoo wood grows strong as she takes the soap from me, but the scent of soap cannot overpower the scent of her desire. It grows stronger by the minute, overwhelming my senses and urging me towards the apex of her thighs. When I fear I can no longer resist, she steps behind me.

The thread between us snaps tight as the tension grows. It is all-consuming. Her fingers comb out my braid, massage my scalp, and run the length of my horns as jolts of lightning snake over my skin. My cock jerks. Fingers dig into the muscles of my thighs. My shadow no longer fights for control, but it is ever-present. Hungry. Ravenous. Not for violence, but for pleasure. *Her* pleasure.

Amara's knees make a quiet sound as they meet the tile behind me. Her soft thighs part and slide around my hips, as the heady scent of her arousal rises.

Suds drip down my abdomen and her hands follow, sliding lower until they reach the top of my groin. My vision broadens and my skin attunes to every touch, every shift of air, every drip of water. My breath hitches. The throb between her legs echoes down my spine.

Suddenly, I am standing, towering over her kneeling form. I suck in a ragged breath. Her skin is slick and shining. Her wet hair, the color of night. And her eyes burn with an unmistakable hunger.

I struggle to stay present as her hands roam my legs. The bar of soap makes a quiet thunk as it hits the floor. Her teeth catch her bottom lip. In one swift motion, I lift her to my chest and walk us towards the bedroom, leaving a trail of water in our wake.

Her legs wrap around me as her lips dance over my neck. Her teeth nip my ear. She falls to the bed. Bright skin against dark fabric. Veladoo colored lips. Pink cheeks.

"I need you," she moans breathlessly.

"I know," I whisper, kissing down her chest before taking one of her peaked nipples in my mouth. Her pleasure rolls through me, strong and intoxicating.

Gods, I forgot how good her pleasure feels.

Her fingers run through my wet hair as I lick and kiss my way down her abdomen, the taste of her skin exploding over my tongue. I move her legs over my shoulders, eager to taste her, but she pulls her knees to her chest, stopping me.

"You're hurt," she says, propping herself up on her elbows and crossing her ankles.

"I do not care," I growl as I move her legs back. She tries to pull away again, but I hold the tops of her knees and nip the inside of her thigh. "This is where your legs belong. Now, lie back."

She narrows her eyes. "Is that an order?"

"Yes."

Her brow arches as a devious smirk curls her mouth. A second later, she rips her legs from my grasp and starts to roll away with a laugh. My jaw tightens with suppressed pride. I love her fearless rebellion and endless desire to provoke me. No one has ever acted like this with me, and it is electrifying.

"Are you sure you do not want to obey?" I ask, my voice dark and rough—the voice of my shadow. It is strange hearing it speak, strange the way it shifts my thoughts and actions, but I can no longer fight it. It has woven itself too deeply, and I cannot tell where I end and it begins.

Her eyes burn with a silent dare as she pushes herself to all fours, ready to crawl further away. My hand darts out, grabbing her ankle and pulling her back. She lets out a playful squeak, and a second later her legs are back where they belong. I band one of my arms around her hips, and place my other hand on her chest, holding her in place. Her moaning whimper of defeat sends a throb through my cock.

"Good human," I say, feeling pleased. Her chest moves rapidly with her breath, and when her eyes meet mine, I run my tongue up her slick sex.

"Umph ... fuuuuck," she moans.

Her hips roll, searching for more, and I smile against her, enjoying the way her face contorts and her breath hitches.

"I ... fuck ... I'm going to come already," she grunts.

I hum a sound of confirmation, and the moment she nears that peak, I stop.

She tries to sit up, but runs into the weight of my hand. "What the ...?"

"You should have listened," I purr, my cock straining.

She lifts an eyebrow and says in a defiant tone, "Oh?"

Somehow, that simple reaction nearly sends me over the edge. I grunt and clench my muscles, willing myself not to spill my seed on the deck. When I am back in control, I lower my mouth between her legs and in less than a minute, I have her gasping and nearing climax again. Just as she's about to fall over the edge, I stop and wait for her pleasure to wane.

She groans. "Really? This is what we're doing?"

I do not answer, and when she is just far enough away from that peak, I resume. I do this again, and again, letting her frustration build alongside her appetite. Colorful curses and strings of expletives fill the air. Her skin glistens with sweat as she thrashes against my grip.

"You are such a fucking asshole," she pants. "How long are you going to torture me for?"

Instead of answering, I continue my task, sliding a finger into her warmth and holding her hips as she begs for release. When I feel her clenching, I pull back.

Her eyes flash to mine and a whimper falls from her lips. "Ok, ok. I give up. I can't... I need..."

A part of me regrets the ache in her voice, but the way her body is reacting to my efforts makes it clear that this is a good thing. I am large, and she is not, but she is opening for me.

"You can," I say encouragingly.

"God damnit," she growls, her voice full of determination and anger. She is stronger than anyone I have ever met. A stone amongst feathers. A raging fire amongst dry brush. And I love her for it.

43

PLAN C

AMARA

MY BODY IS on the verge of complete combustion from the prolonged edging. The intense, building pressure and full-body euphoria are beyond anything I've ever experienced, but the agony accompanying it is equally profound. At this point, I'm probably a few seconds away from psychosis or violence. Not sure which.

"Breathe," Vexar whispers, and I try. I honestly try, but all I can manage are short gasps. *I need to come.* The tip of a second finger nudges at my entrance, and some of the tension in my body melts as it joins the first. The slight stretch mellows into a simmering, pleasurable fullness that—

"Oh shit," I groan. Every inch of my skin prickles with heightened awareness. Even the sheets beneath me feel like they're teasing my flesh, and I grab handfuls of the fabric as I reach a blinding peak.

"Come for me, Amara," Vexar says, seconds before his mouth finds my clit and he sucks.

I shatter. My vision darkens, body pulses and vibrates as wave after wave of unbelievable pleasure rocks through me. When I come back to reality, Vexar's fingers are gently kneading against my walls in a rhythmic pattern, bringing me back to the brink of ecstasy.

"That was perfect," he purrs into my flesh. "You are perfect."

It's only then that I realize he's using three fingers. Not two. He must have added the third while I was lost in my orgasm. The satisfying fullness and the motion of Vexar's tongue bring me back to an unbearable peak. I'm balanced right on the edge, expecting to fall at any second. But I don't. Somehow, the pleasure builds even higher. His tongue and hand work in perfect symphony. The sensation of fullness is ... it's ... holy shit, it's so fucking good.

Then it's gone.

"Wait, wha..." My words trail off as Vexar starts climbing up my body.

Holy shit.

His eyes are pitch black, muscles bulging, cock hard and bobbing against his stomach, and I suddenly feel giddy. *How in the hell did I end up here? Really though? Did I die or ... what?*

"Are you sure this is what you want?" he asks in a throaty whisper.

I nearly laugh. "Yeah, I'm *very* sure. You're exactly what I want."

Moving with slow purpose, he presses a soft kiss to my mouth before saying, "You have to tell me if I am doing something wrong."

"Just do what feels good, and I'll tell you if it doesn't for me."

For the first time since we met, his cheeks flush. It's one of the sexiest things I've ever seen. When he's propped on one elbow, hips nestled between my thighs, and his free hand stroking my left knee, something runs up the length of my slit. It feels like a ... finger? But his hands are—

I yelp as whatever it is sucks onto my clit. The abrupt surge of sensation has me gasping for air and squirming beneath Vexar's massive weight.

"Did you forget about my virga?" he rumbles quietly.

Holy shit. Holy shit. Yes, I forgot about his virga, and fuck...

"Is it good?" he asks, playfully nudging the side of my face with his nose.

The cheeky bastard. He knows damn well how good it is. But I can't seem to find the ability to speak. All I can do is rock my hips and make strange mewling sounds as my hands grip the back of his broad neck.

The head of his cock brushes over me, and he lets out a ragged breath as his entire body tenses. Tingles run up my spine.

"You are so warm," he says as he presses his forehead to mine, sending trails of cool water from his still-wet hair sliding down my cheeks.

Anticipation curls in me like a snake. "Keep going," I whisper.

There's a shift in his weight, and the blunt head of his cock presses more firmly against my entrance. He sucks in a sharp breath, and on his exhale, the air around us vibrates. *Fuck, his weird alien sounds are so sexy.* He pushes forward a little more. Bolts of electricity arc over my skin. A little more. God, I needed this. A little more.

My moans turn into a surprised gasp as the sensation of fullness reaches past the point of intense. *Holy shit.* He's not going to fit. I don't know why I wasn't worried about this earlier. Sure, I could get the head of his cock in my mouth just fine, but it's not a normal cock. Well, not a 'human' cock. And the head is narrower than the rest of it. So what's it going to feel like when he's all the way in?

A string of incoherent sounds leaves me as he sinks a bit deeper. My nails dig into the back of his neck. His entire body shakes, and I can feel the scattered surge of mixed emotions as they charge through him. Heat spreads, blending pleasure with confused panic. Part of my body instinctively tries to bear down on him, to push away the invasion, while the rest of me pulls at him for more. I'm a writhing contradiction.

"Please, tell me to stop," he says, his voice tight and strained.

I shake my head. "No, I need more." And it's true. Whatever panic I felt is already gone, and all that remains is the unrelenting need for more. But he doesn't move.

His face presses to the top of my head, and that's when I feel his terror. He's spiraling again.

"Hey," I whisper, "you're not hurting me. Everything's fine."

Nothing.

Frustration blooms. I'm not a porcelain doll and I *want* him. I want *all* of him. Every part. Good, bad, dangerous, whatever there is, I *want* it all. And more than that, I want him to believe me when I speak.

I grip his face in both hands and say firmly, "You are not going to hurt me. I will tell you if you need to stop." But I don't think he hears me. His face is hard and expressionless. "Vexar?"

Nothing.

Fuck it. Time for plan C.

I pull my hand off his face and bring it back with force. The crack of my palm impacting his cheek is loud, but the deep growl that vibrates through his chest is louder. A nervous thrill runs through me as his face slowly tilts down. My skin prickles and my hair stands on end. Scary-Vexar has arrived, and he is both sexy and intimidating.

I swallow, and in as firm a tone as I can manage, say, "Let go."

44

MY SHADOW

VEXAR

AMARA SLAPPED ME.

For a moment, I think she is going to apologize, but then she says, "Let go."

Those words...

She repeats herself. "Let go."

Let go, the dark voice whispers.

"Vexar," she says, her voice stern and unwavering, "listen to what I'm telling you. You're not going to hurt me. I need *you*. I want *you*."

She needs you.

Her fingers tangle in my hair, trying to pull me back to her mouth. Her legs tighten around my waist. "I want all of you, not just the parts you think are acceptable. So take my pleasure. Claim me," she nearly growls.

Take her pleasure. Claim her. Let go.

My subconscious makes the connection faster than the rest of me, and by the time my conscious mind catches up, I'm staring at her in complete awe.

How? How is this possible?

I slide my hand up the column of her neck, running the tips

of my claws over her smooth skin, watching her with utter fascination. *She* is my shadow—at least some part of her is. This entire time, I thought that darkness was mine, but ... it is *hers*. It was *her* voice in my head. Her voice I have been fighting.

"You," I whisper, lost in a sea of revelation. In the arena, it was her I gave myself to. It was her rage that pushed me, that gave me power when I had none. Her mind that allowed me to think faster—a blend of strategy, emotion, and brute force. My tact and her rage. My calm and her action. The strongest parts of us both, working together, as one.

"Vexar?" she asks.

Unmoving, I stare at my Queen. My shadow. The woman who has saved my life twice.

"You won't hurt me," she says.

Gods, she is fearless. Fearless and beautiful. My perfect shadow. "Amara," I whisper, claws still pressed to the side of her neck, "gentleness does not come easy to me." She feels like glass in my hands. And even now that I know what my shadow is and what it wants, it is difficult to trust.

Her hands slide to my wrist, and she strokes my skin with her thumbs. "Trust me. Please." Her heartbeat thuds beneath my grasp.

Trust her.

I lean down to her ear, feeling the darkness in me rise. *Her* darkness. "Are you certain?" I ask, letting my nose drag along the side of her face.

"Fuck me," she dares.

Holding her, I give in to her request and I fully let go.

45

FALLING

AMARA

AN ALIEN CRY escapes me as Vexar drives into me with one brutal thrust. I thought I had taken most of him already, but I was wrong. There was more. So much more.

Overwhelming ecstasy narrows my vision until all I can see are his eyes as he slowly retreats and presses forward again. His fear is completely gone, and I watch as he gives himself over to me. Fully.

Our hands roam. Lips dance. And I can feel him everywhere. The honesty of the moment reaches an intensity I didn't know was possible. I've never felt so connected to anyone. Every thrust. Every sound. Every smell. Every emotion. Raw, honest, and perfect.

"*Mek Lysaer...*" he whispers, his voice ragged and unrestrained.

Claws prick into the flesh of my ass. I can't tell the difference between pain and pleasure; every sensation is ecstasy. Love and desire in physical form. Another climax builds. Spots line my vision. My fingers drag through his hair, pulling him closer, kissing him, tasting the salt on his skin, feeling the raw power of his body above me.

"Come for me," he begs, as his teeth tease my ear. "Let me feel your pleasure. Let me hold you as you fall apart."

And I do fall apart. My nails dig into his back as an orgasm rips through my shaking body. I scream his name, rolling my hips, chasing the pleasure, needing more.

"Vok," he rumbles, low and deep.

The feeling of fullness intensifies, and I moan at the strange sensation.

"I am swelling," he rumbles. "Tell me if it is too much."

I just want more, so I nod and keep moving.

"Words, Amara."

"Yes, yes. Just don't stop," I gasp.

"Tell me if I need to."

I nod and rock my hips. "I just need to feel you."

"Gods, you are perfect," he says, as his lips find mine.

With each stroke, there is a slow increase of pressure that has me moaning and gripping his forearms with all of my strength. My hips meet his with every thrust, seeking more as every sensation peaks.

"I do not know how we fit together, but you take me so well," he says as he presses himself up until he's sitting back on his knees, holding my hips to his, and continuing to rock into me. The sensation is beyond words.

My eyes trace the lines of his body, the way his damp hair swings with every gentle thrust, the patterns of scars and tattoos that adorn his skin. He's perfect. Like he was carved by my own subconscious.

His eyes drop to the place where our bodies meet, and I feel his carnal pride. "You look so beautiful stretched around my swollen cock."

"Oh god," I moan, "where did this filthy mouth come from?"

"I speak only the truth."

Another wave of pleasure builds as his shameless, wild eyes burn into me. My very soul is on display. Fully bare. Fully open.

"Come for me, mek Lysaer," he says again, pushing me over the edge and into another screaming release.

He's over the top of me again. Holding my body to his. Rocking into me as my mind breaks. I'm falling. Tumbling through space as my entire being is consumed by a height of sensation that shouldn't be possible. Through the darkness, I feel Vexar's pleasure reach a point of near agony as he groans and buries himself in my throbbing center. Vhorathi words fall from his lips. Muscles tremble. And the feeling of complete rightness settles into my bones as he rolls to his side and pulls me to his chest.

46

MESSAGE RECEIVED

VEXAR

MARA WAKES IN terror again, but instead of flying limbs, her small body shakes as she curls into me, gripping me tightly like I am the only thing she trusts. I am glad to be her safe place. I am glad she does not have to wake alone. But her terror and pain eat through me in the most excruciating way possible.

Eventually, the violent oceans of her mind calm, and she relaxes into me. "It's really over, isn't it?" she whispers, the warm puffs of her breath dampening my chest.

A scent that is entirely Amara fills my nose, and I press my lips to the top of her head. "It is," I say. There is a long pause before I add, "I am so sorry."

"I'll be ok. Eventually." She takes a breath. "It's just going to take time. Time and constantly reminding myself where I am."

I push her hair back from her face before tucking her head beneath my chin. "At least you did not punch me this morning."

She huffs a hollow laugh. "No shit. My hands weren't made for punching stone."

Shifting slightly, I take her hand in mine and inspect the lingering bruises on her knuckles. She is right, her hands were not made for punching stone, they were made for weaving thread, for healing wounds and saving lives, for soft touches and unrelenting teases. And yet, her path has made sure they are capable of tearing down mountains if needed, and in a way, they already have. She broke through the stone of my own certainty and helped me see the things I was once blind to.

I press a kiss to her knuckles and say, "You are magnificent."

A few minutes later, she's sitting and prodding my ribs while peppering me with questions about my injuries.

"I am fine," I repeat. She still thinks I am hiding my pain. I suppose I am, but the pain is manageable, and it is decreasing quickly.

"I swear, you could be missing an arm and you'd be running around like everything was hunky-dory."

"Hunk dory?" I ask.

She waves a hand dismissively. "It means 'all-good', or something."

"Well, unless I am fatally injured, I see no issue with letting things be 'hunk dory'. What is the point in complaining about things that cannot be changed?"

She smiles and shakes her head. "*Hunky-dory*, and the point of pain is to keep us aware of our bodies' limits. Ignoring it isn't doing you any good. Trust me." As she leans back on her hands, a horrifying sound emanates from somewhere in her body.

I shoot upright, terrified. "What was that? Where are you hurt?"

A barking laugh shakes through her, and I frown. I've clearly missed the joke.

"That was my stomach."

Stomach? "Why would it make such a sound?"

"It happens when I'm hungry. Does your stomach not make sounds when you're hungry?"

"Not unless I eat a speaker."

Her eyes narrow and she tilts her head. "Wait, have you done that?"

<hr>

AFTER A FEW MINUTES in the kitchen, I have a decent spread of foods prepared and laid out on the table. I know she will eat almost anything, but I want her to enjoy food, not just tolerate it. And, with so many options, she can tell me what she enjoys the most. We are lucky, this ship is equipped with supplies to last a year of travel. We do not have to ration, and there are many options. Including fresh fruit.

Deep maroon juice spills from the veladoo as I cut it into bite-sized chunks. It really is the same color as her lips, and I cannot help but smile at that.

"Smells good."

I turn and find Amara in the doorway, wearing one of my tunics as a knee-length dress. Her dark hair is mussed and her eyes are still heavy with sleep. I feel a thud next to my foot, but I am too transfixed by Amara to look away.

"That was close," she says, glancing down.

In two steps, I have her in my arms and pressed up against the bulkhead, my mouth claiming hers. She is irresistible. Her legs grip my waist and she groans into my mouth. The sound is quiet, but it's enough to ignite a deep hunger. A hunger that will have to wait.

With a sigh, I lower her to the ground and lead her to the table. "I made a little bit of everything. This way you can tell me what you like."

Her eyes go wide. "Oh, wow. That's ... thank you."

It's obvious she wasn't expecting this, and her excitement and gratitude have me swelling with pride. Eager to add the veladoo, I turn and almost kick a knife stuck blade-side down in the deck. I retrieve it, and after a moment of confusion, I realize what happened. That is what she meant by "close". I almost stabbed my own foot.

With the veladoo added to the table, I start introducing her to the different foods.

"Oh shit," she says, holding a hand over her mouth after taking a large bite of the *yazva* cake, "that's really good."

"And now, this," I say, holding up a slice of veladoo. She lets me place the fruit in her mouth, and her eyes go wide as she starts to chew.

"What is that?" she asks.

"Veladoo."

Recognition spreads and she smiles. "To be honest, I never thought I'd live long enough to taste it. It's amazing."

I take a sip of tea and smile, trying to ignore the painful reminder of how close we came to death. "I am glad that is not how our story en—"

An alarm screams, cutting me off mid-sentence. I push off from the table and jog to the bridge. Yellow alerts flash across the view-screen, warning that our comms are back online and someone has breached the security filters.

47

UNKNOWN SENDER

AMARA

AN ALARM SOUNDS from somewhere in the ship, and suddenly, Vexar's gone. I swear he's way too fast for his size. I pop the last piece of veladoo into my mouth and follow him to the bridge, licking my fingers and wincing as my swollen feet protest each step. The alarm stops as I round the corner and find Vexar leaning over the control panel, radiating anxiety.

"What's going on?" I ask cautiously.

His face is drawn, every sharp feature glowing in the pale-blue light of the display. "The comms came back online," he says.

I glance at the display—which is in Vhorathi and entirely unhelpful to me—before asking, "Why would that make an alarm go off?"

"The comms did not set off the alarm; the data packet that was forced through the security filter did."

"Forced through?" That doesn't sound good.

He straightens and crosses his massive arms over his bare chest. Thankfully, he's wearing pants, but they hang low around his waist in a way that's still very distracting.

"This ship is invisible unless it is receiving a communication signal. That"—he points to a flashing orange icon on the display—"is a message from an unapproved sender. It should never have made it past the ship's security filter." He runs a single hand between his horns and through his long black hair. "And now they know where we are."

I shake my head, trying to organize the heap of information he just dumped on me. "Who knows where we are?"

"I do not know."

Ok. That's not concerning at all. "And you can't just open it and see where it came from?"

"No. It is encrypted. I cannot open it without the correct key."

"And it didn't come from one of the people you approved?" I ask, even though he's already said as much. After we left Calidus, Vexar told me he was setting the comms to only receive messages from a few, very specific people. He made it clear it was for safety reasons and let me have a say on who we included. Not that I had much to contribute, I don't know any of these people.

"If it had come from an approved sender, I would be able to read it."

I bite my thumbnail, feeling my own anxiety rise. "Do you think it's from Gaius? Or Marius?"

"Or my sister," he whispers under his breath.

A chill runs down my spine. "Ok. Let's try to talk this through." I slide into the seat on the starboard side of the bridge and pull my feet off the ground, staring at the view from the external cameras shown on the display. The image is just an endless expanse of stars that would make Neil deGrasse Tyson swoon, but to me, it's a little scary. Refocusing myself, I start at the beginning. "What did you mean when you said the ship is invisible?"

"That isn't important right now."

I sigh. Vexar's more of a 'think in silence' kinda guy, and it's clear I'm going to have to convince him of the benefits of talking things through. "Well," I say, resting my feet on the control panel, "do you have a plan? Do you know how to open the message or who might have sent it? Do you know if it's definitely a bad thing?"

His jaw tightens. "No."

"Alright, then we should talk it through. Review the variables. Maybe a question I ask will spark an idea or something." I wet my lips and repeat my earlier question. "Why are we invisible? That makes no sense."

He leans a hip against the control panel, face still tight with anxiety. "We are not invisible exactly, the ship is just very hard to detect. The hull absorbs and re-emits almost everything it comes in contact with: atoms, molecules, dust, radiation"—he waves his hand—"and other things I do not know the English words for. Essentially, anything floating through space will appear to move right through us, including communication signals and sensor pulses."

"Anything floating through space? Like asteroids ...?"

"No. Not like asteroids. Small things. Very small things."

I take a breath and squint. This is all getting very ... sciency, but I guess that's something I have to get used to. With a sigh, I say, "I thought space was empty."

He scrubs a hand over his face. "It looks empty, but it is not. It is full of many things. Mostly hydrogen atoms moving very quickly, but also dust, and other things. However, that is not the problem. The problem is that some unknown person has our location, and our only defense is stealth."

"Ok. So we're *sort of* invisible." I'm trying to act cool about someone knowing where we are, but I'm freaking out. At least a little bit. "Are there any other reasons someone might send a message like this? Someone who doesn't want us dead?" I ask, praying for some sort of hope.

He turns back to the display and braces his hands on the control panel. "That is the only reason I can think of."

I nod, and despite the slowly rising panic in my chest, I charge forward. "How do normal messages get transmitted?"

"An interstellar message has to originate from a very powerful ship or a planet equipped with a clerk." He waves his hand like he's looking for a better word. "A computer that can package and send messages through a fold-point."

Fuck me. I am so out of my depth here.

I drop my head back and groan. "Why does space have to be a never-ending science lesson?"

"It is not that complicated," he says gently.

With a sigh, I say, "Fine. What's a fold-point?"

"Space is big. A direct path from here to Vhorath is approximately 26 light-years in distance." He frowns and types on the control panel again before looking back at me. "Or 21.06 light-years by Earth's measurement."

I hold up a hand. "I thought light always moves at the same speed."

"It is not the light that is changing; it is the measurement of a year. A light-year is just how far light can travel in a single year. One Vhorathi year is equivalent to 0.81 Earth years. Our unit of measurement is different."

Huh, that actually makes sense. With a nod, I say, "Go on."

"The distance is too vast to travel or send messages in a straight path, so we use ... I do not know the term." He types again and his brows dip. "Wormhole? Is that really the correct term?"

"A wormhole? Isn't that just a half-assed plot device for writers who don't have the imagination to come up with something better?"

He shakes his head, clearly confused by my comment. "It is a fold in space-time. Instead of traveling along the normal plane of space-time, we fold the plane and jump through it. It is much faster."

"Now we're talking about space origami?" I murmur, rubbing my temples. "Ok. So you fold space, or whatever."

"Yes," he says, looking slightly amused by my distress.

"Don't you dare laugh."

His grin grows and he laughs, which makes me laugh despite the effort I'm exerting to hold a straight face.

When he catches his breath, he says, "Ok. Imagine my hands are the universe." He holds his hands out, palms up, with his pinkies pressed together. "You need to travel from the pointer finger on my left hand to the pointer finger on my right. Now, if you travel straight across, the distance is long. You have to cross six fingers. But, if you fold space," he brings both of his palms together so his pointer fingers are touching, "the distance is much less." He taps his pointer fingers together. "You can go from one distant point to another very quickly. This is how we travel and send messages over long distances." I nod, and he continues. "A message sent from Vhorath to a ship in interstellar space must go through a clerk that sends the message to the correct wormhole." He pauses. "Can we not call them wormholes? That term is very ... strange."

I shrug. "I didn't come up with it. Call it whatever you want."

"Good. The originating clerk sends the message to the correct 'fold-point' where the message is received by the jump-clerk there. A jump-clerk is just a controller that manages traffic through the fold-point. The jump-clerk then sends the message through the fold, aimed at the next fold-point, and so on until the message reaches its intended recipient."

My brain is already starting to hurt, but I think I get the

general idea. "So it's just passed along a chain of computers?" He nods, and I ask, "How long does that take?"

"It depends on where the sender and receiver are. Our fold-points are static locations—they are always in the same place—and some planets have fold-points connecting them directly, like Vhorath and Calidus."

"Which is why we could talk to Marius without a time-lag," I say quietly.

"Correct. If there is no fold-point connecting locations, messages take longer. Much longer."

Interesting. "Do the clerks have access to the messages' content?"

"Yes," he says slowly. I can already see the wheels turning in his head, and that urges me forward.

"And who has access to the clerks?"

"The Vhorathi government."

I wince. "Could they read the message we got?"

He scratches the scruff on his chin. "Maybe not. Not if whoever sent it didn't want them to. It takes considerable skill to force a message through a security filter, and I would assume someone capable of that could circumvent the clerks' review process." A deep line appears between his brows, and I feel his thoughts moving chaotically. Then, his face lights up and he starts typing.

I pull my feet off the control panel and sit up. "What? What is it?"

"You are brilliant," he mumbles, still typing. A few seconds later, the flashing orange icon is replaced by an image, and Vexar lets out a husky laugh as he drops into his seat.

"I'm sorry, is that a bean?" I ask, tilting my head to get a better look at the image. "And why are you laughing?"

He laughs again. It's a relieved, incredulous sound. "It is a *valaktur* heart."

"A what?"

"*Valaktur.* A large animal native to Vhorath. When we were young, my brother would tease me by saying I had the heart of a *valaktur.*" He nods towards the screen with a relieved smile. "My brother sent this message."

I look from him to the display, where a progress bar has appeared beneath the image. "Your brother?"

"Yes. Steinarr sent this. I am certain of it." When I don't react, he says, "The encryption key I used is something only he and I know, and it worked."

That familiar sinking feeling grips my spine. "I thought your brother was on the approved list of senders. Why wouldn't he just send the message through the correct channels?"

Vexar's expression darkens, and I think we're both on the same page. Steinarr didn't want his message to be seen by the government.

ANXIETY HANGS in the air between us as the progress bar slowly creeps towards completion. My thumbnail is jagged, but I can't stop biting it, and Vexar is compulsively messing with the ship's controls again. I don't even think he knows he's doing it.

"You trust Steinarr, right?" I ask.

"Yes," he says absently, "Steinarr has always been ruthless and uncompromising, and that is exactly why I trust him."

That's good. "How long until we reach—" The computer chirps, and I sit straight up, eyes darting between Vexar and the display. "Is it done?"

With a hardened expression, he starts clicking through things. Vhorathi symbols fill the screen, and I turn my focus to Vexar. His bright green eyes flick back and forth as he reads, and then I feel it. Dread.

My breathing slows. "What does it say?"

He shakes his head and doesn't look at me. Whatever it is, it isn't good. With a wave of sadness and rage, he says, "Solira, the capital of Vhorath, has fallen." He stands and grips the edge of the control panel, knuckles going pale with the force. "Aelrith has taken the government."

48

DANCE

AMARA

"D O YOU THINK Steinarr can actually pull that off?" I ask as Vexar finishes his fourth cup of tea and sets the empty mug on the galley table. "I mean, does he have the skill to do it?"

Fist pressed over his lips, Vexar leans back in his chair and says, "I have no concern over his capabilities, only over the allegiances of those he chooses to join him."

Every step I take sends a sharp stab of pain through my feet, but I can't stop pacing. "Who would Steinarr ask to join him?"

"His *Sjalbanath*. His personal killers."

I stop pacing and stare at Vexar. "Your brother has personal killers?"

He grimaces and bobbles his head. "It is a poor translation. They are more like an unofficial army. He has been training with them since we were children, and I have no doubt they are loyal to him, but I do not know if they would be loyal to us."

"How many people are in this 'unofficial army'?"

"Approximately 300. Maybe more."

That's fewer soldiers than I was imagining, but it's still a lot.

The variables and logistics alone will be a massive challenge, and if any of them aren't fully on our side, we'll be screwed.

"It's a risk. A *big* risk," I say.

"What other option do we have?"

I groan and sink into the seat opposite him. He's right. We don't have a better option. Stienarr's message included a wealth of intel—everything from news articles to video clips to personal communication logs—and all of it's bad. The capital of Vhorath has fallen into chaos. Aelrith has assumed power. The Senate is fully behind her. Warrants have been issued for our arrest. And heavily edited videos of the events in the arena have been distributed, making Vexar look like a traitor who was willing to throw away his throne for a little piece of ass.

If we go to Vhorath, we'll be executed. If we go back to Calidus, we'll be executed. And we can't go anywhere else, because Aelrith has ordered the Vhorathi fleet to 'protect' nearby populated planets by killing us on sight. So, we're stuck with two options: One, we accept our fate and die by execution or starvation. Or two, we agree to Steinarr's proposal and accept the risks that come with it.

The biggest issue is that we don't have the luxury of open communication with Steinarr. I don't understand the technical side of it—something to do with the clerks and message codes—but we only get one shot. That's it. Any other message we send will broadcast our position to everyone who wants us dead.

"Your sister's an asshole, you know that?" A very scary, asshole.

"She has always been like this," Vexar says.

"I bet that was fun to grow up with." I slide down in my chair, straightening my legs out in front of me until I'm hunched like an old walking cane. "So what do you want to do?" At the end of the day, this has to be his decision.

He stares at his hands for a long while before looking up. "I think we must trust Steinarr and let him do what he does best."

I slap my hands on my thighs. "Alright. Let's write the message."

THE FOLLOWING MORNING, I learn the ship has a gym. It's a decent-sized room, hidden beneath a hatch in the passageway, and it's well equipped with a range of odd-looking resistance machines. Vexar walks through the space and stops next to a panel on the bulkhead. With a devious grin, he asks, "Are you ready?"

I stare at him blankly. "You do know my feet aren't ready for a workout, right?"

His brows wiggle. "I have something better." With a touch to the panel, the room fills with a strange, upbeat music.

My eyes go wide.

"What do you think?" he asks.

I haven't heard music in so long that, despite the overall alien vibe of the tune, I'm enthralled and start dancing in place. "Music!" I shout, pumping my fists like it's my first time at the club.

His eyes light up, and to my surprise, he joins my impromptu dance party. His hips sway, feet tap, and arms wiggle as he moves towards me with a huge, infectious grin. This massive, horned warrior is dancing his way across the room, and it's both endearing and hilarious.

Aware of my sore feet, he scoops me up, wraps an arm under my ass, and starts dancing me around. Laughter fills the room, blending with the strange melody as we spin and bounce with abandon. Concerns about Steinarr's newest mission and the perilous situation we're in melt away until the only thing left is the overwhelming joy that we are together and alive.

By the time the song ends, we're both out of breath and grinning ear to ear.

We spend the next hour discovering that none of the exercise equipment is rated for someone of my size or weight. The whole situation is endlessly entertaining. It's clear Vexar's laughing because I don't weigh enough to use the machines, and I'm laughing because of how hard he's laughing.

Hanging from a machine that looks like a fancy pull-down bar, I say, "Yeah, I'm gonna need a few more pounds to make this one work too." My feet are dangling at least a foot off the ground, and this machine is meant to be used while sitting.

Vexar wipes his eyes as he fights back another laughing fit and helps me down. "You may be a Vhorathi at heart, but you are not a Vhorathi in body."

"And that's why I have an affinity for really big guns." I give him a wink and settle down on an empty bench.

"We will have to find another way for you to exercise," he says as he joins me.

I lean my back against Vexar's good shoulder and look up at him. "I can do bodyweight exercises or something. We'll figure it out." After I mentioned how much muscle I'd lost on Calidus and how I'd like to gain it back, he instantly vowed to help me "get back up to strength." It's sweet, and I can't help but feel all warm and fuzzy every time I remember how much he cares. With a squeeze to his massive thigh, I ask, "Are all Vhorathis as muscly as you?"

"Some, but not all," he says, tilting his head down to see me. "How are your feet today? Any better?"

"They're sore. How's your shoulder?"

"It is fine," he says as he kisses the top of my head.

A few minutes later, he's grumbling at one of the machines

as I stretch while pretending I'm not eye-fucking him. "I do not understand. I think these machines may be broken," he says as he ups the tension again. "I have never needed this much weight before."

"Did you forget how easily you bent that fence?" I ask.

He grunts a sound of frustration and moves on to the next machine, and then the next. Each one, he maxes out the resistance and says it still feels like he's doing nothing. It would be funny if he weren't so freaked out about it.

"This new strength is strange," he says as he walks away from one of the 'broken' machines. He tosses his towel over his shoulder and frowns. "I do not know why I got it and you did not."

I don't mention the fact that he's also healing faster than me too.

THE FOLLOWING MORNING, we land on one of the small moons orbiting the furthest planet from Calidus's star. The planet is a smooth marble of reds and whites that fills the display and hasn't moved since we landed. That's what Vexar meant when he said the moon was tidally locked. It doesn't rotate. The side we're on will never face open space. Good for hiding.

That afternoon, Vexar changes the bandages on my feet with a solemn expression. "Your feet are healing too slowly," he says, smoothing another strip of regen-tape over one of the deeper gouges on my left heel.

"It would seem the magic-bond did not see fit to grant me the same special healing powers as you." I glance at the nearly healed wounds on his shoulder and shrug. "It's fine. I'll heal eventually."

He tenses. "Maybe it is because we never finished the *sasi-temwá*? The blood-binding?"

"Why would you think that?"

He uses his teeth to tear another strip of tape from the roll. "Many things about our bond seem ... incomplete. I can hear your voice in my head; you cannot hear mine. I am healing quickly; you are not. I have increased strength; you do not. And your eyes go black, but not fully. I do not know if completing the sasí-temwá would change things, but it might."

WEEKS PASS, and we fall into a comfortable routine as we wait for a response from Steinarr. Every day, after we've eaten, exercised, showered, and reviewed some Vhorathi vocabulary, we sit on the bridge while I read. Vexar had the ship's electronic library translated into English, and I've been learning as much as I can about the Vhorathi people, their medicine, politics, culture, and warfare, while looking for information on the Zhyrrak.

First off, Vexar's physiology is way stranger than I thought. His super slow heart rate has a range of about 6 bpm up to 240 bpm. Also, he can breathe through his skin. Which is weird. When I asked if that meant he could breathe underwater, his answer was, "Sometimes." So, there's that. Unfortunately, we haven't found much information on the Zhyrrak. The only mentions are buried deep in history books, and the references are either super vague or completely fantastical.

"I don't know if we're going to find any more information than we already have," I say as I swivel my seat while staring at the overhead. "Wait," I frown, "is this a bridge or a cockpit? I mean, technically, this is a *ship*, right? So it would be a—"

Vexar clears his throat, interrupting me, and says, "Come here."

I raise a brow. "Are you gonna give me an answer?"

"In Vhorathi, we have only one term for this, *gutejarve*. I do not care what you call it in English."

"*Gutejarve*?" That's a weird one. "Well, I'm gonna keep calling it a bridge."

"Perfect. Now come here."

I climb onto his lap, and instantly, the anxiety I didn't know I was carrying floats away. I swear, a single sniff of this man is like a hit of opium for my nervous system. My muscles relax, heart slows, and a deep sense of calm fills me.

"That's better," he whispers, letting his eyes close while his hands slide around my waist.

I rest my head against his shoulder and wrap my arms around his neck. "What do you want to do?" We've been talking about completing the blood-binding for a few days now. Neither of us really knows what will happen, but I can't deny I'm curious. Curious, and a little nervous to mess with something that already seems pretty good.

His fingers trail down my spine. "I think this choice has to be yours. I have made enough decisions for you to last a lifetime."

I lean back to look at him. "You didn't make any decisions for me, the bond just ... happened." He didn't mean for me to be covered in his blood and cut my knee. He had no idea we were going to bond at all. None of it was planned. Besides, the bond didn't affect how I feel about him. Sure, it made me a little more desperate, but that could also just be from how touch-starved I was and how insanely hot he is.

He strokes my hair and says, "And yet, too many choices have been made for you."

My teeth work over my lower lip. He's not wrong, but this is a partnership. "If the choice were up to you, what would you do?"

He's reluctant to answer, but does so anyway. "I would want to complete it."

49

THE BLOOD-BINDING

AMARA

TWO MORE DAYS pass before I feel confident in my decision. Tossing one of Vexar's giant shirts over my head, I walk into the galley and find my hulking alien holding a mug of steaming tea and looking absolutely edible in all his naked glory. My stomach flips as I take him in. Is it crazy to want to tie myself more tightly to someone who was a stranger just a few weeks ago? Probably, but I don't care.

Every moment we spend together, I find myself loving him a little more. He's a beautiful enigma. A flower growing in a cement parking lot.

He's kind when he was raised to be ruthless. He's courageous when he should be afraid. He trusts even when he's been betrayed. And he loves harder than anyone I've ever known. It's an all-encompassing, unwavering, full-bodied devotion kind of love, and when I think back to the time we spent in his cell—before either of us knew about the bond—I think he already loved me then. When he said I was "magnificent," I felt it. I was a complete stranger, and yet, his love was already there. Like he knew what we would become.

"We should do it," I say.

He lowers the mug of tea from his mouth and swallows. "What?"

"We should complete the blood-binding ... uh, exchange ... thing." Damn, this man is distracting when he's naked.

"Is that what you want?" he asks carefully.

"Yes."

A ripple of excitement tickles the back of my mind, but his face stays calm. "When?"

"Now."

Instead of setting down his tea, he drops the mug and walks through the splash of steaming liquid without so much as a flinch. Goosebumps rise on my neck as he runs the back of his fingers over my cheek. "You are certain?"

I nod. "Very."

His pupils expand until I'm staring at two obsidian orbs. Heat pulses between my thighs. A deep, satisfying sound vibrates his chest. His fingers curl around my chin and he kisses me before gripping the hem of my shirt. "I both love and hate seeing you in my clothes," he rasps.

"Sounds tough," I say, feeling my nipples pebble as I raise my arms and let him pull the fabric over my head.

"I enjoy 'tough'." His gaze roams my body, and then his mouth is on mine, fingers knitting into my hair, and desire surging between us.

I slide my arms around his neck, and he straightens up, lifting me off the ground and guiding my legs around his muscled torso. As hard as I try, my legs aren't long enough to lock my ankles behind his back, so I just grip him with my thighs as he walks us to the bedroom.

"You're a mountain, you know that?" I ask.

"I am *your* mountain."

Smiling, I kiss my way down his neck, tasting the salt on his skin and feeling his pulse beneath my lips. "Yes, yes you are," I whisper.

He detours to a cabinet on the bulkhead, pulls out a knife in an ornate leather sheath, and climbs onto the bed with me still in his arms. The head of his cock brushes between my legs as he sets me down, and I let out a gasp that makes him grin.

With a quick move, he tosses the knife aside, pushes me onto my back, and buries his face between my thighs. I gasp and manage to say, "I thought we were going to complete the blood thing…"

He shushes me and says, "I am hungry," before grinning and returning to his task.

I can't stop myself from laughing. His fingers cling to me as I relax into the moment, wrapping my hands around his horns, and enjoying the pleasure he gives so freely. When he resurfaces, I run my thumb down the deep scar on his cheek, mesmerized by his perfect imperfection.

"You're beautiful," I say.

He kisses me, long, deep, and so full of emotion that my throat tightens and burns with unshed tears. I don't know how we found each other, or what planets had to align for this to happen, but I feel blessed in a way I don't think I'll ever be able to describe.

"Do not be nervous," he says as he rises to his knees and pulls me up with him.

"I'm not," I say casually. He raises a brow, and I sigh. "Ok, fine. I'm a little nervous." We have no idea what's going to happen, and that's both terrifying and exciting.

He picks up the knife and smiles gently. "I am glad it is just you and me. No crowd, no rules, nothing between us."

I push up onto my knees, scooting closer as he settles back on his heels, dick rock hard and bobbing against his stomach. My mouth waters, and the urge to climb into his lap becomes overwhelming. It's one of those instinctual urges I've learned not to ignore.

I glance up. "Do people usually fuck during these ceremonies?"

He laughs. "Not that I am aware of, no." Then he sees my face and goes still. His gaze heats, and it's clear we're on the same page.

"You said no rules. We can do whatever we want, right?" I ask.

"No rules," he whispers.

The knife makes a soft thump as it hits the bed, dropped from Vexar's relaxed hand, and a second later, I'm standing and pulling his mouth to mine.

Claws trail down my back, teasing my skin until the sharp sensation disappears and the warm pads of his fingers find my ass. Like Pavlov's dog, my body reacts, knowing what comes next. A second later, his fingers dip between my thighs.

"Gods, I will never tire of your body," he says, as his teeth nip my stomach and his fingers continue their gentle movements. "I will never tire of this *need* for each other. Of this hunger. I will never tire of *you*."

I run my fingers through his hair and whisper, "Until the very end."

The most intense sensation of love floods me as he repeats, "Until the very end."

With slow movements, I straddle his lap, gripping his neck and pressing my chest to his. Heat spreads from the head of his cock as he guides it to my entrance. I tremble. Taste his mouth. Run my tongue over the sharp points of his teeth. His hands move to my waist. Our eyes lock. And in a slow, deliberate motion, I lower myself onto him, letting him watch every reaction on my face as he overwhelms my senses. My thighs tremble, heart races, and the rest of the world disappears.

His forehead presses to mine as he gasps for every breath. "It is both agony and bliss," he whispers.

And he's right. It's the kind of pleasure that's so absolute, it digs at your very soul, and in this new position, the intensity is dialed up even further. Thrusting is out of the question. There's no way I could handle that, so I start to rock.

He hisses out a breath and his fingers dig into my hips, stilling me. "Please," he begs. I guess this position is intense for both of us.

A second later, his virga finds me, and a fever-like sensation spreads over my skin as I whimper against his neck. When I asked about how much control he has over his virga, he told me he has less control over it than his own heartbeat. So, despite the overwhelming sensation, I lean into it instead of fighting back.

"Are you ready?" he asks, his voice gentle, but strained.

"Yeah," I say breathlessly.

"Wrap your legs around me so your hands are free."

I do, and the slight change in angle leaves us both gasping. "Holy shit," I groan. I can't move at all now. Don't need to. Just existing like this is pure, overwhelming ecstasy.

Vexar's hands leave my hips, metal rasps over leather, and he asks a final question, "Are you sure?"

I lean back enough to see him. "Very sure."

Light bounces off the blade as he drags it across his right palm, releasing a bloom of crimson that pools in his hand. As if my body already knows what to do, I offer him my left hand. The anxiety I felt earlier is long gone. The burn of the blade barely registers.

His black eyes lock on mine and he nods. Our hands meet, fingers interlock, I feel the warmth of his blood against my palm, and—

Time stops. My vision blurs. Heart slows. And then I see images. So many images, filling my mind's eye. Entire lifetimes flashing by in the span of seconds. People I've never seen. Places I've never been. I'm lost in a rip-tide of memories that don't belong to me. Then the images slow, ticking by one at a time before coming to a complete stop. It's not an image anymore. I'm outside somewhere, massive trees tower over me, and ... I'm staring at Vexar. But it's not the same man I know now. He's young. Maybe a teenager? But it's definitely him, standing in the middle of a sand circle, holding a blade.

There's a woman, too. I can't see her face. Vexar looks over his shoulder, and our eyes meet. At first, he looks confused, but that confusion quickly turns to determination. The woman speaks to him, but I can't hear her. She has a blade too. Her blade flicks out and slices into Vexar's forearm. My hands fly to my face, stifling a silent scream. I don't know what's happening. Vexar looks at me again, but this time an awareness passes between us, as if he's acknowledging who I am—or who I will be. That's when the woman cuts him again, from the base of his ear to the top of his shoulder, and a second later he's gone, washed away by another rush of images that eventually fade to nothing.

Slowly, the present comes back into focus. Vexar, my Vexar, is holding my face and looking at me like I'm the center of his entire universe. The answer to every question he's ever had. The only thing he's ever truly wanted.

"I saw you," I whisper. I don't know how else to communicate what just happened, but he seems to understand. I drag a finger down the scar that runs the length of his neck, the one I just saw carved into his skin, before meeting his gaze again.

"*I know,*" I hear him say. But his mouth doesn't move.

My eyes go wide. I *heard* him.

He smiles and kisses me, soft and tender at first, but growing quickly into an unrestrained celebration. His emotions flow through me easily, no longer a stray thought at the back of my mind, but a deep knowing in my body. It's everything I've ever needed, filling me all at once. Safety. Love. Desire. Connection. Belonging. Certainty. And above all else, purpose. A desperate, hopeful purpose.

I'm moving again, rocking against him, deepening our physical connection while the threads between us pull even tighter. His fingers slide up my spine and into my hair, tugging me closer.

Every sensation is heightened. Every touch, smell, and sound, a broadcast of pure intention, growing and coalescing into an unimaginable peak. Existence blurs as our minds lock, and a thousand thoughts and emotions cross between us in a single breath. Then, we fall together, off that cliff of uncertainty and into something entirely new. As one.

EPILOGUE
VEXAR

"IS IT HIM?" Amara asks as she steps up behind me.

I have already silenced the proximity alert, but the yellow warning lights are still flashing, reflecting off the deep black of Amara's eyes in a strange, ethereal way. *Absolutely stunning.*

"Not sure," I answer. "The ship has no identification tags."

She gives me a knowing look, and I hope she is right.

A few seconds later, the external cameras orient, and a Vhorathi Heavy Cruiser Warship emerges from the darkness like some deadly ghost of myth. Of all the ships in the empire's fleet, few can do as much damage as the one before us.

Her hand slides on top of mine in a reassuring caress. "It's him," she whispers. "It has to be."

Gods, I hope she is right. Embracing her confidence, I guide our hands to the comm button. My throat works as I try to swallow. If we are wrong, pressing this button will be deadly, and yet, we press it anyway.

Amara is calm, confident even. So I focus on that. On the steady thud of her heart, the warm scent of her skin, the relaxed curves of her face. "You are braver than me," I whisper, before raising her hand to my lips.

"Only in some ways." She smiles, and a new alert flashes. When I do not move, she guides my hand back to the controls. "It's ok. Answer it."

Setting my jaw, I accept the request, and an image fills the screen.

"Brother!" Steinarr says, in his familiar, cocky tone. "As requested, one newly liberated warship." He places his hands on his hips and asks, "Do you like it?"

ACKNOWLEDGMENTS

When I started writing this book, I had no idea what it would become. I just wanted to squash my perfectionist habits and get words on the page. To my surprise, it worked! And with the encouragement of my writer's group (and countless rounds of edits), it's become something I'm incredibly proud of.

Joe, thank you for your keen grammatical eye, your consistent and thoughtful feedback, and your selfless desire to see everyone in our group publish good work. Ben, thank you for your endless jokes, for the hilarious brainstorming sessions, and for reading and editing my 'completed' manuscript *twice* (even though you don't like spicy scenes). Melinda, thank you for convincing me this story had potential, and for giving me the confidence to keep going.

Thank you to my parents, who heard I was writing a sci-fi romance and were proud rather than judgmental. I will forever be grateful for your openness and support, and for teaching me that love is always better than violence (on that note, sorry about all the violence).

Thank you to my fiancé, who kept a roof over my head after I decided to make a rather absurd career change. I love you and will be forever grateful that you helped me live this wild dream of mine.

Thank you to Jamie, who answered all of my random Marine-related questions, even on deployment. You are amazing, and thank you for your service.

Thank you to my ARC readers who took a chance on me

(you're my heroes), to my author friends I met on TikTok, and to the entire BookTok community. You all make being an indie author possible, and I love you for it.

And thank you to every person who has read this book. You have no idea how much it means to me that you were willing to take a chance on Vexar and Amara's story. I can't wait to share book two with you!

-Maeve Brooks

ABOUT THE AUTHOR

Maeve Brooks is a lover of all things sci-fi and has a serious soft spot for unconventional romances. She holds a bachelor's degree in English - Creative Writing, and after spending ten years in the beer industry—not writing—she's back at the keyboard and thrilled to share more steamy sci-fi romance stories.

Want exclusive access to a *Thread and Stone* bonus scene and early access to Book 2? Sign up for Maeve's newsletter! You'll get updates on new releases, ARC opportunities, short stories, sneak-peaks, exclusive content, and more! **Sign up at: maeve brooks.com**

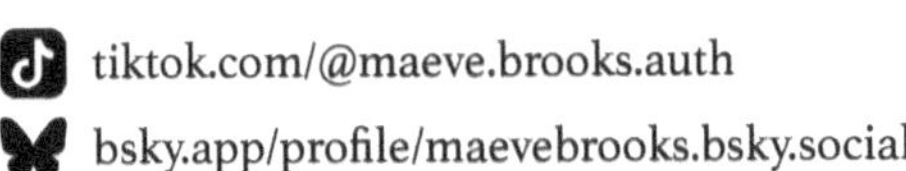

tiktok.com/@maeve.brooks.auth

bsky.app/profile/maevebrooks.bsky.social